CODE 3-M

Third Millennium Road Map for Peace

John Moody Presley

John Moody Presley

LUTHERS
New Smyrna Beach
F L O R I D A

Published by
LUTHERS PUBLISHING
1009 North Dixie Freeway
New Smyrna Beach, FL 32168-6221

PRINTED IN THE UNITED STATES OF AMERICA

COVER DESIGN, CHARACTER SKETCHES AND
CODE 3-M LOGO BY MICHAEL HALEN

LIBRARY OF CONGRESS
CATALOGING-IN-PUBLICATION DATA
Presley, John Moody, 1926–
Code 3-M: third millennium road map for peace
by John Moody Presley.—1st ed.
p.   cm.
ISBN 1-877633-59-3 (pbk.)
1. Peace movements — Fiction.
2. Pacifism — Fiction.
3. Peace — Fiction.
I. Title.

PS3616.R47 C63 2001
813'.54 — dc21   200129306

To Jane,
my devoted wife

Preface

The quest and hope for peace is the highest priority of mankind. This worthy goal has eluded us. Multiplied millions have died in vain.

The fundamental hope is to reach into the minds and hearts of individuals who can eventually band together and end the incredible human slaughter and needless suffering by adhering to reasonable philosophies of fairness and genuine concern for other people.

Inasmuch as any religion promotes ethical behavior and moral values that foster peace, it is, and should be, supported. Conversely, if a religion fosters any aggressive actions that counteract these principles, strong condemnation is and must be accorded to these negative actions.

As the dawn of the third millennium is upon us, the challenge for each human being is to examine their views of life to make certain that, as an individual they will not only refrain from doing anything that causes suffering or death but will earnestly seek out behaviors that will promote peace and genuine brotherhood for all mankind.

In this book, an attempt is made to address impacts of the religions on the two preceding millenniums, extract truth and common sense evaluation from any source in order to create a code of living that each person might use as an anchor for his or her life. To the extent this volume inspires new insights, its success can be measured.

John Moody Presley
Daytona Beach, Florida
May 2001

Table of Contents

Chapter I
An Idea Is Born   1

Chapter II
A Unique Selection   8

Chapter III
Who I Am — Some Things I Believe   19

Chapter IV
Open Topics and Discussion   39

Chapter V
Sexual Issues of Humans   92

Chapter VI
Item Lists of Participants:

Al Green's List   106

Lu Chang's List   128

Rev. John Hayes' List   151

David Preakness' List   175

Tony Tweedhurt's List   200

Rachel Brooks' List   234

Bridgette Thompson's List   250

Chapter VII
Compiling Individual Lists   276

Chapter VIII
An Adventure to Remember   281

Chapter XI
Guidelines for CODE 3-M   287

Chapter X
Romance Blooms   296

Chapter I
An Idea Is Born

Looking out over the familiar waters that couched the tiny twelve-acre island called Liberty in New York Harbor, Rudolph Plutonius Morgan could see, as he did almost every day, the magnificent Statue of Liberty with arm and torch raised high toward the mighty Atlantic.

The colossal statue was given to the United States by France in 1885 to commemorate the birth of another democratic nation. It stands as one of the world's most imposing scenes. It probably was a descendant of the famous Colossus of Rhodes, one of the seven greatest wonders of the ancient world. It was created by Bartholdi and with the granite pedestal, it is 305 feet high. Its skin consists of 300 copper sheets. Rudy, as the billionaire was affectionately called by everyone, had read the inscription many times written by Emma Lazarus: "Give me your tired, your poor, your huddled masses yearning to breathe free, the wretched refuse of your teaming shore, send thee, the homeless tempest-tossed to me: I lift my lamp beside the golden door."

Years ago, both parents of Rudy had glimpsed the Statue of Liberty as they entered New York Harbor. They were a young couple, with all of their worldly possessions packed into one trunk and two suitcases. They were bright-eyed and full of hope for the future! Life, at first, was very difficult as thousands upon thousands poured through Ellis Island. However, they had a dream and persevered until they were able to obtain a small home and begin a family. They named their firstborn Rudolph Plutonius Morgan.

From humble beginnings, Rudy adapted to his country and its wonderful opportunities. He studied hard. He worked hard for many long years. He began to invest his small savings very wisely. By the time he was 25, he was upper middle class. By age 35, he was a millionaire and now at 65, he was among the world's billionaires. His parents were extremely proud of their son's success and shared it with him before they died. They were even more proud of the type of person Rudy had become. Rudy was known as a man of his word and a rich man with compassion. He gave large amounts of money to help many worthy causes. Still, he paced across his huge office on the top floor of one of the twin towers of the World Trade Center, wondering if he had done enough to help others.

He stopped again at one of the spacious windows and for some strange reason, he began to count the vessels carrying passengers from foreign countries. He adjusted his binoculars to read the names of the ships and see the flag on the stern. Most people were coming to America by air nowadays but many could not afford to fly, so they came by cabin and even steerage on ships just like his mother and father.

The challenge from Ted Turner, who had recently given one billion dollars to help the children of the world, had been made to other very wealthy people to do something on a huge scale.

Rudy felt assured that not only had he contributed huge amounts of money, but he was proud that his extensive network of commercial enterprises had contributed to the opportunities and achievements of many people who were willing to put their shoulder to the wheel — to learn, to work, to seek and obtain the good life. He had faced many so-called impossible challenges during his climb to the top.

Yet, with a driving personality like Rudy, he felt he could do more. A moral sensitivity developed in early childhood told him he should do more. What could he do? What should he do? How could he meet Ted Turner's challenge? The desire to contribute more to humanity became a consuming challenge, which bordered on an obsession and burned in his consciousness like a stubborn ember in an abandoned campfire that refused to be extinguished.

"Which direction should I take?" he mused. He had made many deals in a lifetime in business and most proved to be successful ones. He had survived the failures. The actions that brought him the greatest satisfaction were the ones that required the daring decisions for the toughest challenges.

Suddenly, as he traveled down memory lane, his mind bolted back into present reality. He asked himself, "What is the greatest need in the world today?" A long list began to pop into his mind. Most of them were problems concerning lack of funds, especially medical research. All were worthy but none seemed to ring out above the others.

Then, a unique thought occurred to him almost like a revelation. Perhaps the greatest need in the world today was not money but a directional map for each human life! How should a person live to gain fulfillment and purpose for himself and others on this planet? But wait, wasn't this supposed to be what thousands of religions had claimed to do? Had all of them failed? Perhaps so — perhaps no.

There was still so much suffering, outrageous hate, violence and incalculable fear among most peoples of the world. Most were innocent of serious wrongdoing yet struggled to keep alive; many were still victims of useless and senseless wars. What were the causes of all of this human misery? The second millennium was the bloodiest time on earth. More people were slaughtered in the name of religion than ever before!

What could be done at the beginning of the third millennium to prevent the carnage of war from happening over and over again? There had to be some universal values. Man had indeed accomplished some incredible things in the second millennium. He dug through the bottom of the English Channel to connect England with France and fashioned canals like the Panama and Suez to send gigantic freight and passenger ships on a shorter route. He fulfilled his dream of flying, not only far above the eagles' flight, but he flew to the moon and walked on it.

A magnificent space station is in progress and the vast and intriguing universe will be a continual source of scientific study. Man has used his inventive mind in so many new endeavors. He has sent trains hurtling over 200 miles per hour piercing mountains with ingenious tunnels. He has devised apparatus to go to the bottom of the seas to study sea life and retrieve sunken vessels. Through intense and dedicated research in medical science, he has developed drugs to cure a thousand maladies and taught skillful hands to save multiplied millions of lives through elaborate and intriguing surgery. His construction knowledge is matched by unique architectural acumen that has dotted the planet with new pyramids and skyscrapers and prolific bridges that serve justice to ancient wonders and even make a quantum leap in size and beauty. His artistic mind has made possible music masterpieces that excite or calm the spirit and spread on canvas a singular delight that has thrilled billions.

Athletes have traversed a measured mile in less than four minutes and jumped over a cane seven feet high. They have scored dozens of goals throwing an inflated round ball through a 10-foot high hoop in one game, hit 70 home runs in baseball, kicked and passed a football over two-thirds of the playing field and lifted over 500 pounds of iron. On and on, athletic feats flash before one's mind. Women have also excelled in the sports arena to awesome heights since they have been given the opportunity to participate in dozens of sports. The fun and excitement flashed on by two of man's inventions, the television and the computer, have been a pioneer binding cultural factor and a mighty positive force despite some of the obvious negative impacts.

From the profound writings of Shakespeare to the penetrating poetry of Angelou Maya, we have been moved by the written word. We have created plays, live theatre and movies, both powerfully positive and damningly destructive.

If we could just appreciate all of the outstanding creations of man that have become a part of our life, it would inspire us to forget most, if not all of our problems and travel down life's road with a smile of inner confidence.

Yet, man has also turned his fabulous genius toward creating weapons of destruction. From the stone to the knife and spear, from the bow and arrow, to the rifle and bullet, and exploding cannonball. Devastating bombs have been dropped from airplanes. Atom bombs and high-tech missiles can deliver a demonstrated cataclysmic extinction, shocking the world by instantly wiping out huge cities with deadly radiation extending many miles away from their epicenter.

Alas, there is clear evidence that the wonderful talents of mankind can be used in an incredibly negative fashion. It is an enormous paradox that man can create so many wonderful and magnificent things and yet devote so much time, energy and genius to destroying other humans often for the sake of insane, selfish, religiously enraged leaders.

Why can't we, as a human race, care more about our kind all over this unique, delicate, life-sustaining planet? Are we destined to be barbarians forever?

Peculiar doubts crept into Rudy's thought process. People with the highest intelligence had grappled with these issues since the beginning of the written word. They faced the same array of difficulties: the nature of man, the need to survive, greed, selfishness, the desire to control, the lack of compassion for others especially if they were different from themselves, dishonesty, the lack of trust and a thousand other problems. Still, the challenge remains. A new millennium is here!

Is it futile to even try to wade through all the barriers and corroded bastions of doubt to pierce through the morass to see a new light?

Rudy said to himself, "The only hope is truth. The only hope is truth. Truth is the only hope. How can we discover the truth?" This is and always has been the hope of science, the hope of mankind's indomitable spirit and the hope of the future.

What are the causes of man slaughtering man? No doubt there are many underlying forces. All are complex and hard to comprehend. How can we look in the mirror and say, "I don't care as long as I am okay and my family is okay and not killed in war or crime?"

Perhaps one could prioritize the causes and begin to tackle them. Is there something fundamental about the causes of war that humans have inflicted upon themselves? Is this quest an impossible dream? And, even if that impossible dream of identifying prime causes was achieved, could anything significant be done about it? Well, you might as well have two impossible dreams. Are the twin challenges too grandiose? Identify and alter the causes. We can and we must! Should we have allowed humans to keep believing the world was flat and not try to teach them the truth because it violated their sincere heartfelt belief that it just could not be a sphere?

Several days of questioning brought on a considerable amount of mental fatigue, but he finally hit upon what seemed to be a fantastic idea.

The Quest was a beautiful clipper-style yacht owned by Rudy. It seemed the name was on target. The ship was both adventuresome and practical. You could sail whenever desired and/or go by powerful motors by a flick of a switch. It was equipped with state-of-the-art safety devices and had several powerful computers on board.

Why had he named this exquisite yacht *The Quest*? He did not exactly know but at the time he was on a quest for financial security — as much as he could accumulate. Prophetically, he no longer desired money but had a burning quest for a workable, truthful philosophy of mankind that would at least reduce murders and wars and hopefully someday, almost eliminate them. Now, he knew he was seeking the highest goal, a quest, seemingly impossible, but worthy of all the energy and finances he needed to muster up to support this cause.

The idea kept him excited all night long. What if he put together a highly intelligent group of relatively young people to come up with some answers? The group should have varied life experiences and it should be diversified. *The Quest* could create an exciting environment and money could provide a powerful incentive. Rudy decided to motivate the individuals with a generous salary and possible bonus, but depend on a selection process that sought people who would not shrink from huge challenges. They had to have a background of success and individual creativity. Their formal education could vary but a broad informal education and inquiring mind would be essential. They must possess good people skills yet not be wishy-washy and dependent on others to always lead.

Rudy continued to frame in his mind the type of people who could mix it up and yet respect other individuals even if they totally disagreed with their views.

Where on earth and who on earth are such people? He whimsically thought, "Certainly not many in the US Congress or the British Parliament." How many should be in the "think tank?" *The Quest* could easily accommodate a dozen people besides the crew and have room to spare. There was the captain's room that made a very comfortable gathering place with food and beverages.

Rudy finally decided to have seven people in the group. Cruising in a leisurely fashion might stimulate the minds of the group members. Recruitment should be a piece of cake. Who would want to turn down such an opportunity? Applications would be taken on the Internet. The cruise would be basically from Miami, where Rudy kept *The Quest,* and cover the Caribbean Sea and ports of call, as the group desired. The cruise would embrace three to six months, allowing members to drop their defenses and desires to impress, then gel into an honest working group.

Equipment of all sorts would be available on *The Quest* and any special computer programs or books could be acquired at any port-of-call.

The individuals selected could be of any race, gender or nationality. They could represent a particular religion or none. They could be extremists in their views or middle-of-the-roaders. No conscious efforts would be made to select a quota of anything including gender, race or religion. The merit of the individual and how he or she would meld into the group and the significant contributions that they might make would be the key to being selected.

A selection bonus of $10,000 cash would be given up front and the cruise salary would be $100,000 for each participant.

If Rudy approved a document or report, a $25,000 bonus would be given! The crew of *The Quest* would receive double-salary during this special cruise and while not participating formally with the seven, they would be encouraged to put in their two cents worth about any issue with any member or members who might be on deck. Rudy felt the working man's common sense opinions were often underrated in human society.

It should be a lot of fun and yet be a very thoughtful mission in this gorgeous environment. Rudy almost wished he could go along but he was afraid his ideas and comments would carry more influence than they might deserve since he was the sponsor of the entire project. If the group made a report as he believed they would, then he could add comments and decide what method of distribution the report would have, if any.

The procedures and topics would be the challenge of the group themselves. Once Rudy made the selections and watched *The Quest* sail out into the blue waters off the coast of Florida, he would bow out. He promised not to see them again until he received some kind of report from this seven-person "jury."

Chapter II
A Unique Selection

The response to the call for applicants to cruise the Caribbean, as one would expect, was monumental. Rudy wondered if it was the money offered or the intellectual challenge. He hoped it was both. He knew he would be absolutely overwhelmed by the thousands upon thousands who responded, so he hired 150 people who were so-called experts and ordinary citizens to screen the applications. They were divided into panels of three people each and requested to nominate only the very top candidates.

Rudy asked them to present him a list of 25 applicants. He would personally give an interview to a short list of 25 and select seven. The 25 nominees who had gone through the three-person screening process would arrive for his final approval that was very thorough. Regardless of the list of criteria that his screening people might use, they usually went by "their gut feeling" and "fly by the seat of their pants." He had found this to be a method quite successful for him in the commercial world.

After giving the 25 nominees over an hour interview and reviewing statements explaining why they were on the short list, he felt at least 14 of them would be near perfect. Finally, he made out a list of seven ensuring a measure of diversity, but he was not chained to any quota. He made the selections honestly and without outside pressure from anyone; he felt good about each person selected. He had not known any of them beforehand. There would be no alternates. If anyone got sick or so disgusted they left, it would not matter. There was nothing magic about the number seven.

There was, however, something magic about the individuals selected. Rudy could tell that each one of them was totally ignited with curiosity about the project. They were anxious to prove they could take on the world and meet this remarkable challenge. They all wanted to plow new ground, bring their fine minds into focus and create a product that would be not only significant but also inspiring!

He put his list of seven in alphabetical order: Rachel Brooks, Lu Chang, Al Green, Rev. John Hayes, David Preakness, Bridgette Thompson, and Tony Tweedhurst. They all received their notice of selection at the same time.

The cruise began. There is very little on this planet that equals the glow of the setting sun against the heavens as it sinks slowly in the west when you are experiencing the pull of beautiful white sails engulfed with a smooth, steady wind. The ship glided gracefully on the surface of the ocean like an accomplished ice skater on a frozen pond.

This tranquil scene was suddenly interrupted by an emotional outburst. "I've got it! I've got it! I've got it!" Tony Tweedhurst exclaimed.

He had been seated in one of the anchored fisherman's chairs at the stern of the ship. He had it all right. It was a beautiful swordfish that had been playing with his bait for many nautical miles.

J.W. Davis, the captain of the ship, was not at the wheel at this moment so he looked at the catch and helped Tony reel the monstrous fish aboard.

"It's a great example," Davis said, almost excited as Tony.

"Just think," said Tony, "this fellow and us probably have some of the same ancestors!"

The captain was rather astounded. "What do you mean? I have heard some fools say we came from monkeys, now you are telling me we came from a fish?"

"Not exactly," responded Tony, realizing he had unwittingly upset the captain. "What I mean is that a fish is no doubt on the lower end of the phylogenetic scale than man but still branched off the same living being."

"Yeah, yeah," said the captain. "I had better get back to the wheel."

J.W. Davis climbed the little stairway up to the pilot's room. He knew Tony was not crazy. He looked fine and was supposed to be highly educated, but he must have a loose screw somewhere.

In fact, all seven in this group were better looking than the average person but the boss had indeed selected some real weirdos. "Well, I did not come from any fish!" he growled to himself.

As Captain Davis arrived in the wheelhouse, he noticed a beautiful lady peering toward the open sea. Davis inquired how she was enjoying the cruise.

"Oh fine," Rachel Brooks replied. "I feel like I could just sail and sail and sail through the pearly gates and meet my Jesus face to face and walk with him down the golden streets as I begin singing that precious hymn, 'Thank you Lord for Saving my Soul.' This ship gives me a heavenly feeling and I'm just glad my sins are underneath His precious blood. Now I can sing, 'There's a Beautiful and Pearly White City' and keep my mind set like a flint, you know, like the Apostle Paul."

Speechless, the captain paused a moment as he kept walking on through the other door. He smiled as best he could. Finally he said, "Have a nice day."

He would warn his crew of ten that they should be extremely courteous to this special passenger group. This was not the usual run of the mill business group or favor-seeking politicians to which the crew had become accustomed.

In fact, they could talk to the members of the group as the boss had laid out, but their minds would wind up like scrambled eggs if they tried to figure out what the deuce these people were doing in this floating think tank.

The first formal meeting of the group took place in the exquisitely appointed captain's room. Rudy had personally served as the overseer of the redecoration. It was spacious and relaxing.

Soon the members found a seat and Al Green spoke up. "I know we are all leaders, all very brilliant," he laughed, "and all of that stuff, but we need one person to guide us in this important effort. Therefore, I nominate David Preakness to serve as group leader. Are there other nominations?"

After quite a long pause, David said, "This is a surprise to me. Perhaps someone else will volunteer."

No one responded.

"Well, I will do my very best but before it is over, you will all probably wish you had nominated someone else. Really, I do appreciate your confidence in me and I accept this challenge with humility. I just can't seem to say no to a tough challenge."

DAVID PREAKNESS

David, in his late twenties, was built like a linebacker and had the looks of a movie star. The men liked his straightforward but unassuming approach. His biggest fault was an uncompromising dedication to his career, which gave him little time for a social life. Two or three of the female members thought this should and would definitely change before their cruise was completed.

David had developed a strong sense of self-esteem that gave him confidence to praise others. He genuinely displayed a keen interest in their lives, their problems and successes. He could be tough when necessary, but his modus operandi was to be laid back and relaxed.

He always showed tremendous respect for what people believed about metaphysical matters. He actually felt that no one really knew the whole truth so it was folly to be overly dogmatic about any particular position. He wondered all his life if there was any way out of the religious confusion that the human race had created for itself.

He did not really believe that any particular religion, despite their claims, had exclusive answers and recoiled at their intolerance of other religions. However, he learned to admire devout people in all religions. His logical mind told him all of them could not be true because of their diametrical conflicts, so he asked himself which one is true. Should this be left up to chance — a roll of the dice? And, were any of them really the whole truth?

Sometimes he thought it would be very nice and easy to simply accept some faith blindly as billions have done and forget about his burning quest to seek the truth. However, his intellectual nature and considerable education would not permit this road of life to be one he could travel.

He always imagined being born into a family which might have been any other religion than his family. If his mother and father bowed to a statue of Buddha each morning or Indian totem pole, he would have done what he saw and followed what he was told. There would have been an emotional attachment to the statue or the pole even if he abandoned the faith of his parents.

David gradually made a momentous decision. He would back off from everything he had been taught as truth and start over using his own mind to draw a line between truth and myth — between productive behavior and behavioral practices that are negative and destructive. One of his natural concerns was the impact of his views upon others, especially his devoted, devout family and life-long friends.

He finally reasoned with them by saying, "If I am punished to go to Hell and burn forever and ever for seeking the truth, then so be it. I am not concerned about an imagined destiny or anything in the so-called hereafter as long as I know myself that I am honest and sincere in the questions that cause me concern. I do believe honesty insulates a person from fear."

RACHEL BROOKS

Rachel Brooks was an extreme believer in the old time preaching, praying, singing, shouting, Bible thumping, "hell fire" or "heaven with Jesus" kind of religion. She was bound for the pearly gates and fully intended to walk with loved ones and the saints of all ages on the streets of gold . If ever a tiny doubt tried to enter her mind, she quickly quoted some scripture from the Bible (King James Version) that she believed was designed to cast out that particular doubt.

Rachel had been born into a Pentecostal family in South Carolina, not only was she an avid churchgoer, she honestly believed that every word in the Bible was true from cover to cover. She believed God answered fervent prayer, that people could be forgiven of all their sins through the blood of Jesus. She believed God performed miracles and still does every day. She gave 10% of her income to the church and sent generous offerings to TV evangelists like Oral Roberts, Benny Hinn and others.

Rachel Brooks had been chosen "Miss South Carolina" in the beauty pageant. She was a beautiful all-American Doris Day-type of girl, full of exuberance, who loves the ocean and the mountains and nature. She was sure of herself, sure of where she was going in life, and planned someday to marry and raise a Christian family.

She was more than a pretty person. She won valedictorian honors in high school and college. She had a quick wit in conversation. Although she had many suitors, she was waiting for "Mr. Right." She believed that God would provide the right person, just like He provided Abraham with the lamb in the bush just at the right time, if she followed God's will.

Rachel was thankful for her good looks but was not stuck on herself. She viewed her attractiveness as a talent given to her by God and that she would use any influence this might bring her to further God's cause. She often down played her looks and charm; she preferred to be recognized for her brainpower.

The people who knew her best were very proud of her selection to this project because they knew this would finally be the perfect forum for a legitimate and powerful display of her beliefs and intellect. This desire, rather than the fun and the money, was what really motivated her to respond to the announcement she saw on her computer.

She was a leading graduate student majoring in child psychology. She was already preparing a thesis on "Moral and Ethical Training Necessities for Youth." She was still single at age 24. Many men wished they could change that marital status. She was nice to be around because she was so positive and had a great sense of humor.

ANTHONY "TONY" TWEEDHURST

Anthony Tweedhurst was a complete and vocal atheist who frequently declared no one can prove any God whatsoever. Anyone who worshiped or bowed to any deity, an imagined great God or a Japanese Emperor was a pitiful example of a person who had surrendered his brain to others.

He was excited to be in the group to hear the silly arguments of the religionists so he could respond. Being generally a likeable fellow, he kept telling himself to try not to be abrasive and come off like a scrooge. One could disagree and not be mean about it. He did often have a difficult time avoiding ridicule for championing reasons.

He was able, however, to distinguish between the belief and respect for the person even though blinded by the belief. He quoted other atheists often and seemed to have swallowed their thoughts as his very own yet felt religionists were under a type of slavery.

A member of the Harvard Religious Department at one stage in his life, he retired to writing in a variety of areas gradually becoming a dyed-in-the-wool atheist. He was viewed as a brilliant individual who tried to dress like Einstein but had inadequate gumption to fix a simple broken lamp. He really did not care for the mundane things handymen do. He would get in out of the rain if he chose to, not because everyone else did. He often just stayed in it, reverting to his childhood unabashedly.

Wearing mostly flea market clothes, he seemed to exist in his own intellectual world. Trying desperately to avoid style and conformity, he actually surrendered to the rigid style and conformity of the Ivy League super-intellectual. This true adult nerd just might be the person who would give the most insights to the question of what is the greatest need in the world.

He was an original thinker in many arenas. Anthony or "Tony" really believed in himself and often said, "I may seem

weird to you, but you seem weird to me — so we are even. Let's
be friends."

This attitude, though a little strange, was nevertheless
endearing. Whoever met someone proud of being weird but
also regarded you just as weird in a different way? Who do you
know could joke about it? Tony was cocky all right, but at
times he could make you think you were sitting at the feet of
Solomon or Aristotle while he was explaining step by step how
he came to a certain conclusion.

Someone as deep as Tony could be eccentric as he pleased
without offending others. If one could catch him alone, one on
one, he was refreshing as cool water yet in a group he, at
times, could pour cool water on everyone's ideas but his own.

One thing was for sure. This unshakable atheist would
bring an abundance of fire and controversy to the effort of the
group!

REV. JOHN HAYES

Rev. John Hayes, married and in his early fifties, was a
Jerry Falwell-type Christian believer somewhat similar to
Rachel in believing in fundamental Christianity but not as
charismatic in her worship style. He was the classic Baptist, a
so-called mainstream religion.

He believed he was "born-again" and that Jesus was his
personal Savior. He had a pleasing personality who laughed
heartily and very often.

His Afro-American heritage gave him pride, but he just
loved everybody, period. He was very tolerant but he declared
with Biblical authority, "as for me and my house, we will serve
the Lord." He believed in the word of God. John was a very
successful father and a community worker. He had life experience that would be invaluable in the cruise project.

Besides delivering Martin Luther King, Jr.-style sermons,
he served as a lead soloist in his church choir. He could
mount an electric enthusiasm among the congregation. He
believed that striving to live the Christian life before others
was his calling and if he continued, he would have a mansion
in heaven.

He was often disgusted with hypocrites and felt you were
either a Christian or not. Yet, he rarely confronted anyone and
if he sensed he had offended anyone, he would flash his great
smile and say, "You know, you are one of God's great creations
and I really admire you."

One just couldn't get angry with John. He was very bright,

loaded with common sense and sensitive to the feelings of everyone, rich or poor, young or old. He was going to add a little something including pepper to the effort.

BRIDGETTE THOMPSON

Bridgette Thompson, a 25-year-old multiracial beauty, could really pass for an Afro-American, an Asian, a Hispanic, or an Italian. Her perfect bronze skin and long beautiful black hair was a delightful background for her beautiful brown eyes and gorgeous smile. Her eyebrows arched naturally when she conversed and whether the exact racial genes would ever be determined were of no consequence since she was charm personified.

One of her heroes was Tiger Woods because he spoke of his multiracial background and, of course, his great golfing ability. Bridgette, a good tennis player, was better known as a singer. She had turned down contracts but appeared for one-night performances several times a year

Yes, she was exotic and beautiful. She knew poverty and developed street survival skills because she was raised by her grandmother in a large tenement building in New York. She observed human life on many levels. She saw triumph and despair and through it all determined to make something out of her life. She had done just that and with flying colors. She worked hard in a tough job, attended night college and joined a top business firm.

She fell in love only to learn that the guy was an illegal drug merchant. She gave him an ultimatum — choose the drugs or me. She never saw him again and wondered if she could ever love again.

Men dated her once and thought they loved her, but Bridgette was afraid they were falling in love with the outside. How could they really comprehend what she was like on the inside in one date?

Bridgette was a strong believer in what the world needs now is real love somehow. She thought of the peoples of the world everywhere, not just her own country. She was a congenial person but gave no quarter and took no quarter from anyone. She really felt that she was as good as anyone and that she was not superior to anyone.

We are equal, not by religious decree certainly, and not by most governments. We are equal by something stronger — fairness and common sense. "Does not everyone have some shade of skin color?" she would ask.

Such ridiculous insignificant notions that one skin color was superior to another were beneath her dignity. What did seem of tremendous importance to her were the issues of religion, the road to peace, and she jumped at the chance to join the cruise.

She told herself that this would be the most fulfilling period of her lifetime. Bring it on!

ALBERT "AL" GREEN

Albert Green, born in the 1950's to Jewish parents, came from a very large, closely knit family. He was a true believer in Jehovah God, the Torah, and other pronouncements of Judaism, but he was not an Orthodox Jew. He was concerned about the interpretation people in Judaism and outside put on the "chosen people" of Jehovah concept. He was constantly trying to resolve certain emotional hangovers from the many persecutions of Jewish people. He lost both grandparents in the Holocaust.

He was a concert pianist before his early retirement because of ligament problems and joined Green Mercantile Company to work with his brothers and sisters. They always viewed him as a philosopher and musician rather than a merchant trying to advance the company.

He was a very clever person who seemed at times like he missed a great career in comedy. Perhaps so, but beneath that veil of humor was one of the profound minds in the group. He also could have been a great scientist or whatever. He chose to become a family man after his musical career and never looked back. He looked to the future. He wondered about new technology and scientific advancements. He tried to envision a world of the year 3000 A.D. It boggled his mind but he still thought about it from time to time.

LU CHANG

Last but not least of the selections was the stunning Lu Chang from Hong Kong, China. She had it all, whatever that meant. Lu was the type of beautiful woman that you could just stare at and wonder how anyone could be so pretty and so smart. It often happened that very attractive people are taken at face value and their equally potent intellectual capabilities are overlooked.

It seemed to many that it was unfair for people to possess beauty, charm, wit and a thoughtful mind. Yet, one could hardly blame Lu. Although she was not responsible for her heredity, she was to be credited with the resolute manner in which she had excelled in academics and music. She had been unwavering in her pursuit of excellence when obviously she could have been highly successful as a model or actress.

Since she was a little girl listening to everyone call her a "Chinese doll," she had been attracted to the proposition that although people looked different on the outside, what really counted was the real person on the inside. She saw a host of Caucasians in Hong Kong and later on, many members of the Negroid race. There were outer differences, but she soon discovered that neither beauty nor intelligence was an exclusive possession of any race.

She wondered, as a child, why people got so uptight about another human's skin appearance that was different from their own whether from race to race, within the race, whether unattractive or severely handicapped, slightly deformed, tall, short, fat, skinny or whatever. She still was concerned that these porous, weak indications of who the person really might be comprise so much of the criteria that people use to judge others. Instinctively she realized this approach was inherently wrong and devastating. She vowed to do her part in changing it as much as possible.

Lu had been fortunate to have successful parents who operated a huge business firm in Hong Kong. She often accompanied them on exciting business trips into the mainland and many important cities around the world. These experiences gave Lu a wealth of valuable experience even though she was just 27 years old. She had visited places, met interesting people, conversed with national leaders and had the opportunity to be truly educated to a level that would dwarf the achievements of most college professors.

When asked about her favorite countries, she would reply, "All of them for different reasons." But when pressed, she would say she would consider China, England, and the USA since most of her life had been lived under these three influences. Basically, however, she considered herself a world citizen, a human being without the walls of any country. Her "don't fence me in" attitude, along with her other many assets made her an outstanding person.

All her life, she was taught of a beautiful place called Heaven and a place where bodies burned in Hell. Lu Chang had struggled to believe, as her parents would have her believe, yet she was filled with doubts and felt dishonest at times when she was a young girl going to Mass. Finally, learning of the religions all around the world and looking for answers, Pope John Paul II decreed something that was the straw that broke the wagon. The Pope declared that Heaven and Hell were not physical places. Lu rebelled against the whole set-up of religion because she felt that people everywhere in all faiths adjusted the religion to fit their ideas and no longer adjusted themselves to fit the religion. She had many questions and comments for the group and was eager for the sessions to begin.

The seven people selected certainly had different backgrounds and experiences. Could this handful of people ever get together in friendship and common direction enough to accomplish anything? It was up to their own ingenuity and desire to be successful or stubbornly refusing to accede to another's viewpoint as being worthy of any serious consideration. All had come to the table with present notions; some were bolstered by logic-tight compartments. Yet, they were such an interesting group and so highly motivated, something good was bound to happen!

Chapter III
Who I Am—
Some Things I Believe

You can imagine the sheer excitement of the seven individuals chosen to sail on one of the world's most prestigious yachts to tackle the challenge to provide a road map for human conduct that might help eliminate or reduce the bloodshed in useless wars, terrorist killings, and domestic violence including murder, assaults, and all kinds of abuses in the third millennium. It was such an honor to have been selected to this project and each one thought, "I don't want to foul up. I want to make a real positive contribution."

All seven had promised to begin with an open mind and enter the debates, which were bound to occur, with objectivity. However, each participant knew this was next to impossible for each person had become a part of everything in their lives which they had experienced. Perhaps they could and would be willing to compromise a little on things not really important but deep down there was a determination to remain true to previous beliefs and ideas in the main. How could it be different? If only one could look inside the minds of the seven eager individuals, there would be a panorama of thoughts and ideas sufficient to fill a small library.

The challenge was before them. How could these private thoughts be laid on the table, rationally discussed under an umbrella of appreciation and love and still arrive at a useful conclusion?

The yacht vacation atmosphere in the Caribbean was enticing and the money was alluring. However, opportunity was the prime motivation driving the group. The "think tank" situation offered the greatest challenge for these thinkers beginning the third millennium.

David Preakness was the first to speak at their first semi-formal forum-type assembly. He spoke softly at first before becoming rather evangelistic.

"The imperative to point the way humans should regard life, living and destiny is tailor-made for our inquiring minds. The fact that we will be relatively isolated and challenged to form a team-like group, despite vast differences in our backgrounds and beliefs is before us. It will be very interesting and intriguing. Can it be accomplished? Will it be accomplished? Or will this effort be a worrisome waste? Could some negative things come out of this venture? Could some very positive things result from this venture? Will the positive far outweigh the negative? If not, why are we bothering to do this in the first place?

"Even if we, as a group, develop a cohesive and useful team-like atmosphere, how can we translate this attitude to the real, large world? How are we going to handle the intense criticism of some religious leaders whose economic well-being and fame depend on gaining followers and building disdain and hate for other religions? How will the people in the ivory towers of academia view our work and should we care? What is going to be the reaction of our family and friends if we can devise a product they don't like? If the product is halfway reasonable with even a partial ring of viability, would that suffice or do we stand disappointed if the unreachable wall of perfection is not achieved? Who will defend the actions of the group if we don't defend our conclusions ourselves? Do we have the courage to proceed knowing criticism will come like a driving rain? Have we considered that whatever we produce may spawn a new kind of religious type loyalty producing a host of demi-gods who perceive a chance for personal profit? All of these questions and a huge amount of others will loom in our minds. Yet, if we have the possibility of turning this big ship, Earth, even a few degrees, it could land upon a dramatically different shore."

David could see the six participants were giving him very close attention even though their minds were racing at the top speed listening and thinking at the same time.

"Opposed to the many questions about our challenge is the proposition, why not do it? Mankind has come this far, whether through evolution or creation and in general has failed to create reasonable, attainable guidelines about how one should live his or her life and know peace and happiness fitting into one's true purpose and destiny. The technical advances, the economic revolutions, the man on the moon stuff is wonderful in its proper sphere. Yet, wars are still raging on the planet and there are too many sociopath individuals who rob, rape, maim, and murder others.

"Despite the wonderful advances made by humans, we still have not learned to reach a sensible way of living together in peace and harmony on our beautiful and bountiful planet. Certainly, an honest effort at some kinds of solutions is worthwhile regardless of any negative barriers mounted by naysayers. And, what is their solution? Do they even care? Isn't it time to stop straining the water and get the hog out of the spring? Is that hogging the aggressiveness and dogmatism of the main religious in the world? Do we dare examine this proposition? Are there other fundamental causes of our colossal failure to achieve peace and brotherhood? No doubt other causes exist and we need to examine any and all of them to see which ones rise to the level of a major negative cause. Shall we shrink from our task because it is not simple? Shall we not admit now that we are a very diverse group and on any proposition, we may be the only person who honestly regard it in a certain way? Shall we use the power of persuasion and honest debate when possible before we vote? Cannot we recognize that if the vote results are 6 to 1 that the one may be right and six may be wrong but expediently, we must move on?

"I may say once in a while, 'You are butting in too much.' Let the person complete their thought or just say 'Let's cool it' and hear so and so out or I may have to say, 'This is not the US Senate, no filibusters allowed here.' We cannot allow our honest differences to create any hostility toward one another. In a sense, we are a little tiny miniature world. If we wind up like the larger world full of hate and discrimination, we are wasting our sponsor's money and our time. The world has learned well how to let disagreements lead to hate and slaughter. We need to show it does not have to be that way.

"My purpose for this little keynote speech is to encourage us to focus on the necessary gentleness of our process and pledge to love and appreciate all others even though their view may be 180 degrees from our own. It has been my experience with groups that some gel quickly and some are slow to reach a cohesive mode of operation. Better acquaintance is the glue that usually brings a group together. So, as your leader, I would like for you to draw a number out of this baseball cap. The number you draw will be the order in which each of us will give a sketch of our life and beliefs or whatever to

the group in about an hour or so. We need to know you better
— your hobbies, recreational interests, unusual experiences,
achievements, awards, and even quirks if you desire. You may
wish to give us parts of your application that got you into this
august group. We will begin tomorrow at 10 a.m. As your
leader, I really do not know what I am doing and don't want to
dictate procedure. Hit your little voting machine and vote yes
or no on my suggestion."

The vote was 7 yes, 0 no.

"That may be the only unanimous vote we will see," John
chuckled.

"See you tomorrow," said David. "Don't be too modest. We
all know you are special or you would not be in this group."

While leaving, each member drew a number out of the cap.
Little friendly smiles were on everyone's face hoping they
would not draw number one. David felt in his heart that this
group was going to fight it out, but in a productive manner. He
believed they could prove that love and harmony could exist
despite vast differences in outlook. This very spirit was what
the world needed and must develop.

The rising sun shot beautiful silver arrows across the horizon. The small whitecaps on the sea reflected the morning
glory as the sun drove the darkness of the night away. Sunrise
at sea was awesome as the vari-colored beauty was mirrored
faithfully by the relatively calm waters. A soft wind glided the
ship forward. It must have been seen from an overhead airlin-
er as a little chip of wood moving rather aimlessly on a gigantic lake. Indeed, there was no destination, just a small group of
people brought together to tackle the most challenging issues
in life. Hopefully, a feasible direction could be achieved for
this project even though the sailing yacht just cruised along
lazily without a single adversity.

This was the day of self-introductions. Everyone knew Al
would begin and probably set the tone for all of the introductions. He had not complained about the fact that he had only
several hours to contemplate his introduction. He was very
confident concerning who he was and what he could add to the
group discussions.

AL GREEN

"My name is Al Green. I wanted to draw the number 7,
which has always had a religious significance among Jews. I
am Jewish and proud of it but before I try to enlighten you as
those in the group may do about my religion, I would like to

say a few things about myself.

"I was born in New York City. My parents were more Orthodox than I tend to be and this distresses them to no end. However, with my two sisters and one brother, I can say we all get along well together. Of course, we argue quite a bit but in a civil way. We learned that family really means something special and nothing is more important in life than family except service to Jehovah.

"I once thought of becoming a reformed Rabbi but decided to become a physician. I am very interested in cancer research and I believe my work has contributed significantly to the battle against this terrible disease. I am married to a non-practicing Catholic girl and since I am Jewish, you can see the challenge and the fun. Perhaps this cruise will enable me to communicate better with her concerning religious differences as I learn from you. She is my true love and I know she feels that way about me.

"Honestly, I can't help but wonder how many people in the world have fallen in love with what seems 'forbidden fruit' to the guardians of certain religions. It is really a hassle. Some seem to resolve the situation very amicably while others seem to struggle all of their life combating the snide remarks and misunderstandings. Many inheritances have been withheld because of interfaith marriages. I suppose it is not as tough as an interracial marriage but I am not sure whether religious intolerance does not rise to the level of racial intolerance. It certainly does in many people, including my own.

"Many times there is a sinister mixture of racial and religious intolerance that irritates me to no end. The main reason I applied to become a participant in this group was to see if I could give some substance to addressing the situation we are all in as humans on this planet. I believe as has been acknowledged for other religions, that if everyone would accept Judaism, the problems of the world would be solved. There would be no more wars, pain or heartache. All would be peaceful and wonderful. I also know that the likelihood of this happening is like a snowball surviving in hell.

"Nevertheless, I want to present some of the basis of Judaism. Like the rest of you in the group who are religious, I believe there is a massive misunderstanding about my religion. How religions are portrayed in the media seem to dip only into the surface. All religions seem to become a stereotype of what the Hollywood perception is at the time and what the powers that be want to portray. Although Jews have played a prominent part in the Hollywood saga, I personally do not feel our people and beliefs have been properly portrayed. I supposed this is only natural since the storyline and money bottom line is given such preeminence.

"Judaism was not founded by a single religious leader like most religions. It developed among the various tribes who were called Semitic. Later on they were known as the Hebrews, Israelites and eventually Jews. We are all of the names and the anti-Semitic movements continued with the Hebrews, Israelites, and Jews, though the name changed at various times and in various locations.

"We seem to go in for name change. Actually, my forefathers were named Rosenberg, but for anti-Semitic reasons, my name was changed to Green. I have thought of changing it back to Rosenberg but too many legal papers are signed Green. I do dream of a world where someday this kind of nonsense will not be a reality but I have to accept this as present policy. If I did not think we as a human race, could change these large and small prejudices, I would not be on this boat.

"Judaism regards Abraham as its traditional patriarch to whom God promised a land of plenty. The lawgiver, of course, was Moses, who received God's commandments on top of Mt. Sinai. They were written on tablets of stone and should be followed religiously. There are basically five 'Thou shalt nots' and five 'Thou shalts.' Many people I have encountered say to me, 'If we live by the Ten Commandments, we'll make it into heaven.' Judaism is more complex than this one peak episode.

"Jewish scriptures are read and studied in the Hebrew language. The Torah contains the first five books. They proclaim the sacred covenant Jehovah made with the Jewish people and give laws other than the Ten Commandments that Jews are required to observe. The remaining 34 books explain additional history, hymns, psalms for worship, poetry and the proclamations or exaltations of the prophets. The scriptures are full of wisdom as in the book of Proverbs.

"The early Hebrews worshiped only one God and this is true today. Their contemporaries often had a plethora of gods. Jews believe that God created all things and is the god of all things. We see God as both the source of judgment and mercy. And, though controversial, we believe that God made a covenant with the Jewish people that promised them His care and protection. We are, of course, obliged to follow God's laws as laid out in the scriptures. We do not accept the New Testament.

"We believe that a Messiah is coming and that Jesus was

not the Messiah. This is naturally a major conflict with the world's largest religion that says they believe Jesus Christ is the Messiah. With over a billion and a half, about 33%, or one out of three people on Earth believing in some form that Jesus is the Messiah, how can Jews which are only four-tenths of one percent of the world's population about 18-20 million continue to defy these odds?

"Well, we believe as Christians believe that we are the foundation for the one true God and that Jesus himself could not have been the Son of God and was not and is not the leader that the true Messiah will be. We believe that four-tenths of one percent against 70% of the world (Christianity, Islam, and Buddhism) should be judged on truth not on overwhelming numbers. Religious beliefs are handed down from high authority. This is a common belief and not up for a popular vote! We now have part of our homeland back as the nation of Israel but here are more Jews in America than anywhere else.

"Most Jews are concentrated in New York. Some are in huge cities like Miami in America and London in Europe. There are a few in small towns and villages where they worship in small synagogues on Saturday, the Sabbath. In the world there are some very large and architecturally beautiful synagogues. A day of rest and worship is the meaning of the Sabbath. Worship for Jews means the reading publicly of the Jewish scriptures, the chanting or singing of psalms and some other songs of prayer and praise to Jehovah God.

"I am a follower of reformed Judaism. I believe in the spirit of Judaism, but I do not follow the ancient rules of conduct and ritual as strict as the Orthodox Jews. I do not observe the laws concerning clean and unclean foods. I also do not follow the beliefs of Hasidism, which is a fundamentalist sect mostly in Eastern Europe. I attend a synagogue, which has a pipe organ and a choir similar to some Christian churches. My brother, for example, calls himself a conservative Jew and tries to bridge the gap between Orthodox Jews and reformed Jews. You should see and hear the discussions when my father, an orthodox Jew, myself, a reformed Jew, and my brother, a conservative Jew, get together and the topic is the true religion. So, frankly I will not be offended by any differences that arise in the group when it comes to religion. I have been there. My wife and I co-exist very well.

"Most people know of blacks being subjected to slavery and slavery is an awful thing regardless of what group is enslaved. However, blacks are not the only people who have tasted this bitterness. For example, the Babylonians confined the Jews in the year 587 B.C. and kept my ancestors in prison for 50 years. They destroyed Solomon's temple. Jews tried to revolt in 66 A.D., but the power of Rome came down and destroyed the rebuilt temple of Solomon in 70 A.D. Jews had to flee in all directions. They had no land for approximately 1900 years. In Europe especially, the Christians persecuted the Jews and caused laws to be passed against Jews owning land or engaging in certain businesses. At times, mobs of angry people destroyed Jewish settlements and killed everyone.

"The Holocaust came about because Hitler blamed the Jews for Germany's defeats and suffering. I am proud that the United States, my country, and Britain strongly supported the creation of Israel in 1948. Yet, religious prejudices and old hatreds between the Muslims and the Jews still exist and most of you here know that all the attempts by everyone involved to solve these problems have not been successful. Well-meaning leaders on both sides have been assassinated, although I personally believe the masses of people on both sides have a deep desire for peace. The extremists keep the pot boiling and so many innocent people have died. It is stupid. This is my burning reason for my passionate interest in this venture. My God, can't we stop the killing because of religions?

"At some point, I will attempt to tell you about Islam. The sad part is that both Jews and Arabs are descended from Abraham and the extremists still fight each other. I pledge to listen and learn and contribute. Something different has to happen in this millennium. I want to be a part of it if I can just learn what to do."

RACHEL BROOKS

"My name is Rachel Brooks. I suppose there was a sustained effort to make certain that our group was composed of people with divergent views. Obviously, we are of different races and gender and I think this is an excellent approach to considering the challenging issues we are facing today.

"I have always believed that peace and understanding is possible through our Lord and Savior, Jesus Christ. I believe every word of the Bible is true and that there is a great revival sweeping across the world as we sail on this journey to attempt to solve grave issues. Naturally I feel and believe that a commitment to Jesus Christ is the answer. Although I was the valedictorian of my high school and graduated from college with the same high honor, I have learned that there is a world of secular knowledge that each of us will never know no matter how educated we may become. So, along with my quest for knowledge in textbooks, and elsewhere I have decided to follow Jesus and learn of His precious love and power. I believe that He is abiding in my heart and I want to use whatever talents I have to further His Kingdom. I love to sing the hymns that exalt Him and find that they give lots of peace and comfort to my soul.

"After graduate school and my studies in psychology, I am planning to go to a school for missionaries and learn how to devote my life for the cause of Christianity. I am full of love for the Lord and have a passion to go into the world and spread the gospel to every land. I am so excited about what God is doing in these last days and I want to stay in tune with Him. To accomplish what I desire, I believe I need a good partner in life and I want to raise children who will glorify god. So far I have not met the person that I feel God would have me marry, but I know he is out there somewhere.

"I am appreciative of all the awards that have been given to me; even the beauty pageants that I have won but I would trade all of this for the knowledge that my life had been lived in such a manner that other souls would be saved.

"Yes, I am an old-fashioned Christian. I believe that the whale swallowed Jonah and in fact if the Bible said Jonah swallowed the whale, I would believe that also. Surely, God could shrink the whale to the size of a goldfish and students swallowed goldfish for fun in some of our most prestigious colleges in the 1920's. Nothing is impossible with God.

"I also realize most people in the world do not believe as I do. The Bible teaches that narrow is the way and few people find it and broad is the way and many people enter therein. I want to be and plan to be in that small number. You will have to excuse me for testifying more than talking about my little life and accomplishments, but when I start praising Jesus, there seems to be an 'anointing" that engulfs me. The Holy Spirit gives me words to express my complete trust in Him. Praise His holy name!

"Having testified as it were, I am practical enough to realize that we are not here to try to convert the other people in the group. Each person here is probably comfortable with their religion or other beliefs or with the high intelligence you possess, you would have changed your beliefs. I am not here and I doubt if you are here to change beliefs. So what are the beliefs we hold in common? What will constitute the wholesome ideas and tenets that will make the world better? I am certain that all of us desire this result. Is there a way to cut through all the religion and philosophies of all people and create a reasonable map for each person on earth to follow?

"I am sophisticated enough to realize that so-called Christians have persecuted and killed others and vice-versa. This to any fair mind is patently wrong. My compassion must and does extend beyond my particular brand of faith and if we all can mount our compassion to a level beyond our culture and religious beliefs, there may be a way out for the human race. Without doubt, we are bogged down now in an incomprehensible morass and so many people are feeling desperate and depressed about the whole idea of what life is all about.

"I think I know, but if there is another effective gateway that does not call for me to surrender my relationship with Jesus, then I want to be a part of its creation. I want to dust off my mind, be willing to listen with loving patience and individuality to all of you and respect you, not only for who you are and what you have accomplished, but also for your burning desire to forge a new more effective way for humankind.

"Please do not interpret my rather extreme old-time Christian beliefs as a barrier to seeking new paths for people. The world has suffered and suffered and suffered. One cannot help but be brought to tears when today we see starving children, destroyed homes and bombs and bullets being used to destroy others. It seems that any reasonable, compassionate person would cry out, 'Stop, stop the killing!' I am not a big person and have a limited influence but with all the force of my being, I cry out, 'Isn't there something that can be done? Doesn't anyone care?' On this cruise we will answer, 'Oh yes, we care, we know we care and we will meet the challenge!'"

REV. JOHN HAYES

"My name is John Hayes. I was born and raised in Atlanta, Georgia into a staunch Baptist family. As a little boy, I enjoyed the many things that Atlanta offered in the way of fun and excitement. I could not understand the 'birds of a feather flock together' attitude among all races.

"My closest friend was a little Filipino boy and we shared many things together. I had two sisters but what did they know about the thoughts and needs of little boys? Tiki, my friend as a child, is still my best friend. We went to the same college and critiqued the same girls, the genuine and the fakes. He gave his opinions, not only about girls but everything else. I always envied and still do the people who have a sibling about the same age and the same gender to share the pains of growing up, particularly in adolescence. Tiki and I shared that need and comfort.

"My best friend, however, is Jesus Christ of Nazareth. I believe he was born of a Virgin Mary and that He is the Messiah and the Son of God. You might say I am a Billy Graham or Pat Robinson-type Christian. I consider myself mainstream basing my faith on the Bible. I do not proclaim that Baptists are the only true way as some do, but I do believe that our beliefs are the best way to exercise the Christian faith.

"The Baptist churches comprise the largest group of Protestants in the United States. Although the roots of the church are traced back to reformers like John Calvin centuries ago, it was in the south in America that both whites and blacks embraced the faith in huge numbers. In almost every little town and hamlet in America, you can see a Baptist church. I am proud of this and proud that we Baptists are not a centrally controlled denomination. We select our own preachers and in fact credential them for the ministry. We believe that Jesus was baptized in a river by immersion by John, the Baptist, and that a Christian should reach an age of accountability and accept Christ before he or she is baptized. 'Ye must be born again.'

"The size of the Baptist church would be much, much larger in numbers if we counted children as some groups do. We do have the most missionaries preaching the gospel winning souls to Jesus. They serve around the world in almost every nation of the world. We build schools, hospitals, clinics, and recreational facilities because we believe that faith without works is dead.

"About one out of every four people who accept religion in America are Baptists so we are strong enough and blessed enough to carry the message all over the globe. Still, there are many that have not heard of Jesus.

"While we do not consider ourselves fanatics, we are strong believers in the word of god, the Bible. We believe in the crucifixion of the Son of God and that His blood can forgive the sins of any person.

"If you were to ask me, if Baptists have been able to stop wars, I would have to admit that we have not. And, though I do believe the Bible, it bothers me that it teaches that there will always be wars and rumors of wars. I believe this scripture, but I do not want to believe that we, as human beings, can never solve our problems without the horrendous bloodshed that has transpired. I know we have to defend ourselves and I have lost loved ones in three wars. I have come to believe that man is so sinful that many wars are started by evil men who have their own selfish agenda and lead their people through lies and false repeated phrases into unnecessary wars.

"I am somewhat pessimistic that one will ever stop the bloodshed, but I promise to listen to you about your beliefs and ideas. Maybe, just maybe we, as a diverse group can offer a meager beginning to a path that will lead to more peace if not permanent peace. War is the worst thing in human history. I know it is not necessary for me to elucidate on this subject because everyone in this group and each member of the crew on this ship would agree.

"If we the people — not politicians, not the kings and queens — can devise any way that will lead to the prevention of war and bloodshed, we must. Though pessimistic, I am overpowered by the raw need of doing something. That is why I will be as sincere as I know how to be and make contributions to this project. Who knows? We may be more successful that we can envision at this early moment."

ANTHONY "TONY" TWEEDHURST

"My name is Anthony Tweedhurst. My friends call me Tony. My parents were rather poor but honest people. They raised six children so I suppose they had a right to be poor. However, they were rich in compassion and love and most of all, they believed that their six children should be encouraged to think for themselves.

"My mother was a faithful churchgoer. My father never attended except for weddings and funerals. He kept his religious beliefs — if he had any — to himself. I went to work at age 14 and have been working ever since. My education has been at night school, night college and the vast opportunities in public libraries. I deplore TV junk programs but love the educational and informative programs. I've also learned a little from a few movies but mostly acknowledge they are for entertainment. I did think the first 'Planet of the Apes' was very profound. Then, of course, Hollywood beat the idea in the ground with all those sequels.

"When we use the word 'minority,' I think that people like myself, an atheist, need an even stronger word because we seem to be so few in number. The truth, however, may have never been told about the real numbers of people who have decided for one reason or another that man created the Gods or the one God. We were not created by any God but are the imperfect product of millions of years of evolution.

"No one knows how many closet atheists are out there; I suppose it really doesn't matter. But, when I try to learn of the major religions and the minor religions and find common threads, I find it is a most different task. The problem is different deities. They either don't believe in the same God or divine leader or their interpretation of God and what man owes god is vastly different.

"Most religions teach some type of concern and compassion for others yet wage wars with extreme vengeance and hate. In the Old Testament (I Samuel 15) when God supposedly told Saul through Samuel to go kill all the Amalekites, utterly destroy all they have and don't spare them anything. Kill the men, kill the women. Yes, even kill the babies. Talk about hate and vengeance!

"The Bible says God told Saul to kill the oxen and the sheep, the camels and the asses. So what happened? According to the Bible, Saul got together two hundred thousand people and they did kill all these people, babies, and all except Agog, the King. Samuel chopped him into pieces himself. "Of course, Saul did not fare much better. He asked his armor bearer to kill him. He refused and so Saul fell on his own sword.

"Now theologians can give a thousand interpretations to this terrible mess, but I will not and cannot serve a God who is a killer of innocent babies. It is so strange to me that so many otherwise wonderful and compassionate people can go along blindly and accept this awful God. There are dozens of simple reasons to reject this God, but if this were the only one I would not serve him. I would not in any way cause an innocent baby to be slaughtered and I refuse to serve a God who ordered this. Today, this god, Jehovah would be a war criminal.

"Most people steer away from discussing religion and politics because the discussions usually end in fierce arguments and no minds are changed. I must say that the most hatred and venom that I have experienced in life is because some 'loving and compassionate religionist' discovered that I was an atheist. I do not seek to convert anyone to atheism. I am not trying to impose my personal and private views or enlarge the number of atheists. However, when I am attacked or requested to explain my views, I feel it is natural and right to clarify what I believe and how I feel.

"As a member of this group, I will respect each of you as an individual and your right to believe black is white and white is black. My remarks or concerns will be directed toward what you believe and why it makes no sense to me. Obviously, I represent a tiny minority and therefore just by statistics, an extreme view, but that has nothing to do with whether I am correct or not when I declare that there is no God. It is just a figment of man's ego and hope for immortality and all gods and the so-called one god is not a Creator but was created by man. I believe all religions trade on the natural fears of man. If there was ever a sin, this is it. Having given one illustration of why I am an atheist, I will save other reasons as time goes on in the discussion when it seems appropriate to me.

"I am also very proud to be a member of this group, which has a real challenge before it. We may or may not make much progress but there is a warmth and peace that I feel that finally a sustained effort will be made to have a decent start. If we can accomplish even a small beginning on the correct and sensible path for mankind, every divergent view expressed and every hidden moment of disgust will be worthwhile.

"I, like you, intend to hold on to my convictions, but also like you, I want to seek new paths, new enlightenments. It is not enough just to disbelieve in God. I owe you and others to help formulate what it is that is critical and positive for the human race. And, I really believe that there are many wonderful precepts and teachings in most religions. Our task, it seems to me, is to ferret out those good and proper things that are obvious and hold fast to them.

"I am not bound by fear. I owe allegiance first to myself to be honest and thoughtful. I hope I can be a very positive contributor to this cause even though my concerns about faith and religion might be regarded by you as spoken by that awful atheist. I hope to gain your admiration and respect not for my beliefs or lack of them but because I am equally sincere and honest as you.

BRIDGETTE THOMPSON

"My name is Bridgette Thompson. As you can see I am not white. I am not black. I do have some Oriental blood so I call myself multi-racial. I used to identify totally with African-Americans because in America if you have any black ancestors, you seem to be considered only black.

"I totally reject that idea. I am proud of being Irish and Chinese as well as black. I have one sixteenth Negroid ancestry and that was the old standard in the South for being a

Negro. The blacks became just as unreasonable as the old big-ots in the South did by pressuring one to be a black if you have any black ancestors. What a silly notion. I accept the facts as they are. I simply have ancestors who are black and white and yellow. And, if I knew my whole family history, I probably have some brown in me as well.

"I salute Tiger Woods, the great golfer, for referring to himself as multi-racial thereby not denying his Oriental moth-er her dignity and also honoring his father who had black and red ancestry. If we think of people as being lots of different colors and most people in American are mixed blood, how can we perpetuate hatred and racism that exists mostly on the white side but also on the other sides?

"Many people have told me that I am beautiful. I appreci-ate their compliments. If I am beautiful, then I have to realize that I have a greater responsibility to help others in life because I have always had people of all races treat me fairly. I remember when I was a pre-school little girl when everyone was saying how cute and smart I was. Compare this fortunate beginning with a child who perceives herself as ugly and dumb and has little support from even her parents.

"I believe life is a tough struggle for all of us. We all face trials and tribulations. We all have misfortune, sickness, crooked people with which to deal, and calamities of many sorts and the most talented of us do not know at times which road to travel. All of this climbing the mountains of life is magnified many times for some people so those of us who have had it generally good like me should not forget the ones who are not so lucky.

"This is the source of the true blessings of life. It is not serving some strange God that we really do not know whether it or whatever exists. It is serving our fellowman through love and compassion. The purpose of life is not appeasement of some unreasonable and inconsistent duty generated through fear and perpetrated by the followers of some brand of reli-gion.

"No, I cannot accept this way of life. A life based on fear is a stressful, unrealistic life and contrary to what I believe is the true nature of man. Surely we have evolved beyond the age of sacrifice to the Gods. Surely we have advanced beyond the notion that this life is merely a preparation for some imag-ined home of golden streets and gates of pearl. Surely we can look around and see so many thousands of ways to make the world better and help someone in it to be better rather than

waste multiplied billions of dollars on edifices and TV evangelists. Surely we can imagine ourselves in a colony on the
moon or a space station and look at this beautiful blue planet
and gain a true perspective of mankind.

"The handed down deity concepts of all religions do not
make sense to me and while there are a few wild notions like
devil worship, people cults that mark our age, most of this dri-
vel was jealously guarded by evil selfish men who had less
than a noble purpose in protecting their particular brand of
religion. Certainly, most religions embrace some concepts that
are right and good and should gain our favor but for example,
most of the so-called Bible is a self-serving history of a so-
called chosen race.

"The New Testament claims to fulfill the so-called prophecy of Isaiah, but the Jews do not accept Jesus as the Messiah
and only Savior. Neither do the Muslims who regard Christ as
a prophet. What kind of confusion is the world in as far as religion is concerned? I believe it is a very big mess because of
outrageous religious beliefs and especially the dedication to
these beliefs even to the point of destroying others who don't
swallow their particular ideas of human destiny and how to
get to glory.

"I have always questioned the wisdom of the emotional,
explicit perpetration of parents' religion upon their children.
A child in all of these religions, at a very, very early age is
practically forced to believe. If the child loves its mother (and
practically all children do from the beginning of life) and the
mother brainwashes the child by perpetrating her own religion, this emotional quicksand is bestowed on the little fellow
for life. Later, even if he or she chooses to break from the
shackles of Buddhism or whatever, the emotional hangover is
deeply imbedded in his subconscious. What a miserable thing
to do to a child. If the child sees his mother bow down to a
totem pole or a statue of some kind, he must think that is the
thing to do. We should be teaching right from wrong.

"You can label me anyway you desire, but for one voice, I
will proclaim that all of this stuff is wrong and hurtful and
devastating to the march of humans into the future. Then,
what is the answer? As others have suggested, we all must
look beyond any deity and try to assimilate what is right and
wrong and hope this endeavor will begin to put an end to the
heartache and suffering it has caused.

"I know, as some of you have expressed, that hell nor high
water can make you give up your faith. Then hang on if you

must. But I implore you to put it in another box for the purpose
of this cruise and bring out only those things that most of the
people of the world could accept as truth and a practical guide
for human behavior. I am not here to convert anyone away
from their emotional beliefs, but I hope all of us will agree on
some things that are common that do not violate religious
beliefs.

"If this little group cannot do that then there is little hope
for the greater population of the world coming together. I am
an optimist. I believe we can find common ground if I respect
your right to continue in your religion and you respect the
rights of other religions and those of us who have no religion.
I also believe that racial prejudice many times finds its roots
in religion. People who follow religions seem to me to be
anchored in the idea that their little group or huge group has
the answers and they are better than other people. This seems
as a foundation for all sorts of internal hatreds and often boils
over into overt insults and acts against the others that are not
'one of us.'

"I realize this is a condemning type of statement but I think
our task is to thrash out root causes of hatred, violence and
destruction and while not condemning any individual, condemn the perception. I think it is very important that we support or find fault in our systems and notions in our honest
effort to seek truth.

"I am often asked if I am married — a legitimate question.
I smile and say, 'I'll have time for that when my hero comes
along.' I have learned to take little personal questions and big
insults in stride. We all know that what someone says does not
necessarily make it true.

"I find myself saying things that I really don't intend to be
personal or offensive but it may be taken that way. I will try
my best not to offend anyone personally in our discussions
unless not swallowing your religious belief is offensive. A
good fair process will be to love each other regardless of their
beliefs as long as there is no aggression and physical hurt.

"This is an opportunity for me to try to understand why in
the world people can believe what appears to me to be so many
questionable things in religion. Maybe they are not so strange
if I can look through your glasses. Maybe I am stupid for questioning them.

"So if you will try to understand who I am and why I believe
as I do, I will return the courtesy. Perhaps the sport of tennis
can help us. I love to play and I try hard to make my points and

win; I lose sometimes and still in tennis you go to the net and shake hands and remain civil, often with your closest friend. Hopefully, this can be our modus operandi in this enormous task. I am looking forward to a one-on-one session with each of you as we have planned. Getting to know each of you I believe will be a pleasure."

DAVID PREAKNESS

As you know, I am David Preakness, your "fearless leader." Actually, I am hiding all sorts of fears concerning my ability to do the job well that you have laid out for me. However, those fears are balanced off with the excitement and interest you have shown and as they say, 'Somebody's got to do it.'

"I was so fortunate to be born in a loving, happy home during my early childhood. At 16, I thought life was just wonderful and I had nothing to worry about until that day when a drunken driver careened his pickup truck into the side of my mother's car. She was killed instantly.

"When the news came to me, I was in a state of shock for a few hours. I went through all of the phases of denial, the why's, the gloom and desperation. Then, my opinion of my mother and myself shook me out of it. I reasoned that she thought of me as a well-balanced, strong person who could experience anything, mourn if necessary and grieve of course, but to move on and adjust to reality.

"I have often counseled people who have lost a close loved one that they would never get over it, but they could adjust to it and move on with a productive life. And, as a matter of fact, I do not want to get over it. I think of her every single day and those precious memories are permanent in my life. I found the strength to face the future without her through my knowledge of the trust and belief she had in me and my own will to conquer this awful experience by living a life that would make her proud had she continued to be alive.

"I do not share this with you for your sympathy. I do not need it; however, your understanding of me, who I am and want to be, is important to me. Cataclysmic experiences often shape our lives and choices, even little so-called insignificant choices like where we choose to go to college can cast a journey that is forever influenced by that choice. What married person would not say that the mate they chose was a profound factor in their life? I sure hope I am wise and lucky in that choice.

"There are some choices that one can make that are not

dependent on others. I choose not to use tobacco in any form. I choose not to involve myself in any addictive chemicals including alcohol. I choose not to harm anyone physically, certainly not to murder anyone. On the positive choice side, I choose to help others. I choose to dedicate my time and talent to understanding what living is all about. I choose to be my own man yet trying not to infringe on the freedom of anyone.

"On and on I could enumerate choices I have made and do make that require a no or a yes. I am not a half-hearted person. I give 100% to any job. I try to give 100% to my studies and continue quest for knowledge and truth. I try hard and do my best. If I lose, I try to be an outstanding gentleman and good sport. If I win, I speak of the talent and effort of my opponent and endeavor to ease the burden of his or her losses. If I work, I give it all I have. If I relax, I want to lay back and let the rest of the world go by.

"After all, my mind tells me that there are far more intelligent people who lived before me, who are living now, and who will be alive long after I am gone. I like the philosophy my parents taught me, 'Son, you are no better than anyone else and remember, no one else is better than you.'

"Of course, I can do some things better than some people and many people do some things better than myself, but the philosophy is still rich and true. It is a great life if lived on these principles. It has to be genuine. Folks can detect a phony a mile away. To be happy and make life easier for others is my goal. I have learned to first respect and like myself so it is very easy for me to respect and like you. Now I will show you some respect by ending this self-introduction. Don't fret or worry. You will be hearing much more from me as the cruise continues.

"I am not the last but perhaps least. I am very proud to be in the group. I can already feel an abundance of warmth and appreciation."

LU CHANG

"My name, as you know, is Lu Chang. You may have noticed that I am Oriental. In fact, I am Chinese, born in Hong Kong of Chinese parents. Orientals go through the guessing game with other races. How often have I heard, are you Korean, are you Filipino, are you Japanese, are you Chinese, are you Hawaiian and a dozen other names. While some Orientals are inwardly or outwardly offended by this barrage of questions, I find it extremely amusing.

"If I find the person is an appealing male, I say, 'What country do you think is my heritage?' Oh boy, the game goes on. Really, what difference does it make? Some of the best people in the world are Japanese and this can be said of any group of Orientals, white, black or brown people on this planet. So it is so ridiculous to pre-judge any other human being.

"The fundamental and only question of merit is whether this person is a human being. If so, he or she is endowed with every simple right and opportunity that any human being has and should be treated in that manner. Separatism and labeling of others to make lesser people is wrong. It always has been and always will be. If this group can somehow get most people in the world to acknowledge this truth, we can stop war and murder in the third millennium.

"I don't know how much substance I can give to the group, but I have already given you a true and emotional rendition of what I believe. Who said Orientals were not emotional?

"When I was a little girl and traveled to many parts of the world, people often stared at me although I never thought the children stared. Mother told me that they stared because I so pretty. I was too young to know any different.

"Like others, I too believe in giving 100% and I make this pledge to Mr. Morgan and to all of you. I will be honest and attuned to your viewpoint as well as my own. I will strive with all that is within me to significantly help forge a map for the peoples of the world to follow that will be fair and just and cause the swords to be fashioned into plows to churn up the earth and eradicate famine and hunger everywhere.

"If I become too opinionated and too argumentative, Mr. Leader, tell me to cool it."

She gave David a cute wink.

Chapter IV
Open Topics and Discussion

The self introductions had been rather brief and somewhat guarded although some of the members pulled back the curtain enough to get a glimpse of their real self and feelings. The activity that usually brings out feelings and helps a group to really mesh is open discussion or free association on any topic a member feels is important to address.

Quite a bit of socializing and biographical information was exchanged last night on deck after the self-introduction sessions. Barriers are always let down when it is one on one or only a few people just chatting.

David had already been impressed with the beauty and personalities of Rachel, Bridgette and Lu. He purposed to get to know them better. However, he kept these intentions to himself until he could be assured one of them or all of them would be interested in him in a romantic sense. Time would tell. He kept saying to himself, "Don't rush things. They are not going to jump off this yacht and swim the sea all the way to some shore."

These ladies too were playing their cards close to their chest patiently waiting for the perfect time to let David know they were fascinated by him. Other little subtle nuances were already occurring but for the most part, the members seemed to enjoy fraternal friendships and perhaps a buddy relationship.

As the group gathered around the huge table in the captain's conference room, you could sense that the participants were feeling more at ease with each other. The tone set by David had created a positive impact.

"Let's get the ball rolling," said David and the little groups that were chatting and gesturing enthusiastically quickly began to disperse. Each person found a comfortable chair.

"Without objection, we will go around the table to have any topic presented. You may present or pass on any given day. We will try to steer away from present-day politics unless it is pertinent to our mission. This may be impossible, but we will try never to attack any person while questioning or objecting to their belief. I hope this will be possible. If I feel you have crossed the line, I will intervene as I have indicated. What we need is a free-swinging discussion that can lead us to truth. Let's hope that is the method we will follow. Al, you are up to bat and we will try not to give you a nasty curve ball."

"David, thank you for that long and kind introduction. I am unworthy of the many nice things you said about me," Al Green responded. The group gave a hearty laugh.

"I have quite a list of topics or ideas or questions as I am sure most if not all of you have by now. I think the Ten Commandments ought to be the underlying principles of any report or code that we develop. They have stood the test of time and people in every part of the world feel these commandments are a fine starting point for human behavior."

Bridgette spoke up, "I accept some of them and I reject some of them."

"A few of them seem to me to be obvious, but most of them are irrelevant. May we consider them one at a time?" Tony chimed in.

"Why yes," said a somewhat startled Al, "but they were given by God as a group as you know to Moses on Mt. Sinai and written on stone tablets."

"So the story goes," intoned Tony, "but the story also says Moses got mad and threw them on the ground, breaking them. We can at least break them up to discuss them one by one if that is permissible."

Al agreed. "Sure, we cannot only discuss them one by one but word by word, if it can shed light on their power and veracity."

For sure, the open discussion was off and running. Everyone was focused on the First Commandment. Al read it with the inflection of a seasoned Rabbi, "Thou shalt have no other Gods before me." This commandment refers to the one God and the supreme nature of that one God.

David said, "The problem with the First Commandment as far as using it in a practical code for all earthlings is that the majority of the people simply do not believe in the Judeo-Christian concept of a Jehovah God. The majority should respect the rights of people who believe the First Commandment, but it should work the other way also. I don't think it should be in our report."

"I agree with David, period," Lu offered.

Bridgette added she felt there was not proof of a God and truth is what the project was all about.

"You cannot prove or understand many things in life, Rachel responded. "You accept them as true and real — electricity for example, how the swallows come back to Capistrano each year, how homing pigeons do their work or how black and white cows give white milk and yellow butter. We accept these things as truth. You could list hundreds of examples."

After a spirited pro and con discussion that lasted for 43 minutes, Tony called for a vote on whether to include the First Commandment in the report. Quickly, three votes yes and four votes no flashed on the wall.

Al continued with the Second Commandment, "Thou shalt not make unto thee any graven image or any likeness of any thing that is in the heaven above, or that is in the earth beneath, or that is in the water under the earth; Thou shalt not bow down thyself to them. For I, the Lord, thy God am a jealous God, visiting the iniquity of the fathers upon the children unto the third and fourth generation of them that hate me. And, showing mercy unto thousands of them that love me, and keep my commandments."

Again, the discussion was very pointed but did not cross the lines of civility. Bridgette remarked that a Supreme Being with all knowledge and all power would not and could not be a jealous being of anyone or anything.

Lu asked, "What kind of God would punish children in the third and fourth generation because their ancestor or ancestors did not obey Him and His commandments? If there is a God, He certainly is above this kind of cruelty!"

You could see her dark brown eyes, almost black, flashing with fire as she spoke. There would be little doubt concerning her vote on this one.

Rachel said she knew that one of the commandments was against worshipping idols but did not know about the jealousy and visiting the iniquity of the fathers upon children even through the fourth generation.

Rachel reminded the group she did believe in God but presenting the Ten Commandments in *Reader's Digest* form and omitting any part of them seemed deceitful. Using partial truths was a dastardly trick of politicians of all stripes.

John said, "I knew of the entire Second Commandment and

I have witnessed the punishment of children, grandchildren and great-grandchildren because of the sins of a distant father. We must remember that God means business when He says to obey Him!"

Rachel said the positive thing in the Second Commandment was the promised mercy unto thousands of them that love me and keep my commandments.

"Is there any more discussion?" David asked. "Hearing none, we will vote."

Two for yes and five for no flashed on the screen. Lu's comment or question about the innocent children evidently won one person over to her way of thinking since the First and Second Commandments were so closely related.

Al was visibly shaken because he had never seen these commandments challenged in this manner. Perhaps he felt his efforts to use them were not going anywhere in the group. However, like a good soldier, he braced up and read the Third Commandment. "Thou shalt not take the name of the Lord in vain; for the Lord will not hold him guiltless that taketh his name in vain."

Again, Lu led the discussion saying, "I supposed saying hell or damn is not a violation of the Third Commandment. Some of the vulgar cursing must not be in violation if the word God is not used. I wish all the excessive cursing and profanity in today's society would cease or at least cool down. And Al, I am going to agree with you that a deity should not be included while one is cursing or swearing. This is disrespectful to the believers in God.

"I also cringe at swearing on the Bible and saying 'So help me God' while knowing you are going to tell one lie after another in a court of law. I don't think it is fair to Buddhists, Hindus or atheists for the President to be sworn in with his right hand on the Bible. This constitutes the government favoring and propagating a particular religion or two of men and this is exactly why people left Europe to build a nation free from such efforts. I could live my life and enjoy it better if I never heard the word damn with God in front of it."

David said, "I thought I had heard just about every slant on religion yet I was wrong. In just a few hours, I have heard things I never heard or read before. I do think that if an individual does not honor any God, he has the freedom to curse as he pleases — but it certainly would show more class if he refrained from using the name of any deity in vain.

"In this open discussion, we are voting to place ideas and

concepts on the table or to screen out ideas that should not be considered in our road map for human behavior in the Third Millennium. So this is a screening out process as well as laying constructive concepts on the table which will be gone over with a fine-toothed comb to see if after reflection, they rise to the level of our proposed code."

When the issue was changed to respect those who believe in their God, the vote was seven yes and zero nos.

"Surely some of the concepts in the Law of Moses will survive, if not the exact words, so don't be discouraged Al. You are just reaching the fourth inning and there are ten innings."

Al smiled rather obligingly, "Remember the Sabbath day to keep it holy. Six days shalt thou labor and do all thy work. But the seventh day is the Sabbath of the Lord thy God. In it thou shalt not do any work, thou, nor thy son, nor thy daughter, thou manservant nor thy maidservant, nor thy cattle nor thy stranger that is within thy gates. For in six days the Lord made heaven and earth, the sea, and all that in them is and rested the seventh day. Wherefore the Lord blessed the Sabbath day, and hallowed it."

John was concerned with confusion concerning which day is the Sabbath. "There are Saturday Sabbaths, Sunday Sabbaths, Tuesday Sabbaths, and probably some I don't even know about. I am going to observe Sunday as my Sabbath and there is no way I would try to force Sunday on you, Al, so you can see this commandment has to boil down to an individual decision."

"Bravo," exclaimed Bridgette. "I think with many people the practice has boiled out. You can read the old Sunday blue laws and see that this commandment has been used rigidly to force religious ideas upon unwilling citizens. Now all types of stores are open, ball games flourish, and lo and behold people even go joy riding in automobiles on Sunday, which used to be quite a sin in some circles."

Tony agreed the commandment was so ridiculous that it deserved no comment, just to be ignored like most people are doing.

Al asked David to call for a vote because he knew this would never become an item in the code. David agreed with the day of rest concept. Two yes votes and five no votes.

Al tried to keep his composure by cracking, "Well, so far all have been more or less tossed out. Let's see if this group wants to toss out their mothers and fathers."

The group gave him a reassuring laugh and some clapped

their hands softly. Al read, "Honor they father and thy mother. That thy days may be long upon the land which the Lord thy God giveth thee."

Lu asked Al if it was possible to vote on the first part and the second part. "Why?" Al wanted to know.

"Because the second part promises a long life to those who honor their parents and we all know that millions have died long before their parents and at all ages who loved and honored their parents with all their hearts."

"Lu," said Al, "I hate to admit it but I think you have a good point. I'll agree to that if the group agrees." Al turned to David and said, "I think we are ready to vote."

"Okay," said David. Seven yes votes were cast for honoring thy father and mother.

"Hooray!" cried several of the members realizing that finally a full concept had made the report level even if not in the same exact words.

"Thou shalt not kill," Al read on. "Surely everyone will accept this commandment."

"On the face of it, you appear to be right — but how about self-defense, the battlefield, capital punishment, or indiscriminate destruction of animals just for sport?" asked Bridgette.

"You do open up a number of issues which I think are important, but just for now can we use this commandment in the context it was intended. It refers to murder of another human being. If we can agree on this, I will be happy to join in the discussion of the issues you raised later on," Al replied.

Rachel wondered if Bridgette would feel comfortable if the wording of the commandment were "Thou shalt not murder others." Bridgette said she could accept that wording. Al looked at David. He was reluctant to subtract or add any words to one of the Ten Commandments, but he remembered what David had said about trying to find common ground for everyone. David knew by Al's look of desperation that he would like to have a vote and move on. David paused. No one said anything else. David again said softly, "Vote."

Almost as soon as he spoke, seven yes votes registered on the white wall.

John mused, "We have at least two things as a foundation — honor your parents and don't kill anybody." Everyone smiled. John had that great ability to express things in a unique, concise and interesting manner.

"Thou shalt not commit adultery," Al continued. "Is there any beef on this one?"

Lu said, "I don't have a beef on this commandment as an ideal in a monogamous marriage, but many millions of people have plural wives or spouses. Is this adultery? Is lusting committing adultery as the Bible indicates? Many people have been killed for this violation and will be killed as a religious mandate.

"I can agree to prohibit the act of adultery in a traditional American Jewish-Christian marriage as an ideal. Are there any mitigating circumstances which might allow, from a practical view, adultery? Some examples would be if a spouse has been unconscious for years, if a spouse refuses to have sex or uses it as a weapon to control the other spouse, if the spouse has contracted a terrible social disease that may lead to death, if a spouse is marooned on an island with no hope of escape and isolated with a member of the opposite sex alone on a raft drifting. It just does not seem practical or possible in many cases even for a good dedicated person to honor this flat out commandment in every imaginable instance.

"Surely, we do not wish to prescribe the impossible and fall into the trap like Christianity has when Jesus said, 'Be ye perfect.' Yet, we know promiscuity is a bad thing and ordinarily wrong. How can we resolve such a dilemma? I am not sure. I think we will have to eventually come to categorizing our recommendations into something like absolutely no, ideal, practical or whatever.

"Excuse me for thinking out loud, but this is a free association session. I cannot support a simple prohibition of adultery. Under the Law of Moses, if a brother died the living brother acquired his wife along with other wives and had sex with a variety of women. There is something wrong with this picture. Do not commit adultery unless you do it the way God says or allows it. What I am trying to say is to refrain from adultery as most people perceive it as an ideal thing, but an absolute is not practical nor possible in human behavior on this planet as we are constituted."

Lu had tried hard to choose the best words to explain her feelings but feared she had not made very good choices. She carefully studied the body language of the members of the group and senses what she was saying made them uneasy. As she was beating up on herself, she got support from one of the females.

Bridgette spoke up and said, "Lu, I agree with every word you have said. I might add that we take it upon ourselves to condemn adultery quickly and vehemently in others, adorning ourselves with a crown of righteousness, but we do not really know how we would respond if we were in the same set of circumstances. I am not saying adultery anytime, anywhere with anybody is an ideal. The ideal is the opposite but there are circumstances of abuse and coldness that make people vulnerable and I know women who have 'cut off' sex from their husbands to 'get even' for other unrelated things.

"This is not a simple black and white issue. I have experienced cultures in my relatively short lifetime and the boy/girl or sex issue has not been solved in any of them. I suggest we table the whole sex thing and discuss all of the aspects we think are pertinent later on in our discussions."

There was quite a long silence before John spoke, "I think we have opened up a very grave and significant topic. I agree with the suggestion that we bisect it into all its pieces and ramifications rather than accept one aspect that is mandated.

"I have always accepted the Ten Commandments, but the qualifiers that some of the members have put on them today really have my head spinning. I need more time to hash this out alone or with one or two people before I commit myself to this far reaching and universal commandment.

"I feel Lu and Bridgette made some excellent points, so let's postpone a vote on this one," John suggested.

Al again looked simply bewildered.

David said, "All in favor of postponement of this commandment vote yes; all wishing to decide now, vote no."

The unanimous vote was yes.

"Thou shalt not steal," read Al who refrained from making any comment.

"I know it appears that we are tearing the Ten Commandments apart," observed Tony, "but this will be the case in any presentation. I suggest adding the words 'for any selfish or personal reason.'

"In an ethics class I said imagine you were the superintendent of an orphanage in Germany out in the country during World War II. A bread truck broke down near the orphanage and you went out to see what was happening. The driver had gone, evidently to get help. Next you noticed the bill of lading listed Hitler's party at Berlin as its destination.

"Since your kids were without bread and surviving on bean soup, what would you do? Would it be ethical to take the bread for the children or would this violate the commandment, 'Thou shalt not steal'?

"The members of that ethics class almost lost their tempers

in the discussion. 'Stealing is stealing!' yelled some. Others said they'd take every loaf, ask God to let me give it to the kids and have it all eaten up before the driver returned. Most of the class appeared very stunned and wished my proposition had never been made.

"After the professor calmed everyone down and called a halt to the melee, he passed out little slips. Would it be stealing and a violation of the commandment? Write yes or no on this slip. The tally showed two for yes and 26 for no.

"Then, Professor Turkington asked me, 'Tony, what would you do and feel if you were in that circumstance?'"

"I replied I would take all of the bread, disable the engine further because the higher good would be to feed the children. I know you tread on soft sand when you introduce the realm of the higher good and who has the power to decide. The case should always be very, very clear cut."

"So I believe if we say 'Thou shalt not steal for any selfish or personal reason,' it would be a very good guideline."

There was silence. David motioned to "vote on the suggested addition." There were seven yes and zero no.

"Thou shalt not bear false witness against thy neighbor" was the next commandment. The vote was seven in favor and none against. Everyone agreed lying against a neighbor is always wrong.

"Thou shalt not covet thy neighbor's house, thou shalt not covet they neighbor's wife, nor his manservant, or his maidservant, nor his ox, nor his ass, nor anything that is thy neighbor's," Al read.

"I'm having a problem with this manservant-maidservant thing," said Bridgette. "It is demeaning in today's society. I suggest we change the wording to employees of thy neighbor."

After a brief discussion, all agreed reflected by the vote, seven yes and zero no. The principle of the Tenth Commandment would seem to please everyone except someone like maverick Bishop Spong of the Episcopal Church who believes this commandment demeans women by making them like property.

After over an hour's recess in many small group discussions and one-on-one conversation, the group gradually assembled again.

Al asked if he could continue on some other thoughts he had wanted to present. All agreed.

"We seem to be taking apart religions, so why not consider the fact that Muslin women in some cultures are expected to commit suicide if they have been raped so their blood will cleanse the family. Is this barbarism to be accepted in CODE 3-M? Many Muslin women are forced to deny rape so they can live and not disgrace the family but stay alive!"

John interrupted, "Before you go any further, I admit what you say happens in some cases, but any clear-thinking Muslin like the ones I know would not want that custom to be a way to behave in CODE 3-M. Let's go on to your other items, if you please!"

"Okay," agreed Al. "Let's consider the fact as Americans we are a litigious nation. We have so many petty lawsuits going it is disgraceful. And, the appeals go on and on and on. I have a friend who installed razor wire on her eight-foot fence to keep neighborhood kids out of her pool. She did not mind kids using the pool if adult supervision was present and the kids asked for permission. Hers was the only pool in that neighborhood and the kids treated it as their own.

"However, the real problem was the fear that if any one of them received an injury or faked an injury, or drowned, she could probably be sued for everything she owned. Some jury would be persuaded to give an incredible award. When she could not keep them out with an eight-foot chain link fence, she put up razor wire.

"I told her she probably would get sued faster now if some kid cut himself or herself to ribbons still trying to climb over the fence. I suggested she put up very definite signs of private property, keep out, a pool is a dangerous place and the owner would not be responsible if someone swims without permission and climbs the chain-link fence to get in. Maybe this would help in court, maybe not. The point could be made with thousands of cases. So why not a principle in the report of CODE 3-M that forbids trivial lawsuits for personal gain."

"I agree," shouted several members.

"And," said Rachel, "we need to talk about suing rich tobacco companies when the individual knows tobacco is dangerous to their health. This brings up two important issues of outlawing dangerous drugs like nicotine and alcohol and who has the responsibility."

David intervened softly suggesting, "You are right on, but for the sake of efficiency, let's see if anyone objects to considering the inclusion of trivial laws suits in CODE 3-M."

He paused. No one objected. "Let Al continue on his items. I'm sure there will be ample time for discussion on these other very important topics as the presentation continues."

"I have quite a list of issues and on my next round, I will present more of them so I'll quit after one more, at least on this turn," Al promised. "The movie, 'All Quiet on the Western Front,' was recommended to be shown once a year in every country until war is stricken from the dictionary. Germany at the time would not allow it to be shown because the movie featured a gung-ho German youth who volunteered for the battlefield. After tremendous suffering and loss of the lives of his buddies, he realizes war is not a glamorous adventure but a horrible nightmare! It ain't what it's cracked up to be and fear is the prevailing emotion.

"I think we should support all such movies realistically depicting war. We should face the fact that soldiers die on both sides for the so-called cause of their leaders. The I-regret-that-I-have-only-one-life-to-give-for-my-country attitude is great poetry but pales when you are facing death and destruction or your 18-year-old son or daughter is on the line.

"The poetry should be 'I'll defend my country if attacked and I feel it is absolutely necessary to stop conquering, insane tyrants, but I'd rather devote my bravery and energy to trying to reason with others and see if we cannot devise some way to stop war!'"

Unrehearsed, the group jumped to their feet and gave Al a standing ovation. David wisely declared that no vote was needed and ended this day's session of the forum.

It was another calm day at sea. It is remarkable how the calm sea can calm the human spirit as well. President John Kennedy said something like, "We are so fond of the sea because we all come from it. We are intricately related and it supports not only our well being and needs as it gives up food, but our spirits."

On this beautiful day on this luxurious yacht, the group gathered informally around the captain's huge round table again. The intense interest in the topics soon caused formality to wane and almost disappear. Lu Chang was introduced and spoke in soft tones, which would not always be the case.

"I like these short or non-introductions, but I won't repeat Al's clever remark," said Lu. "You really get to know a person not by their long list of training or accomplishments but by what they say and believe, and the passion they give to certain core beliefs."

"I too have a long list of issues, items, topics, comments, whatever and I know you will feel free to agree or disagree with me and express your biased opinion as easily as I have expressed my personal, and I hope, considered views."

"Yet I confess they are biased also by my life experiences and the choices I have made as I pondered many times. First of all, I wonder why most religionists, regardless of their particular faith, are so afraid of death that they fail to concentrate on productive living. They want to have their soul saved first and receive a great reward, a type of honor for having avidly believed in something they are not sure about and have no real evidence the method is right or the goal exists!

"Why can't we simply turn it around and concentrate on living a useful productive, caring for others life as the primary effort instead of umbrellaing these great and wonderful things in after we make sure our souls are saved from a hell and made certain for the pearly gates? I think the world would be much better off if we considered this choice to be the better of the two. Let people believe in any God or Gods they choose but not to the extent that life and its many wonderful opportunities pass them by.

"So, the first thing I present for the report of CODE 3-M as we are calling it is: Focus first on how you live on this earth instead of getting to heaven with a saved soul from hell. The two are obviously related to those of you who are committed to a religion but the primary focus is the issue.

Rachel spoke up quickly and said, "Lu, you may think it strange, but I agree with you 100%. We could never get the members of the group or the world at large to agree on one faith, although that is what Christians, Muslims and the others are trying to do. I would like to see the whole world believe in the Lord Jesus Christ as I do. Then there would be no peace problems anywhere between individuals or nations. But logic tells me and the Bible tells me it will not happen."

Bridgette responded to Rachel's comment, "I appreciate your point about impossible agreement on one faith, but please don't forget that both the Union soldiers and the Confederate soldiers in most cases had the old-time Christian religion. Some came from the same communities, churches and homes and they killed each other in the most telling war America has ever known. Anyway, I'll cast my vote with the issue Lu raised as being very, very important."

There were other comments pointing out both pros and cons but the vote flashed on the wall, seven unanimous votes for giving the highest priority to living, not what happens after we are dead.

Rev. John Hayes, at the end of a long, passionate speech on

the topic finally declared, "Don't worry, if we live right, we'll make it in . I'm going to live good and right and I'll make it in through those pearly gates as well! Remember Churchill said, 'A fanatic is one who can't change his mind and won't change the subject' so I'll say amen and stop."

"The next thing I wish to discuss is gender prejudice," Lu said. "Those who care little about this will point out the number of women on the Supreme Court, in Congress, and various office holders around the world. I believe the stereotypes concerning women are still deep and that gender discrimination is by and large a reality for most women.

"I will concede it is wrong to hire a woman in heavy construction work just to fill a quota when a dozen better qualified men are turned away. Likewise, it is often difficult for a man to obtain a so-called woman's job in many instances. Yet, the overall picture in America while improving still is lacking in the realization that women are extremely capable in many jobs where they have been left out or hired only on a token basis.

"We still have to perform over the standard for men in most situations. Hewlett-Packard, a Fortune 100 company, has set a fairness example by hiring Ms. Carleton Fiorina from the Global Services Group at Lucent to become their Chief Executive Officer. She is effectively handling the challenge of transferring Hewlett-Packard from a traditional engineering company to a creative Internet player making a universal change in the culture and attitude of this huge, well-known company.

"I could cite many other examples of women breaking the glass ceiling and inspiring success stories. But here we are faced with what should humans feel and do to lead happy, productive lives in a matrix of decency and fairness. The problem in America, though real, is microscopic compared to the gigantic oppression of women around the planet. All religions that I personally know much about have minimized women with the exception of the over-emphasis of Mary as Mother of God in Catholic Christianity.

"If we are to be credible, we must address this issue head on. Let it be written in our report that the female human being, while biologically different is entitled to equal respect and equal opportunity when equally qualified. The present organizations fostering a gender war are hurtful and irresponsible.

"Extreme feminists have all but declared men will no longer be needed since sperm can be frozen and kept indefinitely. They should stop and consider also that the female egg can be preserved and a zygote formed with sperm and incubated to create birth as we now accomplish with fowls and animals. Experts estimate that there are 200,000 embryos in cryogenic states already.

"The media, knowing that its lifeblood is controversy, continues to stir the pot with silly shows cutting down men in some formats and rendering the same treatment to women in other shows. It is irresponsible to perpetuate these gender wars. I have never heard a man say that women will no longer be needed — not even an extremist.

"Let us take a sensible, rational view, which exalts the glorious differences in male and female. Let every man think of his mother, sister, daughter, aunt or grandmother as he contemplates fairness for females. Let every female do the same. My father, brothers, uncles, and grandfathers do not deserve the jibes they receive. We know the answer. Let's proclaim it and practice it!"

A provocative and emotional discussion followed this moving presentation. Everyone in the group got in their two cents worth. The vote was 6 yes and 1 no. The exact wording was to be refined in all cases that pass to make the CODE.

"Since I'm on a roll, I would like to present one more topic," Lu said.

"Fine," David acknowledged. "If we were on land I would rent a revival-type tent for you because you can put lots of fire-breathing hell-fire evangelists to shame."

The group nodded in agreement. David gave a loving smile to Lu who thought, "At least he likes me. I hope it will develop far beyond that seductive smile."

Lu continued, "I am deeply moved by the intense disappointments people suffer by crying out to their God. I have seen or read about people who lash themselves with chains until their backs bleed, starve themselves to death, throw their babies into the Ganges River, give up all their belongings, petition their deity in a thousand different ways with prayer wheels, incessant kneeling, going over beads at an altar or shrine, and soliciting prayers from millions on and on.

"Yet, their supplications are ignored by a coldness and arrogance that crush the spirit. When things happen paralleling the prayers, the deity gets all sorts of praise and glorifications. When the deity ignores the prayers, it is not God's will and still commands unbridled allegiance.

"Doesn't anyone care for the poor Hindu who measures

himself for hundreds of miles, by standing up, falling forward and standing again, falling again until he reaches some muddy river or man-made shrine? How many people have actually killed themselves or others to get their God to do something or to save their souls?

"Read the Old Testament and tell me this is a merciful loving God rather than a vengeful, arrogant, fear-producing, man-made deity! We should have a movie shown continuously around the world of all the agony and suffering of people praying to God while being wiped out by famine, flood and violent storm.

"Doesn't common sense teach us that prayer for protection is a farce? Who cares? It is not mine to question; it is mine to follow and worship God regardless. God knows the answer. I don't. The people getting placed back in the ambulances to go back with the same condition plus the disappointment behind the circus tent of an Oral Roberts crusade as well as hundreds of other faith healers does not seem to faze the faithful who give so much of their time and money and incessant prayer to their ministry.

"A few headaches and arthritic walkers and blind claiming sight are continually charged up enough to yell out, 'I'm healed, I'm healed,' at the command of the orchestrator who has a so-called special connection with God. Doesn't anyone care about the poor disappointed? What good is prayer for the sick? God is all-powerful and He is going to do it or not according to His whims. Then, why subject people to all this crying out and in some instances committing physical harm? Do they worship a type of Baal or heathen God as well? The tears being shed around the world crying out to Gods as we ride these calm seas in this luxurious yacht could float it from a dry dock into the sea. Again, I cry out, doesn't anyone care?"

Lu seemed emotionally spent as she searched the group for assurance. Her dark brown eyes seemed to connect with the blue, the hazel and the other brown eyes in the group. A long moment of silence ensued.

Rev. John Hayes finally questioned, "I, for one, do care for the disappointed and don't agree with the intense self-inflicted suffering and sacrifices you describe, but what do you want us to do about it?"

"My solution would be to eliminate all religion from the face of the Earth," Tony suggested.

"You have to balance the comfort and answered prayers against those disappointments which I will try to clarify when

I make some of my points," Rachel replied. "I will agree somewhat with Lu because I can sense she is speaking from the
heart and very sincere but not to the extent we eliminate
prayer and God.

"For the purposes of the group and in the spirit of moving
on I think the CODE should include the prohibition of self-
injury. I know someone will chime in and say it is also mental
suffering, but at least we can agree not to endorse any kind of
human sacrifice or physical self-infliction. Surely, we have
come that far as so-called civilized people. Al, it goes back to
your 'Thou shalt not kill' commandment and killing to please
any God is patently wrong."

David watched Rachel as she held to her faith and yet condemned the extreme. Her beauty was more apparent when he
saw her considerable intellectual powers displayed. He mused
to himself that it really wasn't fair for these ladies to be so
beautiful and so bright.

Enough fire had been kindled to keep the group going back
and forth for over an hour on Lu's point. A vote was held; yes
votes were 5 and no votes were 2.

David waited around while the group left the captain's conference room until Lu was collecting her materials. They were
alone.

"Lu, I admire your passion and your ability to present your
ideas, but most of all I see a depth in you that is really charming. Why don't you meet me after the evening meal on the top
of the Captain's Wheelhouse so we can talk further?"

Lu was really excited but played her usual strategy with
men. She paused for a while and whispered, "Don't worry, I'll
be there."

It seemed cupid had boarded the ship and was doing his job
well.

Rev. John Hayes had drawn the Number Three. He made
certain to eat his soda crackers; they seemed to keep his incli-
nation for seasickness in check. He kept a box of crackers on
the table in front of him and wondered if he would ever make
the entire cruise. However, he would make a special effort
since he felt his contributions would make a huge difference
in the final report. He began by saying he could supply enough
issues to keep the group busy for six months, but that he would
present only a few as others have done. John began full blast
as everyone anticipated.

"Is there any person on the face of the planet Earth and
from the beginning of time who had anything to say at the

moment of birth about whether they would be male or female, rich or poor, black or white, Hispanic or Asian, tall or short, homely, handsome or pretty, brilliant or dull, normal or handicapped from birth, war, accident or disaster, born under a dictatorship or a democracy, with one parent or no parents, born in New York City or Yazoo City, Mississippi? Of course not!

"It is the height of arrogance for anyone to decide they are better than others because of a birth happenstance. It is the decision of a fool. Any form of racism or elitism is a sign of an ego gone wild. It is a detestable social cancer. It must be absolutely and completely eradicated in all human interaction and communication on Earth, spaceships and anywhere else mankind may venture!"

Bridgette interrupted, "John, my friend, why don't you tell us how you really feel! Keep going baby. You know I am with you all the way."

The other five spoke out together enthusiastically. A number of supporting statements were made. "Keep going, John." "You are telling it like it is and like it should be." "We are behind this concept 100%."

"I'm sick of this stuff," John continued. "All my life I've faced this demon, but God has given me the strength to know I'm His child as much as anyone. He loves me and gives me strength from day to day to face any trial and tribulation that devil can sling at me. I condemn racism whether it is from white to black, black to white, brown, red, yellow and any combination. No one is inherently better than anyone else, period. If you want to live better than others live, then give your heart to Jesus and He will deliver you from the demonic bondage of sin and help you live a better life."

"John, the problem I have with that is from what I have experienced, most people who have the deepest racial prejudice are from the Bible-belt South, so what good has Christianity done for them on this issue?" Bridgette said.

Rachel jumped in, "I'm from South Carolina and the deep Bible-belt South and you make a good point, I am sad to admit. I sang from my childhood, 'Give Me That Old Time Religion, Makes Me Love Everybody.' We would have been more accurate if we had sung, 'Give Me That Old Time Religion, Makes Me Love Everybody If They Look Just Like Me.'

"I asked my mother when I was six years old why we had a penny march for missions. She said it was for the souls in Africa and Asia. I asked if we want them saved too, why don't we invite them to our church like we do white people? She began to cry, pulled me close to her and challenged me to always feel that way.

"I went to the neighborhood where African-American people lived and invited them with great sincerity. One elderly black lady told me I would be a good person until I died, but explained that the adults in my church would not be pleased if she worshiped there.

"I was mad as a hornet and determined to give all the energy I could to change this wrong. I did not get very far but at least today some progress has been made in the Bible belt. I mean real, sincere progress, not the hypocritical progress Meredith found in New York when he said, 'I'm going back to Mississippi. I know where I stand there. If I'm hated by a white person, I'll know it. If I'm loved and accepted by a white person, I'll know that too.'

"It's a genuine change of hearts that was needed to make progress and John, we still have a long way to go. I see you as a fine Christian like me, just as good as me in every way. Any Christian who hates anyone for anything has not learned to forgive and is really not living a Christian life."

"I agree with most of what's been said," Al interjected, "but if you expect me to forgive Hitler and his kind and serial murderers and their kind, I will never forgive. I loathe the things they did and the persons who did it. This forgiveness bit has been misused. Do you forgive O.J. Simpson? I don't and I never will. Some dastardly deeds go beyond forgiveness!"

David said, "Great discussion, but go ahead John. You know how to stir our hearts and minds. You got a 7 to 0 vote on that principle."

The status of marriage in the Third Millennium was John's next topic. "I have a heavy concern about how marriage and family values are developing these days. Where are we headed? Many single men are shacking up with single women and adopting children. This practice has an upside and a downside.

"The upside is the fact that in most cases the child is the beneficiary because having a home with so-called parents is superior to no home at all or being shifted about not knowing what to call home. The downside, I believe, is the avoidance or desecration of marriage. So many young folk and some older have lost faith in marriage. They say, who needs the hassle?

"Our entire society is founded on the family and traditional family values. I know that the term family values means different things to different people but most people understand the basic idea of family. Some of us have worked down in the trenches — school teachers, social workers, pastoral services, prison staff — and we have firsthand knowledge about the positive influence of a good family.

"Most dysfunctional people and criminals, not all of course, have a very poor family background. They have encountered few role models that they actually know and trust. Celebrity role models have their place but at best, the effect is artificial. Often, when used as a role model, such as Jimmy Swaggert, Bill Clinton and Magic Johnson, dramatic failure occurs. This can and does have a devastating effect on our youth.

"So, the family is crucial to human life in the Third Millennium if we are to dwell in peace and experience a fulfilling life. I believe the Bible teaches family values and CODE-3M needs to make a stand in this area."

"Which family style in the Bible do you recommend?" asked Tony. "There is the Old Testament family with a plurality of wives and the New Testament with a type of monogamy."

"It seems that God allowed many wives at one time," John responded. "Solomon had one thousand wives. Three hundred were concubines. I know what you will say. God changed His mind and this does not reconcile with Hebrews 13:8, 'Jesus Christ, the same yesterday, today and forever,' if Jesus is God. Again, I do consider the trinity doctrine to be true. God, Jesus and the Holy Spirit are the same, but I guess God does change His mind because He allowed divorce for a period of time and later condemned it.

"The only thing I can say, Tony, is that we need more family units today if we even hope to keep society together in one piece. It is splitting apart at a rapid rate and going in all directions. Children are becoming dope addicts, tobacco addicts, alcohol addicts, sex addicts, criminals of every stripe and committing suicide at an alarming rate! There has to be a better answer!"

"John, we can argue about the problems of youth, yet these same problems have been faced by every generation. You are right about the acceleration of these negative things engulfing our children. However, the polls show a very high percentage of people believe in the Almighty and church attendance is at an all time high," said Bridgette.

"I just have a hard time equating religious teaching to morality, though it tries. There are so many immoral and unethical things permitted in all religions. Perhaps a good family that teaches right from wrong and sets the example is the best solution. Would you agree to that?"

John replied, "I see you are hell-bent on extracting God and religion from everything. I strongly disagree but for the purpose of the CODE, I will narrow my item for inclusion to be: 'Foster a good family unit that teaches a child morality, ethics and love for thy neighbor.'" The vote was 7 to 0.

"Since we seem to be bringing up controversial subjects," John continued, "let's talk about homosexuality, so-called gays and lesbians and a few other terms. I want to say flatly it is abnormal, sinful and not accepted in the eyes of God. Yet, I believe in hating the sin and loving the sinner. This topic is somewhat linked to my family unit concept. There is no future to the human race if we follow the examples of Sodom and Gomorrah.

"The schools, in some instances, are teaching this is a legitimate life-style, not an abnormality. The media has gone hog-wild promoting this dangerous perversion. Politicians eagerly give up all of their gut feelings and righteous instincts to court the gay vote. The Clintons are the most brazen of all and I need say nothing about his moral character. It is well documented and confessed to in part by the President himself.

"This type of moral decay will doom humanity in the Third Millennium if this trend continues. I really don't know exactly what to advocate about homosexuals. They should not be persecuted; in turn, they should not be allowed to flaunt their sickness with the in-your-face parades and frivolous lawsuits. Nor would they be allowed to marry and adopt children."

David replied, "John, you sure do know how to liven up a session. I see several hands raised to offer rebuttal or agreement. Please let me call on you one at a time and let's be as civil as possible on this hot subject. Rachel, I saw your hand go up first, so I will just follow around the room beginning with you."

"John is taking a traditional Christian view on this important topic," Rachel said. "And, as you know, even the Pope is strongly against this sin. Most scholars and objective people would be willing to classify homosexuals into two broad categories: those who have an imbalance of sex hormones and those who are learned or non-biological homosexuals.

"Exodus International, a non-denominational Christian organization, is a fellowship dedicated to helping homosexuals change their orientation. Most secret sharers who attend their meetings are in the 20's and 30's. They are racially mixed and determined to change, united in purpose. Full-page ads have been taken out to attract those who need and want help. 'We changed and so can you.' Their meetings are weighted with many scriptures and it has a religious nature. The gay advocates naturally fight this brave effort arguing that it is a deliberate campaign to make homophobia acceptable.

"Psychologists differ in their approach to whether change can occur, but most do not deny in many cases, Exodus can document sincere change. I believe Jesus can change a homosexual."

Al was the next speaker. "Well, I suppose if it takes Jesus to change homosexuals, then the vast majority of the world which does not accept Jesus as their only true God is simply left out. I say this is nonsense! Why not accept the two categories you describe, admit that those who are biological homosexuals cannot change basically who they are and remember John's beautiful statements about not discriminating against them even if they are handicapped in this manner. And, if learned homosexuals can be changed by behavior modification, or whatever and they desire to be changed, more power to them!

"I appreciate what has been stated and much of the relevant ground has been covered. However, I might add that an emotional issue this large produces extreme statements and predictions by the opponents involved. Senator Trent Lott, one of the most powerful people in Washington, compared homosexuality to alcoholism and kleptomania.

"The learned man should know better. Alcoholism is an addiction with the most far-reaching social impact in the world. Kleptomania is a mental disorder that afflicts people in every financial stratum. A truly biological homosexual cannot help that fact any more than he can his blue eyes or dark hair. There is psychological help for kleptomaniacs and most that receive therapy stop stealing.

"Extreme statements and demands come from the advocates as well. The advocates have won over the American Psychological Association by getting the majority to vote that reparative therapy is scientifically ineffective and possibly harmful. Yet in a well-known and accepted national poll, 56% said gays could become straight. And so, the controversy rolls on. The CODE must address the issue and I hope will follow basically the sensible direction our group has taken so far."

Bridgette was the next speaker on the matter. "I have been quiet so far really surprising myself at the amount of discipline I could demonstrate. Yet, I think I do have a point or two to add to this discussion. The answer to whether a person can practice homosexual acts and then refrain is found in women's prisons.

"Many women prisoners, if not most of them, develop homosexual practices though they had always been straight on the outside and cease this type of activity when they are released. This is done with or without a belief in Jesus. In fact, they convert easily to heterosexuality.

"Men prisoners at a less rate than women become gay in prison and find it more difficult to go straight upon release. Yet, many do so with or without the help of Exodus. These are facts. The peculiar group is the group that accepts the Bible or in the Catholic Church the Pope's infallibility when integrating scripture and prescribing edicts and laws of conduct both practice their religion and their homosexuality. Is this not oxymoronic behavior?

"The problem I have is what should we recommend for the CODE. Since I believe we will vote up homosexuality to the CODE level to be addressed and a course of behavior not to be recommended. I need to do more thinking on this matter so I can be sure I am truly fair to gays and society as a whole."

David said, "I can see that you have been doing quite a bit of research and thinking already. My Buddhist and Islamic friends would agree that if the world were to accept Islam or Buddha, this would not be a problem. Realizing that neither conversion has or probably would take place, we will concentrate on the best wording when the issue is debated for inclusion in the CODE. We can defer it for our sex discussion."

John started another issue. "I have the hottest issues, it seems, so why not face the issue of abortion? Abortion is murder. What possible agreement can we get to say that murder is permissible? I get sick and tired of people who say they are against abortion except in cases of rape and incest. Is that little fetus responsible for its parenthood?

"No, no, a thousand times no. If any fetus has a right to life, then every fetus kicking in the womb yearning to be born has that same right. This is definitely an issue that has to fit the up or down concept. You are for abortion or against it and I am against it in any instance. I know that caesarean birth is fine, especially when the life of the mother is threatened.

"Today, with the advances of medical science, we should let the babies have a chance at life on the outside of the womb if they have life as an individual inside only attached to the mother. They can live on independently at birth if they don't face murder before they are given that chance!"

Bridgette asked, "What do you feel are the mother's rights for her own body? Doesn't she have the right of choice?"

"Oh yes!" responded John. "And she made that choice when she made love knowingly without protection. That is the time for choice, not after life begins. Life is sacred especially for humanity. Lots of the world's greatest people had handicaps that would have been aborted in today's society.

"Where do you draw the line? I draw the line against killing a live human being before it is born. Millions of parents want children so if the mother does not want her child and the father does not or the family, then let it be given freely to couples who will love it for a lifetime. Be done with all the red tape and the black market. It is simple.

"Children are on the way, unwanted by the parent or parents. Create a computer list of every couple on Earth wanting an infant. Even if you draw their name or number from a fish bowl, it would not be much different. You would never know what that fetus might look like, how it would develop or the personality it would have. I know I'm a fanatic on this subject and have an inordinate amount of passion in my voice, but how passionate would I be if I saw a baby crawling out on a window ledge eight stories high and the screen was out?"

David said, "And, I for one, appreciate your passion. But before we hear more passionate speeches pro and con on this issue, can we by unanimous consent include it as a necessary item to address one way or the other in CODE 3-M?"

Seven yes votes appeared. "John, you are on a roll. Have you another issue that might be less controversial or more controversial?" David asked.

"That remains to be seen," John replied, "but thanks for the humor. We need to emphasize in this group all the wonderful things and accomplishments that religions have fostered. Look at the orphanages, the hospitals, the medical missionaries, the contribution to the arts, unparalleled literature, and the soul saving stations flung around the world bringing inner peace, joy unspeakable and full of glory and happiness!

"I stand for a Christ who can change lives, gives peace above understanding and offers a haven in the time of storm. He was wonderful in His miraculous birth, wonderful in His life, wonderful in His healing ministry, wonderful and glorious in His death. For all of us, marvelously wonderful when He rose from the dead and sailed back to heaven on a cloud.

"Who knows? He may have that same cloud parked outside the pearly gates just waiting to jump on it and return to this sin-cursed world and catch His waiting bride away. Even so, come Lord Jesus even before this project is over if it be your will."

Tony spoke up, "I don't know whether to stand up and holler Hallelujah or try to refute this joyful explosion, but I will say the basic thrust has been many, many good things to come out of religion, especially Christianity. It is an indisputable fact. I just hope all of us will be as honest when we weight the negative things like the war in Ireland, the crusades and so on to balance the scales."

Other members expressed their views pro and con. "Since the point was to recognize the many values of religion, let's vote on that issue," David suggested. The vote was 7 to 0 — not for the parked cloud but for the positives religions have brought to mankind.

It was time to move on. Next in the spotlight was David.

"I have been asked to be a resource for all the major religions, except the ones represented by some member of the group. Al is Jewish. John and Rachel are Protestant, Rachel a little more radical than John, if that's possible. Some in the group may seem a little confused as to exactly what they believe. Lu, Bridgette, and Tony do not subscribe to any faith. Neither do I, but I am not an atheist or agnostic. I am a quester or a seeker. If it seems like I'm from Missouri and often display a 'show me' attitude, I apologize. I just want to be honest.

"Religion, by nature, cannot be proven. Faith is not proof. Which religion merits my faith? Anyway, as the appointed source of the main historical religions, I will give you a glance at some of the ancient religions. Man has always tried to figure out why he is alive, where he came from and how should he act. That inquisitive nature is indeed a wonderful part of the nature of man.

"The effort has been messed up by man's almost total fear. There was reason for this overwhelming fear; he was being killed by animals, catastrophic natural calamities, and people from other tribes who hated him just because he was not from their tribe.

"Among the highest developed peoples were the Egyptians. They were quite advanced in learning, architecture, agriculture, nautical vessels, and the essential beginnings of math and science. The ancient Egyptian religion embraced all kinds of hard-to-imagine gods and played to the fears of mankind.

"The Hebrews were slaves in Egypt and knew of their history and culture. Some of you in the group believe that all religions are based on these same fears but the Egyptians developed a very elaborate scheme of gods to handle the various fears. I chose Egypt over the other many god peoples because there is evidence that humans began in Africa.

"The Great Annead called Atmu was the creator. She was the God of Air. Tefnut was the God of Moisture. Geb was the God of Earth and Nut was the God of the Sky. The mean God Shonsu had an imagined hawk-head on the body of a man. The Karnak Temple was built in honor of Anun (the Hidden One). He was the god of Thebes and his sacred beasts were the goose and ram.

"Some scholars believe this God (the Hidden One) was the genesis for deity belief for religions to follow even to this day. Mut was the mother of Gods and could be the genesis of the belief in Mary as the mother of God. And Ka, the soul of man who was the ghost-like spirit, was the genesis of the third party of the trinity. Ka supposedly lives in a tomb and receives offerings to nourish the body.

"Ra traveled Egypt with a solar deity called Hor-Behotet. Ra seemed to be a top God. The solar deity warded off evil from Ra and conquered his enemies. This god was used as a symbol, often placed over doorways to ward off evil. The tangible symbol looked like a two-headed eagle with wings spread. The heads were joined by an open circle.

"There were many more gods and I will run through most of them with just a brief explanation. Apis, the sacred bull who was the sacred animal of a cult who worshiped a god named Ptah, Beg, the Earth god was part of the many triads of gods, Geb, Nut and Shu was such a triad or trinity nut. The sky goddess, the wife of Geb begat Shu, the God of Air, so we have to some a beginning of the idea of the Immaculate Conception.

"There were gods of the chaotic forces. Their names are Seth, Setekh, Suty, Sutetekh or some such similar name. Nephthys, Neb Hut were the protectresses of the King. Anubis or An Pu was the God of Cemeteries. He had a jackal head and manlike body. You can't help but wonder if something deep inside the Egyptians' psyches was the possible notion of future biogenetics whereby human genes can be placed into animals and vice-versa. Who knows?

"Khnum, known as the molder of men, was a ram-headed god regarded as the Creator God of the Nile and also the creator of life. Khnum had a consort consisting of Satjit, Satis, Satet, who were guardians of the southern frontier of Egypt. They wore a white crown on antelope horns. Anukis or Anket

was mistress of the Nile. She was the daughter of Khnum and
Satjit. She was sometimes a caring nurse, sometimes a
vengeance-seeking strangler. This is a good psychological
insight to the nature of man and the Hebrew God who has
extreme capabilities. Anukis had the gazelle for her sacred
animal.

"Osiris or Ausar was 'highest of all powers.' He wore a
white crown and plumes, carried a scepter and flail. This
notion that God seems to be all powerful and can bless you,
send you to heaven — or flail you and send you to hell —
appears to be a very ancient concept. Osiris was the son of Seb
and Nut, the husband of Isis and father of Horus who was murdered by his brother, Seth. He was the god who civilized
mankind, gave them laws, and taught them agriculture.

"Don't we see a little of God and Moses in this Egyptian
God? Isis or Auset was known as the 'The Great Enchantress.'
She was a moon goddess and wife of Osiris, mother of Horus
and daughter of Nut, the sky goddess. The great temple at Phi-
lar was dedicated to Isis.

"Horus, Heru or Hor, avenger of his father hawk-headed
god, was mentioned before the son of Osirus and Isis. He was
known as the Living Horus when used as part of the King's
title. Today, most religions refer to their Living God. Horus
takes on many forms. The best-preserved temple in Egypt
depicts him in the form of a bird. The bird is used many times
in modern religions to represent various ideas.

"Ptah was the god of craftsmen who had a golden face and
his consort was the lioness Sakmet. His son was the Imhotep
who was also deified. On and on Egyptian gods seem to never
end. You can imagine the confusion among the people — like
the world is full of confusion today about religion. Sakhmet
had a lioness head and human body. She was the wife of Ptah
and was known as the Powerful. She was an avenger goddess
who once nearly wiped out the human race. She reminds one
of Noah's God.

"Imhuter was deified. Some believed he was the son of Ptah
and Sakhmet who was the builder of the step pyramid. The
practice of giving sainthood for good works looks to be the
result of this practice in ancient Egyptian religion. Aten, the
solar disc, had rays leading down to touch the persons of the
royal family being protected.

"Uraeus or Ariar was the serpent worn on the forehead of
gods and kings. It was the emblem of divinity and a protecting
evil eye to the owner. The book of Genesis in modern religions

doesn't afford the serpent such high distinction.

"Uazit was the goddess of the North from Buto with the vulture goddess of Nekhbet. She became the royal symbol and shared the title. Hat Hor or Het Hepu was the national goddess of love, beauty and joy. She was a mistress of the gods. Her temple at Dendera and Chapel at Deirhel Bahei are both intact today. Maat, goddess of law, truth and justice was the daughter of the sun god Re, living by the rule. This refers to the stability of the universe.

"Bast or Bastet was the national cat goddess. She had a human body and a cat's head, sometimes in a sitting position. The famous sphinx that still exists uses the opposite — a human head on a cat-like or lion body. Bast represented the flame of the sun. Neith, Nit or Neit, was a war goddess and one of the original goddesses of dynastic Egypt. She wore the red crown of Lower Egypt and had, for emblems, crossed arrows or a bow and arrow. Pahket was a lion-headed goddess representing the heat of the sun. She had a cult in the Beni Hasah area.

"Selkhet was the goddess of nature; Aah, the original moon god; Herishef, the ram-headed fertility god. Sobek had a crocodile head and a human body. His temple at Kom Ombo is still intact. And, there was Khepri also known as the Creator. He was a national god who wore the Khepra beetle as a headdress, depicting the rising sun associated with the resurrection concept in other religions.

"A cobra-headed god, Renenet, was the goddess of good fortune. Reshpu, the God of War, was strangely enough associated with the love goddess, Qetesh. The hippopotamus-headed goddess presided at the birth of children. Nefertum was the nature god representing the heat of the rising sun. He was man-like with a lotus blossom on his head. Bes, ugly little dwarf god, presided over music and dancing. He was sometimes seen as evil and sometimes worshiped as a god of birth.

"Behu a bird-headed man's body was sacred to the sun god, Re. He rose in brilliance from some type of destruction hence the Phoenix rising from the ashes. Hamhit was queen of the gods — represented with a fish on her head. Safekh was the goddess of learning and writing. She carried a reed and palette and the king's names on the sacred tree of life in Heliopolis.

"What a bunch of deities! As people became a little more educated, the masses didn't really believe in all these gods but they did harbor lots of fear. This is akin to people in the world today. There are so many voices and religions calling out 'I am the way, the true way.' Most people are dubious about all the modern gods regardless of what they tell the polls.

"The people in Egypt became dubious about all of their gods. This was true for the Greeks and true for all the areas on earth where people were taught plurality of gods. I will not go into detail concerning these other places where a plurality of gods were once in vogue, but let me tell you what happened in Egypt. This may be very pertinent to our project on this smooth-sailing ship if we can understand the foundation and changeableness of religions.

"We can go back in history to about 3100 B.C. when writing was introduced in Egypt. A king named Narmer united upper and lower Egypt into a unified state. The old kingdom, dating from 2700-2200 B.C., was the age of the pyramids and aloof God-like rulers who were remembered in legends. Social and economic disasters came and finally the country was reunited, known as the middle kingdom in 2050 B.C. This era lasted about 400 years and was a period of great literature and massive state projects to improve Egyptian irrigation and secure Egypt's borders.

"About 1650 B.C., after the Middle kingdom fell into confusion, a line of foreign kings from Palestine known as Hyksos, subdued Egypt and ruled it for a century. Then a line of active energetic kings from Thebes led the war of independence, drove the Hyksos out. The new kingdom began the age of Egypt's greatest wealth and power. As you can see, mankind has a long history and pattern of conquering other people by force and the people uprising and throwing them out by force. This resembles American and other histories; revolution has many precedents.

"King Tutaukhamun, popularly known as King Tut, was the son of Akhenaten. Akhenaten threw out all of the multi-gods I have mentioned and demanded the people worship only one god. The god he chose was Aten, the sun's physical presence. He closed the old temples to the gods and built new temples to Aten on a new site. Thus the idea of one God probably began in Egypt. It demonstrated if you have enough power, you can force people to believe as you do.

"This fact is being demonstrated today all around the world. Our founding fathers fought this notion like a rattlesnake, but people in power often try to dictate religious belief. I resent anyone forcing me to believe as they do, or to believe anything for that matter. Faith is a personal thing."

"David, I appreciate your presentation today and your comments," Bridgette remarked. "I would like to ask you a question. Do you believe that the ancient Egyptians' ignorant belief in all these stupid gods is any different than the variety of wild notions modern man believes today?"

"That's a tough question, Bridgette," a puzzled David responded. "At first glance, their beliefs do seem far-fetched, made up and unbelievable. Yet, I have to be honest. When I study surviving religions, they seem to have a kinship to the ancient Egyptian worshippers. And, I suspect other people around the table feel the same way about some religion other than their own. There are some very peculiar beliefs in all other religions except our own, which we have been forced to call sacred. Unbelievable. Your point is well taken. Logically, you are correct, but I cannot bring myself emotionally or intellectually to completely abandon what I have been taught from my early childhood."

There was a very somber mood among all the participants. David sensed it and dismissed the session saying, "This has been an unusual morning. We have much to ponder and we must be honest. No one said this effort is going to be easy or we could all agree. Thank you for the respect you are giving one another. Somehow, someway, we will arrive at something worthwhile if we maintain this attitude. See you tomorrow."

Each group member eventually found a spot on the ship they called their conference spot. Sometimes they would invite another member or members to discuss matters. Other times they would just meditate alone. The night times offered an opportunity to get to know one another better as a fellow-thinker, friend — perhaps more.

Lasting relationships were bound to emerge with such a limited and beautiful environment. This always seemed to be the case when humans take time to learn about each other and focus on understanding another human being. Maybe this was the hope of mankind and the basis of eliminating harm to individuals and war.

David was comfortable; he had made the right decisions so far. He admitted to himself that he was somewhat fond of these attractive ladies. He had single chitchats with these members more than all of the others combined.

"If each of the three would have me, which one would I choose to spend my entire life?" He honestly did not know and wondered if he would make a choice before the cruise ended.

Now, back in session, Tony Tweedhurst presented the

group's most anti-religious presentation. He blamed religion for much of the world's woes.

Tony began, "I would like to preface my remarks today and for any comment or conversation I may have, with the fact that I respect all of you as fellow human beings. As far as I am concerned, we are all intelligent and honest in what we perceive and believe. If we can change how we perceive events, then automatic emotions will change.

"We are emotional beings, preferring emotional beliefs to realistic and logical interpretations. Our emotions cause certain automatic actions and our overall behavior is incorporated from these perceptions, emotions and actions. You could use many words to describe this process. A simple example might be lying in bed at night and suddenly a loud noise occurs inside your house. The burst of noise is the event. You perceive that a burglar is in the house up to no good.

"When that perception is made, your emotion is one of fear and anger, mostly fear. Feeling that emotion, you go for the pistol under your bed; this action has evolved from your perception of the event. You explore the situation, gun in hand, and finally determine the noise came from the cat knocking over a pitcher of milk you inadvertently left on the kitchen table.

"When you see that, you change your perception of the event. The event did not change. There was a burst of noise. Your perception changed after discovering the facts; therefore, your emotions automatically changed and your action or behavior automatically changed. You laughed at yourself, put back the gun and went to sleep.

"This process works when any event occurs. We perceive, we automatically feel and act accordingly. Now, I fully realize that none of us are going to change our minds about anything unless we change our perceptions. That includes me.

"The Apostle Paul behooved us to 'come, let us reason together' and that is what I wish to do. I will not beat around the bush. I do not believe there is a God. I believe man made God and that God did not make man. I know many of you disagree with this perception and you can feel free to give me reasons why I should change my perception. So, I hope you will grant me the same privilege, as I will present from time to time my views.

"In the first place, if you designate the same powers to any imagined being in which modern religionists believe their God has, there could be similar perceived positive results and also many doubts would arise. The process would be the same from a psychological perspective. Any focus of worship, if given omnipresence, omnipower, omniscience, could be the creator and judge and have the power of ultimate reward and ultimate punishment. The being or thing would serve the same purpose as the particular God in each modern religion.

"One could worship a cow, an eagle, a cat, the sun, the moon, the heavens, a statue, a painting, a mountain, a tree, a person you make a saint, a celebrity like Elvis, Marilyn Monroe, Babe Ruth, Frank Sinatra, FDR, JFK and on and on. Sometimes the person need not be dead like Father Divine and a host of others claiming to be a God. People are so gullible and so fearful that they worship inanimate things like totem poles, statues of Buddha, the so-called Virgin Mary, and the like. They hang St. Christopher on auto mirrors and to their dismay, Chris is demoted and no longer the powerful saint who can ward off evil dangers.

"If one believes any of these has the package of powers unusually given to a God, then add a few miracles and downright lies to the pot, mixed in with the power to reward and punish for eternity in a fiery hell, then you have a workable religion for many, many millions of people. If we laugh at the ancient Egyptians, we had better examine some of our own wild notions about God impregnating the Virgin Mary, Jesus walking on water, raising the dead, and all His purported other miracles which no one can validate.

"The calling down of fire makes a fine tale. Again, I would like to examine it in more detail. Baal supposedly was a Canannitish and Phoenician God of Fertility, the principle male deity corresponding to Ashtoreth, the main female goddess called the supreme goddess. Baal worship was concerned primarily with fertility. Its central theme was the death and resurrection of God. The Baal worshipper believed it was necessary to perform a certain ritual that God would rise again.

"The Israelites, at various times, adopted this form of worship, notwithstanding the horrible consequences as that which happened to Jezebel, Ahab, Elijah, Jehu and Gideon. Worship of Baal was conducted at high places and on housetops. The Phoenicians, great sailors and missionaries spread their religion far and wide throughout the world at that time.

"In the 19th Chapter of Jeremiah, the Jewish God is raising hell about Baal worship vowing He would bring evil upon this place, noting that they have burned incense to other gods and filled the place with the blood of innocents, burned their own sons for burnt offerings to Baal. The Jewish God really gets mean. He says he is going to make the city desolate and cause the followers of Baal to eat the flesh of their sons and daughters and break the people like a broken potter's vessel so they could never be made whole again. The Jewish God is so mad at them because they burned their sons for sacrifice to Baal that he is going to destroy them and bury them in Tophet until there is no place to bury.

"It does not take a rocket scientist to see in this vengeful battle of the gods, people do not amount to a thin dime. Control is paramount and the lust for control starts wars and multiplied millions have suffered because of this type of nonsense. All wars have not been started or fought because of religious control but think of the hundreds of wars that were fought for a certain religious control and it will turn the stomach of any decent human being.

"Gideon destroyed the altar of Baal, then hung out a fleece beseeching Jehovah God to keep the fleece dry. As the tale goes, the dew was on all the ground and the fleece was dry. Many Christians say they put out certain kinds of fleeces to know God's will even today. Jehovah was put on the spot when His prophet made a deal with the followers of Baal. They would pray for fire to descend and see which God would respond.

"The Baalites cut themselves and went through all kinds of agony like many in the world today calling on their God. No soap. Yet the Jewish God according to the Jewish author of the story invoked his God to deliver. Supposedly, He did.

"Now I have a proposition. It may appear to be arrogant and self-serving to atheists, but I will convert to the winning God along with millions, yes even billions of others, if a God can produce. Let's build altars for any faith or religion that wishes to participate in Yankee Stadium or the Rose Bowl for example. Let's invite the Pope or his designee, Oral Roberts, Jerry Falwell, Jesse Jackson, Billy Graham, Louis Farrakhan, Jimmy Swaggart, Jim Baker, Benny Hinn, and the heads of the Methodist, Baptist, Presbyterian, Pentecostal, Mormons, Buddhists, rabbis, Muslims — whatever church.

"Have these leaders to pray to their God to send down fire. They would not dare because they know they could not get results from any God. They would all pussyfoot around the issue by saying you cannot tempt the Lord, thy God. Well, why was God called on against Baal; why did God supposedly answer and win over Baal? If no faith would accept such a simple challenge, one that has already been done, does this not reveal the extraordinary hypocrisy in the church, mosque and synagogue leaders?

"There are many books detailing the unimpeachable inconsistencies in the Bible and the other holy books. There are so many mess-ups it would take all of my time allotted to go through them. However, a few of them should prove helpful as we move along.

Rachel could hardly hold her tongue. When Tony paused, she said, "Are you personally ready to die?"

"I do not want to die," Tony answered. "I want to enjoy living more because I love life and want to help others as well as continue my own happiness. If you mean, am I afraid to die, the answer is a big no. I don't swallow the fear tactics of a hell. And, pray tell what sin could earn a fiery hell where your body burns for a trillion years and then the pain and suffering would have just begun. And, furthermore, what kind of a God would do this to the vast majority of people on earth? Please don't ask me to worship that God."

Rachel lashed back, "You have a right to choose to go to hell, but it will be your own responsibility. I know I am not going to hell because I have been washed in the blood of the lamb and Jesus is in my heart and life. I know the devil brings temptation, but I know He gives us strength to overcome. So I rebuke Satan and all his influences and continue to place my trust in the God of Abraham and his son, the Lord Jesus Christ!"

"Hallelujah! I'm glad you are happy with your religion. Likewise, I am most happy I am not in the category of those who have surrendered their minds to something made up by man. There is not a scintilla of evidence to prove any God exists, let alone a glorious heaven with streets of gold or a fiery eternal hell where one burns forever and is not consumed. It is much easier for me to believe in Santa Claus and flying reindeer."

David intervened, "I sense that we have a slight divergence of views, so let's get out of here and mull over what we have heard today from these two wonderful people."

The group needed a break from the tension. They chuckled at David's remark and left the room buzzing and mumbling to each other. They wondered if Tony would be so blunt and candid the next round. Yet, somehow his remarks did activate a new level of thinking both pro and con concerning the issue of God and religion. They hoped their ideas would also open new levels of thinking and understanding. There would never be a dull moment in these sessions if the heated discussions continued.

As the almost daily event occurred watching the large orange setting sun settling in the west, Rachel was slowly strolling the starboard side of the yacht. As David stepped out of the mess hall — really the exquisite dining area — he saw Rachel. He felt a suspicion that things were not right. "Are you okay, Rachel?"

Rachel turned. Captivated by her unusual beauty even when she appeared distressed, David welcomed this opportunity to lend a shoulder.

"I'm okay, I suppose — just a little mad at myself," she said quietly. A powerful yearning to take her in his arms, kiss the gloom away and let her know his feelings for her came over David. However, he quickly told himself don't blow it man. Be attentive. Go slow. Remember you don't know how she would respond to such a bold move.

So he said amicably, "You know, sometimes I get teed off at myself and that's the worst kind of feeling, one with which it is hard to cope. It's lots more fun getting upset with someone else."

Rachel, somewhat embarrassed that David had caught her in this reflective, somber mood, whispered, "That's the problem, I did get upset with someone else but it was no fun."

David moved nearer to her for two reasons. He wanted to be close to her and he did want to hear every word she spoke. In a flash, he wondered if Rachel had subconsciously lowered her voice to draw him nearer. Girls have subtle ways to charm a man and men take the bait often not knowing what is happening. David didn't give a hoot whether it was conscious or subconscious. He moved over and placed his hand on top of her hand as she gripped the rail. Though they had been engaged in a number of conversations previously, they were mostly academic and not personal.

"I'm a good listener. Do you want to talk about what is bugging you? If not, I'll understand and we can watch the waves together."

Rachel moved a little closer and the touch of his warm body gave her a special thrill. For a while, they said absolutely nothing but communicated through the touch. Sometimes this can be the best communication of all.

Several minutes had gone by before Rachel spoke, "I jumped all over Tony and should not have asked him so bluntly if he was ready to die. I feel terrible about it."

"Never mind, Tony is a big boy. I thought he handled it pretty well; he didn't impress me as being angry. You shouldn't beat up on yourself because of one exchange like that in a setting where give and take is the norm."

"Thanks, David. You always know the right words to calm the storm. It seems to be a special talent that you possess. I've admired the way you can diffuse a hot atmosphere and move on. However, we know ourselves better than anyone else and the reason I feel down is because I know I was mad at the time I challenged him. It was a deeply felt emotion and here I am proclaiming that I am a dedicated Christian and setting a bad example like that."

David just listened remembering that Carl Rogers had in essence said, "Listen, stupid." When the catharsis seemed complete, David suggested, "Well, if you feel like you goofed, just tell Tony you are sorry and will try to cool it."

"That would be the easy way out," Rachel frowned with determination. "I owe Tony, you and the whole group an apology and I'll do it. In fact, I'll do it tomorrow to preface my presentation. I was shocked at his lack of faith and blunt remarks, but you told us to be frank and candid. He has that right. I should have bitten my tongue and countered his views, not attacked him personally, which I did even though he may not have taken it that way. I will straighten this out tomorrow in my first statement, then I won't seem to be the unpleasant person that you are with tonight."

It was time for chow, but there was time for a spirited hug between the two young people. Both of them wondered how far their acquaintance and friendship would go. Could it ever reach the level of fulfilling love's eternal dream?

Next day, Rachel was presenting. "First, I want to say that I owe an apology to Tony and the whole group. I crossed the line when I asked him if he was personally ready to die. I am sorry, Tony. I had no right to be judgmental."

Tony jumped up, rushed to Rachel and gave her a big hug. The group applauded for a long time. There was no need for anyone to say anything else. A sincere apology is a powerful phenomenon in human relations.

"David," began Rachel, "I really appreciate the detail you gave to us concerning the ancient Egyptian gods and how mankind has always been searching for something outside himself in which to believe. My little presentation will focus on the folly of the theory of evolution. You notice I referred to evolution as a theory because that is exactly the case. Charles Darwin did not create the theory. Anaximander, who lived in the 6th century B.C., was the first known person to develop a beginning cosmological system and he was quite a philosopher. He accounted for the origins of life, which began in water through the action of heat. The first animals according to Anaximander were sea urchins. Even human infants were produced first in a fishlike creature. Most people, even the ancient evolutionists, do not follow Anaximander or completely the precepts of Darwin.

"Professor S. Alexander developed a more acceptable theory and a person with whom he had great influence was Lloyd Morgan. Morgan propounded 'emergent evolution,' considered by myself and many others to be one of the best examples of the theory. It makes more sense than the other many, many evolutionists to me yet it also has tremendous problems, which I would like to briefly point out to you. Several in this group speak as though evolution is an absolute proven fact and if you don't believe it, you are an uneducated type who has let the times pass you by. Now, hold the phone everyone!

"There are many brilliant people with Ph.D.'s, Nobel Prize winners and what have you that do not swallow the evolution theory! I want to be brief and fair to Lloyd Morgan and his views. Although his ideas developed years before, his crowning presentation came in 1923. His final work in 1933 concerned the emergence of novelty. In an age-old attempt to explain adequately those things that exist before us involving life, two well-formulated theories are advocated.

"There are mechanism and vitalism. Mechanism as its name indicates interprets organisms as mere machines. Matter of which organisms are composed is reducible to the same chemical elements as are found outside the body. No new matter is formed in the body or disappears from it. The energy liberated in the body, whether as heat, mechanical work or other forms, can be traced to sources outside the body.

"It concluded that all-living organisms, even human beings are governed by two great physical laws, the conservation of matter and the conservation of energy. All behaviors may be analyzed in terms of the laws of physics and chemistry. There is no real purpose. The thing we call purpose is merely apparent and in its essential reality, it is merely a mechanical purposeless physico-chemical reaction.

"Vitalism, on the other hand, claims that there is an essential and fundamental difference between living organisms and purely inanimate things. This fact should be self-evident. The organisms we see before us are of a different nature than mere stones. There is something outside mere physical and chemical laws that gives life its essential nature and causes it to function in an intelligent, purposeful and harmonious way.

"We can construct a grain of wheat with the same chemical proportions of a real grain and give it proper nourishment, but it will not come up and grow. We can compose an egg identical to the hen's but it will not hatch even if it is fertilized. So, life comes from life and there is no real credible scientific evidence of the spontaneous generation of life from non-life.

"Mechanism and vitalism were both challenged by Lloyd Morgan. He reasoned that all the great steps of evolution — the making of the body, the establishment of a brain, the beginning of the blood, the differentiation of sense organs — were new syntheses with new intrinsic qualities and new extrinsic properties.

"This idea of emergence in biology says the characteristics of an organism are novel, and not reducible to physical and chemical laws. When compounds reach a higher degree of complexity, such wholes develop characteristics not explicable in terms of their parts and they can be called "emergent." Life is an emergent and belongs to the general scheme of emergent evolution.

"So, in a nutshell, Morgan rejects both mechanism and vitalism and emerges with a combination type of emergent evolution. He thinks all things are upon the river of evolution floating towards deity and final development. He believes there should be no disjunctive antithesis between the timeful and the timeless. They are not to be regarded as incompatible contradictories but they should be combined into a higher synthesis.

"God, to Morgan, is an object of contemplation in the same sense that we believe God has what we are seeking. It is more than Alexander's Nisus concept, which is an upward drive and direction of evolution. Morgan wants to view God as being involved in the Nisus, the activity, and the spirit of Divine purpose that serves as an eternally existing goal of the evolutionary process.

"Now, ladies and gentlemen, I have tried to give you a skeleton of what seems to be the best evolutionary theory to me. But, the best has been weighed in the scales and found, I believe, pitifully wanting!

"In the first place, you cannot swallow the concept of novelty of Morgan. He uses the idea that from oxygen and hydrogen emerges water. Is water really new and in an evolutionary process or just what happens when two elements combine? It is merely the same thing combined and the proof is present when you separate water back to hydrogen and oxygen. There is no third thing or emergent. There is only what you began with so, where is evolution or Nisus or anything new going upward? Morgan claims a new relation emerged but nothing with newness that is concrete. So how can we call this evolution? He bases his notions on fromness and withness. Common sense tells me that these are opposing or incompatible ideas. Come on, let's get real!

"The next area of thin ice that he falls through long with all others who accept evolution is the spatial-temporal relatedness or time/space combination. A believer in God is asked, where did God come from? We answer God always was and His being was existent before all things.

"Hard to believe? Yes, it takes faith, but it certainly does not take nearly as much faith to believe way out there a little speck started and developed into a planet or whatever. Where did the speck come from?

"Morgan and others can speculate that the speck came from a point-instant in space-time. What kind of garbage is this? You cannot have space unless an object exists and it is the distance between another object! You cannot have time unless something exists! What is measured? To me, it is sheer nonsense to advocate that space occupies space. Space, again I say, is a relation or a capacity of physical objects and space presupposes physical objects.

"It is only fair to state that Morgan and Alexander and a host of other evolutionists do not use the concept of space and time but space-time. They are wedded together and form a space-time continuum. Sometimes they call it time-space. It does not make any difference what you try to call it, if nothing exists to be measured in a durational sense, then there is no time and certainly there is no space.

"So, I ask the evolutionist, how did everything get started at a point-instant in space-time? I ask in return, which view takes the most faith? I have enough faith to believe God was, is and always will be. I have no faith in a little speck happening somewhere somehow in space-time!

"Again, the evolutionists have a problem with mind. He treats this also as an emergent and brings confusion to the issue instead of clarity. He adopts Spinoza's concept of thought and extension. On one hand, he views the mind as innate and on the other hand, he thinks it emerged. Things cannot be used as immanent, everlasting as in Spinoza's sense, and still be an emergent.

"Evolutionists are very vague concerning the concept of life and Morgan seems totally confused about God. Morgan sees God as a spirit or Nisus that gives the pyramid of evolution a divine purpose or great plan. Yet, he regards the universe as flowing toward deity.

"So God seems to be drawing emergence to Himself, thus admitting that God is eternal. When did God emerge? Why not simply believe that He was, He is and He will be, and He created all things just like the Bible says.

"Evolution tries to do the same thing as religions try to do. They try to make sense of the present, retrospect the past, and predict the future. You cannot believe God created human beings if you believe we came from a speck, then a rock, then a tree or water lily, then a starfish, then a walking fish who later developed legs, later a monkey and apes without a tail, then us.

"This is ridiculous! There is the no beginning. It is a jump to the inanimate world, the crossing of the great chasm to the world of botany, then the great divide to fish and then animal, and finally to humans. DNA from the hair of Egyptian mummies is the same as it is in humans today, so evolution has done little in thousands of years. Just believe God made us from dust and breathed the breath of life in us like Genesis tells us. Why do apes look more like humans than dolphins? Dolphins are higher in intelligence on the phylogenetic scale than chimps and other primates."

Bridgette spoke up, "Rachel, I enjoyed your beautiful detailed attempt to debunk evolution. I disagree with almost every word that you said. I won't waste time debating this issue with anyone who will not reason and always goes back to Genesis. In fact, with due respect for you, I fail to see why this topic has any relevance to our mission!"

David intervened, "Whether one agrees or disagrees with Rachel as many of us do, the topic is relevant because it is now and has been a burning issue in the behavioral issues of mankind, not only of individuals but school boards, courts, and nations. Atheistic nations have waged war on religious nations and vice versa. We want this stopped. Whether humans were created or evolved is highly germane to our guidelines."

After a heated discussion, the vote was 5 yes, 2 no to

address it as a possible item in the report.

Rachel wrinkled her brow. Had she vented herself too much for the group to take her seriously? She broke into a pleasant half-smile. Anyway, she mused, David came to her rescue even though he did not fully agree or mostly agree with her stand.

David wondered why she did not point out the fact that chimps and gorillas look more like humans, but parrots can talk like humans. Apes cannot. David winked at Rachel. Now she thought, at least I've shown some fire and determination and that I'm more than just a pretty face.

Rachel chuckled, "Since I'm following a policy of avoiding controversial topics, I want to speak to the declining standards of morality that we see today. I'm ashamed to say but some so-called Christian nations have a bankrupt morality; other religions that they by and large reject have a higher standard in many areas of human life.

"For example, some practically worship Elvis who died on drugs. Oprah Winfrey is one of the best-loved persons in the world and one of the richest I might add, highly regarded as a role model, yet she 'shacks up' with a guy — no marriage and everyone knows it. This is open fornication and a TV program to spread it, though she rarely mentions her personal love life.

"Most of Hollywood has added the glamour touch to this as well as smoking, drinking, cocaine and other illegal mind-altering drugs. Magic Johnson and Rock Hudson contract the AIDS virus. One dies; one goes on as a great celebrity and says he is straight but does not know who gave him the virus. Sports figures by the tens of dozens have run afoul of drugs.

"President Clinton and Vice President Gore admit illegal drug use but not much. Bush evades an answer to the issue of his use of cocaine, admits alcohol extravagance. Senators, Congressmen and Gingrich are kicked out because of moral reasons. Agnew and Nixon resigned. On and on we could go, until volumes were filled of leaders and role models who live in sin and are proud of it. What does this say to the children of America and the world? Garbage is seen on TV and computers at every hour of the day; child porn is a terrible problem on the Internet.

"The so-called justice system has been desecrated beyond repair by money grabbing lawyers and biased juries letting murderers like O.J. Simpson go free and jailing others for peaceful protest. Folks, we are in a moral pool of filth and anyone who cries out against it can be treated as the nutty far right or a religious fanatic. If some level of decency and basic moral standards are not reclaimed, this country is doomed like Sodom, Gomorrah, and Rome. At one time, America was the torch of decent living for the world. Now we are the leaders of moral rot and indecency. Not only America, some English folk have made Princess Di a saint.

"Even if you reject the Bible, surely this group can muster up the courage to develop some basic moral and decency precepts that are worthy to be placed in the CODE for the third millennium!"

Rachel's eyes were piercing each member of the group. Her passion was unmistakable and her point received a 7 yes unanimous. There was a lot of consternation on most of the faces of the group as they left the session.

David and Rachel agreed to go atop the captain's cabin after dinner. As usual, there were a variety of discussions during the meal including world affairs, politics, sports, jewelry and automobiles. The seven members of the group thought they had one another pegged pretty well and then a person would take a view or ask a question completely out of character— or at least the character one thought they should fit. This spiced up the journey to no end and no one was ever bored. Rather, they wondered just what strange statement would be made at the next session.

The top of the captain's wheelhouse setting was perfect for a one on one. David hoped this meeting would point to a romantic conclusion as they watched the small flapping flags on the vessel. Instead, Rachel's first words were, "Why, David can't you accept the Bible as the true inspired word of God?"

"Oh boy," thought David, "here we go again."

After pondering the many reasons why he did not accept everything in the Bible, he thought of one that just might resonate with his beautiful, alluring companion.

"When I was a little boy, I heard the story of Isaac, how Abraham said God told him to take his beloved son, Isaac, kill him and burn him on an altar as a sacrifice to God. Abraham took Isaac, saddled his donkey, and took two young men also to help out with the wood, the fire and other needed items for a burnt offering.

"In the first place, Rachel, this was an ancient heathen custom. If God wanted us to burn live things to worship Him then, why don't you worship Him now the same way? Then, a terrible thing occurred. He tied his own live son to the wood on the altar. Furthermore, he took a knife and started to kill his own son. This is the same God who later ordered Saul to go kill all the Amalekites — the men, the women, the children, the cattle, everything.

"Rachel, I'm against killing people who are so young and innocent. I cannot serve such a God as portrayed in the Bible. He is a God of vengeance and vindictiveness that equals or supercedes the terror of a Stalin and Hitler. Let me ask you for a simple, honest answer. If you thought God told you to kill your child, would you do it?

Rachel began to weep almost uncontrollably. She finally whispered, "I don't know the answer. Only God knows about those things, but I would never kill my child if I ever have one."

"I am so sorry, Rachel. I apologize for upsetting you in my answer to your question. I spoke too strongly and showed too much passion. I just wanted you to step inside my brain for a moment and see the God of the Bible violates his own laws over and over again.

"Let's talk about the heavens above. It blows my mind to realize we are just a small star in a huge overwhelming galaxy and those galaxies are perhaps as numerous as sands of the sea. Each day the sun shines on our turning planet, the stars and moon seem to be eternal. There are so many, many reasons to believe that there must be a God somewhere. Who He is, where He is and what He is truly like has been my quest all of my life since I could understand what they were saying in church. I hope to get a better focus on the Divine One.

"Right now, it is rather obscure and blurred. I believe this complex, mysterious impression I have of the true God will someday lose its indistinct, nebulous and vague conception and a clear, distinct notion will occur. As I said, I am not an atheist and I am not even an agnostic. I am a quester and a seeker. Right now, I believe God is love. I see God in many things, the baby's laugh, the compelling beauty and smell of the rose, the sunrise, the sunset and right now I see god in the heavens above. So, I agree in part with your scholarly presentation and the dismantling of evolution theories and I, in my mind, dismantled the Bible version of creation.

"Should I lie and say I believe as you do to win your favor? No, my mind is the most important thing in the world. It is me. I must be honest with myself. I don't want you to change your beliefs because of anything I say because I am still seeking. I have ruled out many things and ruled in some things. And, I will add something very personal that I have not said to anyone else because I care for you and want you to believe in my sincerity.

"If there is the vengeful God who has created a fiery hell for people to burn a trillion, trillion years and he sends my soul reunited with my body to suffer this fate for eternity for being honest, then let Him have at it! He has not revealed Himself to me except through the words, preaching, and unproven beliefs of other humans.

"If God is love and the God I seek is certainly that, then His love for us poor humans would cause Him to reveal Himself in all clarity so there would be no mistake, then tell us His rules. Let God speak or write or come on worldwide TV.

"It is cruel for mankind to be gripped with uncertainty and dependent upon other humans to show the way and say what the way is. Look at the religious turmoil the world has always suffered; look at what that mess has caused. Did the Bible God supposedly set up and devise a scheme whereby the vast majority of people would go to a fiery hell? This is not the God of love and beauty I seek. Yet, it is certainly with the Bible God.

"I believe deep inside every human there is a burning yearning to know the truth. Which one a person accepts is up to him or her. So I declare my right to accept the religion that says I am seeking the answer. No one has it for me. I am comfortable and pleased with honest quest. It suits me much better than the multiplied thousands of blind faiths so many accept.

"I respect you for your passionate blind faith in the Bible, but that dog won't hunt for me. I wish we could get beyond this religious talk and learn about each other. You make me feel warm and alive when I stand here by you. The sweetness of your smile, the eyes that express so much are so exciting to me. I know I would like to spend more time with you. Despite our divergent views, I hope you will give me a chance as a person you care for and admire at least a little bit."

"Oh baloney!" Rachel exclaimed. "You know I have been keenly interested in you since we were first introduced. I just wish you were a Christian. You know, the Bible teaches us not to be unequally yoked together. We can be friends — close friends — but do not expect me to give you my heart."

David thought there was something totally unfair about her statement, but he kept his cool and did not reply to her. After all, there were more fish in the sea. In fact, Lu and Bridgette were very beautiful fish who would not throw up a roadblock at his being a seeker instead of a committed person to a certain religion.

"I understand," said David. "I will be as close a friend as you desire. I did not mean to propose to you. I just wanted you to know that I had very sincere caring feelings for you."

"Oh, I knew you were not proposing, David. I already care for you so much that I just don't trust myself. I should not have presumed or even insinuated your feelings could lead to a life-time commitment."

"Have you ever attended a space shuttle launch?" David quickly changed the subject.

"No, but I would like to. They say it is an awesome experience to see man take off to the moon or a space station or to repair Hubbell," Rachel purred knowing she had really blown it for the evening.

"Well, perhaps we can watch a launching together on some special occasion."

"I would love that, David," she said with her eyes revealing a hurt-puppy look he had never witnessed before. When they reached her cabin door, David gave her a friendly hug and kiss on the cheek. Rachel spent the night sobbing and fussing at herself for what she felt was a lost opportunity — perhaps the best opportunity of her life!

Another day, another presenter. In fact, Bridgette would complete the first round of presentations.

David opened up the session by saying, "I'm sure the discussions thus far have compelled many of us to flip our brains and receive some novel ideas. Once again, I'm proud that we have already achieved one important thing. We have proved that people who may have different backgrounds and cultural histories can come together, present ideas that conflict but through it all develop very close friendships."

When he said the word friendship, he looked at Rachel not realizing she had agonized through the night about their conversation.

"You always save the best until the last. Bridgette Thompson is our next presenter and from her previous comments, I know they will be perceptive and thought-provoking. Bridgette, you are our heavy hitter. And we have a lot to clean up!"

"David, before I clean up, I want to dirty the waters some more. I agree that our minds have absorbed some shock material outside of our own little logic-tight compartments. Like all of the others and the style of a congressman and congresswoman, I wish to reserve the right to revise and extend my remarks for the record.

"We do need to activate our brains at higher levels so we

can think beyond the edicts and maxims we were taught. It frightens me to know most of our religious people revere the words of people who did not know the Earth was a round planet. Some of the knowledge they wrote down proves out false when heated in the crucible of truth. Much of it is boiled away as chaff.

"Even the ancient Egyptians possessed valuable and worthwhile knowledge in many fields as has been mentioned. We are still impressed with mummies and pyramids to say nothing of their fundamental mathematical principles, which enhanced their architectural prowess. Their crafts and sculptures were intricate and beautiful.

"Don't worry. I will not try to repeat or add on to David's synopsis, but just illustrate that whatever is handed down to us from the ancients, the various books claiming to be the word of God, the forefathers and self-appointed keepers of a faith should not be dismissed out of hand as having no truth or value.

"By the same token, this information needs to be put into perspective according to the development of science and literacy of that day. One must marvel at how truth has developed regarding the various fields of learning and never disparage altogether the pioneers of thought, religion and science. Still, each part and parcel should stand common sense evaluation to separate the wheat from the chaff.

"First of all, we need to develop a passion for life with all of its wonderful and marvelous things. We need to sing in our hearts each day. I am alive! I am alive! And concentrate our energy and emotion on what we know to be real, discover more realities, and seek to add to this remarkable world and to other people. If we concentrate on keeping our soul out of hell and pleasing some man-made God and system of religion, we miss out, I believe, on what life is all about.

"No one knows for sure that there is a God. No one knows for certain that there is such a thing as a soul. No one has ever been to a place called heaven and returned to tell us it is there with pearly gates, walls of jasper, and streets of gold. If the Bible hell exists, you can see why no one has been there and returned.

"The whole idea seems to me to be a crude forerunner of behavior modification. If you do what I say or the religious establishment says I say, great will be your reward in heaven. This is a powerful positive reinforcement. If you don't obey my word (a compilation of materials made by man called 'my word') you will be burned in an eternal fiery hell forever! If the fears of a child can ever be implanted, this notion of hell — a tremendous negative reinforcer — will certainly do the job.

"How many parents have told their children they would go to hell if they did so and so? How many of the children did some of the so and so and were gripped with a fear that caused them to cry themselves to sleep at night?

I know I was one of these innocent girls who was brain-washed to thinking I was born in sin and would automatically go to hell if I did not subscribe to what the Bible said for me to do. It is a terrible thing to scare a child to death so to speak to control his or her behavior. I do not know which is worse, to beat and abuse the child physically or abuse his or her mind with all kinds of fear of a vengeful God!

"I'll move on a little. The same religious system laid on me taught very little about slavery, addiction, and governmental tyrants. Jesus turned the water into intoxicating wine, said to render unto Caesar what was Caesar's and slothed over the issue of slavery. This little group knew nothing of tobacco, but since Jesus was a full member of the so-called Trinity, was he not omniscient as well? Did he not know tobacco, dope and liquor would someday plague mankind?

"Why so much history of the Jews in the Bible and so many glaring omissions on how people should behave? The early books of the Bible are self-serving to show that God displays great favoritism to Jews.

"Then, like the ancient Egyptians, the Bible is a collection of statements and knowledge. Some of it is real and true. Much of it is obscure, heathen and devoid of practicality in this day and time.

"The Koran and the Book of Mormon, the writings of Con-fucius and Buddha have some truths within, but everyone in the world is called upon to pick the overarching only true one. Even if there were a true religion, how is an honest person supposed to choose on the bias of his or her parents? On the bias of some emotional experience without any facts? Or, as in most cases, on the basis of fear?

"I believe we need to cleanse ourselves from the mud pud-dle of all religions and follow what is right and decent and fair that makes common sense to most everyone. Without going too far in my disgust, I propose that we eliminate all religious deities and edits from the CODE and still allow anyone to choose any religion they wish. I believe a common ideal or CODE can be achieved. We should stop killing each other because of divergent religious views."

The vote to omit a particular religion or any particular deity from the CODE was 7 yes to 0 no. All members realized it would be impossible to please every human with any particular religion or any particular deity.

"Another burning issue to me is society's compulsion to pigeonhole or classify the individual as they see fit, not according to reality or the wishes of the individual," Bridgette continued. "This racial thing and religions thing can cause death and bloodshed beyond description. Oh, I know the movies have portrayed the atrocities, the hangings, the bombings and other terrible things. I appreciate also the printed media in their attempts to describe crime and war, but they can only portray the tip of the iceberg. It is the insistence of rigid classification that is the root of the problem.

"As mentioned, we were taught to hate the Japs and the Huns and a thousand other monolithic groups. Hate leads to killing in so many instances. Since 1970, multiracial children have quadrupled in the USA. Yet the old Southern law clause says if you are 1/16 Negro, your Negro spirit prevails. And Rev. Hayes, I think you know the worst barrier to being seen as multiracial is now from the blacks or so-called Afro-Americans. I love what Whoopi Goldberg had to say about the issue. She declared, 'I am not an Afro-American. I am an American. I have been to Africa and I did not like it. I am a full-blooded American.' We must denounce and eventually eliminate this fad of hyphenated Americans.

"Obviously, I am a person of mixed ancestry and multiracial with some Caucasian, some Negroid, and some Mongoloid genes. If you follow the suggested three large categories of race among humans, I qualify to be all of them, so please treat me as none of them. I am a human citizen of planet Earth. I am very proud of all my ancestry in many ways.

"However, all races have a sordid history of hate and violence against other races. Ethnic hate seems to be at an all-time high and present-day wars are either economic greed, religious, racial, ethnic or a mixture. Perhaps these are the underlying reasons for all wars. Usually, fanatical leaders with egos gone wild are involved.

"In simple words, if your tribe does not look like my tribe or believe like my tribe, we will conquer you by killing you until you surrender. We might kill you anyway while you are waving a white flag, because you are the enemy. Furthermore, our leaders say if we can take your land and possessions, all of us will be better off. It is 'us versus them,' so let's build the largest and best military so we can destroy — or at least control them because they are no good. They are in our way. They are peculiar and strange. We hate them and hate their God; we are destined to be on top, perhaps rule the world. So we must indoctrinate our youth to hate those we hate, whether or not they think it is reasonable.

"Folks, I wonder if we as a human race can ever get beyond this stupid, hurtful tribal philosophy. I, for one, will not allow myself to be sucked into this meaningless morass. I will continue to cry out for fairness, decency and justice.

"Frankly, I see very little of these good behaviors in the many nations in the world today. But, the hope is that we know nations are comprised of individuals. And billions of individuals are sick of the bloodshed in crime and war. They instinctively know killing is not the answer. Many know the human sacrifice of war brought on by egotistical and often insane leaders has been a terrible awful, incredulous price to pay for their personal benefit.

"Of course, wars are not just the ego clash of unworthy leaders. All are not begun by maniacs or tyrants of old. The Gulf of Tonkin fiasco and the over-hype of Serbian and Kosovo atrocities smell alike and one wonders if a compulsion to leave a so-called legacy is not a prime factor.

"Anyway, back to this interracial thing. Billions of people are in the category on the face of the Earth and it will continue to increase. It needs to be increased and needs to be specified. Far surpassing his tremendous exploits hitting a little white ball into a hole the size of a coffee can is the fact that Tiger Woods has used his worldwide celebrity to declare many people are multiracial. He honors his Thai mother and his part-American Indian and black father. It is high time for Colin Powell, the Rock, Geraldo Rivera, Charles Rangel, Bryan Gumbel, and many mixed racial people to stand up and be counted.

"Adlai Stephenson once said that all progress has resulted from people who took unpopular positions. We, who are multiracial, need a fearless leader that will make it okay to recognize that we are multiracial. Martin Luther King is gone, but his multiracial wife is still with us.

"Step up to bat, someone with celebrity status — we need a leader! I hope my little call will fall on the ears and hearts of many who will establish that billions of us do not neatly fit into these three categories that can't seem to fully accept one another. We accept and love them all. We have before us the glorious opportunity to show the world that differences in race are miniscule compared to commonness. Please folks, get this principle in the CODE."

John jumped to his feet, "I agree with you 100%, Bridgette! Pushing people into locked areas is a crime and a sin. Let us be what we want to be. I am black and proud of it, but my God teaches me to love white, reds, browns, yellows, whatever and that includes beautiful interracials like you!"

David chuckled, "Yep, Bridgette would be easy to love. Seriously, she has put her finger on some very important things, especially the interracial nature of billions of peoples. Most of the world is not white and never will be. I do not know how we can word the CODE with what Bridgette has brought to us, but if the issue is voted up for consideration to be included in the CODE, I will offer my help to work with Bridgette on this issue. It is very important!"

The vote was 7 yes, 0 no. Rachel felt her heart miss a beat. Then, she said to herself, "Why should I be jealous of Bridgette or anyone. David does not belong to me." She paused; it was true now, but did it always have to be that way? She determined to jump in the issue head long with sincere thought, but also to keep the playing field level.

"Bravo, Bridgette," said Rachel. "I've always wondered why the personal ads seeking to meet people for possible companionship, romance or marriage almost always list the color of their skin, B for black, W for white and so on.

"And worse, why do they seek the same color to contact them? Does not this prove a deep-seated prejudice emanating from all races toward one another? Why are children taught from infancy that birds of a feather flock together?

"I'm very ashamed of the fact that religious people teach the same philosophy. Jews are supposed to marry Jews. Muslims are supposed to marry Muslims. Buddhists marry Buddhists. Hindus dare not marry anyone but Hindus and so on and so on. No wonder there is so much hate and suspicion in the world! I know the unanimous vote has been cast, but I just felt the need to add this comment.

David looked at her and smiled. Bridgette called on her woman's sixth sense and it told her Rachel was throwing down the gauntlet in a race for David.

"Stay cool, baby," Bridgette thought. "He volunteered to help me and furthermore, he said I would be easy to love. Perhaps he was half-joking. Perhaps not."

She continued her presentation, "One other issue I would like to bring up in this session is the peculiarity of religious people giving God credit for life, health, happiness, daily bread, saving their lives in a disaster when thousands of others are not saved, nor healed of cancer or whatever malady. If God is in control, as they believe, why do they not blame God for doing terrible things to them when the terrible things occur? When misfortune comes in a thousand forms, people who believe in a God simply say, 'Oh well, that was not in God's plan. We don't always understand his plan, but he does so we don't have to worry.'

"Billy Graham said when asked why three young people were killed in a plane piloted by JFK, Jr., 'It's all in God's hands.' Others project a curse on the Kennedy family observing that so much tragedy has befallen that talented, wonderful and caring family. Who placed the so-called curse and why?

"Of course, there is no such curse. If a boat had picked up the three out of the sea after the crash, then millions around the world would piously claim that God had answered their prayers. Isn't there something blatantly illogical here? Are some people so brainwashed that they rationalize any terrible situation as God's will, never blame their God and yet give him all the glory and honor for the good things that happen? What a ridiculous one-sided deal!

"Yet, these same brains still believe the hairs of our head are numbered and God notes every sparrow that falls. We humans thank God for a healthy so-called normal child. Who do we thank for a serious spinal bifida or Downs Syndrome child? I once visited an institution in Gainesville, Florida, called Sunland Training Center. It was indeed an institution of incredible effort and loving care. I saw an entire cottage of little Mongoloid or Down's Syndrome girls. God let this happen. What was the purpose? Multiply this number by a billion and tell me why so many severely handicapped people are born.

"If Oral Roberts and other preachers who claim God hears through their ministry were to go and lay his right hand as a point of contact and each little girl would be made completely normal, then God deserves the credit. The world would rejoice and Oral would not have to beg from people ill suited to send him money. Meanwhile, he bought an expensive bull and flew around in a huge Columbine airplane. It won't happen and everyone knows it will not happen.

"If an all powerful God can heal a headache or sore throat as claimed, why not at least one of these precious little girls so she could enjoy a normal life? Oh well, say the religions, you must not tempt God. He does what He wants to when he wants to according to His plan. If He wishes to change his plan like once allowing Solomon a thousand wives to now just allowing one wife, it is His business. I'm sorry folks; I cannot buy this view. It defies all common sense, to say nothing of scientific inquiry.

"The point I am trying to make is that if we depend on anybody's God to make peace, we are in deep trouble. The Gods of man have led man to believe he must annihilate the enemies of their God. This is precisely what is going on in the world today and precisely why we need to make a declaration. There is no God except the ones created by man!"

David spoke, "One thing is for sure, Bridgette, Billy Graham and Oral Roberts better be glad you're not an evangelist because you would have cut into their followers big time. However, even if you are correct, there is no way to get every religious person to denounce their God. Therefore, it seems plausible to attempt to create a set of guidelines that does not require anyone to drop their faith unless it is aggressively trying to promote violence and war. Could you agree to that?"

Bridgette had calmed down enough to give a demure smile, "Oh yes," she purred. "I just get weary at people claiming their God will bring peace to the world. How many millenniums will it take to see this is pure folly? Of course, you are correct in saying, they ain't gonna stop their crusades. We just need to face a few facts to slow them down. As you graciously suggested, I am not fighting any person. It is the hollow and failed philosophy that turns me off. Eventually, I imagine it will for most of the peoples of the world.

It was a time of long one on one and little group discussions as the seven members left the forum room. One thing was for sure, there were no wallflowers in that bunch! David gave Bridgette a long reassuring hug as she left the room. He wanted to assure her that he had appreciated her spirited presentation. He promised to meet her alone later.

Lu Chang was particularly fond of hanging over the stern of the vessel, watching the wake of the yacht as it glided across the Caribbean Sea. The water appeared to be so clean and fresh; often she could see fish. Sometimes large, sometimes small, they were all a little different she thought, just like people. Wasn't it true the difference was the beauty of life?

She reminisced about Bridgette's presentation. She

retraced her words mentally and wondered if she had sup-
pressed her Oriental pride to the extent of unfairness that
could lead to the disparagement of other races. Could they
really be as smart as Chinese? After all, we Orientals will be,
if not already, the most important and numerous people on the
Earth. We are an infinitely patient breed. Surely the third millennium will see the rise and dominance of the Mongoloid race
which shall become eternal.

Quickly she scolded herself for even thinking that way.
Had she not digested anything that Bridgette had to say? Boy,
would she be upbraided and reprimanded by the other members if they could see what was on the screen of her fertile
mind. It was indeed an offensive series of thoughts.

Quietly, David eased up beside her on the stern of *The
Quest*, not touching but very close.

"A penny for your thoughts, Lu," he said.

Lu was somewhat nervous and frustrated. She finally
replied, "My thoughts aren't worth a penny. I wouldn't know
how to verbalize them right now as so many thoughts are racing through my mind."

She did not include the thought that she was tickled to
death David was with her alone and using his considerable
charm to start a conversation.

"Oh, I know just how you feel, Lu. I supposed everyone has
private thoughts they understand. Sometimes when they try to
share them, something gets lost in the translation. I know I
have thoughts I would not want anyone to know about. Then I
have thoughts I wish could share intimately with someone to
make a connection to see if anyone else is sometimes as nutty
as myself.

"Relationships are like a huge stage curtain. When I meet
someone new, I tend to be neutral or positive about them at
first. Then little dots of radar begin to go on the screen that
tells me what kind of plane the radar is picking up. One or two
dots do not reveal much. I don't know if the plane is military,
friend or foe, commercial, private, large or small. In fact, several dots in various juxtapositions appear and I am still in
doubt, although I often jump to conclusions before I have
enough hard facts or dots. I have to change my perceptions
and this is so difficult because I so wanted to be right.

"But, back to the curtain. When one begins to trust another,
whether the same sex, same age, same race, same country or
whatever, if the trust increases, he or she pulls the cords and
opens the curtain a little more. As a little boy, I found it so easy

to open the curtain very wide with my brother who was just a year older than me. I felt our environment and heritage were so much alike and so many of our experiences were shared that I could put a lot of trust in him even though we had quite different personalities.

"I loved my parents, especially my understanding and loving mother, but I could not pull the curtain back as far as I did with my close brother. Perhaps I was ashamed to do so in many instances. I finally decided at about age 12 that girls were not just a nuisance — they could be sweet, charming and alluring. I had difficulty pulling the curtain back over a foot, so to speak. I did not mind them having a peek at what was the real me, but I was reluctant to show very much. With different people, I have pulled the curtain back as I trusted them and as I perceived they were pulling back their curtain for me.

"Lu, I have not had the opportunity of knowing you very long, but from your comments and demeanor I sense a feeling of trust for you. It almost baffles me. In fact, I wonder why I'm telling you all this, pulling back my curtain even this far."

"I'm glad you feel that way about me, although right now I don't think I deserve much trust from you. I will try to build trust if I possibly can. I find you to be an attractive person, not only in looks, but there is a certain depth of personality that is very winsome." Lu had surprised herself with this frank admission, but she was impressed by his curtain analogy and decided to do a little pulling herself on her own curtain.

She had dated many young men but had not found any of them to be as intriguing as David. In fact, she thought I'll even look over the fact that he is not Chinese. She laughed aloud without realizing it.

"What is so funny?" David asked.

"Oh, I'm sorry. I was just thinking about something that must stay behind my curtain at least for a while."

David was pleased she had bought into his little example and decided not to push her for an answer. They enjoyed the exquisite Caribbean scenery while he shared that gaze with her and at her in a non-conspicuous way. She was strikingly beautiful with long ebony hair and a contagious smile. It was a memorable moment in each of their lives.

Chapter V
Sexual Issues of Humans

David began the session on a serious tone. "If there is a number one issue in human behavior that has more angles and defies intelligent comprehension, it is sexual attitudes and behavior. There are many reasons that this issue has become such a tough nut to crack.

"First, sexual attitudes and practices vary so much all over the world. Second, the influence of religion is not seen anywhere as much as it is dominant in sexual prohibitions. Third, it is extremely difficult to cut through all the information and experiences in human history.

It is almost impossible to determine what is even normal and best for humans. And, what is normal and best for most people may not be the best for a particular individual. So, where does one begin to make an honest effort to establish guidelines that would be useful in CODE-3M?"

Rev. John Hayes suggested, "Why not list attitudes and behaviors. Put 'okay' or 'wrong' by each item and find the issues we agree upon."

The group consented. John then offered the first item to be considered.

"God made humans man and woman and they should stay that way."

Tony objected quickly, "I don't believe a god made anyone. I don't believe it is anyone's business — including the state — if a man feels female and has a sex change operation to become a female and vice versa. So I say put an 'okay' by sex change, not prohibit it."

Others gave their opinions. The vote was 4 to allow the individual to decide and 3 to prohibit it.

Bridgette said, "I can see this session is going to be a ringer, so I suggest one thing that I believe will get 7 votes.

Sexual rape is wrong. No doubt we will have 7 votes for this item, but I would like further discussion concerning statutory rape. Girls used to marry at ages 10, 11, 12, and 13. In some cultures they still marry at an early age. Is the husband raping them in a sexual experience?"

"Tough question, Bridgette," said David. "I do believe you raise a valid point, but I don't know how I really feel. My great-grandmother and her husband raised a nice family of seven children and she was happily married at 13! In 1770, Marie Antoinette, 14, married the future King Luis XVI of France, who was 15 at the time."

Others chimed in back and forth. Finally Lu offered, "Maybe we can all vote against any forcible rape and sexual relations with people of early age according to the laws and customs of their nation and culture."

No one seemed very pleased with this compromise. Failing to think of a better one, it passed 7-0. Rachel said she felt the ideal law for age and rape should be 16 years old. She offered this afterthought because the group had not acknowledged that young boys were sometimes the victims of rape. No one asked to reopen the issue since all agreed.

Tony jumped in with his typical controversial angle. "How do we handle the plural wives issue?" he said halfway grinning like he had taken fresh cookies out of the jar. "A man named Tom sired 29 children in Utah and the county attorney has brought bigamy charges against him. The state is also trying to recoup $75,000 worth of welfare payments. Tom is a former Mormon missionary. The Mormon Church officially abandoned polygamy in 1980 and while Tom had only a few wives, the male founders of the church had dozens.

"Shirley, who married Tom at age 15, said that she knew marrying Tom was against the law but it was not against her religious beliefs. Tom then married June and then the 14-year-old stepdaughter. The conflict is between the constitutional rights of religious freedom and the laws against polygamy which some believe are unconstitutional.

"This brings the issue into focus. Most everyone knows God permitted polygamy on a grand scale for a while and then according to the New Testament was against it. So, how can one expect religion to solve this problem? It seems to me to be in the category of sexual tolerance by society like homosexuality and it is okay.

"For the consenting adults' philosophy, I do not plan to have several wives but if I do, I do not regard this as anyone's business, the church or the state. Studies consistently show that animal parents are rarely monogamous. Among the primates, the animal order that includes humans, only two, the marmoset and the tamarin are truly monogamous. All the rest, monkeys, apes, and humans, often mate outside their partnership. Most primates make no pretense of faithfully bonding for life.

"Perhaps humans are supposed to be like the marmoset and tamarin but we are more like monkeys and apes in our sexual habits. If we are evolving, hopefully, it will be more like the marmoset but don't expect miracles. The ambition to control the sex lives of others is the culprit.

"This is a carry over from Queen Victoria who ruled one fifth of the Earth plus one quarter of its population. The Pilgrims, the Amish, the Shakers and a host of other religious people who sought to regulate the sex lives of other people are examples.

"I think it should be placed in the consenting adults' authority. What about other nations and cultures? Are we going to tell them how to live in the most intimate areas of their lives?"

David replied, "I don't think the spirit of God is to dictate personal behavior, but we are suggesting personal standards. I say monogamy should be the ideal standard, but those religious and cultures who permit polygamy should not be persecuted if they fail to meet this suggested standard. A law violating a religious belief when it is perhaps less harmful than divorce is not the solution.

A very spirited discussion or verbal fight ensued.

Bridgette spoke emotionally, "Our famous founding fathers, many presidents, highly ranked generals, popes, hellfire preachers, both male and female as well as many, many celebrities have created titillating sex scandals.

"Is there not a hypocritical disparity between what we posture and how we really feel and believe? Are all men and women monogamous by nature? Should not the pressure and regulation by society be more in consonance with how we really feel and behave? Religious people acknowledge God once allowed 1,000 wives and only one in the New Testament?

"The feeble explanation for such a turnaround is that man lived under the law and we live under grace. This is a huge rationalization no logical mind can accept. Now then, can Jews living under the law still have a thousand wives and Christian men only one?"

"If we accept homosexuality, we should accept polygamy,"

Tony contended.

Finally the vote was 5-2 in favor of the CODE setting the ideal standard as monogamy with tolerance for sincere religious beliefs to the contrary.

"I'm a Jew, but this issue flips my brain up and down again," Al said. "Adultery, abortion, homosexuality, marriage, birth control, divorce, sexual harassment, family values and other similar topics have been previously addressed. Yet, the issues are still plentiful and all of them can probably never be listed."

"Let's talk about something on the general topic of sexual attitudes," Rachel suggested. "Are we going to suggest guidelines for courtship? I think this area is so full of don'ts that the do's win out in most instances."

"Yes," agreed Rev. Hayes. "We need to show our young people that they can fall in love like grandma and grandpa did, wait for heavy sex until after marriage and have a 50th or 60th wedding anniversary."

Al injected, "What if they are 50 or 60 when they just get married? Do you know many 50- or 60-year-old virgins?"

"I was serious, Al. With the threat of disease and the guilt attached, I still think the ideal is just say 'no' until you hear the preacher pronounce you man and wife," John retorted.

Lu said, "I think education is part of the answer. This is a heavy issue that you have introduced, Rachel. The disparity between sexual urges and economic viability is a huge problem in today's world. No doubt it will widen in the third millennium.

"There was a time when it was common for girls to marry at early ages. They stayed on the farm or at home in the city while men brought in the bread. Today, many women earn more than their husbands do. With some couples, this is a cause for sexual problems especially if the control of sex factor increases.

"Old general conceptions that have guided sexual practices do not work well in our present society and I fear, as a woman, that the cutting down of men by extreme 'lib' forces has been detrimental. Such wild statements like we don't need men anymore, just their frozen sperm, does not help. Nor does the other extreme of the Biblical mandate for wives to obey your husbands.

"Sensible men and women who love each other make their sexual life an extension of that love. The climate is very anti-love, as we traditionally knew it. Most celebrities have not been good role models. How many wives have Mickey Rooney and Larry King had? How many husbands has Liz Taylor had?

"Kids are making kids and bragging about it in all of our large cities and even in small villages. I will stop pontificating and recommend we suggest abstinence as the standard first for the reasons of love and respect for the marriage vow and second for health considerations."

The after-discussion was one of the largest yet. The final vote for the CODE was 5-2 in favor of Lu's suggestion. The degree of petting was the consenting authority of the two individuals involved. Tony had suggested this addition which passed 6 to 1.

Al commented, "The pretense of sexual vitality and passionate interest in romance before marriage soon levels off after marriage. Something has gone haywire. We, as a society, have put too much emphasis on sex and romance outside of love, respect and real passion. The abiding emotional essential corollary of sex has in many instances been reduced to an animal-like gratification. Men tend to forget this importance but most women desperately need the sweetness and caring that accompanied courtship. Understanding each other's needs is the basis for a healthy and happy sex life."

Everyone applauded Al's observations.

Tony said he would like to make some comments about cheating in a marriage. "Flat out I do not think it is right; personal responsibility should be placed on the cheaters. What are the causes for unfaithfulness? Why are so many people guilty of cheating on their spouses?

"The pioneer work in this area was the Kinsey Report. Studies since then give an alarming percentage of people who say they have cheated on their mates. It brings into question if perfect monogamy is true to the nature of humans.

"It is not but the choice to give in to nature or not is within the power of people. In some cases, where no love exists and there are no feelings of caring for the spouse, cheating has led to a much better marriage.

"This whole issue is like skating on very thin ice. The only sensible conclusion is to say that the individual has the authority for his or her own sexual choices, but consequences go hand in hand with these choices, good or bad."

John brought up the subject of AIDS. "There is a huge epidemic in Africa and India. The disease is moving fast in many other countries. Gigantic research projects have greatly helped in the fight. However, at the present time, AIDS is winning. The most unfair situations are cases where the virus is contracted through blood transfusions, rape and no choices are made by the individuals. Even the sexually transmitted cases are pitiful, because they could have been prevented if the person practiced safe sex. Here is an important example of bad choices and consequences.

"With dozens of millions dead and dying from this disease, it is a foolish choice for anyone to have sex with anyone without extreme caution. In many cases, sexual passion translates into uninvited suicide. One's life is at stake.

"I reject the silly notion that this disease is a conspiracy for the white man to destroy the black and brown people. Consider the prominent white celebrities who have made unwise choices and are in their graves. This is a matter of personal responsibility and consequences in the overwhelming majority of cases. The major transmission of this torment is sexual activity."

"Well put," said David. "If your statement prevents one person from losing their life, your thinking on this matter is a very positive thing.

"The pill or the first oral contraceptives approved by the Food and Drug Administration in the middle part of the 20th century turned sexual behavior into a different phenomenon. There were many pharmaceutical advances that had greater medical impact, but no drug has every upended society like the pill. It was a blessing and a curse depending upon your point of view. But, sexual lives of the vast majority of people were affected."

Lu wanted to make some comments about stalking since it is usually a perverted sexual activity. "It is a practice used mostly by men stalking women. Increasingly women have been arrested for stalking men like the 39-year-old woman in Los Angeles stalking a rock star.

"Obviously, stalkers need treatment but the terror they inflict on their victims is real. Existing laws against this have to be enforced."

Everyone expressed agreement.

"It looks like we have elevated or degenerated our discussion into comments that everyone seems to agree upon," David smiled. "Are there any more? I'm afraid we have just begun."

"I would like to put in a good word for trial marriage," Tony offered. "I know everyone will not agree. We need to avoid the abrupt cataclysmic changes in life as much as possible. For example, military induction separates a young person in a sudden and almost violent fashion; it should be done in stages. Often legal separation on the way to divorce is helpful to all concerned. It serves as a kind of halfway house and is less legally complicated and psychologically costly.

"Why not then encourage trial marriage, if a couple chooses it? The point I am trying to make is huge changes should be gradualized to facilitate psychological adjustment."

Tony did not ask for a vote to include it in the CODE because he could sense he did not have enough votes.

Lu answered, "I do not necessarily approve or disapprove. We have the Geisha girls in Japan and similar situations in all parts of the world where women sell sex, and in many cases where men sell sex to women, but mostly to other men. There seems to be a basic human need for sex.

"Yet, this drive varies so much in people. Some people for whatever reason possess ten times the sex drive than others have even in the same general age bracket. We concern ourselves so much about what other people do with their sex lives when it should be none of our business.

"I do not think legalizing houses of prostitution is the ideal, but it might save lots of heartache and sickness. Besides, it could bring in tax money just like restaurants. Then we could at least permit medically inspected houses of prostitution without recommending their patronage.

"This would provide a living for a destitute or hypersexed female and provide relief for desperate males. It would reduce or eliminate the well-known prostitution areas of towns and cities and save multiplied millions of taxpayers money enforcing, judging and housing law violators in this sensitive area.

"Consensual sex and marketed sex should not be a matter of law breaking or crime. It is a matter of morality and desire to be a different, more secure self-esteemed person," Lu concluded.

The group finally voted 5-2 in favor of legally permitting prostitution. However, they did not encourage the individual to participate. The choice like drugs, alcohol, body piercing was left within the authority of the individual.

Rachel said, "Let's discuss sexual harassment. I believe it is wrong. It is a good thing laws prohibit it on the street, in the workplace or wherever it may genuinely occur. Flirtation, if excessive, may be harassment, but not if the other person flirts back. Sexual nuances that are reciprocated are not harassment. Often there is no real basis for sexual harassment. The offended should say so and tell the offender to bug off or that is offensive to me. Please do not do it again. If the party continues, it becomes harassment. (Of course, a physical attack like date rape is in a different category.)

"Extreme claims have often placed a barrier between men and women. The result has been a death of useful friendliness. Adults should act like adults. If one falsely accuses or fails to object to some words or deeds of another, and the issue is not raised, there is no harassment. Harassment occurs if the individual continues whatever over the objection of the offended, pure and simple. A false accuser has violated human decency and CODE 3-M of bearing false witness against thy neighbor. Common sense should prevail in all instances.

"We have great difficulty in human behavior to guard against going to the extreme. We identify a problem and go to the other extreme instead of seeking a sensible balance. People who once exchanged friendly hugs are wary to do this because of the correction of harassment. The pendulum has swung too far. This happens in so many things we try to correct.

"CODE 3-M should recommend fairness in this issue as in all other issues. One who supports fairness to all enjoys an inner consolation that cannot be taken away," Rachel said.

Bridgette asked to speak, "I do not want to have an open marriage and will not, but I do not object to people who chose this lifestyle any more than I do gays. We see today permissible mistresses, sugar daddies, one-night flings, and all sorts of deviations to the traditional marriage. I suggest CODE 3-M make a standard of the commitment of faithfulness in marriage but permit others to conduct their marriage as they decide what is in their best interests."

Rachel and John exploded into filibusters against this suggestion. They denounced switching sex partners, orgies and the like. After a couple of hours when the vote was held, it passed 5-2. It is the adult individual's business. It is also the individual's responsibility for negative impacts like psychological turmoil and possible disease.

Lu raised the issue of online sex chatrooms and believed that an excess of this activity leads to online sex addiction. This concerns many psychologists who are treating these addicts in large numbers.

"It may be harmless to look through a *Playboy* magazine, but to fixate on pornographic pictures and become addicted to sex is not healthy. CODE 3-M should warn of the dangers of sex addiction; however, as in drinking alcohol, it is within the individual authority to choose."

The vote was 7-0 in favor of Lu's suggestion.

"The fundamentals of addiction are very much the same in any enslavery," John observed. "No one has to become addicted to anything unless they make the kind of bad choices that cause addiction. Addiction is the result of bad choices of individuals. The human being does have personal responsibility in the beginning by accepting the environment that can aid addiction. When the medical profession declared drunkenness a disease, it did a dubious thing because it seemed to extricate responsibility from the individual."

"Love means many things to different people," Bridgette began. "*Webster's Dictionary* presents quite a bit of space trying to define its many meanings. In the sex behavior of humans, there can be a difference between the act of lovemaking and loving one with a strong affection and a feeling of devotion to that person. The act of lovemaking ideally should be accompanied by a passionate, deep affection for the individual buttressed by sincere devotion and warm, tender feelings.

"Romantical love is often an elusive and tricky emotion. Most parents love their children with a forever climate. There is so much security in unconditional love. Most children love their parents and siblings with similar attitudes and feelings. The boy-girl thing seems to me to often hinge on little stupid tests that are signs of surface commitment.

"I supposed the purest kind of romantic love is the deep commitment of loving someone whether it is always reciprocated or not. Yet it becomes pathological for a woman to love a man who beats up on her and abuses the children as well. Staying with someone in these circumstances because you were committed to love is crossing the line. Yet, we sing whatever happened to love forever.

"I could spend an hour more trying to explain romantic love and still see only the top of the iceberg. One thing I know from my observation of many, many marriages, successful and failed, you cannot assume that love does not require cultivation and attention in frequent intervals. Weeds of dissension will grow faster than in any garden if the tone of love is not kept in reasonably proper tune.

"The CODE should promote and support true romantic love and its wonderful physical act of enjoyable sex. Humans have suffered for many centuries from the confusion of what to do about sex. I say, suffer no more. Keep it on a high personal plane, fall in love, recognize that reciprocity of feeling and support and live happily ever afterward."

"Bridgette, you have got us on the right track. Can I have a copy of your first romantic novel?" Al remarked.

Everyone laughed, but they supported the thrust of her comments.

"I must add one thing I forgot to say," said Bridgette. "No government should dictate any personal sexual matters whether dealing with the young or the old, the religious groups who favor polygamy or whatever. This so-called Christian government allowed slaves to be sold, tearing families apart. Many of our great founding fathers owned slaves and cared less about the sex lives of these people in bondage but were Victorian for the whites. Let's learn from the past and not allow government to get into the bedroom."

"I keep itching to say something," Lu said. "Hugh Hefner, the Playboy tycoon, in some instances may have gone too far in breaking down puritanical traditions; however, there has been a very positive side to the Playboy phenomena. Men and women have had to face up to the reality that they are sexual creatures. This has liberated many people Freud would say. The sensible path is to learn the truth about ourselves and devise a plan of behavior to follow that is both psychologically and physically impeccable. We have a tall mountain to climb, but it is of the greatest importance."

"What about beach nudity?" Al mused out loud.

"It is disgraceful, that's what!" declared John.

"Would you approve or disapprove of the designated nude beaches in America and around the world?" David joined in. "Most beaches nowadays have almost nude people or near-nudity. I think we are giving guidelines for the individual and like so many of the other topics. I suggest that a person consider the issue and make his or her own decision.

"I would not personally feel comfortable at a nudist colony or a nudist beach. Frankly, I feel the story of the fig leaves after Adam sinned in the Garden of Eden as the tale goes is a confusing element in the distorted perception of sex in the human psyche. Sex has the most bent-out-of-shape attitudes of any human activity. Lewd, dirty, pornographic, indecent, disgusting, and obscene art is called fashionable by some so-called artist master. It is viewed as acceptable and praised. If it is chiseled from a marble block, everyone seems to think it is wonderful.

"The next step of live nude dancers or nudist colonies throws us into a moral rage. Why does canvas and marble in the nude rate such acceptance and acclaim when other examples of nudity bring condemnation, reproach and derision?

"If anyone can figure that out, I hope they will clue me in on it! Pornography is damaging to many people and negative actions can occur. The only sensible solution I see is to put these type of issues in the privacy and the authority of the adult individual."

The vote was 6-1 in favor of David's recommendation.

"Marriage forever will probably go the way of the dinosaurs," predicted Tony. "Why can't we recommend a hierarchy of legal relationship or at least condone something like a five-year contract marriage? What we have is not working and it is an unsavory source for divorce lawyers to line their pockets with money."

"And what about the children?" asked Rachel.

This tart exchange got the discussion ball really rolling. Every angle of marriage seemed to be challenged pro and con. Finally, when everyone was worn out by the subject sensing no agreement, except in the case of children, a vote was taken. The vote was 4-3 against Tony's suggestions of any substantive change in marriage.

Tony quipped, "Let's get on this boat 20 years from now and see if marriage as we knew it prevails."

"I don't think we have to emphasize the fact that a lot of sex perversion exists," John warned. "Worst of all, it seems to be on the increase. Rap stars have gone over the edge with four-letter words, sex and violence. In the US, three million people belong to kinky sex clubs and they are soliciting new members on the Internet as we sail.

"I regard homosexuality practices as a perversion. Worse than that are the modern practices of bestiality. God vehemently forbade people in the Old Testament to stop having sex with sheep. For centuries, this ungodly and base practice was taboo in so-called civilized nations. Now, the experts tell us that the AIDS virus developed in certain primates and was probably passed sexually to human beings. This is the result of a nasty sin!

"There are dozens of rank perversions from beating people with leather whips to cutting them to get a sexual charge from bleeding during sex. All are wrong for the individuals and I suggest CODE 3-M take a stand against all perversions!"

"John, if you will not include homosexuality as a perversion, I think you can get a unanimous vote and we have dealt with sexual identity in other discussions and recommendations," David said.

John reluctantly agreed remarking that people who have sexual identity problems are vulnerable to extreme perversions. The vote was 7-0 as amended by David.

David added, "To further add to the law and sexual confusion a couple was arrested in one state for cohabitation while in San Francisco, the 9th US Circuit Court of Appeals upheld a federal judge's ruling in favor of two Anchorage landlords who said their Christian beliefs forbade them to rent to unmarried people living together. Hopefully, CODE 3-M principles will help clear up some of the many, many examples of confusion.

"We basically suggest the government stay out of the sex lives of adults. One hundred eighty degrees opposed to such a federal ruling and appeal is the Alaska State law which has a ban on housing discrimination based on marital status. Both state and federal governments should resist the temptation to legislative morality. CODE 3-M emphasizes the choices and responsibilities of the individual as long as no definable injustice is waged on others not involved."

Rachel said, "I think that the ideal family circle has two parents if a child or children are present, but I have the greatest respect for the many single women and some single men who are forced to play both roles because of abandonment, death or perhaps prison sentences.

"We speak glibly that it takes a village to raise a child. This is true in many aspects, but that single parent does more than the whole village put together in influencing a child. There are so many wonderful success stories of children raised by a loving and dedicated single parent.

"I do not want or expect a vote, David. I just wanted to get this thought off my chest and into the record of our proceedings somewhere."

Al kept the discussion going. "We could never touch on every aspect of human sexual behavior on this cruise, although I think I can get unanimous agreement we are unforgivably ignorant in this super-important aspect of our lives. We need tons and tons of creditable research in this area, not religious taboos, cultural traditions and old myths handed down for centuries.

"Scientists are discovering some novel things like women are more libidinous in one phase of the menstrual cycle. There may be developed a profile or scale of sexuality hopefully assisting better matches. The differences between male and female arousal need clarification. The early erroneous perceptions that many people have of sex warps their views and enjoyment for a lifetime.

"Collaboration research is vital since the sexual issues are physiological, psychological, sociological, religious and often involve other disciplines. We don't know whether early sex education is positive; we don't even know how to teach it. The difference in individuals needs to be identified and respected.

"We have long practiced the notions: 1) Men are like animals and once aroused will have sex with the first female that is willing. 2) Women are like steam freight trains. It takes a long time to get them in the mood and what works one time will not arouse them another time. 3) They say no when they mean maybe and enjoy frustrating the male to force him to plead or beg. 4) Women go for money, celebrity and power.

"These notions are not necessarily valid, but we need to know the truth. Men are acquiring trophy wives. The song, 'What's Love Got to Do With It?' is timely. One thing is true, we need to cool it as far as the battle between the sexes is concerned. It is not only silly and childish but also detrimental. A certain level of competition in fun is fine, but the arrows being shot from extremists, both male and female, lead to a wider gap and affects natural and beautiful loving relationships.

"Research done by husbands and wives has been very productive. No one can deny or change the basic physiological and emotional differences. The differences are glorious and wonderful. When admired and respected, true relationships can flourish. When one sex tries to demean the true nature of the other, it is immature and foolish.

"Like many of our topics, sex has layers and layers of complex realities that need exploring to gain a sensible perspective. I am not suggesting that we attempt to match-up people by computer. The moon, soft music, looking into someone's eyes and whispering sweet little words like 'I love you so much I can't ever express' cannot be usurped by a machine, but we need to know more about our sexual nature before the full moon comes out. A passionate person who hooks up for life with an iceberg-type is in for lots of frustration and sorrow.

"Sex is one of the best attributes of mankind. We need to know more about it and how to use this gift to the best advantage of the people involved. Some exciting research is in progress but we need to make this a major effort."

The group all responded with positive enthusiasm so a vote was not needed for Al's proposal.

The group was buzzing with small talk when David rapped the round table with his knuckles. "This court is called to order." he said. "Seriously, I don't want to be the judge and I need your help in deciding how we should proceed from here. We have had a presentation from each member and from what each of you have expressed, you have a heck of a lot more arrows in your quiver that you hope to shoot. How can we get to all of these ideas and issues and then hone them into the best CODE we can devise?"

Rev. Hayes had the answer. "I say we all make a list of our issues and give copies to each member. We will at least have a ballpark idea of the substance and quantity of what is going to be before us. Then with the same issue appearing, we can go to the participant and decide who will present it for the CODE to see if the group thinks it is worthy."

"Sounds good to me," Al agreed. "But if only I make a long speech on just my issues we will need a slow boat to China and back, not a few months in the Caribbean."

Others agreed and the vote flashed a 7-0 result. An entire week's moratorium was called on formal forum sessions so the seven participants could work on their ideas and concept lists.

No rules concerning what to list were given. It would be strictly individual and open. Any thought as was demonstrated by the presentations would be heard and scrutinized carefully by the other six members. A majority vote would be necessary to forward it for CODE 3-M consideration. None of the items used in the presentations needed to be repeated.

Chapter VI
Item Lists of Participants

AL
GREEN'S
LIST

1.   Every person on Earth should be taught to read and write so they can learn of other views besides their own tyrants and express their feelings for others. Has not illiteracy been a significant cause of war? Writing is mankind's most far-reaching creation. We should use it as we are trying to do now for a noble purpose. If only we could have the written words unmistakably made by God Himself instead of people, perhaps more would believe. Many do not trust man's writings to be holy and sacred. Computers and TV access should encompass the world to educate.

2.   Man needs a belief in God to sustain him in the hour of crisis.

3.   While every decent person seeks not to discriminate, the fact remains that Albert Einstein was smarter than any of us. And, that's why *Time* Magazine selected him as the person of the 20th century. What? No female, no black, no Oriental? We must face the fact that no amount of artificial hype, legis-

lation, passionate movements and so on can ever offset the natural inequalities of unique individuals. There are brilliant people in every race and every religion and every nation. Einstein would have done poorly as a Jim Brown-type football player or a Tyrone Power actor.

4. Why does money have such an influence in religion and government? People with the most money have the most influence in the world's society in most instances. We must put a premium on other things and more important things.

5. William Shakespeare wrote, "Nothing in this life became him like leaving it." I say we can apply this to Hitler and a host of others. The idea of forgiveness has been thoroughly prostituted by bleeding heart people and has a devastating effort on crime and war mongrels. Some people and their acts should never be forgiven.

6. The attitude toward people with age needs to take an 180-degree turn. We can learn so much from Oriental people and traditional European and Jewish families. We should as a general rule, honor older people for many, many reasons. And, children around the world can be taught to realize that one of their main ambitions should be to grow old gracefully, and use their wisdom to help others. We discard our young and old too easily. One half of our life is fighting to prove we are not too young. The other half seems to be proving one is not too old. No one can be age 34 or whatever but one year!

Age depends so much on one's attitude, temperament and health. Some people act like they were born old so they never experience the joy of growing old. Others grow old in body but keep a youthful spirit until death. Let's address age in the CODE.

7. All Sunday blue laws should be abolished. They are enforced haphazardly and people cannot even agree which day of the week is really the Sabbath. People all over the world select certain days for their holy days. Fine, just do not endorse any government forcing anyone to observe a religion's pick for a holy day. Eventually, you could have more holy days than workdays considering all the holidays for people added to them. For example, Christmas should be not a governmental holiday. Let Christians take a vacation day. The same for other faiths.

8. Hatred is blind and so is love. Look at one. It is so difficult for us to find anything good about some people we dislike, let alone hate and conversely so difficult to find any fault in someone we love. We need some reality glasses to see

through. The pitiful thing is that we dislike or hate people we don't even know. The point for the CODE is to treat every individual as an individual not like a perceived member of that group.

9.   Patriotism is not a crime. Common sense tells us the whole world is not going to change overnight and tyrants must learn that when they touch a red-hot stove, there are consequences. We must have an adequate defense but if we keep becoming the strike first to prevent a domino reaction nation, we will come up miserably short to field a necessary military for legitimate defense. We would be hard put now to produce the type of men who clawed their way through a barrage of fire to liberate France as in WW II.

The 'Private Ryan' movie depicts how futile war is when the purposes are not so obvious. Our alliances must be obvious and reasons to send our youth to die for their country must ring out as clear as the captain's bell on a huge ship. The CODE has to recognize legitimate protection and defense for one's country but the CODE should warn against anyone serving any military outfit that is seeking to expand and conquer. Defense is the key and in some specific cases, legitimate alliances are proper at least until the nations in the third millennium can reduce or abolish war as a way to solve problems.

10.   Violence can never be productive. As I pointed out previously, it may be necessary to defend a nation against violence or in some instances use violence to defend yourself or family. Violence against murders may have to be used but it is still a horrible tool even if warranted. I know we cannot expect the eradication of violence in the next millennium, but we must devise ways of dealing with one another that is higher than the law of the jungle. We do not have to imitate the example of animal predators. So far, we have not only followed them, but we have outdone them in spades. They kill a few at a time when hungry. We have killed thousands at a time and murder for all sorts of psychological reasons not involving hunger.

Can we devise the technology that will steer us away from senseless violence? Are we devoting enough research and effort in this area? We seem hell-bent on improving our collection of gadgets. These seem to have a higher priority than the understanding and cure of violence.

Mahatma Gandhi advised us that strength does not come from physical capacity but rather from an indomitable will. We have discarded the power of the human will and the power of human choice by downrating the individual into some group for some questionable cause. The thrust now is to get followers and supporters for a cause even if it is a war or a so-called holy war.

11. No one head is big enough to hold all the knowledge necessary, but we need leadership of people with purpose for mankind. This starts at an early age. Meaningful awards and recognition have to be given to children for their attitude in helping others and their efforts of scholarship in seeking not only gadget trash but philosophical and psychological understanding.

12. Obviously, the third millennium will be marked as the Internet age. It has such potential for good and a huge potential for bad. It bypasses decency in so many instances, promotes hate groups, and spreads child pornography. CODE 3-M should have goals as well as guidelines and one goal should be to examine ways to keep the good and abolish the bad on the internet. Of course, perfection is next to impossible but can a series of decency viruses attack much of this trash? Perhaps.

13, Conformity versus independence. CODE 3-M should produce some clear basic suggestions of conformity but human imagination and progressive spirit cannot and should not be stifled. Place a premium on independent thinking.

14. Proper balance for adoration of heroes. The deaths of Princess Di, JFK, Jr., Mother Teresa and so many others show us we can have a global emotional village, which has a unifying quality. Mark McGuire and Sammy Sosa's respect and love for each other is so inspiring. We need more heroes. We have now thousands that the media ignores. Sometimes a national network ends its program of crime, trouble and misery with one so-called "nobody" hero. It is wonderful to meet these people and know the positive side of humans. The extent they go thrills everyone. We have too much negative reporting and some billionaire could sponsor a hero section and maybe even add to his fortune.

15. Blind allegiance in "My country right or wrong" is a stupid attitude when you believe wars like Viet Nam are wrong. It is one thing to support our soldiers, our men and women in uniform, right or wrong. It is altogether different to support politicians who for greed and personal reasons support useless wars.

More than 58,000 Americans died in the useless war of Viet Nam and no one really knows the number of Viet Cong and other nationalities who lost their lives. The misguided attitude

of my country right or wrong and my religion right or wrong
is the main cause of the endless strife in the Middle East. This
is an example of how slogans can brainwash little minds. Each
individual must use his or her own brain.

16. The decay of Western culture has begun and is fueled
by a selfish, attitude without ethics. Violate your promises if
you wish, satisfy yourself, throw all decency in the trash can,
go on a binge drunk, to hell with everybody. No wonder suicide
is the leading cause of death in ages 16-25. The cure is teaching the fundamental things that can help ensure happiness like
trying to be honest in most all situations, caring for your
health, caring for others and other things I hope that CODE 3-
M will provide. We need a revival of decency and positive living.

17. Star Wars, TV and so many movies, certain toys only
perpetuate the idea of war and the concept of war. Unfortunately, the Bible and most religions are also sucked in by this
idea. We do not have to have war always and we need first to
implant this idea and nourish it every opportunity we find.
"My Fair Lady" did not have a war or murders and did
extremely well on Broadway and on the screen.

18. We must show caution in the philosophy that it is
America's mission to spread the blessings of American liberty
around the world. Washington warned against entangling permanent alliances as a cause of war. America needs to set an
example of democracy and government and with the corruption and crime that exists, the homeless, the pitiful imbalance
of wealth and opportunity, I'm afraid we have not been the
shining light to the rest of the world we set out to be.

Nevertheless, I think no other nation tops us in an overall
evaluation. Still, it is presumptuous for us to take the attitude
we have arrived and therefore, the world should be like us.

19. Traditional atheism offers no quest for a higher power,
no guidelines. It is a bankrupt philosophy and does not suggest
how humans should think and live. It is not a practical
approach. It is as worthless as the extreme cults we all abhor.

20. Maya Angelou speaks of a private, inviolate secret
place where she goes to get in touch with herself. It is her garden where she goes alone — no family, no friends, only herself.
I believe we must learn to get in touch and stay in touch with
what we are all about. Purpose, the purpose of our lives is the
greatest importance. Fulfilling that perceived positive purpose can bring joy and happiness that is genuine.

21. I visualize a society where, for example, you can hear

the names Jonas Salk, Carl Sagan as often as Babe Ruth, Clark Gable and a million other similar comparisons. The bridges of knowledge between the educated and the illiterate or near-illiterate must be built starting one plank at a time.

22. Respect the worker, the person who makes things, grows things or fixes things. We must achieve a balance of respect for all people regardless of their method of making a living. We do not have to disparage education to do so. We should not want to live off of their skills without due recognition and compensation. College professors, physicians, nurses, pilots and a thousand other professions are needed and respected. Good, let's give proper respect for the people who make their cars and grow their food.

23. The old adage "Action speaks louder than words" must accompany any rational CODE. We know from self-experience that bushels of words do not compare to one good deed.

24. Mutilation of the human body by one's self, by ritual or custom rendered or inflicted by others is absolutely wrong. Where does one draw the line? Is ear piercing and circumcision to be compared with creating Eunuchs and the mutilation of Sabiny women of Eastern Uganda who have their genitalia cut on as a rite of passage? The United Nations calls this ritual mutilation. Fifteen of the 25 countries where it exists along with six European countries have outlawed it. The young women being mutilated know if they cried out during this painful experience it would embarrass their families.

No mutilation should exist unless necessary for health, life or death. Taking off a gangrene leg to save one's life is not mutilation. There is tremendous controversy over circumcision. Being Jewish I favor it, but I have to wonder. Sticking jewelry through the skin does seem to some people like a throwback to savage tribes.

I do not pretend to know the answers, but I would like to hear a group discussion in this area. Are some Catholic nuns still required to shave their heads and are some extreme Jewish groups still mutilating animals? I know there are all sorts of cults mutilating living things. The Romans used the crucifixion to nail people to crosses and Christians use a mutilated' Christ as their main belief to take away their sins much like the ancient religionists. Should not any form of mutilation be condemned?

25. Aggressive Christianity should be condemned in CODE 3-M. Christians are now making a very determined effort to convert Jews. On the other hand, rarely will one see

any Jewish effort to convert Christians to Judaism.

Christians can't even agree on the so-called trinity and they condemn any other beliefs than their own even within the ranks of Christianity. One God is the belief of many Christians, not a triune God with three aspects, Father, Son and Holy Ghost. The one God view is strongly trumpeted by the Messianic Bible Institute which claims the early Christian church saw God as one. Messianic believers say their belief is a deeper view of God, a different description of God. They say all Christians who are trinity believers go beyond the Bible and adopt old Greek and Egyptian philosophy and religious ideas.

David spoke of ancient Egyptian notions that Christians adopt without even realizing where the idea originated. The same charge can fairly be leveled at Jewish beliefs. The point is, however, Christians that are hell-bent on converting Jews should realize that Jesus was a Jew and a product of Jewish culture. If Jews do not accept him as the Messiah, they should be respected for this view, not condemned to an eternal hell because they do not accept Jesus as their personal savior.

26. Radical Orthodox Jews should know someone long ago said, "A ship in harbor is safe, but that is not what ships are built for." There is much danger in resting in our religious harbor and locking up our minds towards any new thinking! This goes for all religionists that cling so tenaciously to strict edits handed down by word, manuscripts and family members.

27. There can be a moral and ethical position outside of religion and I believe this is a great part of our mission — to establish those guidelines. Each person born on this planet should strive, according to their individual talent and opportunity, to promote human rights and recognize that divisive measures and gods that support things that divide have to be countermanded with measures that unite and bring harmony.

28. If we could see a video of all the war machines, the mass destructive weapons and could accurately measure the hate and greed behind these forces all around the world, we would get a sense of urgency to accelerate our feeble efforts at peace-making. The possibility of a war that is more devastating than anything the world has ever experienced is still a reality. It will probably begin as universal terrorists and hate groups form an alliance against all nations striving for peace and then escalate into a war to top all wars.

Therefore, we must go not only to the so-called grassroots but make a sustained effort to persuade each individual born on the planet that the road to happiness is a belief in one's self and respect for each brother who shares this terrestrial ball. We can, we should, and we must live as a loving and caring family.

29. Women have put the spirit of sport in most cases back in the world of sports. They play hard to win and when the contest is over, they as a rule do not deride the other ladies. They exhibit a warmth and respect for them. In much fewer examples, men show the true spirit of sports. Hating the opponent and taking any unfair advantage to win at all costs is now the sporting milieu. This non-sporting attitude can be clearly seen in world trade situations on all sides. We need to live and let live, to compete hard but fairly with the nations of the world.

30. More celebrities need to use their prominence for the good of others. Some do. For example, Paul Newman food products profits go to charitable causes. Paul gets a kick out of helping others with the $90 million going to them. Bill and Melinda Gates recently added $45 million to Harvard Medical School to fight drug-resistant strains of tuberculosis. He has donated far more to other needs.

Ted Turner gave a billion dollars. Hundreds of other celebrities have used their fame in a heart-warming manner. Most are selfish and self-centered only concerned with their image and career and would do next to nothing without the allowed deduction on their taxes.

31. We must spend more on medical research, period. We can afford it and we cannot afford to neglect it. Most people do not have a clue concerning the tasks of the researcher, but they are talented in complaining about the high costs of medicines and surgeries. A thousand dead-ends sometimes plague the scientist who is striving for new truth before one road keeps going.

Nations that support a shotgun approach to research get the best results. The universities, the pharmaceutical companies, the research institutes, the government grants, the bulldog type individual inventors and discoverers all are important. It is happening around the world. New ways to raise and harvest food and a large book of other wonders are in the making. Hopefully, we can devise a pill or a portion that will sterilize those who choose it and another antidote to turn the birth process back on. Hopefully, we can get water fit to drink to the millions who do not have suitable drinking water. The Nobel prizes have proven to be more of a blessing I am sad to say than most religions. We are on the way to new truths.

CODE 3-M should applaud and recommend expansion and

acceleration. This is a ready-made cause for those celebrities and the super rich. Just look at what Jerry Lewis has done for muscular dystrophy and what others have done for AIDS research. Of course, this research is disproportional, but every dollar was helpful.

The forgotten and lean areas hopefully can claim their knights in shining armor to lead their cause as others have done. We should never criticize these efforts but applaud these heroes and try to inspire more to follow their trail.

32. The death of a loved one or close friend does not take away years that were shared. They can live in other hearts and minds of people who cared. Through the power of memory we can raise those shared times to a plateau of preciousness that brings repeated happiness as long as we live. Therefore, do not take a death to bring undue attention to yourself but begin to share with others what a human can really mean to another human. I do not have a video of all the wonderful moments but I do have a diary of wonderful times both written and etched indelibly in my mind. Live so your family and friends can enjoy great memories when your frail tent is folded and time for you is no more.

33. "The right of unions to withdraw labor is matched by an equal right of the employer to withdraw wages," a member of the South African parliament named Fraser-Moleketi declared. The issue of unionism needs to be addressed. Unions have served a great and noble purpose in many instances around the world. In some cases, however, union leaders have crossed the line of fairness and their efforts have punished the employers they claim to represent. What is the answer? Union leaders use a good principle to fatten their own wallets while they live like the multi-millionaires they are supposed to be opposing. Corruption is their middle name in too many documented cases. Yet, management seems to be unable to satiate their greed for more profit and more work from their employees to add to their enormous wealth. A fair and just balance is needed and more employee ownership is part of the answer.

34. I, for one, believe that there is such an entity as the human soul. It is difficult to define or illustrate. Until I can describe it better, I will accept the definition of Josephus who proclaimed that all of us have mortal bodies, composed of perishable matter, but the soul lives forever; it is a portion of the deity housed in our bodies. This concept is one that cannot be proven.

However, I want to believe that something about me is

divine and will live forever. I think every human being has that yearning, but many cannot generate the faith to believe it. Part of the problem is the massive confusion of the different religions. How can we expect the non-believer of the world in the soul concept to ever believe as long as there is so much confusion among the ranks of the believers?

35. In our road map, we need to emphasize those acts of unselfishness and help to others really count. Jumping in front of someone to take the bullet should just about guarantee heaven. We place so little credit to organ donation, blood donation, high percent of income donation to the poor, diligent unselfish research participation by both the researcher and the subject, all acts that impose a real sacrifice and benefit others, big and small. This is so vitally important and it is living at its best. We spend too much time adoring Jehovah or whomever and depending on a higher power at the neglect of using the rod in our hand as God told Moses and Aaron to do.

I do believe in God, but that is not enough. I must earn my way to heaven by my concern for my fellowman. Princess Di and JFK, Jr., are shining examples of young people who were determined to contribute. They could have easily ignored others because of their fame and wealth. Yet, God or something let them die so young. This has always concerned me and others. We cry out, "Why God? Why?" We don't get an answer, so we make up one.

Yet, the good deeds philosophy makes so much sense to me because even if tragedy comes and it seems there is no one and nothing to care for you, you will have received great joy and satisfaction intrinsically. You know your own heart. You know what your motives are. You know if you really care. And if you know it, the reward is there and no one can take it from you.

36. CODE 3-M must take a zero tolerance position on terrorism. Instead of a brave new world, we have reached the moment of a grave new world. The atom bomb is well known around the world, but the nerve agents, germ agents, chemical poisons and the like are just as threatening though the tactics may differ. The advanced technology of weapons in the hands of terrorists on any side can and will wreak untold havoc in cities and facilities everywhere. We have already seen a taste of this destruction and many lives have already been snuffed out.

Can't we at least call for and enforce a worldwide moratorium on terrorism? I hope to God that people will end these religious and ethnic hatreds. They are twin monstrous concerns. Everyone knows this, yet we continue this hatred. Let's begin in this small group to abolish every vestige of hate and learn to love one another. This may be more important than any formal religion, any ethnic groups and any individual nation! People must learn to care for themselves and others.

37. We should not minimize the urgency of CODE 3-M because of many reasons. A main one is the tremendous acceleration in weapons technology like smart bombs, smart bullets and weapons I have mentioned before. Someone somewhere somehow must feel this urgency and attempt to translate it into action to effect a world alert for the next millennium. Not to be sacrilegious for I am a religious person, but wouldn't it be wonderful if God came on worldwide TV and told us the plain truth about everything so mankind would not continue struggling to travel down this dark road of night confronting a thousand turnoffs which might lead to a great goal or to our destruction. Please God, you created us, so give us a break!

38. When one reviews the most famous battles in the devastating wars waged by man on the planet, it is difficult to imagine a more fascinating and meaningful conflict than the battle of Midway. Serious historians mark this battle as the turning point in our war against Japan. It is the history of ordinary people doing extraordinary things fighting for a cause in which they deeply believed. But, let us consider not only the allied military people but also the Japanese men on those vessels that were sunk along with the American ships. They were victims of a strange culture and religion that propounded the idea of giving their lives for their emperor.

Though the cause was wrong, in my opinion, I have to admire their hard work and training and devotion to duty. Thank God thousands upon thousands of our heroic veterans have gone to Germany and Japan, put their arms around each other and looked into each other's eyes with an understanding that only they can share. So, is not this the proof that ordinary people can love one another and not go to war to kill one another? There is no question about it. If we can stop aggression and war-mongering everywhere, the ordinary people, if you please, will do just fine!

39. We should challenge the media to do its part for the prevention of global conflict. The media monguls from all around the world, if allowed, should meet on an island somewhere and devise a CODE 3-M, that is a media code that steers away from religion, politics, and extreme nationalism. There are brilliant people in this wealthy and important group and

their influence cannot be and should not be underestimated.

40.   CODE 3-M should be a guideline that emphasizes happiness for the individual and there are billions of examples where this is achieved despite relatively poor economic conditions. The proven fact of course is that money does not bring happiness. We must all strive to level the economic playing field around the world, but wealth is not an essential ingredient for happiness. Neither is religion a requirement for happiness. Too many people are relatively happy without it. In fact, the most miserable unhappy people in the world are the religious fanatics. There's an old Scottish proverb that says, "Be happy while you're living for you're a long time dead."

41.   Everyone needs to talk in confidence to someone sometimes. Should it be the Rabbi, the priest, the psychologist, the psychiatrist, the physician, the pastor, the teacher, the kinperson, the neighbor, or fellow employee. There is a simple answer. Confide in someone you know you can trust someone who has earned your trust and someone you respect for their intelligence and honesty. A friend or anyone you can trust is worth great riches. By the same token, be a person one can trust.

42.   Educational systems need an overhaul. Most educators realize that we are stuck in a third rate system but don't know how to get out of it. The key is to form an alliance with the students and abandon the old, "I'm going to flunk you if you don't do so and so" attitude. The hostility between teacher and student in some cases is outrageous. The superior teacher (and there are many) know the "Let me see how I can trick them on this test" is no longer acceptable and already hundreds of fine advanced methods and ideas are proving successful.

The problem is moving the big mediocre group or inspiring them to follow suit. Video tapes can be made of every teacher to evaluate how they perform in the classroom and salaries should be based on performance. "A" teachers deserve a quantum leap in salary pay. "B" teachers deserve a huge increase. Some teachers should try McDonald's.

Any change ignites a loud cry from the union type organizations that protect the status quo and could care less about excellence. Their goal is to get better salaries for all and equal pay for all who show up.

The way out involves the business community, scientists, blue-ribbon citizens who know that innovation is not a sin, and a learning unit system that may be from a class, privately sponsored or a long trip to China for a first-hand experience.

Mexico, Canada, and Cuba would be cheaper. A week at the Smithsonian would be a fine educational trip for anyone and similar endeavors. The early years require more regimentation and many parents would form a partnership with teachers if given the opportunity. Our youth are growing up without essential basics. Computers, videos should be commonplace to teach subjects.

The overhaul is coming, but it lacks direction and cohesion. First, we must agree it is broken then fix it. Other nations are leaving us in the dust in some areas.

43. Emotions. People get very emotional listening to music, watching sports, nature's scenery, religion and many other activities. We are emotional beings. However, just because someone has a big tent revival or a huge stadium filled with followers or a million-man march shouting out tired rhetoric does not make it truth and reality. Usually the crowd that yells the loudest has the most insecurity about what they claim to believe. I believe 3 plus 3 gives you six. I don't have to chant it before multitudes with loud-blaring speakers to bolster my true beliefs.

44. I believe in addition to bullets, bombs, germs, genes and other common weapons that man will master the control and use of the weather as a controlling weapon of war. If we ever reach such a level of calibrated control of drought and flooding, it could rival any weapons we have ever seen. What an awesome potential! It may be possible to dry up for instance, the entire continent of Africa or flood the continent of South America to cause havoc unimagined. This is another reason why animosities and extreme nationalism must be addressed.

45. We know that the bright future in medicine will come from biological, chemical, pharmacological and physiological studies. So might the bright future of industry. Microbiology in Japan has reached new heights. Much of their food and food industry is based on processes in which bacteria are used. Computers are still in the T-model Ford stage. Ultimately they may model their electronic components even more like the human brain and open new vistas of development that now dwarf our minds. Florida State University has just installed the most powerful computer of any university in the world.

46. Information is being amassed exponentially. One computer can store more facts and deliver them much faster than anyone dreamed when Univac was built in 1940. It is already phenomenal. The individual can be overwhelmed

without some valid screening process that suggests what is priority and what is superfluous.

Furthermore, the blurry path to what he needs to learn beyond the basic learning levels should be brought into sharper focus. The requirements of learning to be an effective physician or an effective automobile mechanic are changing on a rapid basis and the changes are already legion in the span of one year. Sincere, diligent, dedicated people can go awry in obtaining useless information, thus a challenge to rearrange our educational system is urgent to meet future demands.

47. Self-esteem is one of the most precious qualities anyone can develop. If you can give unconditional love like most of our mothers gave to us, this is the foundation of developing self-esteem. Knowing that you are loved regardless is priceless and loving others regardless is a glorious feeling.

48. Human society is flying out of control not just in America but everywhere. We have a sick social structure. All students need to be grounded in certain common skills needed for human communication and social integration. Things seem to be coming apart more than they are coming together but as an optimist, I think once we can agree on fundamental important ways for a human to act, peer pressure will correct most of the maladies.

49. I am puzzled and ashamed that religious refugees receive most of their persecution from other religions. Witness the pilgrims, the Mormons, the Jews and hundreds of other groups that were severely persecuted. The Jews' religious rulers did persecute the Christ and were involved in His crucifixion and share responsibility with the Romans. History tells that synagogues have been burned by anti-semitist Christians in the south. All of this is wrong wherever the chips fall.

50. Intelligence is essential in the laws of the universe and this implies a divine force of God.

51. In 1829, Charles Darwin concluded species evolve and change is drawn by variations in the offspring. I personally have no problem with weaving in my religion some evolutionary concepts like the big bang theory and I know evolutionists who will accept God as the overseeing force of evolution so why can't we drop this "either or attitude" on how we got here. We are here. We need to make the best of it not by attacking each other on things neither side can actually prove but put evolution and similar knotty unsolved issues in a category to continue enquiry. What difference does it make as far as how a person should live and treat his neighbor?

52. So many of our sexual hang-ups come from various religious upbringings. They are deeply ingrained causing so many people to believe sex is dirty. Cutting off parts of the body as in circumcision is a religious action of my own people, but I was dumfounded for an answer when a Jewish physician recently asked me how the courts would handle a mutilation suit by a Jew's son against his parents?

I did not and do not know the answer. With few, if any, health pluses and minuses, it boils down to a religious decision. Apparel, facial makeup especially lipstick, veils and the like have long been topics of religion. It is a bad mixture to mix up sex realities and religious teaching.

53. James Carvell, the aggressive liberal, and archconservative Mary Madeline love each other, live together and enjoy their family. What a perfect example of how people with honest views that are 180 degrees apart can get along and make a future together. Why can't the rest of the world?

54. Extreme feminists have tried to reduce the obvious importance of men in society. A sense of shame is felt by a few men for just being male. There are serious consequences to this radical push. Religions and men no doubt pushed the pendulum too far against women but the war on boys and men generated by the extremists is equally as unjust and dangerous. Common sense orders that these differences are respected and that equal treatment should be given to both sexes. The sex war is childish and highly intelligent people who discern its destructive elements call for a permanent armistice.

55. Our justice system is better than most but it is in need of major reform. There are many unjust characteristics such as long waits before trial, racial bias (by whites and blacks) and the need to eliminate the jury charade. There must be a better way than to have highly educated, skillful lawyers swaying less capable citizens back and forth while members of the same tribe sit as so-called impartial adjudicators and consistently award huge unreasonable fees to the barristers who make deals and meet in secret chambers to handle highly crucial matters. The US system may be the best, but God help the rest.

Is it fair that the side who can hire the best lawyers win? Look at the DNA freedom releases and look at O.J. Simpson playing golf. Judges should be blue-ribbon type citizens, not attorneys. A three or five judge system should replace juries and shift from venue to venue. Something must change or the judicial chaos we are in will swallow us in trivial lawsuits and estate robbery.

The Supreme Court is not a Supreme Court in the US. It is merely the politically correct position of a majority of nine lawyers at the time. The pure concept of the Supreme Court was prostituted and lost the first time it reversed a previous Supreme Court without a constitutional change or legislative act that met constitutional standards.

Nine people have, in several instances, become legislators and constitutional revisionists. The Supreme Court was not established for this nonsense approach that five people could change the previous considered rulings with no intervening change of law or the Constitution. We really don't have a constitutional government if this practice continues. I am for social justice and many other advances, but we tread on thin ice when we let the nation's future rest on five people playing back and forth with constitutional words and precepts.

The question, "What type of justices will presidential elections produce?" proves the thesis that the Supreme Court is a forgotten dream. Our Constitution was properly ratified. The Supreme Court was set up to give a final ruling on what it meant. No change should be effected until the Constitution is changed and properly ratified. There are many other things in our system that need complete reform.

56. I would challenge each individual everywhere to examine CODE 3-M. It might be foolish for anyone to agree with each guideline. I will not. Perhaps a check mark and x-mark concerning each item would prove useful. Then briefly list why you disagree with particular guidelines. You may be right and CODE 3-M may be wrong.

57. The mass hysteria and mob hypnotism practiced by TV evangelists is an affront to the mainstream religions and one's intelligence, to say nothing of the amassing of funds for the leaders. Some go to jail. Some are disgraced. None do a systematic honest account of the true impact of these hyped-up crusades on people they claim are healed.

58. A government that did not outlaw slavery until the 1860's and did not allow women to vote until 1920 is one that receives too much praise and worship. We can and did do better. We must not regard the US government as sacred. It is still the best thing going but not the best thing that can be achieved.

59. Slavery for blacks versus the Holocaust inflicted on Jews is a useless and unwarranted comparison. Blacks have felt genocide also and Jews have experienced slavery. It is a

dumb argument. Recognize that many peoples have gone through hell on earth and seek to prevent it from ever happening again to anyone!

60. Why don't multiracial people declare themselves to be multiracial and be proud of it? If the Harold Fords of Tennessee made such a declaration, it would be very positive. I have friends who married into gentile Christian families and they teach children to love and respect both sets of grandparents. One can be proud of who one really is. I regret my grandfather changed his name from Rosenburg to Green even though he felt it necessary to get food for his family.

61. When the Internet fully embraces China and people everywhere, freedom will take wings. Increase trade agreements with everyone will include Cuba. The Cold War was won because East Germans saw the quality of life in their democratic cousins in West Germany. Russia, thanks to Gorbachev, and others grew tired of demonizing the west and spending themselves poor to prepare for the Third World War. Inter-trade and inter-travel getting to know people is the key.

62. Thank goodness for the Olympics. It brings the young people of the world together on the sports field instead of the battlefield. President Carter was one of our greatest leaders for peace and people still trust his honesty and integrity but he made a mistake when he kept American athletes out of the Russian Olympics.

63. Muslims possess different views like Jews, Christians and others do. A Muslim school in Memphis welcomes kids of all faiths proclaiming that diversity produces well rounded students while Pakistan, Afghanistan move in the opposite direction. The percent of followers of other religions in Israel is pathetic. All of us must live and let live in respect to our religion.

64. Education and health care for all people on earth is essential. However, food and peace are even higher priorities. Much good is being done in these four areas but so much remains. We need more Peace Corps and more Salvation Army people! I am very proud of the many Jewish charitable services that serve Jews and others in desperate need.

65. I am for religion. I am for morality. I am for ethics and justice. I expect to endorse most of CODE 3-M. However, the individual needs to develop one's own philosophy of life and remember the admonition "to thine ownself be true."

66. If Europe with all of its warring sordid history can see the wisdom of a United Europe in economic policy, why can't

the whole world come together in cooperation so everyone can have the good life? It will happen some day. I just hope I live to see it.

67. Elderly abuse, child abuse, any kind of abuse should be a high priority for police, social workers and judges should be careful to mete out appropriate punishment to convicted offenders and not look the other way as is done in so many cases.

68. A person needs a sense of fairness and willingness to forgive most things. Some things are unforgivable. When that line is crossed, the bleeding hearts should cease. Preying on others and taking their lives is unforgivable regardless of what a religion may teach. It is difficult for non-Christians to understand the unpardonable sin concept in the Christian religion. If you sin against the Holy Ghost, it cannot be forgiven. However, if Hitler had sincerely asked for forgiveness, he could have been forgiven. Could it be that the unpardonable sin is simply a means of more control?

And do we forgive Noah for incest and God for ordering the murder of babies? This kind of stuff seems to create non-believers. This is why I am a reformed Jew. It gives me more latitude to accept what makes sense to me and what doesn't. As an individual, you do not ever have to forgive an animal posing as a man who rapes your daughter and cuts her body into pieces. There is a time and place to forgive most things but not everything. A parent raping his own little child, incest, is unforgivable. Thinking that they can get away with atrocity breeds it.

And, if you would not forgive the guy who raped and murdered your daughter, is it fair to forgive a guy who rapes and murders the daughter of your neighbor? Of course not. Loving others requires the Golden Rule and same fairness standard.

69. We need to elevate and give more honor to people in our society who make real contributions to humanity. Breakthroughs in knowledge, inventions, pharmaceutical advances, new surgical techniques and the like.

If a youth of 16 can name 125 movie stars and sports heroes, it would be especially rewarding if he could name 25 important people in the categories that count even more. We should consider building statues in prominent places to the real heroes of mankind. Some good lists already exist.

70. In 1939, 56% of Americans were anti-Jewish. It has improved but like black and Oriental hatred, the problem is a long way from a heart-felt solution. This is why I basically was

so desperate to join this project and I will say that I have not seen one drop of prejudice and hate since this cruise has begun and that includes the group and the crew. I'm beginning to believe that some day the world will be free of this venom.

71. The Y chromosome does not change and now there is genetic proof that some Africans descended from Jews or vice versa. If we had an infallible family tree of the world, the intermingling would astound us. Isn't this a reason for togetherness and peace?

72. Laziness is a sin. Hard work to help oneself is righteous. Expecting others to take care of you when you are able to do so is wrong, wrong, wrong.

73. Our challenge was well put by one of the most brilliant humans that ever lived, Albert Einstein. He said in 1916, science without religion is lame; religion without science is blind. How does one blend in the truths of this beautiful statement? Extreme religionists sometimes refute the obvious scientific facts and extreme scientists scoff at the possibility of a God.

The answer may be simple. Don't take an extreme view either way. Be open to the truth whenever and wherever it is found. What is truth is determined by study and testing and diligent seeking and once convinced having the courage to embrace it.

74. Without personally offending anyone, I would like to pose a question. If Jesus Christ was the son of God and the Messiah and his primary mission was to bring peace and salvation to the world, why have we had two bloody millenniums of war, destruction and heartbreaking devastation since he came? Why have his followers been involved in so much of this incredible, cataclysmic slaughter?

Did he make a difference or make things worse even though he tried to set a good example himself of peace? Would the world have been better off if he had not been lifted up as the Prince of Peace? Did not the poor desperate people who rallied around him seek a better condition of life, more freedom and more means? Did not many other Messiahs come on the scene and vanish also? Is it not plausible for Jews to wonder and believe that the true Messiah is yet to come?

The Thirty Years' War, 1618-1648, was caused by Protestant-Catholic hatreds and decimated central Europe. Both sides believed in a Jewish Christ. If the true Messiah comes and real peace is spread through the world, will Jesus prove to be just another false Messiah or a great teacher or a prophet? We Jews still await the promise of the Messiah and feel the promise of peace in two horrible millenniums was not fulfilled.

75. We must address the strategic petroleum problem as a cause of past wars and perhaps future wars. Oil has played a very important role in wars. One wonders where the poor Middle Eastern countries would be without the combustion engine, oil furnaces, and the need for electricity and one hesitates to contemplate the future of say a Kuwait if and when oil is no longer in much demand.

Alternative sources of power are already feasible. The leverage oil has given certain areas of the world is a fascinating proposition and unmistakably had pitted nation against nation and peoples against people. In the US, oil in Texas, Alaska, Oklahoma and some other places does not create a War Between the States. Why can't the same principle be followed in a cooperation or unification of all the countries in the world?

In August 1998, British Petroleum and Amoco merged as one proving it can be done. There is so much to be shared if people would not be national extremists and religion extremists.

In 1977, the US created the strategic petroleum reserve, which permitted the storage of 580 million barrels of oil. It was very helpful in 1990 when Iraq invaded Kuwait and President George Bush rallied the allies to save Kuwait from Saddam Hussein. In 1985, the reserve held enough oil to provide a normal level of petroleum to the US for 115 days without import oil.

In just a few years, due to increased energy consumption, and selling Alaskan oil to others, it sank to 78 days and now the country is at risk if Saudi Arabia and OPEC shut down production due to war or a natural catastrophe. Our heavy reliance on foreign oil may be the principle cause of the next war.

A possible new energy source that could compete with and someday surpass oil may be feasible in extracting methane from beneath the sea floor. It may take a half century or more to make the process feasible for public consumption. Methane exists in huge quantities beneath the sea floor. It is normally a gas but there it is locked in an ice-like state. Technology does not exist now to convert it from a frozen state to a gaseous state and pipe it in large quantities to the strategic metropolitan areas of the world but it may exist some day.

Methane is environmentally friendly and the almost unlim-

ited source would solve many problems without import oil. Other solar and wind alternatives are promising. Opponents of a cooperating world order like Europe or the US should seriously consider the consequences.

76. The Japanese belief that the Emperor descended from the gods is like the other myths in all religions. One hardly knows which myths to discard and which to believe, therefore in the final analysis, the individual must decide.

77. No pressure from society or any religion should be made on a married couple or anyone to have children. Many misfits and dope-ridden people give birth who are not capable of raising children. Economic payoffs for having children are absolutely wrong. Hopefully a pill will be developed that will make men and women permanently sterile. A large financial bonus could be given to anyone, regardless of race nationality or creed, who would be sterilized. It would have to be on a very strict voluntary basis, no coercion or force. This would be a positive step in solving many social problems in the world today, save tons of money in the long run, and present indescribable misery. The UN, for example, could administer the fund compiled from many nations like they do for their support. China has made a bold effort in this area.

Something drastic has got to happen or we just go on with our cold and callused conscience like we do today while multiplied thousands die in poverty and suffering each and every day. Each year the world grows in population by 86 million! Getting the world together to stop suffering is a whale of a challenge and many people are trying and doing their part the best they know how but we need some bold leadership and innovative ideas to show we do care and will tackle this overwhelming problem. It is wrong to keep bringing children into the world to suffer and die.

78. We are spending over $500 million on research concerning the aging process using children who age abnormally fast. This is a worthy and exciting effort. Could this be a chance for some measure of immortality in the future? Will we live past 200 during the year 3000 A.D.? There is little limit what science can learn and accomplish when we concentrate on certain fields. This is an example of an area we can focus on instead of new weapons to wipe each other out. It is so clear and most if not 99% of the world see it so let's be done with 1% plunging us into war. FDR proclaimed, "I hate war!"

79. Anything goes versus religious fanatics and Victorian moralists. The sensible balance lies somewhere in between.

80. Religious people, and I am one, know that there are at least three kinds of followers of a religion. These are the true believer; the believer who accepts some but not all of the faith; and the fake believer-type who do not believe but sees needs to be classified as a believer for family, friends, commerce, politics or because it is fashionable.

81. To me, one world is inevitable although it may take centuries. Alaska and Hawaii becoming states, Canada's relationship to England, and the bond between Israel and the US show that it is possible not to mention the unity in Europe and the growing acceptance of the value of Russia and China. There is lots of hope!

82. I honestly endorse the Old Testament teaching, an eye for an eye and a tooth for a tooth to stop the crime wave in the whole world. It works.

LU
CHANG'S
LIST

1.   Food for everyone is a requisite for peace. We must consider bringing fewer babies into the world until we can feed the ones we have. Scientific gains in agriculture are impressive, but we have to work on both ends of the problem — more food production and better distribution and less births.

In some instances, extremists in religion hamper food efforts. The United Nations World Food Program started bakeries in Afghanistan to make bread for the needy sold at a subsidized price. Women baked the bread to help. They were widows and they helped other widows. The hard-line Taliban claimed Islam forbids women from working and shut down the bakeries that were helping the poorest of the poor.

A UN spokesman said that this action would result in increased poverty and possibly loss of life and health for women and children. Religions help food efforts as a rule so this is a strange turn of events. Extremists in religion are the enemy of peace.

2.   In the 2000 year census, an individual was able to mark off more than one race. Tiger Woods could mark Asian, black, white, and native American. I dream of the day when all can just be human and not have the burden of any race label.

3.   We have in the last few decades developed an appreciation for important things of the past and we must accelerate this positive, interesting, and valuable activity. The historical society, though labeled by some as the "hysterical" society, has a solid record of accomplishment. Perhaps they appear radical to some but their determined efforts on the whole are very positive.

Italy could have used them. Only recently did Italy have

even a list of its priceless art treasures and a statement of their condition. What if some group had been determined to preserve the seven ancient wonders of the world? At least Egypt is preserving the only one of the seven in existence, the pyramids of Egypt.

4. "I know God answered my prayer" is a very disturbing statement to me. No one knows that God exists. How about awful situations when God does not answer prayer? Prayer is an emotional beckoning of deity in any religion, usually ignored. When fate coincides with the supplication, some kind of god gets credit. Who gets credit when 6 million pray their hearts out and no one comes to their rescue — neither God nor man?

5. Religion demands so much respect to be fulfilling if fulfillment is ever achieved. Self-respect and respect for most other people is so easy and brings solid fulfillment without chants, rituals and paying out money to foster the religious system.

6. There is no telling how wonderful life could be if we spent the funds we spend on war and religion to further education, science and medicine.

7. The Unification Church, followers of Rev. Moon from South Korea, have large economic interests in America and many other countries. They are building a huge complex in Brazil. This cult is very aggressive and resorts to a type of mind control. Many youth forsake their families for this cult who submit to intense brainwashing. Yet, isn't this true to a certain extent of all religions?

Jews, Catholics and Protestants were enraged when the New York Supreme Court recognized the Moon church as a serious religion. They claim about 2-3 million followers. Who knows? When the Rev. Moon passes on, he could easily be a Jesus-type or Mohammed-type religious hero, prophet or whatever similar title his followers give him and all kinds of miracles and great deeds like walking on water can be claimed.

Fear of a terrible eternity easily controls people and a supposed way of escape from the fires of hell or whatever is immediately appealing. People give their very lives for religious beliefs.

All religions have a long list of martyrs. The Shinto believing Japanese pilots crashed their Zero airplanes carrying one bomb into allied ships, thinking they would be highly rewarded by committing suicide. This is one of the most moving and pitiful stories in history. Lots of precious lives were lost.

On a much smaller scale, the Jim Jones followers drank poison Kool-Aid to show trust in their evil religious leader. The list is almost infinite.

It behooves one to show caution while condemning the "moonies" as one reflects on the death and pillage behind the Christian crusades against the Muslims. I choose freedom from all of this activity.

8.   Must humans always nurture ethnic hatreds? No! The Irish stoned the Welsh workers as they got off trains in New York. The Italians hated both groups. Fistfights were the norm. The old "birds of a feather flock together" philosophy was rampant before the black-white struggles.

My ancestors were mocked and treated like dirt. We have progressed a little — mighty little. America has some sordid moments in its history.

A leading coal mine owner brought the workers all together and declared, this is not Irish coal, Welsh coal, Polish coal, or Italian coal. It is my coal and you better learn to dig it out together for our common good. There will be no more fistfights or bickering on the job. I do not expect you to socialize off the job but on the job you will set aside all hatreds and work in the spirit of respect and brotherhood. It was at least a start.

It took years of ethnic intermarrying before socializing slowly began but the threat of losing their jobs sure changed things at work. Mr. Mitchell, the coal mine owner, has long since passed on and sadly a huge amount of ethnic hatred continues.

9.   There is no way to forgive the United States for two things — the stealing of lands from American Indians and the enslavement of black people. White people sometimes snicker at the drunkenness among some American Indians and the relaxed father responsibilities of some black males, but they were never conquered and exploited and they were never called boy and degraded before everyone.

Perhaps because I am Chinese I can understand these wrongs, but I do wish to challenge all minorities if they can find it way down in their heart not to forgive those who did those terrible acts but to forget and march into the future with head held high. The white people you know did not do these awful things; do not hate them for what their ancestors did.

Indians enslaved and stole from other Indians at times. Blacks were captured by blacks and tied up like animals by blacks as they were delivered to the Dutch boat captains. All of this unbelievable stuff transpired so let's all get on with it. We have a future world to build. Let's do it right so fairness and justice will prevail for all!

10. The world is shrinking is more than just a cliché. Transportation, communication advances boggle the mind. Disease and infection can swing around the globe in a few days. Old drug treatments are losing their effectiveness in many instances. I believe in globalization in trade and commerce and I believe caring for all people are the key to the future. We have medical capability to battle most epidemics far more effectively. We yearn for peace and leadership to get the medicine to the sufferer.

We must rid our thinking that just concerns our part of the planet. We must show love and compassion for the whole world. This concept is so rudimentary. It baffles me why every human does not understand it and embrace it.

11. People use religion if it is convenient for them and even those professing deep commitment often switch to something else for their convenience. Richard Gere and other Hollywood celebrities have switched to Buddhism. There is a sizeable group of Jews who are evangelical Christians; others have switched to the nation of Islam and take an Islamic name. Some Muslims become Christians and many Hindus go to Buddhism, Muslim and Christian religions.

When Castro took over Cuba, it became inconvenient to be a Catholic although 95% of the Cubans claimed to be Catholic. Almost overnight, the vast majority of them became communist and believed in no god at all. Was the fear of Castro greater than their religious fears? Why so much surface belief? Are people in religion that insecure? It must be a fragile thing because all religions think they can and should convert all the others to their faith.

There is a huge controversy now with Baptists and Jews and many other religious feuds are boiling. This is a root problem and a deep cause of conflicts and hatreds. Convenience religion often brings food and medicine. If an opposing religion offers food, medicine, and money, that religion will easily outdo the first in desperate nations. Thusly, religions that back up their beliefs with great rewards often flourish and those who scare the people profoundly often flourish.

Poor people. Would not they be better off if there was no competition for their soul and received help because of man's brotherhood and love, not a fear of a certain deity?

12. The traditional concept of heaven is quite boring. We are supposed to sing praises to God throughout eternity, have no challenges to improve, rejoice for ever more and shout the praises of the lamb that gave us victory continually. We need invent nothing. Everything will be perfect, "In my father's house, they are many mansions." It sounds like a blah environment to me.

13. People speak of a human race that is tea-colored. Why does color of skin matter? Color of eyes doesn't seem to bug people. Is it because whites have dark brown eyes often and they look like Asian or Negroid eyes? Outside appearances are nothing compared to the character, caringness and trustworthiness of the person inside.

14. Religious surveys and polls mean very little, it anything. If you ask the next 100 people who walk by if they believe in God, yes or no, you will get just about all of the people to say yes. But is that an honest answer or just a conventional wisdom, popular expected response? Ask them if they go to church often or what the doctrine of the church is for a blank stare.

15. The dignity of one human being is the basis for peace.

16. We demand proof before most people will accept flying saucers and the like. Yet most people accept a God never seen or heard by them without any proof that He exists.

17. I reject the Bible notion that there will always be wars and rumors of wars. What a defeatist outlook!

18. Closure at death. The Chinese build paper houses, paper airplanes and the like to burn them at funerals of loved ones. The American Indians buried tomahawks and wampum with the dead. The Egyptians put in boats and gold at times.

Psychologically, any type of closure is superior to a continued attention-getting activity concerning the dead. The closure I prefer and recommend for CODE 3-M is the brief litany of the positive highlights and contributions of the individual's life, the love expressed by them to others and the love expressed for them and the sacredness of their memory because of their good life.

19. It is sad that many people think that if they question any part of their religion, that in itself, is a sin.

20. Why did God create a plan of salvation that was devised so most people would go to hell and a relatively few would go to heaven? It seems very cruel.

21. The traditional God is certainly not perfect. Why does Jesus tell us to be perfect like the father!

22. The focus of most religions is to make sure their soul is saved and most of their energy is spent in a rather selfish quest. They rely on faith to save them from hell. Would not it be far more productive to score a high grade of help and caring for others and let eternity take care of itself?

23. Mahatma Ghandi said, "Strength does not come from physical capacity. It comes from an indomitable will." The little frail gentleman used that indomitable will of his to free hundreds of millions of people from a foreign power.

24. Situational morality is too popular like Pope Pius XII being soft on Hitler but there are rare occasions when flexibility in rigid commandments can be used like taking food from a tyrant to feel starving children. Flex good moral absolutes only in justified very rare cases.

25. Some people go through their lives bravely fighting the battle of time. Many people want to get their life over with so they can land on that beautiful shore where there is no sickness, no sorrow, no more tears, pain or heartache. They get in this mindset and become rather useless in the only life they know is real. What a tragedy!

26. Corpse allegiance that borders on worship is ridiculous. How about those who are cremated and the ashes cast into the sea. Perhaps JFK, Jr. and others chose the best form of closure. The ultra-orthodox Jews go overboard in this area. They go by the painstaking procedures set down in Halacha, or traditional religious laws. It is just common courtesy not to disturb graves of the recent dead without the permission of any family member that may be still alive. But how about the mummies on display?

I see nothing wrong with historical explorations that find humans a million years old and examine their bones. A sensible balance is needed, but the furor over bones is ridiculous. When life leaves a body, the life is forever gone. I personally want my body to be cremated after all healthy organs are given to help others.

There is something bizarre and haunting about a corpse and I believe people put too much money in disposing of it and follow silly notions about it, but I grant them the right to feel as they feel. I look at the valuable land in New York and New Orleans taken up by corpses and wonder how many children could be vaccinated around the world. Are we obsessed by the notion of a future heaven and immortality? We, as a human race, are and always have been but it is gradually improving.

27. The so-called soul does not exist. I agree with Thomas

Edison, a brilliant man who said, "My mind is incapable of conceiving such a thing as a soul. I may be in error, and man may have a soul, but I simply do not believe it." The concept of soul is a heathenistic concept adapted by religions because of their obsession with immortality and wish to control others.

28. Why do religious people get depressed? Is it because they have committed to an impossible standard and fail or because they are burdened down with so many doubts and questions about what they are supposed to believe? Where is the "joy unspeakable" they boast of in their religion?

If they really believe the deity is all powerful, loves them and can lift all of their sorrows and heavy crosses they have to bear, why the blues and doldrums that most of them have? Why do they need so many "booster shots" or organized worship to keep them going in the faith? One has to wonder if the whole set-up is not mythological and imagined.

29. The joy and reward of atheism is not worrying about heaven or hell. You begin to focus everything on what you know. You are alive, life is wonderful. Live it fully and share your life with others. Try to accomplish all you can. Score as high as you can as a good person does. Leave the world better because you lived!

30. Religious disagreements often decay into political disagreements and that can bring on bloody wars. It has. It does. And, it will. Religion may continue to exist for a few centuries but it should not exist at all unless it becomes non-aggressive.

31. Few people define prayer the same way. The dictionary describes it as an earnest entreatment obtained by begging. It is made to some type of God spiritual or material. This is a crutch or a curtain of refuge when one fouls up or seeks something to happen that they want to happen.

The ridiculous true story I can share in this area is the prayer of a friend who asked God not to let the bad guy on a soap opera hurt the little child he had kidnapped. I was amused, but she figures God, being all-powerful, could change the script and the video if he chose and the child would be okay. This is really getting into the drama. I dare say, her prayers were not answered.

People make all kinds of claims about prayers answered but say very little about the ones that are ignored. Perhaps it was not God's will to heal my husband. Who knows God will? The prayers of a thousand people were for healing. "By His stripes we are healed" was screamed and healing was beseeched and begged for over and over again. His head was anointed with oil. The husband died.

Prayer for the dead is too far out to discuss. Prayer is a misguided activity. What is going to happen is going to happen. Prayer does not make it happen or keep it from happening.

32. Earrings, body tattoos, tongue rings, and rings in various other parts of the body in some cases are for aesthetics, aids to beauty. If it is done for raw, rabid rebellion, it is an important caution flag of deep and serous conflict and a tremendous lack of self-esteem. It could cross the line into mutilation for some maladjusted people. Yes, most people, I hope think they are just being fashionable.

The wooden discs placed in the lips of older tribes in Africa and elsewhere might have been fashionable, but it was also self-mutilation, which carries a host of psychiatric problems. Binding little girls' feet in China was finally outlawed.

Cruel practices inflicted on the body of others is awful sadism, but if inflicted upon oneself, the masochistic monster really shows up. Approaching this body-piercing fad with caution is good advice. If you have seen the extremes as they exist, I think you will agree.

33. Religions that teach that one is sinful, carnal, bad, possessed with inbred sin, lost and inadequate are psychologically destructive. People are basically good and spend a lifetime effort in bolstering their true self-esteem. They don't need this type of untruths laid on them. They need positive support.

34. The competitive nature in man is no doubt a positive trait. It can bring lots of fun and sportsmanship. So-called sports activities that are designed to permanently cripple or kill should be outlawed. We outlaw rooster fights and permit bullfights. We permit boxing in men and women and boys and girls sports.

I know the purpose of boxing is not to kill an opponent, but boxers with the most knockouts get the most money. The matador gets more acclaim as he tortures the bull to death. Wrestling though skillfully rehearsed on the performance level filters down to backyard kids who are banging each other with chairs and breaking each other's limbs. Can't we progress beyond this bloodthirsty competition?

No doubt if you throw people in to be eaten up by lions like the Romans did, some people would buy a high-priced ticket to attend. At least in car racing and football, the purpose is to get a car or ball across a line, not to kill or maim the opponent. Where do we draw the line? I don't know but I draw it on the principle that the sport has rules against intentional permanent damage. Block hard but not in the back. Throw a hard baseball, but do not bean a player on purpose.

The strict enforcement of player violence in hockey, football, and other contact sports is essential. Tennis and golf cause little problems. Where would our group draw the line? To be sure they don't want to see the Christians thrown to the lions again so a line needs to be drawn somewhere.

35. Why would a Pope declare in 1948 that Mary went up to heaven on a cloud like Jesus did if Catholics did not believe that for all these centuries? Is Mary a God that is supposed to be worshipped also? How do people swallow these changes? St. Christopher is not to be considered a saint anymore. Pope Paul XII may be voted into sainthood? Strange indeed. Religions surely mess up people's minds. About the time they are sure some tenet in their church is true, it collapses.

36. Jerry Falwell said he intended to stock up on food, sugar, gasoline and ammunition in case the computer bug caused a huge catastrophe. He declared Y2K might be God's instrument to shake this nation, to humble this nation. He sold a video for $28 each giving a Christians' guide to the millennium bug. Is there no shame left for TV evangelists?

37. Did you ever wonder why God just talked to people in Bible times in an audible voice?

38. Don't talk to me about the wonderful American justice system while O. J. Simpson is playing golf and innocent blacks are being executed.

Jose Luiz Howarsh Silva has become one of the most dangerous Satanists according to Christians living where he lives in southeastern Brazil. Silva, born Catholic, was preparing for his first communion at age 7 when he had a supernatural experience that guided him to Satan worship. Lucifer appeared like a beautiful woman like the Bible's Holy Virgin and convinced him to serve the devil.

He says today that God is not wise or perfect otherwise he wouldn't have created the enemy. If God can't destroy Satan, then he is weak, Silva argues. He calls the Bible a bunch of lies and claims life was given to us by the devil. He has a growing number of followers.

Most people would be shocked at the number of devil worshippers on the planet. This is no surprise. When it comes to religion, people will follow almost anything and anybody. Satan is a myth just as much as God is a myth and neither have to be destroyed because they never existed.

40. Gen. Colin Powell was asked who was the most impor-

tant person of the 1900's. He replied that he would not confine it to one person but suggested it was the GIs in WW II who saved the world from Fascism and Nazism.

William Buckley, that brilliant philosopher of sorts, disagreed with Powell stating that the German soldiers fought valiantly for their country as well even though psychologically duped. Buckley makes a good point.

Americans also have done some duping of their own which may be an effective method in military training. Demonize the enemy. We made outlandish posters making the so-called Japs look like crazed monkeys and posters of Germans looking like insensitive, cruel monsters. We called them Huns and our movies made them look like buffoons. Hitler and Tojo were prime targets. We demonize Saddam Hussein and Fidel Castro.

No doubt these evil men deserved being demonized but the deeper concept is well taken that all foot soldiers and other military forced into a war have to show unbelievable courage. Some forfeit their lives. Any caring person grieves when they have seen the awesome atom bomb devastation.

Tactically, it was justified, but look how many babies were slaughtered. It was in the Old Testament days. Wipe out the enemy. None are any good. War is such a horrendous thing on both sides. We must stop it. We must. There has to be a better way! On that, both Gen. Powell and Bill Buckley would agree.

41. The economic element in religion sickens me. Look at Oral Roberts. He bought a Columbine-type airplane and a $10,000 bull way back. Benny Hinn is planning a $30 million plant in Dallas. Some healing evangelists with worldwide ministries take in untold amounts of money. There is more gold in the Vatican than most anywhere in the world besides Ft. Knox. England, France, Switzerland, and a few other spots.

Yet, I have seen Italian children in need of food and clothing. It's big money folks. Send in your love gifts and I send you a book or whatever. The money each day baffles the mind. You can't outgive God so send me money and you will prosper. Flash pictures of starving children and more money rolls in. A precious little goes to the children. As I say, it is sickening.

42. Bishop Spong, the novel-thinking Episcopal priest, usually in hot water with the powers that be in his church gives a breath of fresh air here and there. He said most people's prayers sound like letters to Santa Claus. He declares that God is not Mr. Fix-it and that human sacrifice is a dumb way to communicate to people. There are many closet doubters and more are emerging. Spong still wears his collar backwards

and hangs on to a part of the faith, but he will not swallow the
company line completely. May his tribe increase and be
blessed a thousandfold.

43. God is not up there deciding where the next earthquake will kill off people, where He will send the next
Andrew-type hurricane and stop rain for a couple of years.
Bad things happen to the faithful and the non-believers; so do
good and wonderful things. It seems so childish to thank God
that the storm only killed half of one's family and praise him
that the earthquake was in Japan instead of California.

44. Why were there no women or minority disciples? Did
Christ not even consider diversity when He selected those
highest-ranking followers? The twelve tribes of Israel had the
same attitude of discrimination. Poor examples I would think.

45. Religion does not have a legitimate influence in society
except as it promotes decency, morals, fairness, love, and
brotherhood. Some do this to a point but too much energy and
emphasis is placed on converting others and attacking others
sometimes even killing others in direct opposition to what it is
supposed to represent, peace and charity.

46. President Bush was right when he cited the need for a
kinder, gentler America. New Orleans has adopted a neat rule
for its school students under a new state law requiring them to
address their teachers with a title like Mr., Mrs. or Ms. Such a
law was never mentioned nor needed just a few decades ago.

We need a new motto, "Crudeness is out, gentleness is the
in thing!" Many other countries put American to shame in the
area of common courtesies and respect. Let's shape up. Start
with one person — yourself.

47. As knowledge increases, our wonder deepens. Curious
and searching minds advance human progress. Inquisitive
people are interesting and attractive. They aspire to be more
than ordinary and eventually help others. No wondrous invention or spectacular work of literature is required, just a little
wonder that helps educate one even further.

48. Feminism has gone wild. Any fair-minded person male
or female will acknowledge that women, like minorities, have
been given the short end of the stick and forced to play on an
unleveled playing field. The correction of this wrong has
spawned another wrong called male-bashing. Mothers with
sons should think twice before they support extreme feminism. Mary Daley, a former teacher of feminist ethics,
refused to teach male students because they could not fully
comprehend her precepts. She was not a true friend of

women's rights because she was betraying the cause of equality. Women deserve equality, not favoritism that sets them apart and belittles the other gender.

49. Each human has faced and will face crisis hours. Knowing you have tried earnestly to be a good person can sustain you through any crisis.

50. Without the introduction of the scientific method, and adherence to it for discovery and invention, we would be living today like medieval people.

51. Globalization is inevitable. The world trade organization has imperfections, but it is a step in the right direction. Some type of world government will happen in the third millennium. We have the responsibility as individuals to do our part in seeing to it that it is a fair and just one. We need to pass this principle on to our posterity because it will take centuries to fashion out a great world spirit of cooperation and no war nor ethnic, national or religious hatred.

52. When a man and a woman both fall in love and know it and wish to be married and raise a family or not have children this is strictly their business. No artificial barriers should exist — none period. It is happening and the pace will be accelerated. It will help world understanding and peace.

Heaven and hell are not actual physical places but of a state of mind, whether you are out or in the state of God, is the position of Pope John Paul II. The Bible teaches exactly the opposite. Are the Pope's feelings above the word of God? These changing situational religious rules further weaken any assignment of validity to religion.

54. We need economic justice and we need to teach individuals that they have a responsibility in bringing this about. We seek a balance between handout programs and the responsibility of individuals to do good work. This is the answer to one of the world's greatest needs. Love and care for the needy and expect the needy to appreciate what is given and do their best to help themselves.

55. Mani believed he was a successor to Jesus. He put together elements from Christianity, Buddhism, and Zoroastrianism. He called for choosing the good that is within us (light). The (dark) trapped in human bodies is regarded as inherently evil. St. Augustine followed Manichaeism for nine years before he turned to Christianity. It is difficult to combine religions, so I agree with our effort to develop a code without a deity.

56. Get a life! TV, videos, movies, magazines, books, and

especially computers have captured the lives of too many people. Some of all of this is positive and productive, but computer addicts often surrender the great outdoors, social situations and travel just to be helplessly chained to the mouse for many hours in one day.

There arc psychologists now who specialize in therapy for computer addicts. It is a wonder that the medical profession has not moved to say computer addiction is a medical disease like alcoholism is a disease. Any addiction has elements of a disease, but one does not have a choice if he develops TB or a brain hemorrhage. He does choose alcohol or a computer. That is the clear difference.

57. "Do the right thing because it is the right thing to do." This is of course a popular saying, but I think a very poignant one. You don't do right necessarily to save your soul from hell. Many do right and do not believe in hell. You can certainly do right regardless of religious influences. You don't need to be promised a reward of heaven or any other reward to do right.

Forcing racial choices or religious choices is wrong. Someone like Tiger Woods, can choose to be Thai, Black, American Indian or can choose to be just Tiger Woods, human and great golfer. Geraldo Rivera, Hispanic and Jew, has probably surveyed both the Catholic religion and the Jewish religion and is strong enough to accept one or the other, neither or both.

These prominent, successful men have no serious problem, but the average little child is often caught up in the situation where enormous pressures are made upon them to accept one and exclude the other. CODE 3-M should suggest each available choice be laid out gradually and sympathetically without pressure. The child will observe and learn, and should be given the right to choose or not to choose a race and to subscribe or not to accept a religion. Tearing a child's emotions apart concerning these two entities can scar them for life.

58. We must give proper priority to our quests or seeking. Many quests are laudatory and push everyone forward. Some quests are full of vanity and very selfish. A little handful of quests representing long, long lists could include the quest for power, the quest for beauty, the quest for space exploration, the quest for medical miracles, the quest for recognition and fame, the quest for legacy, the quest for the fountain of youth, the quest for better surgeries and drugs, the quest for solace and contentment.

Towering far above all of these and other quests should be the quest to learn the purpose of man's existence, how his life should be conducted and his niche among all living things. That is the supreme quest. We must seek it with diligence, organize and postulate our findings and be amenable to amending the concepts as truth and science dictate.

59. Equality is simple. I am human. You are human. They are human. Therefore, we are all equal. When this simple thinking engulfs the world, it will be a much better place to live.

60. There is sadness about false religion. People have given their lives for the wrong cause. A particular faith feels this sadness and moves hell and earth so to speak to save the poor followers of the religion that has a different deity.

If they can't save them or convert them, then they wipe them out for it they don't believe like us, they are perpetuating evil. It is heartbreaking to a compassionate, objective observer. All of them spend their lifetime of service and many have died for things they could not prove. This is not the way humans should live.

The disintegration of mainstream religions will accelerate. The ratio of people going to church to the total population is much lower than in 1900. We will see in their place thousands of cults that will parallel the beginnings of the religions that have amassed multiplied millions to their creeds. This déjà vu is already happening and each time disintegration occurs and huge masses leave the traditional powers of religion, the ranks of the non-believers swell significantly.

I do not know how many cycles this will take for it to be politically correct to say, I do not subscribe to any particular organized religion, but I believe that in their hearts, most people have enough logical doubts to feel dubious about the whole religious message and long for a sensible, fair CODE of living for the human race.

61. We must emphasize that up front choices are the most important. This applies to most anything but especially smoking, drinking, doping, AIDS, venereal disease, and murder. Look just a moment at what bad choices by individuals cost the rest of society in heartache and expense. I do not advocate that society just let all these people wallow in their own ignorance and die or execute all murderers.

However, there comes a breaking point when decent hardworking people cannot and should not be taxed to pay for all of those up front bad choices of others. Education has helped but it is not the answer. Let them die out for they don't add much to the human race is a non-compassionate attitude.

We need a balance. People do not have the right to squander their lives at the expense of others. And many have pushed the compassionate side of most people too far. This money could be sent to help starving babies and supply clean water to millions of deserving people. Society has got to come down more on the side of personal responsibility!

62. Take last from me my mind and ability to think clearly and reason. It is my most prized possession.

63. The best hope for mankind is the cessation of brainwashing children to ape the beliefs of their parents.

64. It took an atom bomb to knock out one false imagined God. The emperor of Japan, under the terms of surrender included a mandate that he had to denounce his claim that he was God, as Shintoites believed. It was convenient for this God was a talking, thinking human being. The task of eliminating mythical gods, those who are spirits, is more formidable. However, logic and common sense overcame many ancient mythical gods. If we knew how to erase fear of eternity in mankind, all religions would collapse.

65. An interesting development is the international video matchmakers. Money, of course, is driving the various projects, but it is a legitimate business and has quite a potential in bringing people together from various cultures of the world that otherwise would never meet.

66. One should not charge religions cause mental illness because mental stability is not an issue for most of its participants. However, for unstable people with depression tendencies, neurotic behaviors, and even some psychotic conditions, the monotonous practices of some religions and the dramatic hell-fire preaching can ensure a strengthening of the mental problems one may be enduring. Therapists frequently discover serious religious entanglements in some of their patients.

67. Fifty years has changed the world. The computer burst on the scene with unprecedented power for analysis and dissemination of extremely varied kinds of data in unbelievable quantities and at mind-staggering speeds. Fifty years in the future, something we do not envision now may change our way of life even more. We must at least make the effort to keep up with the appropriate behavior for mankind. Moral philosophy must be emphasized with the unimaginable things that will be created. This is also essential for the biogenetic advances.

68. The traditional hierarchy must be challenged and is being challenged with some success. The old military moral of "I'm over you, you are over him and he is over 16 others" is a dinosaur. Participating management is best. People should

avoid the "control others fever." People resent being controlled and they should. They will cooperate with a true leader if they think they are part of the effort in truth and spirit.

Times have changed and will keep revealing the power of group decisions. The old boss set up is passe.

69. If motivational gurus like Anthony Robbins do nothing more than awaken people to change the perception that they are yearlings and helpless, they do a good thing. Personal power is there in each person and their techniques are needed for many downtrodden people. Weight loss and exercise evangelists have positive results also while ignoring a deity.

70. Beware of those who overemphasize the importance of feeling over thinking. Existentialist promoters, Catholic mystics, Jungian psychoanalysts, Hindu gurus, TV preachers and others exhort people to concentrate on how they feel. If one thinks rationally and gives proper acknowledgement to science, the good, steady, solid feeling is automatic. How one perceives is how one feels. Beware of fads of "emotional blessings." Plant your feet on solid ground.

71. If the UN never does fulfill its full promise, it has been enormously successful already in showing that good people of all religious stripes, governments 180-degrees apart, and cultures strange to one another can sit down, show courtesy and civility to one another most of the time and chit-chat in the halls and anterooms in an enjoyable fashion. So, there is hope!

72. Perhaps those who attack any effort like CODE 3-M attack harder depending on the insecurity they have in their own beliefs. Intensity builds in proportion to their inability to keep child-like faith in socket. Any person in sinking sand yells louder and louder but people who stand on the rock of their honesty, scientific facts and logic to not have to explode in conversation or debate.

73. Human affairs have concerned themselves with too much national, ethnic and religious issues. It is time to focus on the individual.

74. Cloning of humans in inevitable, unfortunately. We must make certain the Dillingers, the Hitlers, the Stalins, the Castros and the like are passed over in favor of the Mother Teresas, the Florence Nightingales, the Einsteins, the Edisons, the Fords, the Gates and the Turners. Clones of the Liz Taylors, Clark Gables, Muhammad Alis, Babe Ruths, Aarons, Sosas and McGuires will be popular. Football players will be cloned for position. Marino, Tarkington, Montana and Elway may have clones to fill needed quarterback positions and so

on. I sure hope this prediction is hogwash.

75. English, now the language for pilots who do not know the other's language and air controllers and in many other human communication situations, will become the world language. I hope this prediction comes true. Chinese can be tough for people not raised in China and there are so many dialects, I have problems myself.

76. Mexico is to get 27 more saints. They only have one now so Pope John Paul II will canonize 27 more. A specialist in religion in Mexico stated it's an international boost that strikes the Mexican collective ego, rather like winning the soccer world cup. This kind of religious pandering is exactly why the CODE must not support a particular religion.

77. Nudity should not be promoted or endorsed by CODE 3-M but permit it as being within the authority and choice of the individual. The Bible in Exodus 32:25 tells us that practically the whole nation of Israel had a nude orgy. Moses got so mad he had 3,000 of the men killed. Peter was fishing naked the last time he went fishing. Isaiah, the great prophet, walked naked and barefoot for three years among the Hebrews in obedience to the Lord (Isaiah 20:2). This was for a sign and wonder for Egypt and Ethiopia.

Most people are shocked when they are told this kind of activity is in the Bible because they do not read but select passages like St. John. The few preachers who do read it gloss over anything that does not enhance their doctrine.

I am not a prude, but most females would look much better if they wore more decent swimsuits. The same goes for men. There is nothing wrong with the human body. Appropriateness is the key. Swimsuits and nudity is an individual choice.

78. People who believe their God is a truthful God and rely on the Bible should examine I Kings 22:22. The Lord put a lying spirit in the mouth of all these prophets. Maybe it was justified. Does not that open the door for man to lie if he regards it as justified? Nixon and Clinton thought so. Don't forget Eisenhower and the U-2 plane that was shot down. Maybe lying in very extreme cases is justified. What a can of worms this opens up!

79. Learn to be positive most all of the time. People don't like to be around negative and judgmental people.

80. No God had anything to do with man going to the moon. Jim Lovell said, "Going to the moon was not a miracle. We just decided to go and we went." Surely if this were some God project, so many people would not have been killed in the effort.

So far, no heaven has been located.

81. The serpent spoke to Eve — stop right there. Serpents talk, reindeer fly, Frosty the Snowman talks too. Where does imagination in the so-called word of God end and reality set in?

82. Jezebel is mentioned in the Bible 23 times. The holy Virgin Mary, Mother of Jesus, is mentioned only 19. The Bible emphasizes wickedness and punishment instead of lifting up the beauty and potential of mankind to overcome for himself.

83. Why pray after the plane crash?

84. In Taiwan, some believe the 7th lunar month is ghost month and spirits of the dead walk on earth. Taoist followers flock to their temples on the first day to pray. Temple priests open symbolic doors to welcome the spirits and beg them not to make mischief among the living. Ceremonies and banquets are given to appease the spirits.

There is no way you are going to get my friend Rachel, a born-again Christian from South Carolina to go along with that kind of religion and vice versa. I just wish everyone subscribing to any religion would pause to identify the many weird and impossible things that they profess to believe in and accept as sensible and true. When they even start to begin such thinking, they pray the devil away and slide comfortably back into their child-like faith.

85. Angel Flights are airplane trips retired pilots volunteer to fly. For example, a seriously ill 11-year-old was flown to the Mayo clinic and hundreds of others — no charge. This really adds to the positiveness and helpfulness of their life. Perhaps you cannot fly the plane, but most anyone can help the child get ready and get on board. Use the talents you have.

86. If a large group of people on earth are looking for something firm to stand on, then the CODE should be a welcome answer. A man was buried in a coal mine. When finally rescued, he said his main problem was his worry that everyone thought he was dead and stopped looking for him.

Who knows their number, but many sincere people are very concerned about the false claims and empty promises of their religion. They are lost and trapped by ancient superstitions posed by people who did not understand the world was round. They have great difficulty switching back and forth in schizophrenic fashion from reality to the unreal. They are disenchanted with the deity-oriented systems and yearn for a compass to find more happiness and contentment in their lives.

They are not alone and not abandoned. Some people with compassion and understanding and facts, not myths, are still looking to help them. We know they are still alive.

87. "Look over this world well, for it is here for all of us," said Wei Jingsheng who was imprisoned 18 years for writing about democracy. Some day freedom of ideas and thought will be commonplace around the world.

88. There is a formula for ongoing war. We get afraid if people who do not look or dress just like us. They do not worship like we worship. We don't like them. That dislike easily turns into hate when one of them does something to one of us.

We turn into a wolfpack and dehumanize them. We demonize them for they are all evil. Kill them. It is so easy to kill them and we must to save our own necks. Sadly, this pathetic tribal mentality formula works.

89. A holy war is an oxymoron. There is nothing holy about any war. It is a stupid human exercise and vile as can be.

90. There is a huge gulf between what scientific minds have accomplished for mankind and religious minds. In fact, the disparity is so great it is astounding!

Twin boys, 12 years old lead a mini-revolution in Asia. How sick can a society become? They kill and order massacres yet have strict behavior for their followers. This outrage has got to cease and it will. Others will take its place, but there is hope that someday, no one will rise to lead the next war. I want to do my little part in bringing this about.

91. People have often tried to deride me by calling me an atheist. It matters not what anyone calls me. I think of myself as a seeker of truth, not an atheist nor an agnostic. If earnest diligent and honest seeking leads to a god, I will embrace the concept 100%. The gods nominated thus far do not meet my criteria for a god I would or could worship.

92. Can anyone top the incredulous story of the Tower of Babel? (Genesis 11:1) Was God afraid one language might produce some facts? Languages at that stage were spoken all over the world by humans that had evolved in their area. There was never one language. It would be helpful to have one.

93. Many humans deeply desire freedom from all isms and people hell-bent on swaying them to their religions, to work out their own destiny. Too many systems think they are the only way.

94. Religion causes wars, suffering and misery. Consider Pope John Paul II's apology for the church in March 2000 for the crusades, the inquisition, hands-off attitude toward the Jews during the Holocaust years? An apology — fine. The millions killed and maimed did not get to hear it. How can people

today forgive what religious leaders did centuries ago? What Jew would ever really forgive Pope Pius XII? I don't remember any apology he made. The present Pope, I believe, would have acted differently. At least, his apology exposes the wrongs of others parading under a religious flag. When will the Muslims and Jews apologize to each other?

95. Isn't it pathetic when we talk about the Catholic vote, the women's vote, the Hispanic vote, the tobacco states vote, the blue collar vote, the religious right vote, black vote, the Italian vote, the Jewish vote or whatever?

I have not heard much about the Chinese vote and I would greatly resent anyone thinking that I would vote a certain way because most Chinese were voting that way. I am not a dumb, easily led sheep. I choose to think for myself. The special interest groups are antithetical to freedom and democracy.

96. Doctors Without Borders exemplify the wonderful spirit of man loving and caring for man. Organizations like this have many true heroes in their number.

97. "Make love, not war," the hippie motto of the 1960's, makes lots of sense. "Hey, Hey LBJ, how many kids have you killed today?" may have had more impact than we realize. We need to create more catchy slogans to stem wars and suffering as well as more cartoons, art, songs, and theater.

There have already been some very effective efforts in these areas. John Lennon had a world vision of peace. Millions have, but the number has not been enough to overcome the hatreds and greeds of the aggressive warmongers. Hang on, everyone. Someday, we will be politically correct.

98. No one has been able to show that religious people die with any greater ease in battle or anywhere else than the non-religious. There is no appreciable difference in the struggle to keep living despite suffering from terminal illness.

If those who say they believe they are going into heaven — a land of beauty, peace and rejoicing — why the inordinate struggle to stay on this wicked, sinful earth?

99. Goth is a passing fad and will not be on stage very long says one religious historian. Let's hope he is correct.

100. Many learned scholars believe that the Apostle Paul hijacked the Jesus movement, skewed it to be a non-Jewish religion and finally was able to extinguish the Jewish matrix and customs that James, the older brother of Jesus, tried to foster.

Paul, of course, never met Jesus. James grew up with Jesus as a close brother along with three other brothers, all the natural sons of Joseph and Mary of Nazareth. Jesus was not born in Bethlehem according to the scholars who present an entirely different view of Jesus than the Pauline influenced gospels in an alternative biography on the birth, life, death and resurrection of Jesus Christ.

There were many messiahs making claims that they were the fulfillment of Old Testament prophecy. Actually, there was no census at the time of the birth of Jesus. The Jesus movement went hand in hand with politics. The Romans had developed collective farms with Jewish collaborators in charge of them. People were poor and oppressed and disgruntled as the Romans drained their resources for themselves and came down with an iron hand to force labor for their benefit.

The Pauline doctrine had Jesus saying, "Render unto Caesar what is Caesar's." The James doctrine insisted on a different course, one of rebellion against Rome. John, the Baptist, was the mentor of Jesus and his brothers. He was fiercely opposed to Herod and the Roman conquerors. He got his head chopped off for these views.

His protégé, Jesus, followed a milder way but met death by Roman crucifixion. Political dissent was not tolerated. John, the Baptist, and Jesus were political threats. The Dead Sea scrolls, discovered in 1947 but not included in the Bible, are authentic documents which describe a large Jewish group who fled from the Romans and were linked to John the Baptist.

The Essenes were a political movement against the Romans. Jesus created his own movement after the death of John the Baptist. Some scholars believe Mary Magdalene was actually the wife of Jesus. She had special access and rights to the body and burial details of Jesus.

Jesus wanted to bring in a New World order. He bristled at Roman cruelty and injustice. James, his close brother, ate kosher food and insisted that new gentile Christians be circumcised. Paul's version did not require either.

The battle between the true legacy of Jesus was on. Paul was highly educated and a prolific traveler as opposed to James being a humble devout Jewish man who did not have the charisma of a Paul but knew Jesus as a brother and close friend, having grown up together. Paul's claims and views came from his experiences on the road to Damascus where he claims he made connection with the heavenly Jesus.

Before that, he persecuted Christians. Saul, a Jew of Tarsus was a Benjamite and Pharisee who changed his name to Paul. He had missionary journeys extending from Jerusalem and Antioch westward through Cyprus and Asia even into Europe.

Among his traveling companions were Barnabas, John Mark, Silas, and Luke. Timothy and Titus were co-workers. Paul wrote many epistles to his Christian leaders, some of whom appear in the Bible. It was obvious through his admonishments and rebukes that he was the man in charge. He emphasized that Jesus was the Son of God and had to come up with the Immaculate Conception to explain this view.

James, realizing that Paul was taking over and making spurious claims, summoned Paul to Jerusalem. Paul offered James a huge donation, but James refused it and then accused Paul of encouraging Jews to ignore the Torah and Jewish law.

There was a great riot. Paul claimed to the Roman government that he was a Roman citizen so the Roman soldiers rescued him from the Jewish zealots. No one knows how Paul became a Roman citizen, but it was common for people to buy citizenship, which he may have done as Saul of Tarsus. At any rate, James and the actual family of Jesus lost out.

Paul, highly educated and crafty, had a free hand to slant scripture in the New Testament according to his deification of Jesus and soft views of the tyrannical Romans. Thus we see Pontious Pilate, a very vicious tyrant washing his hands and being somewhat sympathetic to Jesus who had proclaimed himself to be King of the Jews.

The entwined tale of Judas betraying Jesus has no basis whatsoever in any evidence or fact. The Pauline view needed a scapegoat. Judas means Jew and the skillful Paul was able to make the Jews in general the scapegoat of the crucifixion of Jesus. Simply put, the Romans eliminated John, the Baptist and Jesus because of fear of a political uprising. The Jews did not accept Jesus as the Messiah and according to the Pauline view joined in to get rid of him.

In 66 A.D. the Jews did rebel and try to overthrow the Romans. They were crushed easily; 900 fled to a mountaintop and committed suicide rather than suffer crucifixion by the Romans. Which version of Jesus are we to believe, the Pauline version or Jamian version? The main truth any objective person can determine out of all of these conflicting claims is that one should not surrender their minds to be brainwashed by such a scrambled set of contradictions and wild claims.

One fact is undisputed by all. The Messiah was to come and deliver the downtrodden and bring peace, equality and prosperity to the world. It did not happen!

101. I believe in and appreciate the many positive teachings about love and brotherhood attributed to Jesus Christ. They

are worthy. One can accept the uplifting and the good without assigning deity to this son of Joseph and Mary.

Probably Jesus himself did not think of himself as God until the idea was thrust upon him. The CODE can derive much from his teachings which, though mostly a rehashing of previous concepts, are pertinent today and forever.

102. I need something I can believe in. This is not only the wail of the rock singers but also the cry of the human race. Here is what everyone can believe in: one can add up the total picture of one's life. In most every case there will be much more good, so much more it will be overwhelming despite a number of lapses and mistakes, even a few hurtful things.

Extreme wrongs like hate crimes, rape, murder, felonies, and child abuse can weigh the scales over to the negative side so much it would have been better if that person had not lived. Some people flunk and if they really believed in a grading system for one's life, it just might have prevented some of their meanness towards others.

Most people do not do such things and do many wonderful things and realize that what they do for others count. The average person can grade out 70-80 very easily. The person who is known to be a good, positive, wholesome person can easily grade out 80-90. A number of people I know can reach 90-95, but no one grades out 100 and the high nineties are very rare.

Simply, if you want and need something to believe in, believe that if you do good deeds and grade out well, whatever destiny may be, you're okay. One need not be afraid to die and is not haunted by the fears that accompany people in all religions.

REV. JOHN HAYES' LIST

Since Al and Lu did not prioritize their items, neither did I.

1.   Power of the media. Newspapers, magazines, books, TV, and computers — all have been more of a blessing to people than a curse. Why do we have to have the negative influences? In 1999, alone in the US, there were 1.4 billion hits on computer set-ups for pornography displays.

Have not we beheld what Hollywood has done to our society for decades? The media teaches our youth it is commonplace to kill, do drugs, use tobacco, beat up on people, have babies out of wedlock and almost any sin you can name.

The "everybody's doing it theme" is a persuasive weapon. We have seen the sad results of do your own thing at hospitals, broken homes, inmates in prison and some receiving capital punishment. The individual can help by refusing to buy any of the products of the company which sponsor trash.

2.   The universe and its order is but one vast symbol that there must be a God somewhere. Consider the creation of the heavens and the Earth, the plant and biological world, the animal world and that crowning divine creation of man himself. Surely, there must be a God somewhere.

3.   The democratic process can be a substitute for violence. You don't settle anything with a bayonet or a bullet. Mahatma Ghandi and Martin Luther King, Jr. showed the whole world that non-violence and democracy could be a very powerful set of twins.

4.   The Confederate flag that flew over the capital of South Carolina was divisive and should not have been flown with tax money support since it was used as a negative racial symbol.

5.   Health matters more than wealth. Evidently, most people have to lose their health to recognize this truth. Take care of your body and strive for as good health as you possibly can, given your physical attributes.

6.   God's power is never questioned by me. I wish also to raise the issue of will power. People cop out by saying, "I can't help it." Winston Churchill said, "All great things are decided not by machines or gadgets, but by will power. Whoever has it will finally prevail."

The greatest faculty of mankind is his ability to make choices. Some learn to make them despite pressures to be a sheep and go along. I decided I would not smoke or chew tobacco at an early age. I made that choice and no one had the power to make me do it. Apply this principle to thousands of things.

7.   Over one million Americans say they are atheists. And another group has arisen who declare that God is dead. He isn't for I just talked to Him today. Still another group on the rise says God is suspect until proven by science. Yet, a worldwide revival is sweeping across the lands where people are being converted to Jesus.

Some claim the Muslims are gaining the most converts, but if so, it is because autocratic governments in whole nations are banning every other religion. I know religionists should not fight each other, but we do believe in preaching the gospel to the whole world and giving the individual at least an opportunity to accept Jesus as their Lord and personal savior.

If they refuse Him, then I respect that and just continue to pray for them, but every person needs to hear the story of Jesus and know He fulfilled the prophecy in the Bible. All the prophecies in the Bible have come to pass or will happen.

8.   Love. I won't preach here, but I feel all seven of us will agree that I Corinthians 13 has a beautiful description of what charity or love is all about.

"Love suffereth long and is kind. Love envieth not, vaunteth not itself, is not puffed up, doesn't behave itself unseemly, seeketh not her own, is not easily provoked, thinketh no evil."

If we can try to live up to this beautiful portrayal, the world will be rid of war and violence. I for one am making the best effort I know how.

9.   In the early 1700's British slaves in the Carolina Territory learned that the lives of their counterparts in Spanish Florida was much better. The slaves could sue over ill treat-

ment, work independently and make money to buy their complete freedom.

Word quickly spread among the Carolina slaves about a 1733 Spanish decree that anyone who reached St. Augustine, accepted Roman Catholicism and swore allegiance to the King of Spain would be immediately granted freedom. As you would imagine, many risked everything to get to St. Augustine. They knew very little about Roman Catholicism and very little about Spain or who was king. But desperate men do desperate things. They did know a lot about what it meant to be free.

My point here is that dire circumstances often influence your actions. I am not excusing the lads in the big city ghettos who steal as a way of life, but I hope some parallel can be drawn.

We must encourage the downtrodden to find a proper and honorable way out. This is by changing their perception of who they are and the power within them even if they don't lean on God's power which would surely add to their efforts. They can be free in every sense of the word. If they are willing to go forward, we should be willing to push.

10. The senseless war between Ethiopia and Eritrea in East Africa is a very brutal war. They share a 620-mile frontier; what is so sad is that people on both sides are starving every day through famine while their leaders are waging war. It goes on for a while, then a pause and it starts up again — like the Irish or the Arab-Jew conflicts.

This is where the UN can and should play a major role if the countries will let them. The people of the world would send enough food to get through this mess if they would cease killing each other.

You can claim all the religion you want, but if you cannot show compassion and concern for people far away on another continent, something is lacking. Aside from religion, morality and caringness for our fellow man, give out a clarion call. Do what you can to help.

11. Man needs a higher power than himself. Is religion worthwhile? Yes, so say the vast majority of the people in the world. I realize most of them have the wrong faith but if they had the correct faith in the Prince of Peace, there would be eternal peace on earth.

12. Some push religions too far and hurt the cause. Stick with the word of God is the best advice. Some neurotic people believe their pets go to heaven for it wouldn't be heaven to them without Fluffy or Spot. Just because some people go off

the deep end does not mean that there isn't a true sensible way. Jesus said, "I am the way, the truth and the life."

13. Government control of religion is wrong, but extricating prayer from school and completely separating the church and state is the other extreme of governmental control.

14. "It won't happen to me" attitude. People hang with the wrong crowd and are maimed or killed, but they did not think it would happen to them. People drink socially and drink to celebrate and drink when depressed. They become drunks or the politically correct word, alcoholics. But they did not set out to be an alcoholic.

The same goes for drug addiction. Terrible things happen to someone in Kalamazoo or Wewahitchica; nothing awful is going to happen to me. It might.

15. We are going to live much longer as a species. We must learn to live better for ourselves and for others. Admittedly, people don't read the Bible much and the majority of church members go to church very little so if a CODE can be developed to help us live better and I can still have my Jesus and my Bible, I am all for it.

16. Present drug laws and prosecution practices are unfair especially the crack laws and racial profiling. I am for prohibition, but that will never happen again, so I am now for consistency. Abolish the illegal drug laws, tax it like liquor and teach people to stay away from either one and the like.

I taught my children not to swallow poison and they don't do it. I taught them not to use tobacco, alcohol and mind-altering drugs. They don't do it. They don't tie themselves to railroad tracks either.

17. Faith without works is dead. You need faith, but if you have no good works, what good is your faith? We need to hold on to faith with one hand and work hard with the other to accomplish positive things for other people. The greatest commandment is to love thy neighbor as thyself. The greatest love is to lay down your life for another.

18. Abusing others is wrong. Children are being beaten in some cases to death. Spouses are being knocked around like a volleyball. It is, of course, against the law. We need to provide appropriate punishment and penalties for these criminals.

Child molestation is on the rise and our permissive society and surface-minded psychologists explain it away saying, "Oh, he was abused when he was a child." That is an unacceptable excuse. Most children who suffered abuse do not do the same to other children.

So much nasty and abusive behavior is winked at until it has become the norm in many circles just like different sexual lifestyles. These lifestyles often lead to child abuse according to police records. And the spineless courts turn child predators back into the community.

CODE 3-M is against war and violence and these examples are another type of violence we should strongly condemn. Each individual can impact this desperate issue.

19. The dictates of our own conscience are indeed the most important basis for a person to follow. One can feel free if one's conscience is clear. There is a great variance in the conscience of one person to another depending on what one has been taught and what has truly been accepted.

God expects us to follow our conscience based on His divine word. One may ask, how can there be over 180 denominations that say they believe the same Bible?

Well, one painter was asked to paint a sunset. He brushed great bold strokes of yellow. Another painter saw the blue sky and made equally bold strokes of blue. Soon the two mixed and a beautiful emerald green emerged.

I wish we could get every religion that preaches Jesus to join. We can see things differently and still be honest. As long as we are faithful to the belief as Jesus is the Son of God and our Savior, there can be great latitude. I prefer to worship with people who generally believe as I do in most things and give others that right, but I would not worship with anyone who denied Christ.

20. Faith. Despite my inability to understand, I have utmost faith in God's word although I admit I do not understand some things in the Bible.

An example is the moving of the sun and the sun standing still. Hezekiah asked Isaiah what would be the sign the Lord would heal him in Chapter 20 of II Kings. Isaiah cried unto the Lord and the shadow of the sun moved backward ten degrees. Joshua commanded the sun to stand still. The sun stood still and the noon stayed about a whole day (Joshua 10) so God's people could avenge their enemies. It seems the sun changing direction or standing still would foul up the orderly rotation that is required.

No, I don't understand this or a number of other things in the Bible, but I trust God to do what He wants to and make it come out alright. He is omnipotent, omniscience, omnipresent, and He can do whatever he pleases. I am saying people who embrace the principles of CODE 3-M or at least some of them, will see them change from time to time in the future. They can still embrace their never-changing principles of their religion even if they do not always understand them. Faith is not proof. It is trust and belief.

21. "Whatsoever ye would that men should do to you, do ye even so to them: for this is the law and the prophets." (Matthew 7:12) The golden rule has proven to be one of the best if not the best guidelines for human behavior.

22. Heaven is a place and hell is a place "where there will be weeping and gnashing of teeth." (Matthew 8:11). Jesus' angels will cast them that do uniquity into a furnace of fire. Lazarus cried for a drop of water while he was burning in hell. Hell is in the center of the Earth.

People should fear God who hath the power to cast one into hell forever and forever. Few can grasp the concept of forever. The preacher Charles Spurgeon said to consider the Earth a gigantic steel ball. Suppose a little hummingbird flew once a year from the moon and swished his little wing against this mighty ball.

A powerful microscope could detect some wear after a century or two. When that little bird coming once a year causing that tiny bit of friction to wear down the Earth to the size of an orange, eternity will have just begun! One can choose eternity in a place called heaven or a place called hell!

23. There exists a real devil called Satan. He was once an archangel in heaven, but he rebelled against God and was cast out of the heavens with the other angels who joined him. Satan is in for a rough ending. He will be bound for a thousand years and cannot deceive nations during that time. Then God will cast him into a lake of fire and brimstone and Satan will be tormented night and day forever. (Revelation 20:7)

24. Creation of all things was made by God. In Him was life. Evolution is of the devil.

It is a simple act of faith to say and believe, "In the beginning, God created the heavens and the earth" and it prevents lots of questions one has in life. When creation was accepted by all students in school, you did not see the murder and disruption you witness now in the year 2000.

25. A false accusation against another knowing it is a lie is a terrible sin. Potiphar's wife cast her eyes on Joseph, a Jewish slave, who was made overseer of Potiphar's house. She asked Joseph to have sex with her. He refused.

She caught his garment and he took off. Then she called in others; she said she had his garment and he had participated in sexual acts with her.

He was put into prison although he was totally innocent. This terrible sin exists today. An appropriate penalty should be given to the liar.

26. I agree with Bridgette on some things, but not on most things. When she promotes inter-racial marriage if voluntary, she is right on. Movies like "Guess Who's Coming to Dinner" and "Bodyguard" have been a very positive force in portraying to whites real love blooms among all races. Though persecuted, some people are pioneering this practice and raising another window of freedom. Bravo, Bridgette!

27. Consider addiction to video games and/or computers. It is only common sense to see a carry over in violent video games and school killings and mass murders in fast food places and elsewhere. People become calloused to others being blown up. When they do it for hours themselves, isn't it reasonable to believe the shock and horror are reduced?

Three first graders were discovered plotting to murder a student. You don't need a Ph.D. in Psychology to know this negative influence is a fact. We are suing tobacco companies. Although I do not smoke and wish no one would smoke ever, it is unfair to sue them unless you sue liquor manufacturers. Alcohol has caused far more death and suffering than tobacco ever could.

Why not sue Hollywood for violent movies and video creations if a nexus can be made for a particular crime? We teach violence and then we are appalled when it occurs.

28. I disagree with one of my heroines, the indefatigable Shirley Chisholm who ran for president of the United States, when she says she sees no steady progress toward a wonderful millennium in race relations. I do see lots of steady progress and I intend to keep pushing and do my part by word and example to see all racism is wiped out on the face of the Earth long before this millennium comes to a close.

Martin Luther King, Jr. said, "We must learn to live together as brothers or perish together like fools." I heartily agree with him. When Shirley Chisholm declares it is not enough to sit down and talk, form commissions and refer to committees, she is right — it has to come from the heart.

The largest unsolved problem we have in the world besides war and famine is the age-old primitive fear and dehumanization of other people who are not like us. The DNA genome results should put this to rest forever.

The same standards are true for black people or Asians

who hate whites. Two black men agreed in Jacksonville, Florida, to kill the next white man who walked down the street. It was a mentally handicapped man, age 50; they beat him to death. Many more cases like this reflect whites that are racially motivated to kill blacks.

However, I did not see Rev. Jesse Jackson or Rev. Al Sharpton come to Jacksonville and lead a protest march. No one has within their individual authority to show or feel racial bias toward anyone!

29. Dr. Laura, the famous radio and TV talk show celebrity, is attacked from all sides because she is trying to bring a higher moral level to the nation. For example, 52% of children born in New York have only a mother.

The media is in an uncontrollable frenzy like a gigantic tornado destroying morality wherever it touches down. They portray one as a nut if they bring a Bible standard of behavior for this nation.

30. Christ had doubts and questioned if His father God had forsaken him on the cross. It is not a sin for Christians to have doubts. Everyone does but there is nothing on earth like Jesus to give hope and joy to a saved soul and renew your faith. Let the doubts pass through quickly and read reassuring scriptures or sing a good hymn that will bless your soul and increase your faith!

31. If you could have a computer containing all the knowledge in the world at your finger tips and had the Hope diamond piled on top of an 18-wheel moving van full of diamonds (making you a trillionnaire), and who was known and admired by 95% of the world's population, it would ring hollow to the consolation of knowing you had been born again, passed the test and was headed for heaven's eternal glory!

32. Hollywood cares little about desecrating religious leaders. Time after time, they feature rotten preachers, rabbis and priests. A license for embellishment is appropriate but when a movie depicts Christ envisioning a sexual relationship with Mary Magdalene after He married her, this crosses the line and is patently sacrilegious.

Christians everywhere must unite. Already, the Christ is being taken out of Christmas. I know "X" stands for Chi in Greek, but what is the percentage of English-speaking people who know it?

Commercial interests have replaced "Merry Christmas" with "Happy Holidays" and overshadowed "Wishing you a Merry Christmas" with "Wishing you a happy holiday season."

Christ is taken out of our public schools. All this and hundreds of other attacks and we Christians are fighting over creeds, women pastors, and water Baptism. Even the three main US Islamic groups in American who have had serious rivalries going on 25 years have agreed to settle their problems for the glory of Allah. Muslims and Christians seem to be headed for a huge showdown in gaining followers on the Earth. If one believes in Christianity, why fight one's brothers in the faith?

Emphasize the commonness not the differences like CODE 3-M is trying to do with race and human behavior. This project has taught me this approach can be very positive and valuable. Religions will never unite because their leaders will not allow it to happen and everyone will not accept the same God, let alone the plan of salvation.

I plan to keep my faith in Jesus and follow CODE 3-M also as long as it does not attempt to take away from me my particular faith.

34. Moral absolutes. We have already established some things that every person should adhere to on earth. I hope the basic ones will never be changed. There are many, many more that I hope will be included in CODE 3-M. Time will tell when we see everyone's biased list like mine.

35. If any objective person weighs Christianity in the balances, they will find it has accomplished so much for the world notwithstanding that people in history and today desecrate the loving principles it teaches. What would the world be like if Jesus had not come with His message of love and peace?

36. Responsibilities to God, to others and to self are my motto and I recommend it to all.

37. We have underestimated peer pressure as a main force in guiding our youth. It does not have to be a large group of peers. In Ft. Myers, Florida, four teenagers pledged their loyalty to the Lords of Chaos and killed the band director.

Young people begin to smoke, drink, do drugs and sex at an early age because of the power of peer pressure. We must somehow teach our youth that one person can be strong and say "no."

A leading national magazine, *Newsweek*, declares we are a society that has lost its consensus, cannot agree on standards or conduct, language and manners. Even some staid universities founded on Christian principles are winking at the practice of co-ed housekeeping among their students and some religious philosophers are condoning trial marriages.

CODE 3-M must attempt to heal this broken and cracked consensus by setting some kind of base that our youth can follow and know when they are following a certain path to unhappiness and misery. They are faced with an avalanche of emotion-packed options and for most, they cannot find a true anchor so they follow like sheep the voices of their peers.

38. People, especially mental health people, keep talking about therapy. The best therapy is wholesome activity and dedicated work. A day's work for a day's pay may be out of style, but it is great therapy and builds great self-esteem.

39. People say no one knows now what Jesus looked like. Neither does anyone know what God looks like and Jesus is God. So I fail to see the problem. He did not come to be an actor, but he came to be a savior of mankind.

People say the gospels are inconsistent in places and other criticisms. They say many people other than Christ claimed to be the Messiah. Well, what happened to them? Jesus changed the course of human history which no one can deny.

40. Love, honor, pity, pride, compassion, and abstract thought help define the heart of man. We must never surrender to the notion that man will not endure and always prevail on top of the phylogenetic scale.

We have a duty to protect our species against all intrusions by biotechnology or Hitler-like experimentation. We are unique and should always exist until Jesus returns.

41. "Flip for a Coke" is common and betting on ball games is rampant. Gambling in churches (Bingo) is endorsed. On the face of it, this appears an innocuous thing, but millions of gambling addicts started out this way.

I wonder if the Robe of Christ was offered by gambling tickets, which church could make the most money? I know Christ would drive the money changers out of the temple with a scourge of whips!

42. Registry in heaven's book of life. Man seems to fear anonymity. We register for many things and are included in the census. At an early age we write our names on things, carve our names on trees. George Washington carved "GW" under Natural Bridge in Virginia. The important thing is to have your name registered in that great book of life in heaven.

43. Extremists hurt the cause of true religions. Some faiths and individuals let their children die before they will allow physicians to give them blood transfusions. Others take the position that if God does not heal me, I am supposed to die. God expects us to use the medical advances and pharmaceuti-

cal wonders He has given men the brains and dedication to develop.

44. A holy war, whether by Christians (Protestants or Catholics), Muslims, Jews, Buddhists, Hindus is a misnomer. No religious war has ever been holy!

45. Josephus, the great historian, wrote, "All of us have mortal bodies, composed of perishable matter, but the soul lives forever! It is a portion of the deity housed in our bodies." Making certain that one's soul is saved from sin and the devil by Jesus Christ is the prime purpose of man.

46. One of President Kennedy's aides, Mrs. Lincoln, was summoned to Air Force One; JFK asked her to clear away some papers off his desk. She noticed a little note in the President's own handwriting, "I know that there is a God and I see a storm coming. If He has a place for me, I am ready." There are few people who sense death or calamity that do not turn to God.

47. Fame is such a fleeting thing and people spend too much time and energy seeking fame. Seek worthwhile goals. If fame comes, handle it gracefully and know it is as a thin shadow passing.

Can one name 10 of approximately 75 Academy Award winners for best actress? Can one name 10 vice presidents? Have you heard the name Napoleon mentioned lately or even Columbus?

We all come on the stage of life and pass off rather quickly. Even the famous are soon forgotten. Fame is a false goal to hunger and thirst after. Righteousness is the goal.

48. Self-preservation and rationalizing our beliefs are basic to man. Perhaps it is essential to place our beliefs on a pedestal above the beliefs of others. We should not, however, ignore those beliefs or demean the individual who has them, even if we decide their beliefs are incorrect.

Remember how difficult it is for oneself to even question a long-held belief. I have changed my interpretation of the word of God several times, but it is uncomfortable because I like to feel the Bible is an absolute and not subject to so many interpretations. Yet, my judgment tells me good people interpret the same passage in totally different ways. Still, I must accept what is rational to me.

49. AIDS is a terrible plague in Africa. The number of people infected is past the alarming stage. Other areas of the world are suffering also, but Africa is the area most in peril.

AIDS is not a curse on black people or gays. If any religion

is worth its salt, it should be concerned about suffering people. All religions make this claim. Sometimes I am ashamed of
the focus of my own religion when we spotlight trivia instead
of people in need. Hooray for the Salvation Army that has
lived by its motto, "Soup, soap and salvation!"

50. Fame should not negate moral responsibility as it usually does in our society. Looks and talents do not change
accountability for the individual. Oprah "shacks up" publicly
with a man who is not her husband; Elvis is practically worshipped even though he was addicted to drugs and lived a life
of sin. Frank Sinatra, Dean Martin, Mae West, Mickey Rooney,
Liberace — most any Hollywood character had or has great
impact on the youth of America. Yet we change the rules for
them, not to mention sports figures and politicians. But no one
is above the moral laws of God.

51. Individuals in the media play loosely with the truth.
Often they deliberately slant stories or tell outright lies. There
should be no double standard for the press. They are as
accountable as Joe the taxi driver for truth and fairness. If Joe
charges $15 and the fare is only $7, then we say Joe is a cheat
and a lying thief. I rest my case.

52. People yearn for super beings like Superman, Spider
Man, Wonder Woman, and hundreds of similar fanciful char-
acters created since then. I have wondered about this propen-
sity and wondered why Jesus, who walked on water, healed the
sick, raised the dead, and other super things does not fill this
yearning. He, as God, flung the stars in the sky!

53. Basic unifying things include man's innate sense of
fairness and justice, self-preservation, biological urges, cultural needs and curious intellects. We need to identify all of
the activities and practices that can bring us together. Music,
sports, art, travel, media, philanthropy, Peace Corps type programs and projects, space, environmental causes — all serve
to blend us into one species respecting each member of the
human race.

Sadly I admit the religions of the world have not unified the
people of the world in peace and understanding.

54. Worship can be entertaining, but entertainment can
never be worship. Many worship and so-called praise services
today with banners and dancing. It may be worship or may be
mostly entertainment.

Whatever happened to the preaching of God's word? A
group has the perfect right to worship as they please. They
can whirl prayer wheels, run fingers through beads, speak in

unknown tongues, dance, sing choruses 10 to 30 times to work up a shout with stars before loud microphones or whatever. They have that right and privilege in America and other places in the world. However, I have the right to say we should minimize this outer display and "preach Jesus and Him crucified."

55. We speak of heathen tribes destroying one another. Is this basically any different from the Irish in the name of a different interpretation of Christ destroying one another? Or in America wearing fancy uniforms, destroying the tribe from the South by the tribe from the North?

I think not. There are thousands of similar tribal wars started and perpetuated just because people are different or believe differently. We need to practice dialogue and peaceful negotiation and outlaw war. If a war is started, the remaining people in the world should not fund either side or supply weapons. The warriors should be isolated with severe sanctions. Are we all heathen? Is civilization a mere word?

56. The medical profession is to be honored and praised in most instances for their help to mankind. However, some have made a major error in regards to their attempt to umbrella non-medical things under their wing to enlarge their financial base. Some of these activities enable the individual to escape responsibility and results in a two-fold bad practice.

First, if a drunk senses he had a disease to come upon him, it was not his fault. It would be like contracting tuberculosis. Second, in that milieu of "couldn't help it," therapy can be ineffective and the disgusting situation can continue because who is going to blame the individual if he can't get well from a disease. Of course, the body becomes addicted on alcohol like drug addicts and then it has serious medical consequences. But the individual would not be an alcoholic if he or she had chosen not to drink.

So the choice — not a virus or bacteria — is the cause. If any therapy succeeds, it will involve the choice of the individual. You cannot choose to never have leukemia. You can choose never to be an alcoholic.

Some mild depressions and blues are not clinical depression and people, especially in Hollywood, keep a psychologist or psychiatrist on retainer or on call. These practices have been hurtful to the profession who for the most part tries to help desperate mentally malfunctioning individuals.

For umpteen years, personal responsibility was attached to excessive use of alcohol. What are the reasons this important analysis was changed to disease? The medical profession hems and haws and does not give a plausible answer to this question.

CODE 3-M should place the personal responsibility element back into the alcoholism plague.

57. God is in control. People may declare that He is dead or never existed. Let them explain this fact. Approximately the same number of boys and girls are born on little islands or in China. With the complexity of the X chromosomes and the amount released at conception you might expect the boy-girl ratio would be heavily skewed in small or even some large populations. War and other factors like mothers dying at childbirth have altered the proportions later on. Yet, why over the world or in Peoria is about the same girl babies and boy babies born? My atheist friends, this is not chance! God ordains it. We are to follow the creation of Adam and Eve, which started a family unit.

58. We need a healthy reasoned approach to sex issues. Bishop Fulton Sheen made a rather profound statement on the matter. "The Victorians pretended that sex did not exist; the moderns pretend that nothing else exists." Individuals should recognize that there are various levels of sexual desire and consider the fact carefully before marriage.

59. President John F. Kennedy issued a poignant statement that challenges the mind. "People have not been horrified by war to a sufficient extent. War will exist until that distant day when the conscientious objector enjoys the same reputation and prestige as the warrior does today."

This president fought in World War II and knew what he was talking about. He was trying to emphasize, I believe, that there needs to be a consciousness of the unspeakable tragedies of war. This is why I was anxious to join this group. Of course, there are times to defend the nation, but only after the majority of 535 people in Congress listen to the will of the people and then declare it!

If CODE 3-M does nothing but heighten the horrors of war, it's worth the effort. There is a little chorus from my childhood that goes spiritedly, "Jesus loves the little children, all the children of the world. They are yellow, black and white. They are precious in his sight. Jesus loves the little children of the world."

We should sing "decent folks love the little children" and so on through the song. And, decent folks want to prevent wars because they love the little children everywhere.

Someone or something can perhaps make you despise the tyrant of a nation or adults, but no one can stop a decent person from loving the little children. If we love them, we must do something to help them or that love becomes a "tinkling cymbal" with no melody or power.

60. What is enough? I raise the issue of insatiability of many humans. People are so stressed trying to get more things that they do not need and wonder why they are still unhappy and unfulfilled. They seek a road map to riches and care less about a guide for living.

It is almost impossible to go into a residential section in the US and drive past a house fairly late at night and not see at least two or three cars. Usually the driveway has several cars in it: his, hers and one for each child over 16.

Go to church. You have a tough time counting the expensive diamond rings on fingers, on ears and bordering wristwatches. No, this is not necessarily a sin, but it illustrates insatiability.

False religious prophets are begging on TV, "Send me seed money and God will make you prosper ten-fold." Manipulative letters are being sent out. One of my friends recently got one stating a TV evangelist saw his face in the sky and God told him he was to send him a certain amount of money. Beware of false prophets!

Getting rich seems to be the number one drive for many if not most people. Look at the success of lotteries everywhere. Many people spend their entire lives even after they are worth a million dollars striving to make more money and failing to stop and smell the flowers as they hurry by. They have not learned that money does not guarantee contentment and happiness.

The CODE should caution people that others are starving while they cannot settle for way above enough. I have stopped preaching one may say and gone to meddling, but each person should take stock on his or her possessions, how much he or she eats, how much money they waste and ask, how much is enough? It depends on one's motive to acquire wealth. Many sacrifice health to get wealth.

61. Forgive yourself once in a while. Then, take your burdens to the Lord and leave them there. The only perfect one is up in heaven. You will falter at times, fall beneath the load. Get up, go again. Your life and influence count for something. Make your life worth living and try to be a blessing.

62. Have faith rather than professing faith. Blondin, the

great French tightrope walker, won widely acclaimed fame in
1859 by crossing Niagara Falls on a tightrope. He then trun-
dled a woman in a wheelbarrow across the falls. When he was
about to do it again, another woman greatly encouraged him
saying, "You can do it, Blondin. I know you can!"

Blondin said, "Please get in the wheelbarrow." She ran
away.

The spiritual song I sang as a little boy, "Everybody Talking
About Heaven Ain't Going There," is so true. You have to
appropriate real, genuine faith to be a Christian. If you have it
and follow His word, you will go there. Amen and amen.

A fellow name George sent this poem to the "Dear Abby"
column. It was published, but it has no author's name. I cut it
out and keep it in my Bible.

THE COLD WITHIN

Six humans trapped in happenstance
In dark and bitter cold,
Each one possessed a stick of wood,
Or so the story's told.
Their dying fire in need of logs
The first woman held hers back,
For of the faces around the fire,
She noticed one was black.
The next man looking across the way
Saw not one of his church
And couldn't bring himself to give
His stick of birch.
The third one sat in tattered clothes
And gave his coat a hitch.
Why should his log be put to use
To warm the idle rich?
The rich man just sat back and thought
Of the wealth he had in store.
And how to keep what he had earned
From the lazy, shiftless poor.
The black man's face bespoke revenge
As the first passed from sight,
For all he saw in his stick of wood
Was a chance to spite the white.
The last man of this forlorn group
Did naught except for gain,
Giving only to those who gave,

Was how he played the game.
The logs held tight in death's still hands
Was proof of human sin.
They didn't die from cold without
They died from cold within.

64. Every person has the potential for good and evil. The so-called scientific studies indicating biological genes cause people to rape, murder, steal or torture others is not only misleading, but it is also dangerous. While expressing full wonderment and appreciation for the DNA advances, we must caution everyone not to get carried away with wild unsubstantiated theories.

No chemical or biological studies disprove that man is an intelligent creature capable of making many choices every day of his life. Slow down, science extremists before you get outside of truth and reality.

65. Face the death of a loved one with courage devoid of yearning for excessive self-attention. When a loved one transcends from mortality to immortality, family and friends can pause to celebrate the victory of a life that will be cherished forever. The highest tribute to the dead is not grief but gratitude.

66. Parenthood. Use love and the Bible when it says, "Spare the rod, spoil the child." This isn't a license for cruelty or using discipline when one is angry, but the Dr. Spock type of permissiveness for children has been disastrous. Most children are not accountable to parents, teachers, coaches, adults or anyone else. They think they have a right to do their thing regardless of the impact on themselves or others.

What has happened to discipline? I have no quarrel with people who maintain discipline without the rod. That is the better way.

However, some children do not respond to love and respect and psychology. They need to be told after reasonable explanation, "You do this or else." Sometimes the "else' is a non-injuring spanking. It is Biblical and whether it is politically correct or not, it is sometimes needed.

Never hit or slap a child. For some children a spanking at an early age can point the child in the right direction to learn there are serious consequences. I wonder how many children go on pot who were spanked early on for misbehavior. It would make an interesting survey.

No one knows exactly how to raise children; the same

approach for children in the same family can be faulty. However, somewhere, somehow, sometime a child needs to learn of serious consequences for serious wrong behavior.

67. The Internet is wonderful in many respects, but it is the greatest thing since sliced bread to build hate groups. It has also facilitated a rise in child pornography and other wrongs. Like the invention of the automobile, it is mostly good with some things on the downside. The bottomline is that it is here to stay.

We try to control drunk drivers. We sell them unlimited amounts of beer, wine, and liquor and put them in jail if they kill someone with a car. We will be about as successful trying to control the terrible things concerning the Internet, but we must make the effort to gain even the little success. All that glitters is not gold.

68. What a shame that religious holidays have been degenerated into an economic culture!

69. It may be legal to blaspheme, but that doesn't make it right. Gay Jesus plays and the like try to change what the Bible teaches about Jesus. They are exercising free speech, I suppose. I do not believe in Buddha, but I find no cause to blaspheme him.

70. Can there be morality and justice in the issues of union versus the company? Yes. First consider the mentalities of each side. The owner of the company or management has a set attitude: "It's our money, power and control at risk. The workers receive what we feel is right and fair. They would not have a job if it were not for us."

The workers have a set attitude: "Nothing we have gained in the past is negotiable." How much more money and benefits can we force the company to give us by our uniting together and threatening a strike.

So the adversary climate is created and usually stiffens in the first part of any meetings to resolve problems. Problems are best solved at the first meeting level. Others have to go to voluntary arbitration, or in some cases, to compulsory adjudication or a court decision.

The underlying force is greed on both sides. Both sides throw out the golden rule and self-interest sets on the throne. The company often is dishonest about its profits and the workers often do not care about quality or quantity and put in a partial day's work if they feel like it. Both sides rev up the accusations and a real thorny situation usually ensues.

Some solutions like giving company stock with the paycheck and similar ideas have worked well. However, the old what-is-enough greed grips the rich owners and their surrogates when the ice starts melting.

The Christian attitude — and I hope the position of our CODE 3-M — will be to respect both sides, listen patiently to opposing points of view, apply the Golden Rule, make certain all the facts are on the table, compromise as much as possible within decent, moral and ethical limits and honestly work for a fair solution. Compassion and respect can play critical roles.

You can control how you feel about anything by gaining a realistic and true perception. Eleanor Roosevelt said, "No one can make you feel inferior without your consent."

72. Religious tolerance. Those of us who believe in God and try to practice the principles of God know that we should be more tolerant of others. Possibly the keenest competition in the world today for converts is between Christians and Moslems. Since none of the seven chosen for our project is Islamic, I think we should consider the positive beliefs of this religion for inclusion in CODE 3-M.

I heard that few, if any from that faith, the Hindu faith, the Buddhist faith, or followers of Confucius were interested in this project. Anyway, Islam represents almost a billion people on earth and is now the second largest religious group. Islam means submission to the will of God. It is considered to be a divine revelation communicated to the world through Mohammed, who was the last of a succession of inspired prophets, beginning with Adam based on the word of God, the Koran, and the traditions and sayings and manner of life of Mohammed.

There is no God but Allah; Mohammed is the apostle of Allah (God). Mohammed was born about 610 A.D. The Father, Son, Holy Spirit or trinity is a mistaken concept. There is only one unity of God who is one of power, unity and goodness. Around the throne of God (Allah) are the angels: pure, sexless beings, some of whom bear the throne and some who praise Him continually. They are also His messengers and are sent to help the faithful in their fight with unbelievers. Some are guardian angels of men; some are watchmen of hell.

A Muslim follows five obligatory practices: recital of creed; performance of divine worship five times per day facing Mecca; fasting in the month of Ramadan if able or feed the poor; payment of legal alms; and make a pilgrimage to Mecca if able.

Devout Muslims maintain strict rules of conduct. Women

are expected to dress modestly, some even cover their faces in public. Sale and consumption of alcohol is forbidden. Eating pork is forbidden (like Orthodox Judaism).

Muslim places of worship are called mosques. The principle weekly worship is on Friday at midday. Most Muslims are Sunnites often called Orthodox Muslims. Less than three percent of Muslims are called Shiites. Most Shiites live in Iran and Iraq. The Shiites follow somewhat different rituals than the Sunnites and have additional holy days and holy places.

Mohammed based his teachings in part on Judaism and Christianity. He recognized Jesus as a prophet. Mohammed's teachings are contained in the Islamic holy book, the Koran, and are a distinct new revelation.

During the Middle Ages, Christian Europe mounted a number of attacks on Islamic states to try to free what they believed were holy lands. These attacks are known in history as the crusades. These bloody battles raged for hundreds of years back and forth even to this day. One has to make an in-depth study to understand the deep continued resentment of these two religions for each other, yet many Christians and many Muslims as well as many Jews yearn for peace and respect.

Though I am a Christian, I know there are some very good principles in the Muslim faith. How much better would the world have been, would be now, and would be in the future if we adopted their prohibition of the sale and consumption of alcohol?

There are many other positive practices in Islam. I appreciate the fact that Mohammed made an effort to blend in some Judaistic and Christian principles. There is some common ground to serve as a basis of peace between Jew, Christian and Muslim. The same can be said of the Buddhist, Hindu, Confucius, and other religions.

We must realize that acknowledging that other religions have good in them is not a betrayal of our own religion. This animosity is ammunition for atheists, agnostics or whatever. Back to my point. We must believe in and practice religious tolerance.

73. Separation of church and state. Religion should not seek to control government and government should not control religion. Most people buy that but the devil is in the details. A huge battle is now waging on these details.

I think two key words force and embarrassment should be the basis of regulating this sensitive issue. I will admit that I would not want to send my children to a class where the teacher kept a statue of Buddha on her desk, but I have been derelict in applying this principle if a Bible was on her desk like several of my school grade teachers. These matters are sensitive.

But I do know when moral and ethical teachings are abandoned that student behavior disintegrates. If we keep public prayer out of our schools and fail to recognize there is a God, then how do we handle it?

I would hope and dream that a school code of behavior could be extracted from CODE 3-M, but I'm pessimistic. Forgive me for raising an issue and not offering even a biased answer.

74. I'm puzzled by the fact many humans give their babies milk from animals and do not nurse their offsprings. Would there be less stress and more assured people if they had the advantage of being breast-fed when an infant? Perhaps not if the mother cuddled and loved the child while giving it a bottle of animal milk.

I believe the fragile baby is extremely insecure and needs something like the close loving contact that nursing provides. It seems to me we are producing more maladjusted people than societies that have continued this practice. I am not a pediatrician or a child psychologist, but this seems fundamental for building security and insecure people act in all kinds of inappropriate ways.

75. The color of racism is fear. Returning hate with hate is like biting the dog that bit you.

76. So-called honor killings. Recently in Cairo, Egypt, Nora was on her honeymoon when her father cut off her head and paraded it down a dusty street because she had married a man of whom he did not approve.

Begum was sleeping next to her three-month-old son when her husband grabbed a gun and shot her dead because a neighbor spotted a man not in the family near the field where she was working.

These and multiplied thousands of innocent women have been murdered to save the "family honor." Honor killings exist mostly in Muslim countries even though Islam does not sanction the practice. Any decent, fair minded person on the planet should abhor this act and work toward its elimination. This is one more reason for a workable world justice system.

77. Some so-called sex therapists are recommending sex surrogates. Of course, the surrogates do this for a price. This

is just another form of prostitution and another example of deterioration of the morals of this society.

78. CODE 3-M should make genetic rights an issue. There must be no discrimination by employees or insurance companies on anyone else if the DNA of an individual shows weaknesses. No one's DNA is perfect. One concern is "gene terrorism" might be employed by the enemies of decent people everywhere. It could perhaps be worse than bombs, gas, germs or the other debilitating and destructive methods.

79. It may or may not be morally wrong to allow the Boy Scouts to prohibit gay leaders, but it is the same principle whereby the law allows the Baptist church and others to prohibit gay marriages or women pastors. Government should stay out of religious practices and principles if they are not breaking laws like murder and thievery. The Pilgrims will have braved the treacherous waters of the Atlantic in their pitiful little vessel for nothing.

80. My God in Heaven! What have we degenerated into? Those against capital punishment have no pangs of conscience when a fully formed baby struggling out of the womb is murdered intentionally. Likewise, how can people abhor abortion and be strong supporters of killing criminals?

I must have lost it somewhere. For the life of me, this does not make sense. The crowd supporting baby killing says save the life of a serial murderer. Others say kill the murderer but absolutely no abortions. Can CODE 3-M resolve these illogical antinomies? I hope so, but I doubt it.

81. Wars never rest in peace. Old hatreds are difficult to extinguish. There seems to always exist an element that cannot stand to live in peace. Mix in hatred, political egos, and the willingness for the old cowards to send the young to die, for their cause, demonize the other side, mount false propaganda. Mix to a boiling point and you can have another war most anywhere.

The Vietnam debacle cost 58,000 American lives and over one million Vietnamese lives, for what? I am praying that somehow, someway humans can stop aggression. If so, no one will have to defend.

82. In the year 2000 A.D., Israel's Supreme Court finally banned torture by the Shin security service. Hopefully, other nations who practice torture in the world will also ban this inhuman procedure. Shame on all who are doing it and ever have done it.

CODE 3-M should make a strong stand against it for every

individual. Stand against it for every individual, just don't torture anyone.

83. The proverbs of Solomon are full of wisdom, instruction, understanding, equity, knowledge and discretion. I will list just a handful from over 300 that give the general theme, but I recommend each individual study all of them.

The fear of the Lord is the beginning of knowledge.

Despise not the cleansing of the Lord; neither be weary of His correction.

Happy is the man that findeth wisdom and the man that understands.

When thy liest down, thou shalt not be afraid for the Lord shall be thy confidence.

Withhold not good from them when it is due.

A good name is rather to be chosen than great riches.

A merry heart doeth good, but a broken spirit drieth the bones.

Train up a child in the way he should go and when he is old, he will not depart from it.

Where no wood is, there the fire goeth out; so where there is no talebearer, the strife ceases.

84. The ability to find creative solutions to challenges may be the highest form of intelligence and facing dangers, tragedies and sorrows reveal the innate strength of the human make-up.

85. Some critics of the Bible seemed to hark on the fact that there are four gospels and that they vary in their accounts concerning the life of Jesus.

Let me illustrate. An automobile accident happened. A boy shooting basketball goals heard the screech of brakes and saw the wreck when it occurred. An elderly person, coming out of a nearby store also saw it. A repairman up on a telephone pole looked down and he too observed the accident. Finally, a fourth person, a bread deliveryman, almost got hit in the accident, so he had yet a different perspective of the accident.

All four were asked to file a written account of what happened. The basics were similar, but each had details that the other did not see or know. So it is with Matthew, Mark, Luke, and John.

Matthew was a Jew who was giving his gospel for the Jews. All of the writers were writing under the influence of the Holy Spirit. He goes into great detail of genealogy tracing Jesus all the way back to Abraham to prove to the Jews that Jesus is the true Messiah they were expecting from the prophets. Mark does not emphasized genealogy, but he sees Jesus from his service role and as a servant to his Father and to mankind. Luke, a Gentile physician, highlights the son of man or human characteristics of Jesus and John, perhaps reviewing the other gospels saw Jesus more as the son of God and emphasized that side of Jesus. Four people all under the inspiration of the Holy Spirit wrote of Jesus in different manners according to their own background and personalities. I have no problem with that and I don't see why others would have problems with there being four gospels from four angles but telling of our wonderful savior, Lord and Master.

86. I have great compassion for homosexual people. They have been unfairly treated and deserve equal legal rights. However, I personally have never met a gay person, male or female, who was not burdened down with severe emotional misgivings and adjustment problems.

These problems arise I feel, after a compassionate analysis, have two fundamental etiologies: the bio-homosexual who is persecuted and really has no choice; and the homosexuals who chose homosexuality because of their emotional imbalance. The first group deserves our understanding and Christian love, so does the second group and Jesus Christ can change their chosen sexual identity.

87. The binding power of religion. Others may not believe the idea of a God, but the fact remains that our forefathers believed fervently and practiced a set of rules, though imperfect. The Pilgrims meant something to this nation.

I know there has been great slippage and one asks what has happened to the glue that once held our society together. Belief in God and fearing God was the glue. It has melted to a great extent. We are melting down morally and ethically even though there have been improvements in race relations and advances in science and gadgets.

If my people will repent and return, God will again bless America. We need more Jerry Falwells and Pat Robinsons and Billy Grahams to call us to repent.

DAVID PREAKNESS' ## LIST

1. The whole world needs to be a melting pot. The "us and them" is fine in high school sports and all go to the dance afterward, but adults and nations should know this philosophy carried to the extreme is an enemy of peace. Always has been. Always will be.

2. If we are serious about stopping war and advancing, I suggest this simple formula: just list all the rights that you claim for yourself and then give the same rights to each individual in the world.

3. The ideal is no abortions. The issue has been muddled up by the politicians and the religionists. In the final analysis, it should be up to the individual who is pregnant. Adoption should be easily accomplished and up front choices should be made before pregnancy occurs. Finally, it is the choice of the woman who is pregnant and within her exclusive authority.

4. When religious people murder other religious people because of deep hatreds and beliefs, it causes me to wonder if either side has a God worth man's allegiance.

5. I have admiration and stand in awe of man's basic empathy for suffering people. The good works of people outnumber the sorry acts in thousands to one ratio yet the airplane crash is the story that the media seizes.

I challenge the media to at least balance off the news 50-50. It would lift the spirits of good people and convey a more positive picture to young people.

6. My greatest fear is the pace of cataclysmic change and its enormous worldwide impacts. In the beginning of this millennium, we must discard so many time-worn ideas of the past that were held sacred in practically all of our fields of endeavor. We will be lost in the storm if we cannot provide an anchor.

I believe the answer is truth based on reasoning, logic and science and the abandonment of handed down myths and magical stories that have no evidence of truth.

7.   Man's survival as the humans we know is threatened. We must address the problem. We must set enforceable guidelines for biogenetics on a worldwide basis.

8.   Crime is no longer local or national. It is international in so many areas. We must think and act from a global matrix.

9.   What man has accomplished and will accomplish in the Third Millennium is beyond anyone's imagination. When the automobile was first demonstrated, experts said it would take nothing less than feeble mindedness to expect anything to come of the horseless carriage movement. Only six years later, Henry Ford's millionth car came off the production line.

In 1933 the great scientist Rutherford, who discovered the atom, said the energy in the atom's nucleus would never be released. Nine years later, the first chain reaction occurred. Do not disparage the ability of the brains of men set upon what seems to be the impossible dream.

10.   Humans want to know in the face of so many conflicting systems of religions what are the essential moral guidelines for contentment and happiness. The top priority of philosophical advance and discovery must be the organizing principles for one's life that really works.

We are making a stab at this need by our project to produce a fair and just CODE of living that is functional and founded on truth to give assurance it can produce workable guidelines.

11.   We are hungry for balance and fairness in our judicial system.

12.   One could argue there has always been a keen disparity between what people did and what they pretended to believe. True, but society can no longer pretend to believe irrational myths and cause wars when another system of untrue doctrines clash. The war mind set must go. Religion has failed miserably as glue for the world though it has been an impenetrable adhesive for the groups that believe in a certain God. What is the glue that can bind all humans together in true brotherhood? That is our quest and the essence of what we are seeking.

13.   I don't mean to sound sexist, but I firmly believe that if women were the only people to decide to go to war, there would be far fewer wars and finally none. It must be a terrible feeling to see a son or daughter you have carried beneath your breast marched off to die for a dubious cause. Of course, when

violently and massively attacked like Pearl Harbor women would wage war but how many other wars would they have endorsed? Not many.

14. We make heroes out of people who conquer drugs, alcohol and the like and ignore the real heroes who never abuse these curses. It is easy to understand why our young people look at this fact and reason that even if they do hit bottom, they can get help, be rehabilitated and become a hero.

They don't realize that over 90% are never fully rehabilitated and once an addition overcomes a person they, for example, will always be an alcoholic, straining and hoping not to regress and become a practicing alcoholic again. I would like to challenge all forms of media to show some heroes of boys and girls who refuse to be sheep.

15. A human being comes into this world alone and goes out alone. Family and friends, in most cases, are standing by at both events, but no one can substitute for you in birth or death. So, the responsibility of what one does with one's life is personal. He or she can live a good life that considers others and finds happiness or contentment or squander that opportunity. The choice belongs to each person.

16. Armies brainwash people using tried and proved methods. It is necessary to follow commands without thinking or arguing back on the battlefield. You will wear your uniform correctly. You will go where you are sent. You will salute when we say so and fire a weapon upon a command.

The same psychological dynamics are employed to keep the faithful in line in every religion. You are a Jew; therefore, you will abide by Jewish laws. You are a Muslim; therefore, you will pray towards Mecca five times a day. You are a Catholic; therefore, you will go to mass and confession and believe as the Pope says to believe.

There is little difference between soldiers in an Army and adherents to a religion. Obey the company line or else you get prison or hellfire. It is simple and effective. The old Prussian Army had it down to perfection much like the Jim Jones-type cults. No wonder so many people are filled with guilt and depression. The individual's choice and reasoning is not allowed. The church fathers and the huge following know best.

17. We should make our choices on the basis of moral principle, ethics, fairness and equal justice. Does this proposition ring true to me? Will our guidelines help or harm anyone else? We can learn to improve our actions and will be comforted when we choose the right thing for the right reasons.

18.   What would happen if you took the cost of building one aircraft carrier and its maintenance costs and applied it to medical research?

19.   If the 30-40 billions of humans who have been born and lived on Earth could put a page telling of their life history in a super computer, how many billions would have died from disease, starvation, natural disaster, old age, or war? Old age and natural disaster are tough to change although some are researching longer life and weather control.

We can certainly do something about disease, starvation, and war. We need to hasten the day when all babies can expect a good, happy life like many have enjoyed. It cannot be 100% but 100% is a great goal.

20.   Self-esteem is a primary goal for each person. Most if not all of the other virtues flow from the feelings of self-respect and worth.

21.   There are many impulses that make me wish they were some God to protect me and others and do all those great things. I cannot bring myself to say I know there is a God. I cannot say there is no God. I am not satisfied with saying I don't know so I will classify myself as a seeker or quester.

I really would like to find if there is a God and what the role is for him in human affairs. So far, the beliefs in the strange gods people worship cannot pass my criteria of compassion, reason, logic and science. If I don't use any of these criteria, I could put the Gods in a hat and just pull one out and worship him. That repulses my mind. There is something about humans that yearn for a higher power.

22.   Sometimes the world seems like a giant kaleidoscope, changed with one small twist or perhaps a new invention like the printing press or computer changes the whole pattern of the lovely picture. These small twistings are increasing at logarithmic speed. Adapting to change is one of the highest forms of intelligence. I just hope we can adapt for changes that are happening at a rate never experienced before.

23.   Those of us who fail to subscribe to any particular religion must continue to realize that despite all the hatreds and wars religions have generated, lots of positive things for the human race like hospitals, feeding the hungry, education and thousands more.

24.   Saudi Arabia, the country saved during the Gulf War by the allies, follows a very strict penalty for criminals. Tranquilized prisoners are led into a public square blindfolded their feet shackled, their hands cuffed behind them. With one

swing of the sword they are beheaded for crimes ranging from murder to drug trafficking.

The authorities say this method of dealing with criminals is justified by the need to keep law and order. The latest crime figures show this method is very, very effective. While I am not proposing CODE 3-M adopt this method, a sensible balance between America's slap on the wrist attitude is sorely needed.

25. The transcendence of celebrity should be an issue. It is wrong to accept celebrity misbehavior or crime and practice a double standard. Every person must be equal under the law.

26. Ambition is worthy as long as it does not carry the sinister agenda to control others.

27. Men in mostly European countries often sing together. It is a lost art except for the very talented in America. Music is the universal language and universal participation could be very positive. Each boy or girl should have the opportunity to play some kind of instrument. And all should sing whether or not they are always on key.

This is a relatively small thing but a powerful thing. The world needs more music. I realize a lot of shock vulgar words are in so-called fad music and it is rampant but one can choose to ignore it. Good up-lifting music will never go away. Embrace it.

28. Messianic Jews believe Jesus is the only answer. Beaming a large TV program out of Phoenix, they are converting souls to Christianity. Ultra-Orthodox Jews, Orthodox Jews, Conservative Jews, Reform Jews all consider this a proseliting effort and condemn it, yet they allow individuals from any religion to convert to Judaism.

This type of animosity between religions and efforts to belittle the other and sometimes erase the other believers does not represent a system that attracts the objective, caring, reasonable person.

29. God is love. This is about the only definition our group can agree upon and some don't accept that definition.

30. Racial hatred knows no boundaries. It is not just a white and black issue. In Vietnam, Asian people treat half-Asian and half-African-American children like dogs or worse. Racism is wrong whenever it raises its ugly head and we should recognize it as artificial and eliminate it.

31. Only a century and a half ago, just a small fraction of human history, a person could be an upstanding member of a religious group, even a congressman, an ambassador or a president and still own other humans like a piece of property.

There was no moral compass and they should not be honored today — none of the slave-owners.

Churches that allowed membership to slave-owners should disband in disgrace and have a public burning of their age-old creeds that did not prohibit slavery. Then they should start over again with basic decency.

"Most everybody did it" is a lame unacceptable excuse. It is most difficult for me to honor anything Washington, Jefferson and others had to say and believed because they were slave-owners.

32. The surest way to stop war is to let the populace of the countries involved vote on it.

33. Life should be a continuous celebration. At the beginning of each day, one should pause and contemplate how wonderful it is just to have life. It will be a better day. You know so many that would love to have one more day of life.

34. Some parents who adopt children render unconditional love. This should take precedence over biological parents who claim a change in heart in later years. A little four-year-old Korean boy had been abandoned by both parents, begged for weeks on street corners for food. He did not get very much, so he sneaked into an American battle unit.

One American soldier saw him and held out his hand. The little boy grabbed and felt love for the first time in his life. The soldier built a little shed for him and made sure he had plenty to eat and fathered him when he was not on duty in the front lines. Finally, he took him home to be with his wife and children and adopted him. The family received him as a full member of the family.

The boy later became a successful businessman. His biological parents learned of his good fortune and wanted him to reconcile with them. They wrote that blood was thicker than water. The gentleman wrote back, "It may be, but love is thicker than blood."

35. Good positions can create strange bedfellows in religion. Muslims and Pentecostals, for example, are very far apart in doctrine, but on the evils of tobacco and alcohol they agree and have always agreed 100%. There are other areas of agreement to which all churches would agree. So, if we can ferret out these areas, accentuate them and eliminate the huge disagreements as far as CODE 3-M is concerned, we will have accomplished something.

36. Power needs to be dispensed and control should know reasonable limits. The riddle of the ages is how to get capable

leadership that will not lust for too much power and control. The Golden Rule seems to be forgotten when power and control infect the thinking of once very good people. The masses must make its strongest effort to keep leaders who care and will do the right thing, as they would desire the right thing to be done unto them.

37. Humans have a genius for creation and sadly a genius for destruction. Be a human who creates and never destroys the good and worthy things that should continue. Everyone should know our destructive ability is bad — the practice of war to settle disputes, ignoring the environment, and letting babies starve. Let us destroy these practices.

38. Opinions are fine if labeled as opinions only. The danger comes when a gullible individual takes opinions to be absolute facts. He becomes a mental slave without thinking for himself rather than forming his own opinion based on his own perspective. These may not be factual, either, but it is honest and then one can seek indisputable facts.

39. Which is the largest threat today — atom bombs or anthrax (deadly bacteria) and the like from terrorists? This is a no-brainer.

40. The herd mentality is fine for sports arenas, political conventions and the like, but when it comes to your destiny and the way you should conduct your own life, back off and let the stampede go by.

41. One eulogy statement is my goal. He passed the test of a positive, caring life and the world is better off because David Preakness tread upon it.

42. One thing, among many, the CODE can draw from comes from Confucius, "Know what is right and not do it is want of courage or of principle." Confucius lived from 551 B.C. to 479 B.C. This 72-year life touched millions of people and still claims a following of over six million today.

For more than two centuries, Confucius was the dominant philosophical system in China. It strongly influenced Chinese culture and Confucius is still perhaps the most revered name in Chinese history. He was a pioneer of social reforms and taught "the way" or the one thread that challenged the individual to be a superior man of perfect virtue who helps others in this effort.

He wanted the family to be harmonious and the state to be well ordered. He strongly wanted the world to be at peace. He believed in moral self-cultivation by manifesting one's clear character, loving the people, and abiding in the highest good.

This could be accomplished through his eight steps: investigation of things; extension of knowledge; sincerity of the will; rectifying the mind; cultivating personal life; regulating the family; ordering the state; bringing peace to the world.

I think we have some very worthy goals here. His grandson Tzu Ssu (483-402 B.C.) spoke of harmony of the emotions and operations of all things in harmony. The way of all existence is absolute, intelligent and indestructible. Mencius (human nature is originally good) versus Hsun-Tzu (human nature is evil and needs discipline) was a challenge for people to decide. Plato and Aristotle in Greece about this period had views somewhat similar to the idealistic Mencius.

Both Mencius and Hsun-Tzu were disciples of Confucius and had the same aims as their leader, a perfect moral individual and harmonious social order. Taoist hermits chided Confucius and made him a favorite object of ridicule.

Undaunted, Confucius condemned force as a way of life and opposed the obsession of power and control of the "legalists" who won out. They helped establish the Chinese Empire about 221 B.C. The Confucius school of thought was almost wiped out leaving the "legalists" the sole controller of ideas.

This dynasty, however, only lasted 14 years and the Han dynasty took over, first favoring "legalism" and Taoism and finally turning to Confucius. Tung incorporated into Confucius the Yin-Yang philosophy which considers everything the product of negative cosmic force, Yin, and positive cosmic force, Yang.

In 136 B.C. Confucius was proclaimed the state doctrine but not in a strict religious sense. Though it promoted the traditional worship of heaven, sacred mountains, rivers and ancestors, its influence and supremacy was in the secular realm. The universe originated from a prime force called one or origination. Confucius considered Taoist and Buddhists religions as appropriate only for the ignorant. Transmigration (the supposed passing of the soul at death into another body) was nonsense; the acceptance of heaven and hell was motivated by selfish people who were gripped with fear.

Another teaching was filial piety or the authority of parents over their children. It influenced both Korea and Japan. Japan prostituted the Confucius ethical ideas and formed the CODE of Bushido or the Way of the Warrior. Confucius' followers believed man is not a man of the sword but of moral nobility — never a fighter but a scholar/gentleman.

Confucius avoided discussion of spirits and life after death.

He wanted man to direct their own destiny rather than allow the spirits to do it. Yet he himself worshipped a kind of heaven and declared it was grand. He was and is viewed mostly as the "foremost teacher" instead of being a deity. He taught the natural laws of retribution — acts of goodness and evil will bring their own consequences. He believed in a future Utopia on Earth. Confucius frowned on drama and novels because they often played upon vulgar emotions.

In 1949, the Communists gained control of China and outlawed the national holiday on the birthday of Confucius. However, there remains a huge, cautious following that no doubt will outlive discredited communism. Confucianism will once again rise even to a higher pedestal than ever in China.

Confucius was largely self-educated yet he was the most learned man of his day. He abhorred the wars made by the aristocrats and strongly advocated reform. The rulers of his native state paid him little attention. Yet, Confucius became one of the most influential men in world history.

Those of us who are trying to forge a CODE for human living should know these things and many other things about Confucius for two reasons. First, his unwavering stance against war is to be emulated and his strong promotion of peace are cornerstones of our CODE 3-M.

Second, 25% of the world's population is in China and the proportion will be higher in the future. Understanding some basics of Confucius may reveal a considerable amount of common ground, thereby serving as a foundation for cooperation and peace.

43. The David Dukes, Al Sharptons, Jesse Helms, Jesse Jacksons and other extremists can never solve the problem of racism in America. The Jimmy Carters, Bill Russells, Bill Bradleys, the Doles, the McGuires, the Sosas, the Tiger Woods, and Gov. Jeb Bush and wife-type could.

If people are profiteering from the problem, why would they want to solve it? Better yet would be a bunch of intelligent and caring young people. I hope Mr. Morgan, our sponsor, will consider this for his next project.

44. When one free-associates and has no boundaries, it is remarkable how many new ideas come to your thinking. Some of them — perhaps most of them in my case — should just pass on through. But I feel comfortable that the other six will throw out my extreme ideas like the judges do when deciding who wins the gold, silver and bronze metal in ice skiing in the Olympics. Likewise, I will see some of their items as being off

the wall. Nevertheless, it is worth the effort for me for I have learned so many things I never knew as I pondered and researched some of my thoughts.

45. World people power is developing through the internet and it is a wonderful, glorious thing it may eventually show the politicians that if they announce a war, no one or only a handful will show unless it is such naked aggression that none can deny. And massive peace efforts and global condemnation should come down on the aggressor. Sanctions have not worked because all nations will not enforce them. If they did, the power of the people within the aggressor nation would overthrow the tyrants.

So, come on people of the world, you can change things. It can and will be done by one individual adding his or her weight to the critical mass! Obviously, a complete unification of humans on planet Earth is centuries away. However, there is reason to believe it is inevitable. I wish I could be living during that time. Many steps will have to be accomplished. I will briefly suggest a dozen.

Continued increase in travel and vacationing trips.

Continued increase in trade and economic union like Europe. Fifteen nations of Europe have already developed an Euro-currency to replace individual nation's money. Ireland, France, The Netherlands, Italy, Denmark, Austria, Germany, Luxembourg, Finland, Greece, Spain, Sweden, Great Britain, and Portugal have blazed the path for more nations to fuse together for each other's benefit. May it happen all over the world! Wars would cease and a golden era would begin for all humanity! The Euro could become international.

Continued increase in student interchange.

English language teaching grants and bonuses for students who learn the language sponsored by all English-speaking countries.

Mandatory nation and world culture study in each high school all over the world using videos and students from the various nations. No examinations, just exciting learning. Credits given and average of other grades is automatic grade.

Open more borders gradually on a selected basis that will cause the least disruption

Increase sports leagues to include many more nations.

Interchange of college credits so that 50% may be earned in other countries.

Increase sharing of technical information.

Sharing arts.

Donation of computers, tractors, generators, and other strategic equipment with reasonable tax breaks.

Government and religion non-aggressive pacts and many more such steps.

46. What we know now is like one page of a huge volume. Page 2 through whatever seems to be glued together but the last piece of information on page one has told us how to get to page 2 and this pattern will be followed for the huge volume and for future millenniums. What we do know for certain and scientific fact pales in comparison to what we don't know and what humans will know someday.

Yet, we should be very proud of our page. We have been inquisitive. We have learned by trial and error. We have advanced from ignorant tribes who could neither read nor write nor record advancement. We don't even know when the wheel was invented, but we now know when the first computers were invented and patented.

So we do not stand ashamed of our progress but we stand in awe with just a glimpse of what we will learn and develop in the future. Let's all get excited and turn to page 2 as we enter the Third Millennium.

47. We have entered a number of new eras; we are on the verge of realizing a positive world that is beyond our wildest dreams. We can do it if we stop fighting each other. However, we have to abandon the pervasive stupid philosophy of us versus them. This attitude has got to go in religion, race relations, nationalism and all other things obviously divisive.

We have the time and knowledge to accomplish all of these promising things. Can we muster the will to do it? I believe we can. I know we must.

48. The unacceptable disparity between the haves and the have-nots is a cause of desperation and hate . This often leads to murder, war and destruction. The solution is not as complex as some would have it be. The haves need to show compassion as many already do and create opportunity by sending tractors instead of cannons and pure water instead of radiation.

The have nots should seize any and every opportunity as many now do, take the needed assistance to move forward coupled with a determination like was demonstrated by the people who were welcomed by the Statue of Liberty in the 1800's and early 1900's. Most had nothing but determination. Now many have-nots have assistance but little spunk and determination.

I do not believe anyone accepts the notion that most

humans want to live on handouts or tax handouts by the society. Most want to be independent and make it on their own. The simple answer is for the haves to care and create and for the have-nots to be determined and appreciate. Of course, there are exceptional cases where determination even with help won't do it for certain handicaps and obvious inadequacies. Most people do not object to taking care of these precious people. They object to the sorry, healthy, lazy people who want to sponge off the society and not contribute a dime to it. CODE 3-M will, I believe, emphasize individual responsibility. This goes for the rich and the poor.

49. As a seeker and a quester in religious matters, I will have to formulate the best conception I can to create for me a God. I do not feel capable at this time to do this, although I have not encountered a deity that I could honestly worship. If I ever try to fashion a true God, it will not be a negative God of vengeance and selfishness and destruction but a God of consistent love and support of my efforts to help my fellow-man.

50. People who constantly complain of boredom have a very short list of things that they could list as selfless acts for others for no compensation or glory other than the inner satisfaction that feeds one's spirit. Increase the list and you can throw the word boredom out of your consciousness. And you will not get depressed.

51. A 33-year-old Caucasian man recently decided to donate a part of his healthy liver to anyone high on the list. A 52-year-old Hispanic man received the liver transplant. Both are doing very well. The recipient finally met the donor after a determined search. Do you think the donor is ever bored? Is he ever depressed? I doubt it. I think he deserves lots of brownie points. Let us all add to our list and raise our grade.

52. Algebra and other similar courses should not be mandatory in high school. Latin, a dead language, used to be required in some schools. Why do we persist in turning off our youth in education? Consider the fact 90% of students forced to learn algebra have never used it.

Algebra should be an elective for the few that have a foreseeable need for it. A few other mandated courses are suspect as well. We would be better off if we taught manners and ethics. Yes, I took algebra, solid geometry and advanced statistics. I made very high grades, but it should not have been a have to do-or-die course.

Are we trying to create juvenile delinqueny or just being

stubbornly ignorant? The entire educational system needs a new beginning and adopt a more realistic approach.

Finally, I believe in good standards in education. There should be higher pay for those professionals most of whom are very dedicated. They have to be surrogate parents and are burdened down with paperwork trivia.

53. Advances in technology can be scary. Thus far we have accommodated them sometimes well, sometimes less than admirable. What if someone develops an invisible death ray released from a gun mechanism. Let's imagine it can fit inside a ballpoint pen and its deadly beam of destruction only activates a month or six months later.

Talk about people being eliminated with no clues and no justification. It would be perfect for murderers and for the good guys to take care of the bad guys. Anyway, the thought of the consequences are fantastic and troublesome. I hope such an invention never happens. Who knows?

CODE 3-M would be against any use of this imagined weapon by anyone and try to get it outlawed worldwide like germ warfare. But there will always be a few Saddam Husseins around. We must be very vigilant as unbridled technology marches boldly into the future.

54. Build a new bridge before you take down the old one is sound advice. The new bridge could be CODE 3-M for some. Others will want to keep the old bridge because they have used it before and it did not fail them. Some will reject completely the concept of a new bridge; others will put a foot on the new bridge and a foot on the old bridge.

Another group will sense the old bridge has had its day. After all, many planks are rotten and as soon as the new bridge opens they will use it alone. Some will not understand what I am writing about and just go on the same old way. I believe in the individual's right of choice.

55. When the economy goes up because of jobs to create weapons of destruction, that is blood money. Youths have died on the battlefield as their friends got greatly improved wages in munition factories all over the world. This is not right.

Even worse is some tyrant who puts out false propaganda in order to start a war. People usually rally around their leader, even a despot leader. A brief review of the history of wars turns the stomach of decent people and we know only a few of the inside facts.

56. One can be a righteous hero despite discrimination and many have done it like Mahatma Ghandi and Martin Luther

King, Jr. Gandhi was denied the right to practice law in South Africa although he had lived there for ten years. Why? He was not of white European descent.

King was set upon by Bull Conner's police dogs, but how many streets and boulevards are named Bull Conner? It has always moved me deeply how the oppressed overcame and still manage to love their oppressors. Is not that a most wonderful attribute?

57. I Timothy teaches that a deacon must not be given to much wine. Millions of people drink not much wine and do not give in to alcoholic beverages enough to become alcoholics. Good for them.

However, billions have become alcoholics who begin with wine. Does their example ever cause young people who cannot control the alcohol to begin? Some youths become alcoholics and live wasted lives that cause untold sorrow to others. It is an individual choice. It has great ramifications.

58. A good philosophy from Buddha is, "There is no fire like passion, there is no shark like hatred, there is no snare like folly, and there is no torrent like greed."

CODE 3-M could not say it so eloquently but should support it 100%.

59. I have often wondered how the top intelligent people in Egypt, Greece, Rome, Babylon, and other lands of polytheism really felt about the ridiculous amount of gods they were supposed to worship and their silly rules. I suppose they had to keep their true feelings secret or be completely ostracized or killed.

It is the same today in some parts of the world. In something as crucial as how to live and one's destiny, why can't individuals have the right to choose without the oppression of government, family or whatever?

60. The Miss Universe Pageant is a beautiful example of how people of every religion or no religion can cooperate and live together, play together, sight-see together, and wind up with life time friendships despite religions that hate each other. This type of activity will hasten world understanding and world peace.

61. "The World Is Waiting for the Sunrise" could be a theme song for CODE 3-M. Thousands of songs fit the thrust and purpose of the CODE like "What the World Needs Is Love Somehow" and "We Are the World." Many thousands more will be inspirational to any member of the human race.

62. Billy Sunday, the baseball pitcher who turned into a

fiery evangelist, preached, "If there is no hell, a good many preachers are obtaining money under false pretenses." Right on Billy, preach it! If there were a hell many money-grabbing TV evangelists would be on top of the list to go there with their false claims and outright lies on TV.

63. Character *is* important. The Code must strive to build character in people because it counts.

64. A one on one murder is a small war. Gangs declare war and often death occurs because of "macho" gone wild. You don't have to have a worldwide war for it to be war. Tribal warfare is our ancient heritage. The question is how to rise above the ridiculous concept of killing off people. We have to learn to live and let live, except in a few extreme cases of defense where a person or a nation has to act.

65. Laughter is positive. Laugh often. Laugh out loud. Laugh at yourself, never at others when inappropriate. Laughter when genuine is so contagious. Cause others to laugh. Great comedians can make people laugh without vulgar four-letter words. So can you.

"Jingle Bells" speaks of laughing all the way. It is good for you and you will enjoy it. There are things that happen each day in our lives that are very funny. So laugh all you please. If you can't laugh, then giggle — whatever.

We cannot do what we need to do without a little humor here and there. Humor is absolutely essential for a happy life and good personality.

66. Man has lived in caves, in igloos, tents, houses, mansions, cardboard boxes, trees, cars, vans, shacks, castles, and skyscrapers. The important thing is not the house you live in but how you put purpose to your life. Turn your eyes away from the material and grow the moral, ethical and philosophical to gain enrichment and satisfaction. A certain level of money and things are legitimate but how much is enough?

67. Benny Hinn goes to Trinidad, an island with many Hindus, blurts out, "This is a country full of devils and demons." Evangelical churches are being planted all across Trinidad.

Hindu leaders are fighting back. Sat Maharas said, "We launched a counter campaign." It includes literature pointing out inconsistencies in the Bible and calls the new religion a group with undue focus on material possessions.

Pastor Allen from the Bible Way Church in Virginia Beach, Virginia retorts, "We're in the soul-saving business. He commanded us to make disciples and that's what we are doing."

This is another brazen example of religions fighting for

people's souls. Can't they see that aggressive soul-saving causes murder and wars? Don't they read elementary history or
present day newspapers? Is it ego need and greed?

68. Many psychologists and psychiatrists, along with psychiatric nurses and social workers, have gone off the deep
end. They have come up with a term "dyssemia." This diag-
noses some toddlers with the inability to fit in socially and
suggest therapy.

Our children can't simply be shy, aggressive, loud, bored,
unhappy, and exuberant anymore. Instead they must fit a specific behavior pattern which the shrinks define as normally
adjusted and fully acceptable to the group. Otherwise it's off
to therapy.

Some see this tripe as being incredible and ridiculous. I
prefer the more educated term, "Hogwash." Of course, a small
child can be psychotic, but it is rare. Getting some children on
a therapy train might actually cause mental problems.

69. What if Jews, a religious group, had never existed? The
world would be without many marvelous things and ideas. No
group so small even comes close to the positive contributions
Jewish people have made with such a tiny ratio of the world's
population.

Yet, their extreme obsession to keep Jews from marrying
others is antithetical to world understanding and cooperation.
Today, there is a speed-dating program whereby Jewish men
move from table to table after a seven-minute social
encounter with available Jewish females. They then decide
whether they want a full-length date. But all hell breaks loose
when a Jewish boy marries a Gentile girl that he loves or a
Jewish girl marries a Catholic.

This common prohibition in many religions is an affront to
the individuals. It is mindless malice and poisonous prejudice
wrapped in foolish fanaticism. CODE 3-M should support any
person truly in love and desirous of interfaith marriage to proceed with heart, rather than outside pressures from anyone or
any religions prejudice. We must mix up the races and religions when true love occurs.

70. Many say your immortality goes on in your children,
not a religious doctrine. Who knows?

Another view that is not a physical type of immortality is
the introduction of special ideas and creative thinking. If one
adds anything to the truth or scientific body of knowledge,
composes a useful drama, music composition or lasting poem,
that is a type of immortality.

Joyce Kilmer's "I think that I shall never see a poem lovely as a tree" gives a touch of immortality and as long as it is read and admired, he lives on through this great little poem because it is a part of him that will never die in my opinion. That kind of immortality can be an inspirational challenge for each person. Frank Rooney said, "Immortality is the genius to move others long after you yourself have stopped moving."

71. Each person needs tangibility to validate themselves. Good works you know you did and did not have to do are a wonderful validation act. Helping the handicapped, feeding the poor, saving the environment, and important causes where you see tangible and indisputable evidence is the key. You have to know you made a difference. If you make a positive difference, big or small, you validate yourself as a worthwhile person. The more, the better.

72. National pride at this stage of human development is okay, if not taken to the extreme of aggression. An earthquake in Turkey not long ago killed 18,000 people in a few hours. People from European countries, the Americans, Asians, Australians, and others from all over the world joined in to help.

Yes, we are our human brother's keeper regardless of ethnic or religious differences. We must magnify this spontaneous spirit to help following a catastrophe and help people in starving catastrophes because they are humans and we care for them. It often seems so far away and we are not certain of how we can help.

Find a good organization like the Red Cross or Salvation Army and others. Ask them how you can help. If you are on a close budget, you can wrap packages — whatever. Beware of religious con artists and groups that spend most of their donations on operating expenses. If possible, do it hands on.

There are desperate needs in every community. Check with the fire stations and see if you can help a family that has lost everything. Show the honest feeling you care to help and be your brother's keeper for everyone wherever they are suffering on the planet. This spirit will someday bring us all together in brotherhood and peace.

73. Most of us owe so much to others. We need to concentrate on that instead of what we expect from them. This is the secret of building abiding friendships necessary for a happy and fulfilled life.

We must resist the obsession to discover mistakes made by our public figures in hopes that we can bring them down. Mistakes are part of everyone's life and the quality and quantity of mistakes is important. The Golden Rule must apply.

President Bush is often completely discredited despite all the very positive things he did for America and the civilized world because of his statement, "Read my lips — no tax increases." The fact that the opposition party would not pass any budget without increases does not seem to mitigate the statement at all with some people. This is not fair.

One candidate using the term "brainwashed" referred honestly to himself. Another shed tears about the negative things the press revealed about his wife. The overall grade of a person is what is important. You do not build trust and loyalty by criticizing or bringing down someone.

Most people could not be much of a success if it was not for the interest and contributions of others. We need to not only reciprocate, but also make an effort to boost and contribute to those we love and friends we are fortunate to have made on this earth. Lives are inexplicably intertwined. Easy forgiveness and conscious overlooking is what we need to receive and what we need to give. Remember that no one scores 100.

74.   There is so much confusion about what Jesus was like. If He was a literate person, why did He not write about who He was, His mission and His personally written ideas about human conduct. All we know about him comes from others who wrote of him in somewhat conflicting terms. This assumes Matthew, Mark, Luke, and John were the authors of the gospels as widely believed and it was not written by James, the brother of Jesus. There may have been an unduly influence by Paul who never knew Jesus.

If only He had kept a diary interspersed with His own ideas or if He would appear now on TV and straighten up the tangled mess. The world could know more truth and be rid of so much confusion. This applies to some other deities of other faiths as well.

75.   A miracle is an event or action that apparently contradicts known scientific laws. Miracles are believed to be supernatural or an act of God.

The Bible is replete with such recordings, but there is no way we can know if they are true. So many so-called miracles claimed today have a plausible scientific basis or fall in the category of deceit and false claims for personal or religious gain.

It is strange that Jesus, the disciples and others, performed so many miracles centuries ago and I cannot find a single miracle that rings true today. The acts of Superman and the like keep our desires for miracles, but even children know he is fictional. How much of the Bible is fiction? Who knows?

76. We must oppose genocide whenever and wherever it occurs. A genocide convention outlawed acts committed with intent to destroy, in whole or in part an ethnic, racial or religious groups. Since the Holocaust in Cambodia, one million dead, 1 million displaced; Rwanda, 1 million dead, 3.5 million displaced; Bosnia, 300,000 dead, 2 million displaced are other examples of genocide.

Any decent human being would not partake in such destruction and as an individual, do not do it. Escape from tyrants that force you to engage in genocide. It is terrible and wrong as can be; this is a sound reason for more globalization and cooperation in trade and government. Someday these hatreds will cease, but it appears to be way into the future. We have to overcome our sordid past carried on by tyrants, governments and religions. It can start with me and you can be next.

What are the origins of human sacrifice? It is a tough research challenge. Perhaps polytheism and mythology contributed more than we realize. Minotaur, of Greek mythology was a monster with the body of a man and the head of a bull. Each year he was fed seven youths and seven maidens from Athens until Theseus finally killed him.

Extreme Hindus, believing the Ganges River to be God, have thrown thousands — perhaps tens of thousands — of babies into that river. The Aztecs used humans as sacrifices to their gods. Abraham almost used his only son as a sacrifice. What a distasteful, heathenistic concept!

I don't know the origin of the inhumane and disgusting practice, but it still happens today on a small scale. It should be roundly condemned and outlawed everywhere. This is a perfect example of how ridiculous a religious group can be when it abandons science, reason, love, and common sense.

77. Freedom cannot exist without basic virtues. The foundation of honesty, fairness, and respect for others, all others, is imperative.

78. Anthropomorphism, ascribing human-like characteristics to animals, has been a phenomenon since the beginning. One wonders if there is not such a thing as "theomorphism" as we attempt to make our gods so much like us. Instead of man being created in the image of God, should not it be that God is created in the image of man?

79. The writings of history from the beginning have been

fragmented, sparse and in many instances suspect of actual happenings. Forty-four men over a span of centuries wrote the Bible. The Apocrapha and Dead Sea scrolls are not included, but many claim they too are inspired scripture. It is so difficult to trust such a haphazard set of writings with the horrible stories and conflicts. With the printed press, things improved and with newspapers, magazines, books, library, microfilm, movies, videos, CDs, recordings of historical facts now are much more reliable. They are not fully reliable, however, because many historians feel a compulsion to rewrite history without substantial evidence, according to the conventional wisdom of their era.

Wouldn't it be wonderful if we had a factual video of all of man's history? We are improving and we have already reached the place where it is getting more difficult to distort history. One wonders how much distortion exists in just the last two millenniums.

We must dedicate ourselves to accurate history for future humans that is highly reliable and substantial by irrefutable documentation of many sorts. So much of what we think we know about history probably did not happen at all. Many important things that did happen have been blocked out by religionists of all kinds and slanted beyond repair. The future looks bright and positive for a more accurate and less biased history of man and his doings.

80. My favorite quote from President Eisenhower is, "When people speak to you about a preventive war, you tell them to go fight it. After my experience, I have come to hate war. War settles nothing."

If each human can see the wisdom of this statement and act accordingly, there will be no more wars.

81. Do not take yourself too seriously. You are a very important person. You can make a difference if you do your best. Keep in mind that billions and billions of humans have lived before you were born and billions upon billions will live after you are gone. Strive to make a good grade for your life, but you will always be one little tiny grain of sand on a million-mile sandy beach. Your positive actions coupled with others will count tremendously for the good, but never get puffed up in your own importance.

82. One billion people on earth now at the start of the Third Millennium do not have safe drinking water that can keep them from a number of fatal diseases. The cost of even a relatively small war could change that.

Some big city water plants use chemicals to purify water. Others have found ultraviolet light does even a better job of killing disease-causing bacteria and viruses. And ultraviolet light works in a very short time. A pen using ultraviolet light that will sterilize 35 glasses of water has been developed. So it is only a matter of money and will to get clean water to these billion people.

We shall continue to convert seawater into drinking water and continue to advance methods of water purification. Surely this cause will get a 100% vote of any group anywhere.

83. In so many areas of the world in every nation, people are persecuted, prosecuted, and executed unfairly. Mankind has some basic sense of justice, but it is often blurred. This cannot be corrected overnight, but it can be and it must be corrected.

84. One lingering doubt I do not comprehend is about God, the protector of his people as taught in scripture. It just is not true. You can look around your own little life and list one saintly person after another who had to experience untold suffering, ravaging disease, accident victims, pain unspeakable and death, many of them in relatively early age.

You may have heard them sing, "My heavenly Father watches over me" or similar phrases to assure themselves that God was surely looking after them.

A young missionary called to give his life in service to God in a hostile foreign land served for many years. His wife was ravaged by four soldiers as a gun was held to his head; he became mentally imbalanced. Where was God? Now, they both fear that they may have the AIDS virus.

Is not this an honest fair question? The lists would fill libraries of dedicated, good people who called on God like the 6 million Jews and billions of good servants of God. God did nothing. He protects no one.

85. Prayer, interceding, begging God is antithetical to building self-confidence. It portrays you as weak, unworthy, and dependent. This can be psychologically harmful.

86. Walk away from negativity whether it comes from a person or a group. Seek positive people and positive organizations. Be an optimist. Do not hang with naysayers and pessimists. It will rub off on you. The positive people will also influence you. Stick with them and be positive for them as much as possible.

87. Some religious leaders in every organized religion seem to have the ability to mesmerize their congregations or

TV audiences. They possess a scintillating wit, incomparable timing, and are viewed as prophets of the Divine. They easily adapt the accustomed preacher tone of magnificence and project sweeping authority with their thundering words.

When all else fails, they demand the people in their audiences to repeat chanting words in kindergarten fashion. They are able to hype the people up to a high crescendo like an enthusiastic cheerleader at the homecoming game. The less logical and less educated are the most susceptible to the hype although some of the gullible are quite educated and capable of independent decision.

The hypnotic atmosphere is heightened by the charismatic, moving person who has a powerful microphone and no one to challenge his or her wild harangue or pompous speech. The tirade has no time limit and often goes from one to two hours. Mentally and emotionally beat down, the crowd easily obeys orders to lift hands and shout praises or bow heads and be silent. Almost to a person, including believers and non-believers, there is child-like compliance.

CODE 3-M should advise against the loan of one's mind and emotions to any "sales pitch," whether it is delivered by a skillful medicine man or a self-appointed messenger from God. One needs to get a grip and hold on to common sense reality.

88. A web of interdependency is fast developing, as the world's nations are becoming neighbors and family. It is an exciting unstoppable change. The G-8 members — France, Italy, Germany, Russia, Canada, Japan, Britain, and US — are all working in unison to help economically. One can further this cause by being educated about other people and their customs and being friendly and supportive of people not exactly like us.

89. All kinds of negative or distasteful events will be a part of everyone's life. Times of stress will arise as loved ones and friends die. Disease may overtake one. Money problems can overwhelm. Divorce involving oneself or a family member or friend can be taxing. Accidents may disrupt whether lightning strikes and the house burns down or an automobile crash.

Thousands of tough adverse winds will blow. Into each life some rain must fall. The issue is how one is able to respond to this rainfall of untoward happenings. The individual needs to build a reservoir of strength to call upon like a savings account in a bank. Accept adversity. Handle it with dignity and grace. The reservoir can be built by your own good deeds.

90. Technology is advancing and in logarithmic style. There are many heroes in this momentous effort. The quest for new technology grows strangely dim as a few brave people search for some truths. These truths will shed light concerning the purpose and role of mankind in regard to his responsibilities and how one should conduct themselves for contentment, fulfillment and reasonable happiness.

91. If I were confined to one meaningful word to suggest how man should live his life, I would offer the word "balance."

92. Atheists say there is no God and some of them reach over to the side of religious zealots in their obsession or extreme zeal to convert everyone to their point of view.

Religionists blindly accept a version of god and usually various holy writings or sacred ceremonies. They demand no verifiable evidence for their God or their scripture.

Agnostics chicken out in a sense by saying, "I don't know whether there is a God or not," and let the issue go at that.

Questers and seekers are willing to be open-minded and pursue the idea of a true God hoping to find the answer. However, the existence of a God for them must be one of love and consistency and verifiable in a scientific or logical manner.

93. With the fantastic information storage ability and communication of modern computers with bigger and better coming down the pike, we need to have citadels established whereby people all over the world can critique our little beginning effort and help forge a more ideal CODE 3-M.

Imagine 10 million brains churning on this subject perhaps the most important one in our existence. It is exciting just to contemplate the positive possibilities. The ship of humanity needs a common rudder even though the cabins will house many kinds of unchangeable faiths. The common ground is there and must be discovered and revealed.

94. Right, wrong, choice, and accountability should be four cornerstone concepts in CODE 3-M. A moral compass can be constructed with or without worship of a deity.

95. Many generally accepted the notion it is wrong for a nation to try to conquer another nation. However, it is extremely difficult to find any nation that has not been involved in a territorial dispute. Why do we not condemn any religion that tries to uproot and eliminate any other religion and replace it with their own true religion?

96. I am fond of little uplifting sayings like, "Keep hope alive," "Give peace a chance," "Faith without works is dead," "What the world needs now is love somehow," "Brotherhood of

man," "We are all in this boat together," "Hang together or hang alone," "Am I my brother's keeper," "All for one and one for all," "If at first you don't succeed, try, try again," "When you get to the end of your rope, tie a knot and hang on," "No pain, no gain," and thousands of others.

They are short but say so much like a one-frame political cartoon. Some of them are absolutely profound. We can create sayings about the CODE like, "I really did my best, I really stood the test."

97. Veterans. They can never receive the honor and admiration they deserve. We must keep their bravery and sacrifices before posterity and us. Medical care should be automatic for any honorably discharged veteran. It should be completely comprehensive with free medicines, free care of any kind as long as he or she lives.

It should be at VA Medical Centers, clinics if the veteran is close to one if he or she desires their services. It also should be free at any other medical service in any city at any time.

The bill should be sent to VA who will have received appropriated funds to pay for outside care, if chosen for distance, sophistication or any other reason. It is a national disgrace for veterans to have to go through the red tape and questioning procedures they face.

Upon honorable discharge, issue a plastic card usable for medical care and drugs anywhere at home or abroad. Congress and Presidents send the military to put their lives on the line and fail to do what is right and fair when they return.

Most Americans think veterans do have free care for anything. Certainly, they would be outraged if they knew the true story of how we treat veterans with superficial classifications and stingy budgets reneging on recruitment promises. It is no wonder that we are so far behind in obtaining enough people.

If we promise free medical care for life any place that medical care is given for anything, this is an earned benefit and will solve lots of problems. Any prosthetic a veteran ever needs should be free. How can decent citizens do otherwise? Many veterans have suffered the insufferable and endured the unendurable. The public should be made aware of the hassle veterans have to endure. This is the least our military veterans deserve.

Parading congressmen and women who scream they are for veterans have been deceitful or ignorant of the true situation. Veterans do not automatically get free medical care like they did when in uniform. We must correct this injustice!

98. Every human advancement originated by the wonder and questioning of the human mind.

99. Choices are so important because there are always consequences. No one has ever made the correct choices all of the time. So, the goal may be to make the right choice each time but the practical way is to score high.

TONY TWEEDHURST'S LIST

1. Why are religious people as a world group so very judgmental and extremely punitive? This is counter productive in the quest for world peace. Why do they hate each other and go to war to exterminate each other? They have done it many, many times in human history sometimes fomenting wars that last 30 years and they are fighting each other in a number of hot spots today. Religions, all of them, have failed to bring peace.

2. People in religion often claim they have a personal relationship with their deity. This is strange since they have never seen God nor really talked with him except in their imagination and blind sheep-like beliefs.

One could claim a personal relationship with Adam, Moses, Aristotle, Zeus, Venus or whomever, real people or made up beings using the same faith criteria. It is imagination gone to seed and becomes so addictive that people surrender their minds to a system of religion they know practically nothing about often based on dubious contradictory writings. The fear of eternal indescribable punishment and the promise of glorious rewards drive these weak-minded people as described by one of our leading governors.

Billions of precious people have been duped, brainwashed into a dozen main religions and thousands of other cults. Each system of religion is basically a cult of people who subscribe to the same ridiculous ideas and beliefs of which there is no proof whatever.

3. It is a fact that the more an individual reasons and tests the wild religious claims, the more unbelieving one becomes. Conversely, the more mythical, mysterious, apocryphal, fanciful, fictitious, visionary, imaginary, and leg-

endary the claims and doctrines are, the more intense and fanatical the followers become.

One can start a religion worshipping the Loch Ness monster and get some fools to follow. Witness the Roman and Egyptian god entities that people prayed to and believed to be real. A so-called TV evangelist can make a thousand wild lying claims and more money rolls in. The appetite in some humans for the miraculous tales that could never be proven even for a million-dollar reward is pitiful.

Some people are so gullible they think Alex Trebek knows all the answers on his show, Jeopardy. They do not realize he has all the answers written down before him. The gullibility of mankind is only exceeded by fear that some made up and imagined God is going to destroy them if they do not adhere to the system dictated to them by the prophets, Popes, bishops, elders, and all sorts of titled people posing as God's appointed leaders of the particular religion.

These so-called leaders of the various groups sometimes wear ridiculous garments and costumes, carry a little statue of a dead man that just endured a crucifixion and make weird hand signs while mumbling so-called prayers caressing beads or twirling prayer wheels. Some followers of some religions get into mutilation, torture, beating themselves to serious bleeding with chains, and even human sacrifice to their Gods.

If an intelligent, thoughtful human being reviews the religious history of mankind, he or she does not know whether to laugh or cry. There are so many ridiculous and unreasonable practices in all religions that make one laugh. Yet, gullible people, precious people, in each of these made-up God systems are so sincere or at least act like it, that a compassionate person is deeply moved by their dedication trying so desperately to appease a vengeful God.

Some shysters are bilking people out of millions of dollars removing curses that have been placed on them. This elaborate scam netted $500,000 from just one poor woman who was convinced she was cursed by God and her soul was doomed unless she complied.

The style of worship in some Protestant churches and others is getting bizarre. It is more like a rock concert with blaring speakers, strobe lights and the leader yelling commands that are so repetitious that it reminds one of the chanting of jungle tribes or Buddhist monks.

The chorus singing and haranguing goes on a long time until the crowd is worked up the hill of the emotional roller coaster. The roller coaster comes down at a fast clip. Are they unconsciously creating manic-depressive people? At the least, it is unhealthy mass hysteria!

There could be no such thing as the imagined soul, but they spend enormous amounts of energy and often money trying to get their soul saved. It is indeed a pitiful situation and most human beings on the planet Earth have been scared into one of these improbable systems.

Any religion is very much like quicksand. One gets in it and most of the time one just sinks away from his or her own individuality and is surrounded by the sands or peer pressure. Their lives, while not necessarily wasted, are in the clutches of an overwhelming force that grabs their emotions and dictates their actions. It is a sad way to live.

It is true that some of the most intelligent people in the world have religion. Many just get a foot or a toe in the quicksand and can pull out on their own power. However, most religious people are doomed to a slave-like attitude that tightly grips their mind.

Some do manage to shift to another side of the pond of quicksand like when a Jew converts to Christianity, but they can never get out of the religious quicksand pond mentally or emotionally. They can see others in the pond and feel some bizarre consolation if they attack each other's particular faith. In fact, they have killed for this bizarre consolation and are still doing it.

So, the point of this item for CODE 3-M is to foster peace and brotherhood in the world. The first and most important thing you could do is to eradicate all of the religions. Of course, this is impractical, but it is practical to refuse to endorse any single religion, take any positives from all of them and forge a common ground road map. We seek to do the impossible but we must. We can craft a code that is better than anything we know of in the world today, however crude it may be.

4.   Education is so vital for understanding. Education comes more from non-academic environments but a basic education whether from school or the library can greatly enhance anyone's life. No one can stop you from becoming educated. Slaves were not allowed to learn to read or write but many did despite the threats of severe punishment. Still, some folks are satisfied with the lowest mandatory formal education.

The religious systems have historically been concerned that followers would read other religious notions and book banning, though almost eliminated because of so many lines of communication now, is still tried by insecure people who have a vested interest in protecting their system of myths against the light and power of truth.

Many people will wish to ban CODE 3-M and some will try. If what you believe and stand for will not hold up against other positions, then you better be shopping around so you can really say, "I can truly accept this philosophy of life." Beware of those who put down education and broader learning.

5.   I am proud of every Holocaust memorial that has been erected. Rarely, if ever, has so much hate been manifested against a religious group. We should never forget it and prevent it from happening again.

However, the Jews, according to the Old Testament, launched their own Holocaust against the Amalekites. I have not seen a single memorial to commemorate the atrocities suffered by the Amalekites. What a merciless and cruel God Jehovah must be to have ordered this Holocaust. I can't believe God had anything to do with it.

Of course, Jehovah is a God made up by the Jews. Anyway, they were supposedly ordered to destroy all the Amalekites, women, children, cattle and wipe out every living thing. The Jews did a rather thorough job with 210,000 warriors but failed to do exactly as Samuel said God's orders were to slay man and woman, infant and suckling, ox and sheep, camel and ass.

Saul utterly destroyed all the people with the edge of the sword but spared Agag and the best of the sheep, and of the oxen, and of the fatlings and the lambs. The Lord got rather upset and told Samuel that he had regretted setting up Saul to become King because he had not followed his commandments to kill everyone and all the animals. This is the same so-called God that wrote the commandment, "Thou shalt not kill" on the tablets of stone Moses brought down from Mt. Sinai. Samuel got angry and hewed Agag in pieces before the Lord in Gilgal.

Now the apologists for the followers of Judaism and Christianity can try to explain away this holocaust of murdering men, women and babies, but there is no other reasonable interpretation. God told the Jewish people to do this. How can anyone serve a God that takes revenge on women and babies?

Now it is the Jews versus the Arabs. Will Jehovah order a wipeout of precious little Palestinian babies? How can honest, sensible people ever expect peace in the world when all this religious animosity exists?

6.   Hinduism. Since the group does not have anyone who follows the Hindu religion and several have asked about this religion, I will give a very brief and hopefully accurate sketch of this religion with over 700,000,000 followers — about 14% of the world's population. Hindus say their faith is a way of life, not a religion. The modern educated Indian of Hindu origin call themselves a Hindu but do not adhere to much of the ancient precepts of original or true Hinduism.

The doctrine of transmigration of souls, with its corollary that all living beings are in essence the same as the basis of their attitude for example that cows are sacred. It believes in a complex polytheism yet all of the lesser divinities are aspects of one God. It gave religious sanctions to the caste system contrary to Western religions.

Hinduism gives some validity to all religions. Their incarnate god Krishna does say however that whatever god a man worships, it is I who answers the prayer. In place of the more narrow view of the universe held by traditional Jews, Christians and followers of Islam, Hindus postulate a very huge universe in size and view it to be immensely long in duration going through a process of development and decline that is continuous or eternal.

The family is considered paramount. Offerings are made to ancestors. Paterfamilies or father families have authority over the younger members even when they are grown. Marriage is indissoluble and widows may not remarry. Immolation (sacrifice) was outlawed in India in 1829. Though not required by sacred texts, it was a widespread practice to sacrifice widows when their husbands died.

Polygamy is permitted but not looked on with favor in most castes, except when the first marriage did not produce living male children. Elaborate requirements exist for followers, especially men and boys. There is very little congregational worship. It is mostly in the home.

The self-tortures among a relatively few Hindus are thought by some to be a degenerate Hinduism of recent times, but many believe they were practiced centuries before the Christian era. The influence of Western ideas has been significant in modern Hinduism such as widow burning, child marriage, and polygamy. Mahatma Gandhi attempted to hold on to Hinduism but adapt the beliefs to the needs of the times.

In most instances, the more educated a Hindu becomes, the less Hindu he becomes. Before Western brainwashed Judao-Christian religious leaders begin to hark on the strange and weird practices of Hinduism, they should identify such off the wall practices in their beliefs like God telling Abraham to kill his son, Isaac, or God telling Christians to pick up poisonous snakes and they would not be harmed. One could fill volumes of really bizarre gruesome and grotesque practices in all of the religions. Often the more bizarre, the more sacred it becomes. People really believe shocking rituals and practices, so it is wise for us, in my opinion, to think it will be centuries before they have lost their allure for the majority of human minds.

Weirdness in the religions is so deeply ingrained and held sacred it will take a long, long time, but it will happen. It has to follow like the general decline or dying out of polytheism. Not many today worry about Thor, the God of Thunder and war, who had a magic hammer that destroyed the foes of the gods. We might as well believe Harry Potter is a god.

Education, science and common sense will practically eliminate God worship and religion, but it won't happen any time soon. Too many humans have too many vested interests in the complex machinery of hierarchies in the organized churches. There are many religious leaders who are true believers.

However, the leadership is rampant with self-promotion money grabbing charlatans. All or the vast majority of them are doomed to disappear as the light of truth exposes this God stuff thrust upon humanity from every quarter. Humanity has carried this burden too long. When it happens, lasting peace will have a much better chance.

7.   Arab terrorists killed 11 Israeli wrestlers in 1972 at the Munich Olympics and Jews kill in revenge. Even worse is the Protestant-Catholic killings. Both sides serve Jesus Christ, the Prince of Peace. The same thing happened in the US Civil War and in essence, the Revolutionary War was our first civil war where Christians wiped out other Christians. Tyranny can reach a point of injustice where people lay aside religion and "kill the enemy." This is Bible-based.

8.   One could list a hundred or thousand milestones to illustrate the triumph of science over religion. I will list just a few. The Islamic Empire, roughly 800-1,000 A.D., believed their phenomenal discoveries in astronomy and mathematics would give a new glimpse of God. The discoveries have had an opposite effect. They made a positive contribution also by preserving the ancient Greek and Egyptian texts.

Thomas Aquinas, around 1268-73 A.D., wrote about Aristotle's physical studies and attempts to synthesize scientific findings with the Christian religion. This enabled a well-deserved climate to exist for scientist who could pass off their role as uncovering the divine plan without being branded a heretic and being excommunicated from the powerful Roman Catholic church.

Scientists knew the world was round and Columbus in 1492 verified this radical view. In 1543, Copernicus concluded the Earth revolved around the sun, challenging man's long held belief that the earth was the center of the universe.

Just 90 years later in 1633, Galileo was censured by people of the Inquisition who were formed to search for and punish nonbelievers and heretics. Galileo was ordered by the Pope himself to refrain from teaching the Copernican system. Galileo continued. Finally, he was made to recant or face excommunication and placed under house arrest.

What a tragedy! A religious leader not only involved himself in something he knew nothing about and tried to stamp out science. The Scopes monkey trial in Tennessee was similar, except the populace was worked up to a froth fighting evolution. Scopes was indicted, put on trial and convicted for teaching evolution.

New ideas that threaten religion whether irrefutable or theoretical frighten the religious people half to death. Why? Because they are so insecure in what they believe. Most of them have a very difficult time explaining what they truly believe.

Imagine the dilemma of an honest church member who grasped the scientific proof concerning the claims of Galileo. He had been taught to embrace truth and yet he did not want to be branded a heretic and suffer house arrest. This dilemma has plagued humanity long enough. One should muster the courage to say, "I will accept the scientific fact and proof that the world is round regardless of what my religion teaches or what penalty they lay on me."

Poor Galileo! In 1992, Pope John Paul II apologized for the Roman Catholic Church's condemnation of Galileo and in 1996 the same pope endorsed evolution as part of God's master plan. What kind of rotten baloney is this? Had not the powerful church silenced Galileo, there is no telling what this brilliant scientist could have accomplished.

In 1687, Isaac Newton advanced the mechanistic vision of the cosmos and demonstrated gravity as being a force by which every mass or particle of matter attracts or is atttacted by every other mass or particle of matter, their tendency toward one another. Newton knew of the religious power that existed, so he fashioned God as a first cause some say to appease the religious powers.

Little publicity has been given to Chevalier de Larck, the great French naturalist who preceded Charles Darwin by several decades, proclaiming acquired characteristics could be inherited in his theory of organic evolution. In 1842, Richard Owen found dinosaur fossils. One questions how a male and female of those animals would have fit in Noah's Ark along with millions of other species of animals.

In 1859, *The Origin of Species* shocked the world and still shocks a large percentage of the world. Along with *The Descent of Man* in 1872 it undermined the biblical doctrine that humans are a divine creation by suggesting humans evolved from apes.

In 1905, John William Strutt determined the age of a rock to be two billion years old officially disproving the 1650 declaration of James Ussher that, according to Genesis, the universe was created on October 22, 4004 B.C. How these precise determinations are made may be suspect, but the pile of evidence of life on this old planet far, far exceeds 4004 B.C.

In 1948, George Gamow coined the term "Big Bang" to describe the theory that the universe began in a primeval explosion. Everything is moving away from that explosion. This theory found support when Arso Penzias and Robert Wilson in 1965 discovered that space is filled with background radiation. In 1989, the COBE satellite made an image of this radiation.

No one knows what science will learn further in the next century or the Third Millennium about man — if we last that long. One thing is certain, the power of religious leaders to muzzle their findings is gone forever. Hallelujah!

9.   Demons, angels and saints are man-made concepts. The danger is the power ascribed to those fakes. They are no more real than Mickey Mouse, Santa Claus or Harry Potter.

Shame on people who say a child is demon-possessed! Study 101 Psychology or just use common sense. Jesus supposedly drove a batch of demons into swine that ran into the sea. A demon is supposed to be spiritual and is destroyed when a hog runs into the sea? Give me a break!

10.   Multiple millions of religionists believe in inbred sin, whereby Adam's sin became an inheritance for all humans. They point out when a baby cries in a temper tantrum, it is caused by inbred sin. Not only is this a foolish belief, it is

counter productive and hurtful in one's attempt to build self-esteem.

The Born-to-Sin crowd usually are people with very little understanding of the psychological characteristics of human beings. Humans must learn to appreciate and accept themselves to build a healthy self-esteem, which is so essential for a happy successful life. This inbred sin notion is just another attempt of control by the churches that expouse it. But if one gets sanctified, the blood of Christ washes away inbred sin. So follow their instructions and believe and you can get rid of your inbred sin. How ridiculous!

11. The Kansas School Board has removed evolution teaching from school curriculum and urged the teaching of creation. Already they are considering a reversal of this decision. Why not teach a course in alternate doctrines of man's beginnings and learn about anyone's ideas on the subject? They are so insecure about the creation theory. Are they afraid the students would choose evolution as the plausible explanation? The Kansas School Board cannot stop truth because of their religious prejudices. This is not the 1920's.

12. The ease to forgiveness practiced in some religions may contribute to people's ease in doing wrong, even criminal activity. Christ on the cross told a thief, "Today shalt thou be with me in paradise."

Can one live a terrible life, mumble a few words and float on into heaven? Would Jesus have forgiven Hitler just as quickly and easily if Hitler repented of his sins down in his bunker in Berlin? Is this fair to bring horror and destruction upon millions and then get to heaven?

Death row conversions are common. Knowing forgiveness is so easily obtained fosters wrongdoing. Kill, rape or anything you please. Knowing He will always say, "I forgive." This is a dangerous doctrine. What about the victims?

13. Death and funerals should not be celebrated as a time when an oppressed burdensome soul enters a so-called heaven. It should be a eulogy to the individual if he has lived a good, productive life and shown love for others. The goal of one's life is not to get an imagined soul saved but to go about being content and doing well.

14. Over 10,000 amendments have been offered to change the US Constitution. Only 27 passed. The so-called Supreme Court of the land has usurped the powers of the Constitution and in a number of occasions made themselves into a legislative group. The worst possible scenario is for the court or any

other branch of government to submit itself to the religious whims of the times.

15. Behold all the wonderful things man has accomplished without any so-called miracles from a divine power. And, the best is yet to come if we can continue to break away from the myths and false promises of religion.

16. People say they know their dead loved one is looking down on them from heaven. Then, how can all the dead rise and meet Jesus in the air at His Second Coming? How about those who were cremated and the ashes cast into the sea? Will their body be resurrected?

Do we have to abandon all common sense to become a Christian? Do we have to literally believe as a child as admonished in the scripture?

The apostle Paul said, "Come, let us reason together." The problem with reason and logic when applied to religious beliefs is that none of the beliefs sacred to the religions can withstand that kind of scrutiny. There is nothing left, so why not build a system of action and behavior that eliminates gods and myths?

17. Evidence of God is extremely weak or non-existent. There is also weak evidence for flying saucers from another planet, the Loch Ness monster, Yeti, Big Foot, and other similar things. Yet millions believe in this kind of speculation and billions believe and have believed in all sorts of gods.

While some display photos of spaceships, I have not seen or heard of a photo of any God. If God is a spirit, then it would be a likeness of Jesus whose body was supposedly resurrected from the dead and His body ascended on a cloud to heaven.

People do not require much evidence when it comes to a religious belief. All that is needed is way-out dogma, lots of fear mixed in with a natural desire to live forever and you have a religion. One could be generated each month and a branch seems to be born that often.

18. All humans on earth are very similar in DNA (Deoxyribonucleic acid), a set of instructions for creating organic and physiology with the same range of emotions. We have similar fears and joys and all search for answers.

Where we exhibit one of the greatest differences is the level of searching for correct answers. Some people hardly ever question anything and they easily accept whatever they are told to be truth. This is fertile ground for any and all religions. Declare whatever boldly and threaten coupled with promise of soul saved for heaven if you immerse yourself in our belief. It is relatively easy to drum up a following.

A man called Karesh in 1893 declared the sun and earth were inside a big ball and a number of other wild ideas. He drew a sizeable following and bought a huge tract of property between Ft. Myers and Naples. Karesh, whose real name was Dr. Cyrus Teed, claimed he had experienced a vision while living in Chicago where he was told to establish a New Jerusalem in Florida.

He named the city Estero. He devised a beautiful elaborate plan for the city that was supposed to be self-sufficient. Exotic trees and plants were brought from all over the earth. This was the start of the Kareshan Tropical Gardens which have been growing ever more luxuriant to this day.

There were a number of communal businesses in the beginning, a bakery, general store, boat building shop, machine shop, and facilities to make arts and crafts. In the Art Hall the visionary leader displayed his unique geodetic diagram of the earth. Earth was a hollow sphere with the sun in the center and life on the inside layer of the shell.

This religious movement died out quickly since one of the virtues was celibacy, like the Shakers religious movement that died out in Kentucky.

The Shakers, an offshoot from the Quakers, established a village in 1805 on the Kentucky River. Men and women could work together and worship in the same building but remain apart at all times. They did not believe in sex so they died out in a relatively few decades.

However, they did believe and practice racial equality and gender equality, real advances in the early 1800's. Had they not been so weird about sexual relations, they could have been a strong force eventually for righteous causes.

Religions always get involved in sex practices; most have a very negative view towards such an important function of humans. Some people do not cultivate their minds to question this type of psycho-visionary hype.

One has to wonder if most or all religions were not founded in a similar manner. The ones that have engulfed millions and even billions, caught on and pyramiding much better prove to adapt better.

Personally, if I am to be true to myself, I must question all religious claims. So far, I am not convinced that anything came from any God, but I am convinced man can make up just about anything, make any claim and get a following. History proves this thesis.

19. Psychological studies have proven that monotonous sensory stimulation produces confusion — a disruption of the ability to think clearly. It can cause hallucinations and impairs judgment. Every religion I have studied and witnessed employs some type of repeated monotonous type of ritual to muddle the rational thinking of the flock. These practices are often so subtle that the individual does not realize these techniques are being used to drive their behavior.

While some individuals do realize they are being corralled, the emotional highs they receive are worth it to them. The letdown aftermath from extreme emotional build-ups can be very troublesome.

20. Apparently, people are not concerned about the brainwashing of children in other false religions as long as they can indoctrinate their own children in the true religion they follow. Why not teach children decency and ethics along with courtesy and kindness until they can choose a religion themselves when they are 11, 12, 13 or so? Is it fair to try to make your child believe exactly as you do especially when so many of your ideas have changed since you were a child?

Perhaps broad beliefs in a loving God and the like are not harmful, but extreme beliefs that must be followed or the child will face hellfire is obviously wrong and debilitating. Some children are independent enough and strong enough to keep their own counsel. However, most are gripped with fear if they don't believe as mom and dad and the rabbi, priest or preacher say they must.

We all cringed and were deeply moved as the fires at Waco burned up those precious little children. They were helpless in the battle between their parents' religion and the forces directed by Janet Reno. Who proved what? What kind of parent would force their child in the Jim Jones Kool-Aid death line? Isn't there some way we can emphasize this wrongness and evil?

21. Jerusalem and a large part of Palestine have been leveled to the ground five times. It has changed rule 26 times and is still one of the worst powder kegs to foment an atomic war on the face of the earth.

Several religions lay claim that this is their holy city. It is one of the most bizarre and ridiculous stories in human history. No other city on earth has been the focus of such lasting hatred and erupted in so much despair.

Today, the Jews control Jerusalem and the whole nation is only 1-2% Christian. What a desecration of the word "holy." If there were a Satan, Jerusalem would fit well as his capitol city.

"Sha alu Shalom Yerushalayim" (Pray for the peace of Jerusalem). Will it ever happen?

22. Juneane Garofolo, a young, beautiful beauty queen, was asked whether God exists. She replied, "For other people, yes. I don't have a particular allegiance to one."

A high percentage of today's youth feel the same way, but many are wary of proclaiming their views for obvious reasons. There will come a breakthrough someday when all people can say how they really regard their God and religious believers. When that happens, the world will be "born again." I may not live long enough to see that day, but I want to go on record that I believe it will come. I cherish the thought when people are set free enough to declare independence from all imagined religious ideas.

23. Death cults sadly are alive and well around the world. In Uganda, not far from one of the world's most beautiful lakes, over 900 have fallen for a strange religious teaching: Jesus went to heaven after death. His mother went to heaven after death. Who are you to go to heaven without dying?

Graves of the young and old turn up daily. This is a sick situation brought on unfairly in the name of the Jesus religion. It is only one of thousands of examples where rational thinking eludes the faithful.

24. The mixture of government and religion has been one of the largest curses on humanity.

25. People who reject any form of evolution are like people who insisted for centuries after Columbus that the world was still flat.

26. Catholics fight birth control for one simple reason. It increases Catholic control, if eliminated.

27. Praying to selected saints for special needs is preposterous and just plain silly. One prays to St. Anthony to find lost things; St. Dominic's statue is placed in gardens. St. Christopher used to be the patron saint for safe travel, but he was demoted.

Don't people realize that saints are nominated, lobbied for and voted on? And was not Lucifer an archangel before he rebelled against God and became Satan? Why did not God destroy Satan so humanity would not have to suffer so much?

It is a puzzle to me how some highly intelligent people can swallow all this hokum, never questioning its truthfulness and reality. It must be a sterling illustration of how fear can cloud the rational mind of a human being.

28. Some people worship nature. This is a step up from most organized religions. Frank Lloyd Wright, the great architect, said, "Put a large 'N' on nature. That is my church." The American Indians gave much credence to nature, but their scary totem poles told of their fears.

29. All religions have overplayed their hands by promising so much and producing so little. It has caused the people of the world to be lost in a sea of confusion.

People pray until they are exhausted, but their child still dies. They keep praying for sons and daughters, but rarely do they come back to the "old time religion." They fast. Some beat on themselves as the followers of Baal did, screaming for their God to rain down fire.

The Jews in the concentration camps of Hitler prayed and prayed. Where was Jehovah, the great and only all powerful God, who wrote "10,000 shall fall by your side but I will protect you"? Yet, they kept praying as they were marched into the burning death furnaces. Where were the wonderful promises of their great religion? If you visit those camps of doom, you can almost hear their screaming cries out to Jehovah. If there is a Jehovah and he turned away from those cries, who wants to worship Him?

30. Globalization is inevitable. McDonald's sells hamburgers in many countries today and so on. CODE 3-M should recommend this concept and support its early completion. The important thing is to retain our essential values as we make the plunge.

The coming together of the peoples of the world is wonderful, but it has to be accomplished step by step holding on to hard fought freedoms and openness. We cannot and should not swallow up other cultures much older and richer than ours. Our experiment in democracy and the positive parts of our culture should not be sacrificed.

A blending process using the best in all countries and cultures is most appropriate. We have a lot to learn from Europeans, Asians, the Middle East, and Africans. The pyramids had been pointing their peaks toward the heavens long before Columbus arrived and beheld the native Americans.

31. Open marriages are the style in many Hollywood couples and elsewhere. I fear the consequences. Does this lead to plural wives and plural husbands?

If only adults were involved, it would not phase me, but when children have to endure this type of environment, I am deeply concerned. My thoughts are centered on what I feel is the urgency of adapting to this fast approaching cultural change by devising the best course to follow or find the best advice to give to protect the children from irreparable harm. It is new territory for us and I have not seen a trail that leads to a good outcome, but I throw it out for discussion hoping someone will have a revelation or insight that will help.

32.   The unconcern of present day humans for the 20-30 billion people who preceded us in matters of life, death and destiny is baffling. So much dogmatism is being communicated throughout the world by print, TV, radio, and crusades.

The thundering preachers thump their big black King James Version of the Bible and declare without any fear of contradiction that no man can enter the kingdom of heaven unless Jesus saves his soul. Do not these people have a concern for all the billions of people that died before the birth of Jesus?

Don't they care about Jews, Hindus, Moslems, Buddhists, and whatevers? Do all of these non-worshippers of Jesus burn in hell? Many Jews are dead including Moses. Is he in hell?

The only sensible way out to me is to say Jesus evidently taught some good things for mankind, but He was not God and though He believed, He did not know there was a God.

The claims He was supposed to have made about Himself can be attributed to others. They were not even recorded until many years after His death.

If Jesus is the only focal point for the largest group on earth who follow a religion, then where is their compassion for people who were never born again? Not only is their compassion empty, their arrogance declaring that they are the only ones right shows a strange malfunctioning ego.

33. Jesse Jackson says among his unique interesting quotes, "When faith takes on fate, faith will prevail." It sounds good, but of course it is not true. This type of blind allegiance to religion is irrational. Humans who never heard of Moses or Jesus have died with great comfort and dignity. Humans who suffer phenomenal loss collect themselves and go forth with their lives.

Some Christians go into depression, moan and groan the balance of their days casting negativism wherever they roam. Faith in any God does not necessarily cause one to believe in a certain manner. Behavior is the choice of the person as noted in the examples given.

Would Jesse Jackson's faith overcome the fate of JFK, Jr.,

or the son of Dr. J? When a mother and father fervently pray and believe God for a normal healthy child and fate delivers a Downs Syndrome baby, who was the winner, faith or fate?

34. The blood sacrifice concept is the most disturbing thing in the various religions and so very much is made from it. This notion crosses the line as far as legitimate rational thought for humans is concerned. In ancient times when knowledge was at a minimum, human sacrifices were common place. The Jews and others sacrificed animals trying to raise this blood offering to a better level.

But God demands Abraham sacrifice his son, Isaac. The story says he finally got a ram and slaughtered it on his altar to appease his God, but the fact remains that human sacrifice was in the Hebrew consciousness.

Jews wrote some of the gospels and reach way back in time to suggest Jesus was the blood sacrifice for all humanity. Why would God who saved Abraham's son from the same fate not save his only son? Because the blood was needed to cleanse and forgive people's sins. This emphasis on the dead, bleeding body of Christ goes back to heathenism and decent compassionate people should be repulsed by this doctrine.

Catholics believe they are actually or literally drinking the blood of Christ in Mass because the priest has performed his ritual over the wine. The transubstantiation doctrine is worse than gross. Why should people drink blood? Of course, they don't. It is still wine.

If anyone believes it is blood, let a couple of chemistry professors — one Catholic and one non-believer — examine it after the priest blesses the wine.

Bloody situations run through religious thinking like red adorned British uniforms in colonial days. It is not wholesome and it is thrust on very, very young children.

35. The subtle sex implications of women chanting "I love you Jesus" hundreds of times working themselves into a frenzy and the corollary of men's interesting prayers and love sayings to Mary are not considered fair game for discussion, but they exist.

36. Awesomeness of the universe. The more we learn from Hubbell and other magnificent telescopes, the more we are struck by the universe. We are just a tiny part. What state will it be in thirty more billion years? Will the subtle changes in humans continue and a much superior brain develop in time?

Scientists point to the lack of need for the appendix, tonsils, wisdom teeth, and the increase of brain size in humans. These are but a few of the questions that one can ponder as he is stargazing. The heavens are more than elegant and overwhelming. They are spectacular, radiant and majestic.

If one needs a refilling of one's spirit, stand on the bow of this luxury yacht during a full moon and contemplate what nature hath wrought! If it pleases you, say God started it all. Every human should treasure this free exhibit and should view it more and more for inspiration!

Perhaps the practice of beholding the heavens will be a significant unifying event for mankind. The poorest infant in the poorest environment can share these wonders with Bill Gates, the richest man on Earth. No charge for this window, eh Bill?

37. People speak of human beings having a spiritual experience and spiritual beings having a human experience, bodies rising in the air and angels appearing. People really want to believe in the supernatural. In the final analysis, it is only a belief like the statement made at funerals, death is really the beginning of life. These things make no sense to me, but I would defend people's right to believe anything they wish to believe if it does not trample the rights of others.

38. A minister told me that he was not concerned about anything God did. God has the right to wipe out nations from the Earth and He has done it before. He is God and He can do what might appear to be murder or a sin to us, but He is not under the same rules. For the life of me, I cannot understand that type of thinking.

39. The contrast between some of today's Christian worship and that of the turn of the last century is absolutely remarkable. Hebrews 13:8 says, "Jesus Christ, the same yesterday, today and forever." One thing is for certain, He is not worshipped the same way by His followers and even within the exceeded 200 denominations that do worship Him, it is not the same as yesterday. It will not be the same tomorrow.

The same is true of their doctrines and prohibitions. The anything goes attitude has infected the organized churches must to the chagrin and disapproval of the old timers. So how one would worship Jesus Christ would depend on the era, the particular church rules, and adaptation to the style you preferred.

You can go from little shouting tent meetings where you can hear speaking in tongues to staid, cold cathedrals where until a few decades ago, someone was reading Latin. The dress of women has always concerned the devout and you can find any extreme you can imagine in that no-business-of-religion area. If worship were not such a serious subject, it would be very funny to note all the variations among people worshipping the same god.

40. The so-called word of God to Christians is the Bible. The Bible has to be put in perspective. Very few people could read or write when the Bible was written spanning a number of years. All sorts of fights and disagreements have occurred concerning what should be included in the Bible.

Remember one of the greatest technological advances in the second millennium was the Gutenberg printing press. In 1456, a very long time after the death of Christ, he printed the Bible in the Latin language. Even if God had inspired some of the authors whose writings made it, imagine the amount of distortions monks could have produced in their handwritten copies. They did not even know about the Dead Sea Scrolls or other writings that may have been burned, stolen or lost. They included the Apocrypha, but the Protestants threw those books out. If everyone's eternal destiny is dependent on this colossal haphazard compilation, we are indeed all in jeopardy.

41. Will humans be the same yesterday and forever? No. A number of humans are already part material and part cells. We will install specially designed parts that are better than original and provide the user with superior capabilities.

Genetic engineering will produce super-people outstripping the slow pace of evolution. Sports figures can have extra capacity lungs and hearts. Sculptors may have a neural device to increase sensitivity to texture. Viagra has already increased sex ability. Many will be part protoplasm and part electronic.

When will we be more like something else when compared to the human of the 20th century? When will the so-called soul be gone? Don't worry. It never existed in the first place. Will we mix animal protoplasm, fish other water beings with humans like the minds of men once imagined the centaur and the mermaid? I don't think so, but technology always surpasses any moral corollary.

CODE 3-M must recommend specific guidelines for mechanical, chemical, electronic, and genetic possibilities that could call for a new classification of beings that would not pass muster as a human being.

42. Despite the New Testament doctrine putting down women by telling them to keep silent in the churches and the Baptist prohibiting women pastors, God evidently looked on at least eight women very favorably by making them prophet-

esses. A prophet outranked a deacon or a pastor and most
other titles. They were the sisters of Moses; Mirian, a judge in
Israel; Deborah, Huldah, Anna; and the four virgin daughters
of Philip, the evangelist. Scripture is inconsistent in its views
concerning women. I would say the fair thing is equal rights
for women in religion including a woman pope, but I don't
think Pope John Paul II would agree.

43. Outrageous events in the Old Testament have helped
fill many books and I have mentioned only a few. There is one
that you almost never hear about. A bunch of children in II
Kings 2 made fun of Elisha's bald head whereupon he cursed
them in God's name who honored the curse by sending out two
female bears who tore up all the 42 children.

Did the punishment fit the crime? Laughing at bald heads
is not nice or appropriate, but it hardly deserves the death
penalty from Elisha and God. Elisha's vanity is not worth the
life of anyone, certainly not 42 children.

Unreasonable vengeance by God in the Old Testament
should give pause and concern to every Jew, Christian and any
other religions that subscribe to the Old Testament.

44. Masonic principles offer much good material. Much of
masonry is full of myth like the religions. Masons split on religion. The Scottish Rite is mostly for Jews and the York Rite is
mostly for Christians as one seeks to go from the Third
Degree to the Thirty-second Degree.

How can two walk together unless they reason? If they
can't reason together, put them on separate tracks. Masons
have found common ground in many areas, but on the issue of
whether Jesus Christ is the Messiah, they fail. They have not
learned that no deity is essential to practice the positive parts
of their order.

45. Common ground often cannot be found within one
organized religion. Recently, dozens of Jewish women, some
draped in prayer shawls, prayed out loud at the Western Wall
on a Sunday. This was a week after parliament passed a bill
that could become law that would sentence them to seven
years in prison if they prayed there out loud.

Ultra-Orthodox Jewish men in the adjacent male section
shouted "shame" and "quiet." Four men were caught with eggs
they planned to throw at the women. How cowardly can a religious fanatic get against his own kind?

Some Orthodox rabbis have ruled that a woman's singing
voice is lewd and women must not wear skullcaps, prayer
shawls, phylacteries (small leather cases with scripture in

them attached to the forehead and left arm with thongs), used by men.

Is this any way to treat women or attract anyone to become a Jewish Orthodox? I hope the bill will be voted down and never become law. One can see how difficult it is to get an extreme Muslim and extreme Jew to agree on anything, yet both groups belittle women and think their way is the only right way.

46. Ridiculous Christian admonitions can almost match the cruel vengeance in the Old Testament. Such teachings like in Matthew 5:38-39 instructing Christians to turn the other cheek to get hit again if someone hits you. If one steals your coat, give him your cloak also. And in the 27th verse, same chapter, we are told that if men just look at a woman and lust, they have committed adultery in their hearts.

In the 43rd verse, we are told to love our enemies. If someone comes in and kidnaps your four-year-old daughter, takes her out and repeatedly rapes her, then chops her little arms and legs off one by one until she bleeds to death, you should love that scoundrel — never!

Such unfair and impractical behavior guidelines can never be followed by most intelligent and decent people and they should not be honored regardless of where it is written or who says it. Jesus could not bring Himself to love Lucifer after he rebelled against God and became Satan, so what authority does He have to tell others to love their enemies?

47. Lots of unbelievable errors are in the Bible. Books list hundreds of them. One that always fascinated me was the ages of seven men who lived passed 900 years. Methuselah almost everyone has heard of topped the group as the oldest man at 969 years. The others were Jared – 962; Noah – 950; Adam – 930; Seth – 912; Cainan – 910; and Enos – 905.

Biblical scholars and believers admit there is not proof that anyone lived that long and no proof that a year was only a few months in the counting. This is not too important except it undermines the belief that every word in the Bible is the truth position.

48. Even without the clarification of evolution, Genesis would remain a very weird fairy tale — man from dirt, woman from one his ribs?

49. Carl Sagan was a very enthusiastic outstanding scientist, a happy man who loved the heavens and spent most of his life exploring the wonders of the universe. He concluded there was nothing for God to do — every thinking person was there-

fore forced to admit the absence of God in the universe.

So many have come to the same conclusion, but are wary in declaring that position because of the vile and depraved recrimination that would follow from the guardians of sacred interpretations of the universe.

50. A few decades ago the cry began to ring out, man is basically good; God is dead. The first part resonated well with me. The second part did not because how can someone die who never lived?

51. I recently saw a map of all the trouble spots in the world. Religion was at the center of almost every one. If the world ever exists without war, it will exist without evangelical or aggressive religion.

52. Clarence Darrow said, "There is no such thing as justice, in or out of court." In a perfect sense he is right, but in a practical sense CODE 3-M must urge for a perfect system as we can devise. We have a long journey to reach even a fair system, but we must make the journey.

53. The need to celebrate seems to be a basic human need in primitive life, in politics, in sports, marriage, religion, and many other areas. Celebrations are counterproductive when some drunken fool ruins everything and many celebrations have led to violence and death. As an individual, it is your duty and responsibility to learn to celebrate with as much gusto as you like but not abandon common sense and the Golden Rule.

54. Incest is a horrible act and is a crime in most jurisdictions around the world. It is physically dangerous to any offspring and the emotional toll cannot be calculated. I don't know how the grandchildren of Adam and Eve were conceived and born unless there was incest and I have never been given a plausible answer. Anyway, I've never bought the Adam and Eve story as truth.

Noah was guilty of incest and drunkenness, yet Ezekial (Chapter 14) tells he was a righteous man. Still the CODE can and will make a stand against this tragedy even if one of Jehovah's favorites committed this crime.

55. Most of the Bible is antithetical to peace, but none exceed the mystery and harm dished out by John's wild Book of Revelation. It is the result of a sick mind, colorful and imaginative, but to proclaim it is truth from an Almighty God has had a negative effect on mankind. It may have value as fiction, but it is a menace when presented as truth.

56. No church property should be exempt from fair taxes. It is unconstitutional and places a heavier burden on legiti-

mate business and homes. If a group wants to propagate or sell their religion, fine. However, it should not receive tax exemption on its property.

It becomes ridiculous when people like in Los Angeles put a big church sign on their homes, have small groups to worship sometimes and the owner pays no taxes. The Catholic Church has invested in property, especially in Florida and fast growing values, paid no taxes and later sold the property for great profit.

Others have done the same. This is wrong and they should regard it as sinful.

57. Jews are partially responsible for the hatred spewed out on them since they claim superiority in God's eyes. They say they are God's chosen people. Of course, they are not, but the claim does not endear them to others.

If there was a God who chose a small group like this to be worthy of his protection and favor above all others, that alone should make a fair-minded person reject that God, Jehovah.

The persecution of Jews is still an evil thing, especially when they have contributed so much to humanity. However, people do not admire people who draw a line around themselves indicating they are special to God — you are not special like I am because you are not chosen or from the 12 tribes of Israel. Where was God when the chosen people suffered the holocaust?

58. We are engaged in cultural fatigue. So many separate groups are desperately trying to perpetuate their culture from the old country and they are having a difficult time. The young people really don't care even as much as their parents, let alone their grandparents about the dances, costumes, ethnic food and so on. Hopefully, some of the distinct culture will be preserved, but the greater hope is that people around the world will begin to think more about their commonness and brotherhood for everyone.

Extreme separate identities and creating fear for young people to cross over and marry in other cultures have been and will be a detriment to peace. Some culture clinging is okay. Extreme devotion to the past of one's family homeland and culture is a negative phenomena. Refrain from being a hyphenated American. Whoopi Goldberg does. It is divisive.

59. Civil wars since people could read, write and be educated even to a small level are hard to fathom. In the ancient tribal wars in Europe, Africa and Asia, the foot soldier knew little about the rest of the world and could not read about it.

He marched almost like a dumb animal into the fray hoping to kill off the enemy without asking, "Why I am fighting this war?" This did not concern him as much as it should have for the soldiers in later civil wars.

In European countries, the US, Ireland, Greece, almost any spot on the globe, there have been so-called civilized people fighting their own people and many still are in conflict. Have we remained so close to tribal warfare? Can't we learn to settle matters like boundaries and communicate at a negotiations table? Nope, not yet but all can hope "I have a dream" will someday be a reality.

60. Robert Ingersol stated, "Our hope of immortality whether old doctrine or new propaganda does not come from a religion, but all religions come from that hope."

It is okay to keep hope alive, but to translate legitimate hope into hundreds of mandatory and punitive systems of religions and scare billions of people including precious children to devote all their life so to speak is in itself cruel and unusual punishment. It is a root cause of war and suffering and untold mental anguish.

Imagine little boys and girls all over the world crying themselves to sleep, afraid they may go to hell and burn forever. No wonder some of them never get over horrible nightmares. Some brainwashing may be relatively harmless, but the incessant hell fire preaching that practically everything is sinful and one sin, unforgiven, will land you in the eternal lake of fire can and does have severe psychological consequences on a child. It should not happen.

61. We need to spend more time thinking. Bertrand Russell said, "Most people would rather die than think; many do." We need to think about what life is all about and what our individual life should be; what we might accomplish for self, others and perhaps mankind.

As we think, we find the need to revise many of our long held ideas and beliefs. We should not grab and embrace the first thing that comes along to change our body of truth as we see it. Neither should we lock in old ideas in a compartment that can never be altered.

For some, reading a good book on logic can prove most helpful. The people who handle poison snakes, drink poison, and do anything dangerous are not thinking. Perhaps most of them do not have much to think with, but some of the people are not intellectually challenged and they need to think.

Thinking honestly might eliminate many more illogical

beliefs about all religions and non-religious things as well. Thinking is what made some brave people declare the world could not be flat or people would go off the edge somewhere, so it might be round, cylindrical or maybe slightly oval. Don't lock up your mind like most of the world did. Listen to logic and reasons why the world must be round. People did not have those beautiful, inspiring photos from satellites and space shuttles then. They reasoned.

Of course, this is only one example of millions. The principle is the same. Hold on to what seems truth to you, but when it is challenged, think! Then keep what you still feel is truth or change with the ability to give reasons for that change. For example, does a miscarriage have a soul?

Pentecostals preach that with the infilling of the Holy Spirit, one speaks in tongues as the spirit gives utterance. Acts 2:2 speaks of a sound as loud as a rushing mighty wind accompanying the infilling and the third verse says there appeared unto them cloven tongues like as of fire and sat upon each of them.

How can one accept the speaking in tongues as necessary evidence if they ignore the great sound and actual appearance of cloven tongues like fire sitting on the head of the receiver? This never happens in Pentecostal gatherings nor has anyone ever seen it on TV. Yet, most of us have heard the mumblings and gibberish claiming to be real languages of the Pentecostals. It is time to think and reason.

62. Religious people try to cover every loophole, but the covers are transparent and there are too many loopholes. One worth mentioning is the putting God on the spot to produce phenomena.

Baal was worshipped by a large number of people, sometimes by some Hebrews and throughout the story in the Old Testament, he is the main nemesis of Jehovah God. Elijah set forth to call 450 prophets of Baal's hand by challenging them to see which God, Baal or Jehovah, could send down fire.

They set up altars on Mt. Carmel, took a bullock apiece for a burnt offering and proceeded with the contest. The prophets of Baal cried, "Oh Baal, hear us." No fire came down. They yelled and screamed to Baal and cut themselves with knives and lancets until blood gushed upon them.

Elijah just ridiculed them saying, your God must be talking or gone on a journey or perhaps he is asleep. He mocked the prophets of Baal. Finally, it was Elijah's turn. He poured barrels of water on the bullock and twelve stones and the wood.

He did it a second time and third time and filled a trench around the altar with water.

Then Elijah prayed, "Hear me, oh Lord, hear me, that this people may know that thou art the Lord." Then the fire fell and consumed the burnt sacrifice and the wood, and the stones and the dust and licked up the water that was in the trench.

Elijah took all of the 450 prophets of Baal down to a brook called Kishon and slew every one of them there. However, this putting God on the spot was rejected by Jesus when He refused to jump off the pinnacle of the temple and trust the angels to catch Him. Yet, He walked on the water to prove He was divine.

Consistency in the Bible is so lacking and these examples indicate God is willing to put on quite a show and murder His opponents on one hand and yet not dispatch angels to catch His Son if he jumped. I'll tell you one thing, if a rabbi builds an altar inside the International Speedway at Daytona Beach, Florida, with 12 stones, puts a bull in it, builds a trench around it and pour barrels of water on it three times then he prays for God to prove Himself and fire comes down and burns up the bull, the altar stones, the dust and no water is left you will see 200,000 people cast away every doubt that Jehovah is God and raise their hands shouting praises to Him.

Do you believe this could happen? Of course not. We just have to believe in the ancient tale that no one can verify except through religious faith and belief. Well, many billions on earth don't believe the tale and I am numbered among those billions.

63. "God told me to do so-and-so" can be a dangerous approach. In the first place, how do they know it wasn't the devil that told them to do it like the murderer who said God told him to wipe out his victim.

A young couple recently refused to feed their little boy because God told them he was a prophet. Anyone can have a desire or an impression and attribute it to God.

When Richard Roberts, who tries to be like his Dad but does a pitiful job of it, says God just told me someone has a cancer in his side and God is going to heal it, this is blasphemy. Then Richard does his little power thing and declares that God healed him.

This is fakery. Impressions can fool those TV evangelists, but they don't say I *believe*. They say they *know* God told them. How arrogant and self-praising and downright disgusting can these egos become?

64. Do women accept religion and participate more than men because of their emotional make-up? It certainly is not because women have achieved equality from the teachings of religion. Perhaps the dependency syndrome is stronger in the female gender. I don't know, but I think it strange that they are cut down so hard and yet are the more faithful gender. It is not due to less intelligence.

65. Bethlehem was full of Jews longing for a Messiah the night of the birth of the Christ child. One wonders why they did not see the very bright star that hung over the manger and rush over like the shepherds and the wise men who came from afar. Was every single Jew in Bethlehem dishonest or in denial?

66. Strange rituals. Is the lighting of candles, drinking of wine, burnt offerings, animal sacrifice, and even human sacrifice kin to some type of voodoo or pre-civilized practices? Practically all forms of worship are traceable to ancient oddball, weird practices.

67. One wild group of religionists seems to astound us then we discover another has topped them. A religious group in Brazil believes that a spaceship hovers above a certain spot on earth in Brazil. They go to that spot to be cleansed.

How different is this from the hallowed sacred spots of religions that have millions of followers? In 1858, a French girl, Bernadette Soubirous, claimed to have seen Mary at Lourdes. Millions have gone there to hear that miracle and pray.

68. The Big Bang happened 22 billion years ago according to leading scientists. Earth is about four-and-one-half billion years old. One's life span even if it exceeds 100 years is like a small pen dot on a line that would stretch from earth to the sun; and we have no idea where to place this dot that represents our life span. Would it be one third, one half of the way? There may not even be an end, but there was a beginning of time. One wonders if evolution moves forward on a steady pace or could it have bursts of speed or a period of slow or little development.

What if man some day could find a key to speed up the process of evolution. Twenty-two billion years is a very long time to our finite minds. If we are evoluting upwards, what will we be like in say another two billion years? Will our religious views last one more millennium? It is doubtful that they will endure even a few centuries and people will look back at the beliefs and rituals as we do the ancient Egyptians.

69. Let me present a real positive fact. The great human spirit is so often demonstrated in huge disasters both in war, disease disasters and natural disasters. People scramble half way around the world to help people they never knew and will probably never see again.

It does not matter if they do it with an organized group or on their own. It is so uplifting and wonderful. A sacrificial act from one human to another is a great principle to include in our CODE for living.

70. Depending on and believing that the religions of the world will ever get together and bring peace is sheer folly. It is a no-brainer. It is impossible because the very nature of religion demands exclusiveness for its particular god. And, you could not convince them that they are all made up by men and not that essential.

71. Some mind-warped terrorists think their violence and destruction will hasten the coming of the true Messiah. The individual must weigh this intolerable view and not give support to such notions.

72. Just a little humor, if I may. Someone tell Dan Marino the ancient Greeks used to worship dolphins very fervently. Seriously, this wonderful giving person who has been a great role model for everyone deserves the new Dan Marino Boulevard honor.

Many people do not know of his outstanding work for children with severe challenges, especially those classified as autistic. He gets a very high grade as a quarterback but more importantly as a person.

73. Slow the growth. The human population is expected to reach 8.5 billion in just the year 2025 and most of the growth is in the poorest areas of the world where babies are dying from lack of food and medicine.

As mentioned before, valiant efforts are being made to slow population growth. We must catch up with the needs of the people we have before we go over the critical number we can sustain. Science and the ingenuity of man may raise that critical point but first, our distribution of food and basic needs have got to improve by leaps and bounds.

74. Richard Pryor defended his vulgar foul-mouth utterings by saying Don Johnson shoots someone in "Miami Vice," Arnold Schwarzenegger kills dozens of people in the movies, and people criticize Pryor for foul language. He says the critics are ignorant and should grow up. He uses cursing for emphasis.

Many of us who are not ignorant object to the negative influences of the violence and the lack of class in the incessant cursing that our society has embraced. If you cannot emphasize a punch line in a joke without a four-letter word, then try a new profession. I hope this principle makes our CODE for living.

75. Swearing on a Bible that is full of God-ordered useless murders and full of so many other horrors is ridiculous!

76. Why did Jesus gloss over such heart-breaking issues like slavery, tyranny, liquor, opium, and foreseeable to him, nicotine? When he showed up at a wedding feast, he became part of the greatest problem the world has ever experienced besides war — the alcoholic. He turned the water into intoxicating wine (Oinos) — not grape juice.

77. Pope Paul XII was told of the round up of Jewish people in Rome. Fearing Hitler, he did nothing to save them; he placated Hitler throughout WW II.

Now the saint historian and others are recommending Pius XII for sainthood and the Jews, rightfully so, are up in arms saying it would be a colossal shame. I could care less when people vote someone in to be a saint but to deliberately slap the Jews in the face with this guy crosses the line.

It would be like putting King David the president of a college that taught morals. All David did was take Uriah's wife, Bathsheba, for adultery and send her husband out to die. Yet, he was forgiven and was close to God's heart.

What kind of debauchery do religions expect people to swallow? Pope Pius was no saint. Neither was David.

78. The ritual or practice of confession in Catholic confession booths and in Protestant altars is a childlike process, but it is enormously psychologically helpful to people whose views and emotions are childlike and immature. Often a child knows Santa Claus is Dad, but he loves the scenario and especially the presents. So he goes along with the charade.

Catholics know they are talking to a man who calls himself a priest or father, but the unloading of guilt is worth it to them. Especially when father says it's all forgiven. Sometimes a certain number of "Hail Mary, Full of Grace," is required and other little penalties, but the lifting of the guilt and fear is a positive thing if one is childish enough to believe it.

79. People always cry out to their God in the times of disaster. If they survive, they say it was a miracle or an answer to prayer. A train wreck occurs or an airplane crashes. Some survive, most die.

Why would God be so selective and choose sinners and religious faithful to live? Which side was God on in the sinking of the *Titanic*, the people in the pitifully few lifeboats or the hundreds who went down in the sea? How did God make these choices?

80. Oregon has been on the cutting edge in many areas especially in their granting citizens the legal right for assisted death. This should be a right within the authority of the individual when circumstances are so overbearing, one chooses to terminate their own life.

Self-euthanasia is a practice that has gained widespread attention. Videos show one how. Some physicians cooperate. Some will not, just like abortion. Our CODE should allow it, not promote it, but in any case emphasize appropriate safeguards.

81. Inability of people to sort out religious fears and demands may enter the etiology of a number of mental illnesses.

82. Religionists' faith is so weak that they constantly seek tangible evidence to back up their beliefs. Some claimed to have found Noah's Ark, which stayed frozen most of the time. They did not. They flock to see a picture of Mary crying, an image on a church wall, a black stone in Mecca, a wailing wall in Jerusalem, and a shroud supposedly placed on Christ.

If they really believe, why all of the far-out desperation for tangible proof, which they ordinarily dismiss as not needed when their beliefs are questioned? It is a strange antinomy yet the need for holy things and holy sites have become an obsession with the faithful in almost all religions.

83. Hitler was not religious, but he mastered the use of regimentation and played the indoctrination card so well he might have been a powerful religious leader had he chosen to become one.

84. "There is only one success — to spend your life in your own way," wrote Christopher Morley. That is only partially true and needs clarification. Every serial murderer lived up to that saying. If you have a successful life, you can be independent, but without care and concern for others, your life is F, a complete failure.

85. Being a non-religious or atheistic nation does not guarantee peace. On the contrary, Nazism, Fascist, Communism, and other ruthless philosophies are created to control, exploit and degrade mankind. Religious hatreds do cause wars, which no one can deny, but if all religions were abolished, would there be no more wars?

Wars would continue unless some common behavior CODE or road map is generally followed loaded with morals, decency and fair play wrapped in an abiding love for human beings. This, to me, is the essence of what our project should be about. It is our over-arching challenge.

86. What is the difference between ghosts and angels? None. Neither exists.

87. The so-called closely woven wheat field designs were done by men at night and proved to be a hoax. They used ropes and boards in a skillful manner. The gullible still want to believe in beings from outer space.

Let us concentrate on the reality of the problems of this world and do something about them instead of imagining little E.T.s with big heads. A phenomenon with some religious people is seeing miraculous gold dust manifestations raining down from heaven. The gold dust is really plastic film. People still believe.

A good rule of thumb for religion, scientific studies, wild tales is to test it with your common sense and reasoning powers.

88. Shintoism deserves very little attention. Ancestral spirits inhabit all aspects of nature and its belief in the divinity of the Japanese emperor is weird.

The bulk of Japanese after defeat and surrender in WW II began to question this belief. Before 1945, it was the state religion. The Kamikaze pilots proved they would die for their beliefs. Some still worship their ancestors as Shinto believed.

Similar ancestral worship existed among Egyptians and American Indians. CODE 3-M should not interfere with such bizarre beliefs as long as they do not seek to evangelize and control others like Japan hoped to accomplish.

89. How far should society go to try to rehabilitate people who have chosen crime, alcohol and dope? How does society rehabilitate a murderer or child molester? We spend multiplied millions for counselors begging people not to commit suicide. We spend small fortunes keeping a preemie baby the size of a mouse alive that will probably have severe problems the rest of its life. We spend ridiculous amounts of time imprisoning non-violent criminals because they took or sold crack.

I don't know how far we should go, but we have to balance this against the clean water, vaccinations and other things so many children in the world all crying out for so desperately. We should care for dope addicts but at what cost to the depri-

vation of precious little innocent children around the world?
The addicts made a choice. These precious children have no
choice.

90. A rather disturbing and disgusting phenomena is for
people who gain wealth, success or celebrity status to say God
did it and without Him, it could have never happened. How
about Ted Turner, Donald Trump, Babe Ruth, Dennis Rodman,
Magic Johnson, and the atheist Russian athletes who do so
well in the Olympics?

Is this claim made to try to convince others that God has
made them something special and selected them to be wealthy
and others to be starving to death? I doubt if that would fit
most definitions of the great merciful and loving God. A poor
wretched person in India may be one of the best Christians
ever and die in abject poverty.

91. Thomas Jefferson cut out all of the miracles from his
Bible and from his history with Sally; he paid little attention to
the rest of it. The people who say they believe every word of the
Bible know very little about how the Bible came into being and
very little about all the things voted out or discovered later.

92. Ellen Church Semple wrote in 1911, "Man is the product of the Earth's surface. This means not merely that he is a
child of the earth but that the earth has mothered him, fed
him, set him tasks, directed his thoughts, confronted him with
difficulties and whispered hints for their solution."

This is about the most ardent nature worshipper I know of.
She opened up new vistas in a sense in 1911, but it is too comprehensive for my thinking. I will admit it raises the appreciation for the surface of the earth like we have tried to raise
appreciation for the wonder of man. Man does not need imagined gods.

Continental dissonance occurs when one strongly believes
something and finds it to be untrue. One can easily see how
upsetting this can be. However, one should rest assured that
truth will win a place in their hearts.

94. I had rather have a bugle to play "Taps" at my funeral
to bring closure to my family and friends than some preacher
talking about my soul being whisked away through the pearly
gates by the angels. Nothing said will have changed the life I
lived and hopefully that life would speak for itself in good
deeds rendered.

95. It is promising to know we are mostly living in a secular society. People say they believe in God, but check out the
number in church, synagogues and mosques on worship day.

Only a fraction seriously practice their religion and many look for any little reason to skip out. The faithful usually consist of old people. Then there are people with social needs, "dress up to be seen" needs and youth who are forced to attend. Most of the congregation consists of old people and women. Yet others are highly welcome and encouraged to attend. The services are extremely boring as a rule.

Non-mainstream churches have learned that you have to have somewhat of a show and entertaining to attract crowds. Rock gospel is popular. Preachers crack clever jokes and rail at the people. A few loud guitars and electronic organs help and wild-type yelling preachers run all over the place.

There is a charismatic movement that emphasizes praise and worship. They click the words of choruses on the wall that guests or visitors have never heard and sing or chant those choruses, usually Old Testament psalms until an ordinary person is drained out of patience or interest. However, this is the proven formula that works. Some add dancing to the program.

These services will eventually overcome the traditional styles of worship for mainstream churches — Episcopalians, Catholics and whatever. It will rejuvenate things for a while, but will eventually go the way of the Big Tent revivals.

The so-called dead services churches are on the way out. This is no longer a Christian nation. It is indeed a secular nation and most people already could care less about the old traditional religions that existed when the Constitution was written.

96. If the time comes, and I hope it does not, when a human is genetically part animal and part human, will the theologians claim it too has a soul?

97. Brotherhood on this planet is the very price and condition essential for the survival of mankind. Division is the enemy. We have to find ways to work and enjoy life together and as "equals" in rights and opportunities with no hatred.

98. A tee-shirt caught my attention recently. It read, "Never underestimate the power of stupid people in large groups."

99. Humor is a great tonic for people. Where is Will Rogers when we need him? Most comic strips are refreshing and helpful and useful like Peanuts, Snuffy, Dagwood, Mickey Mouse, Popeye and a thousand-and-one picture scenes.

Political cartoons seem to say it all and they keep us from taking the politicians too seriously. Oh yes, there are a few statesmen in the group. Taking life too seriously can be antithetical to happiness. Learn to laugh at yourself. Everyone else laughs at you. Comedy can be great!

100. The Hebrew God gave power and blessed many bloody heroes besides Saul and Elijah. A long list of them is in the Old Testament, but I must highlight just a few more.

Simeon and Levi killed all the men of a whole city with their swords to avenge the defiling of their sister. Shangar delivered Israel by slaying 600 Philistines with an ox goad. Samson, as most people know, killed a thousand Philistines with the jawbone of an ass.

King David's chief of army captain killed 800 men with his spear in one battle; of course, David was just a lad when he killed Goliath with one smooth stone and then chopped off his huge head.

God wiped out everybody but Noah and his family. One could go on and on. If this does not give the picture of a vengeful, bloodthirsty God, nothing will.

101. One of the most unreasonable commands of Jesus is "be ye therefore perfect." This is unrealistic and guilt-producing and if He said it, it should have never been recorded for people to have to follow. Humans cannot be perfect like the father (Matthew 5:48). Who would want to be like Jehovah?

102. Religious prejudice spills over into politics. Why does a distinguished senator like Orrin Hatch get a pitiful amount of votes when he looks like a president and has such a splendid record for the people? He's a Mormon, that's why.

He should run as a mainstream religionist or even if he ran as an atheist, he would get more votes. Religious people seem to hate religious people.

103. Laws against someone's idea of sin will never work. Pot is illegal. Arrest them and prostitutes, then buy a six-pack of alcohol drinks and go home, watch TV and be proud that you have done your duty as a police officer.

104. Isn't it strange that no one ever came back from the grave like Lazarus who had been buried quite a while? Houdini faked it with a recording. Even the powerful modern TV healers can't pull this one off. Again, common sense and reason go a long way.

105. Cannot God protect his own house? Roofs fall in and people are killed. One man admitted burning 26 churches to the ground. People rush for more insurance. Why did not God strike the church arsonist down before he wreaked all this havoc?

Surely, some of those churches if not all were sincere

places of worship. God makes claims to protect his people, but He seldom if ever delivers. Yet, people rebuild their churches, bury the dead and still worship that same unseen God who could not or would not protect His places of worship.

106. Peace on earth depends on many things. Food is an obvious essential requirement. Jehovah rained down manna for the Hebrew people when they were starving, but He has neglected so far to rain down food for the starving in old China and present-day India and Africa? Does God discriminate? The Old Testament says He does. Yet, billions of minorities have worshipped God anyway.

107. Is Jesse Ventura, Governor of Minnesota, correct when he says organized religion is a sham? People need numbers to give them a license to stick their nose in other people's business. Religion is a crutch for some weak-minded people.

Rarely will a politician be so candid. He has paved the way for others. What politicians believe in religious matters should never be an issue. The hypocrisy, claiming to believe when they are lying, is an issue.

108. Atheism was set back a hundred years when Hitler, Stalin, Chinese leaders and others embraced it, coupling it with aggression and horror. What a shame! It is now time to realize that most atheists are compassionate and caring people who grieve at the horrors religion has brought to humanity.

The CODE, in essence says to people to reach higher than atheism or religion and promote brotherhood among everyone whether in religion or whether they are non-believers.

Atheism is the belief of millions of people around the world. The highest percentage — about 20% — reside in Europe. North Americas about 10%. Asia is about 20%. Compared to 1900, there has been a sharp surge in atheism. Millions simply reject the notions of God.

I appreciate what David said about seeking a caring and merciful god who practices what he preaches — love, fairness and peace. None have showed up yet in human history, but I admire David and others who quest for the impossible dream. Our CODE should not be impossible, but practicable and useful to each human on the planet.

RACHEL BROOKS' LIST

1.   Most people know so little about Jesus. Some know He was born in Bethlehem in a manger at Christmas. He did miracles, was crucified, rose from the dead, ascended to heaven, and promised to return. Some know Him as their Savior because they believe He died on the cross that through His blood they could be forgiven of all their sins and become a Christian.

If you do not know much about Christ, I suggest you read the Gospel of John, the fourth book of the New Testament in the Bible, to learn of His life and purpose for mankind. John has only 21 very short chapters and it gives the words of Jesus himself. It is not necessary for a person to read all of the Bible to become a Christian. Faith in Jesus makes you a Christian.

Many criticize the Bible and have never read it. When you can, the whole Bible from Genesis to Revelation should be read. Few people have read it from beginning to end.

I believe everyone in the world should read the Gospel of John. It might make a huge difference in the world. I realize we are not here to promote a particular religion, but this step is recommended if you really want to understand me and the topics I will offer and discuss very briefly.

2.   A university researcher surveyed 17 developed nations and found that Americans are most likely to accept the Bible as the actual word of God and it is to be taken literally, word for word. And Americans are least likely to call the Bible an ancient book of fables, legends, questionable history, and just moral precepts written by man without divine inspiration.

I wonder if there is a connection to this fact that America is the greatest of all nations. When we lose respect for and allegiance to the Bible, our country will go the way of the

Egyptians, Babylonians and Romans. We will become a "has-been" power for morality and freedom. Unfortunately, we have been moving in that direction for several decades of "anything goes."

3.   Good people around the world are sick of the race issue. The CODE must be clean-cut on its stand and declare all humans are equal period. Extremists on all sides should realize that race is nothing but a social label. We are all God's children, brothers and sisters.

If, as I believe, the vast majority of people feel this way, why do we allow extremists to keep the racial pot boiling? Each individual should purpose in their own heart to be cleansed from all racist feelings and their acts will reveal this cleansing.

4.   Who decides what mainstream churches are? The godless ultra-liberal media has proclaimed that the fastest growing movement in the world, the Pentecostals are considered outside of the mainstream religions.

I believe people who believe the whole Bible and the fundamental things in the Bible like being "born again" are the mainstream. And, if one will search the history of the more elite and acceptable denominations, they will find out all of them were fundamentalists in their origin.

The Presbyterians for example used to drive big stakes in the ground so the people could clasp their hands around them and shake under the anointing power of God. I have yet to see the Pentecostals do that one. It is no wonder many people dismiss religious organizations because of our internecine bickering.

Yet I am prepared to go forward with good things even from Muslims who are to be commended when they forbid alcohol, drugs and a number of other beliefs they foster. CODE 3-M can be a force that is not submerged in my particular faith, mainstream or radical. So let's get on with it.

5.   Many good efforts are in progress. The Council on American-Islamic Relations is trying. Recently, they led a fight to keep a debasing TV show off the air called "God, the Devil, and Bob." It was supposed to be a comedy, but the council labeled it as being a tasteless and trivial portrayal of God.

NBC said it was never their intention to offend anyone. Of 215 affiliates at least a dozen refused to air the show; others are considering the same path. It may not be much, but it shows that decent people with moral values can be at least partially successful when they stand up against blasphemy and negative influences.

6.   During the Third Millennium I believe all separate races will largely disappear and the race issue will be moot. Perhaps it will become politically incorrect to mention it. I hope so.

7.   Abortion politics are a disgrace. I would not ever have an abortion nor would I stick my nose in the private, delicate, sensitive and personal issue of a woman who had an abortion. It is a terrible shame this issue flowed from improper religious influence to even worse, political influence.

Personal choice on private matters are no one's concern. If you are against abortion, don't do it. If you find yourself making this choice after due consideration, do not be intimidated by anyone. I don't recall the Catholic Church making a big deal about giving miscarriages last rites and praying them out of purgatory until the baby was born independently of the woman.

The male preachers whooping and hollering against abortion have never been pregnant. I have every right to my personal belief and so do other females. I hope our CODE 3-M will take a similar stand.

8.   The majority of families in the next century will raise their kids without the presence of both biological parents. The trend is frightening according to the report of the General Social Survey from the National Opinion Research Center. In 1972, 73% of children lived with their original parents who were married. By 1988, this dropped alarmingly to 51%.

Of course, there are good reasons for some of this, but the facts are that families are smaller and less stable, marriage is less central and co-habitation more common. The value of children and the values for children have changed. Gender roles are blurred and in many cases, disciplines of any kind have gone out the window.

The face of the American family has greatly changed and sadly not for the better. Tolerance for premarital sex increased from 36% saying it was always wrong in 1972 to only 27% in 1998 saying it was always wrong. These facts disturb me and I will vote that the CODE 3-M be in the 27% which is probably 25% now in the year 2000.

9.   I love my country. I love my flag. I get cold chills when I sing the "Star Spangled Banner" and "America the Beautiful," but as I have been contemplating and praying about people everywhere in the world. I am convinced that God thinks of all of us as his children, regardless of nationality.

I have a vision of a world without any artificial boundaries, like you might see from the Space Shuttle. It is a vision of people all over the world, working and living together and enjoying the good life together, just like we all are doing on this ship which can go anywhere there is six feet of water. I am not smart enough to say when or how this will be brought about, but someday it will happen.

When it does, the birds will chirp new songs of victory. Stars will seem more beautiful and brighter than ever. Faces that are bowed in sorrow will smile a new smile and rejoice because love and respect will have been triumphant over hatred and war! Man has been endowed with enough intelligence to make this happen someday, somehow, someway.

10. On January 16, 1920, prohibition of alcoholic beverages in the United States under the 18th Amendment to the Constitution was passed. It was repealed by the 21st Amendment in 1933 because people said it didn't work. People still say it didn't work before and it won't work now.

My grandmother says it did work then much better than the legal drinking going on today that robs families of decent parents or spouses and inflicts untold economic disaster. Today it takes the lives of innocent people on the highways. Twenty-five times more people are shot by drunks than during the days of Prohibition

It did not work perfectly, but there was little, if any, binge drinking in colleges. Bootleggers abounded, "rotten booze" and "white lightning" killed many, but it showed young people it was disastrous. It worked to brand people visiting the speakeasies as vile, unprincipled sinners. It worked to save God only knows how many lives.

Yes, Prohibition on balance did work and we should bring it back. Although I never experienced those days of Prohibition, there are many people, probably not most, who agree with grandma. What is the answer to the binge drinking of our college students and the ruination of precious people in every strata of society? Society condones alcoholic participation without being cognizant of the tremendous cost.

11. Can anyone see the movie or read "The Diary of Anne Frank" and not have their heart strings plucked out in caring sorrow? If so, they may be alive physically, but they are dead spiritually. This is but one example of horror and inexplicable agony man will inflict upon man.

Can't we, mustn't we do something about the repeat tortures and violence going on in the world today? Perhaps the only effective way is to get one individual to feel as we feel, another individual and another until the number is over-whelming enough to cause and continue peace.

Surely most everyone in the world would agree to stop the suffering. You, as an individual, may be surprised how much influence you have in this mission. Perhaps you have said, "Alas, I'm just one small person with no money to speak of and no power." I challenge you to challenge ten other people to try and get them to challenge ten others and so on until almost everyone says they are against war and acts accordingly!

It may take centuries, but you will know what you did for the cause of peace. No, the world is not perfect and may never be, but as an individual I vow to lay a brick of perfection now and then when the opportunity arises. I will do my part to leave the world a little better off because I was born and lived in it.

12. I vote for music. The power of music takes one to a higher place. In music, as in poetry, one can sense an effort to understand human nature, the various forms and moods par-allel human feelings and often create them or appease them. Music can boost the immune system and make one healthier.

Musicians and composers, when interviewed, allude to something larger and greater than the song or instrumental strings. It may be our basic need to stand in awe or worship. We sense that there is something greater if only we could get a handle on it.

(One caveat please, rap is not music. It has no redeeming quality. It builds hate and decent people hope it is a fad that will blow away.)

People should be allowed to choose the type of real music that lifts them to become a better person. Tax money should not go to support opera and symphony music nor should it sup-port country or jazz or gospel concerts. If people do not sus-tain it, let it fail; the same is true of poetry, literature, paint-ings, sculpture, and any art. The self-ordained definers of the arts are fallible. There is universality in these things that are positive, but folks have a choice. We should be broad-minded as religious people.

I love it when Barbara Striesand, a Jew, sings "Ave Maria." It should be very moving to every Christian who believes in the Holy Virgin, the mother of Jesus. Artistic expansion through the dance, theater or whatever can be a strong posi-tive uplifting and energize all kinds of patriotic and good moods, especially romance.

13. Jesus gives hope of forgiveness and the hope of heaven. The Bible does not seek to prove Jesus is the Son of God. It declares it! Well, many may say if He is the Son of God, why do we have war and poverty and such? The answer is simple. The Son of God did not take away choice from human beings. It would reduce us to animals.

Our misery and negative things on earth are because of bad choices; the positive and wonderful things renown to our wise choices. None of us would want to be lowered to the level of the nature of animals so we must use our choice power prudently.

14. Being drunk or "smashed" is not a laughing matter as Hollywood and TV comics often portray. A drunk at a Presidential inauguration party is just as obnoxious and indecent as a drunk in a cheap bar. It is not funny but a public disgrace!

15. Severe penalties for severe crimes. The Lindberg law has proven to any intelligent and fair mind that severe penalties work. They must be quick and fair to all.

16. Devil worship, witchcraft, fortune telling, astrology, tarot cards, cults, psychics, bones, soothsayers, medicine men, and similar fakes do not deserve mention. Avoid all these people. They have nothing to offer that is good.

17. Sincerity and dedication are noble attributes but do not suffice if they are given to a false notion. Every religion has had sincere, even practical followers. So there have been billions of people who were very sincere in their worship but wrong like the poor Egyptians believing in all these made-up gods.

A lady was riding on a train in 1929 going through the snowy mountains at night with her seven-month-old baby in her arms. She was going home for Christmas. She kept pestering the conductor to be sure to tell her when the train got to Elizabethton. He told her not to worry; he would come back and tell her when the little town was the next stop. Finally, he did return to her seat and said, "Get your things together. It is snowing pretty hard. The next station is Elizabethton. Do you have far to go?"

" No," said the lady. "My folks live only a block away and they will be there for me."

The old steam driven train rumbled on. They halted to take in water from one of those old water tanks by the track. The lady with her well-wrapped baby got up. She grabbed her suitcase and stepped off the train. At this time the train had received the needed water so it moved on. When they stopped a little later at Elizabethton, the conductor went back to help her off the train. She was nowhere to be found.

The next day she was found frozen to death with her frozen baby clutched in her arms. She believed she was getting off at the right place. She could not have been more sincere and striving to do the right thing. She believed incorrect information and stepped off into disaster.

I pray for so many everywhere who believe in a religion that is not the true way taught in God's holy word. Jesus said, "I am the way, the truth and the light. No man cometh unto the father except by me. Ye must be born again."

It is a fallacious argument that says as long as people are sincere they will get to heaven.

18. Love and care for yourself because you cannot love and respect others if you are incapable of loving yourself. Of course, you can go to extreme and love nothing but yourself and become disgustingly self-centered and non-caring for others. Keep the scales well balanced by loving inward and loving outward. What more important guideline could I list?

19. I am a deeply religious person and I believe it will help me follow the principles of the CODE very easily. I don't believe we can ever get agreement to put all my ideas in the CODE, but I know one can keep the faith they have and adopt the CODE in a basic sense. If a guideline in the CODE is contradictory to my faith, I will skip it and follow the ones that I can give my honest allegiance. If every person will do the same, great progress will have been achieved.

20. Our society has become infected with too much "psychobabble." If a murderer is caught, someone points out he may have been abused as a child. Then all the more reason he or she should not abuse anyone else. Millions upon millions of children down through the ages have suffered unprintable abuse and did not ever even consider murdering anyone. This dodging accountability has turned our society upside down already and explaining away things is exactly the wrong thing to do!

21. I could never overstate the power of peer pressure on youth and all people. We must develop the strength within ourselves not to become sheeplike pawns for the manipulation of others.

If everyone's drinking poison like in the Jim Jones cult disaster, do I have to do it? No, they could shoot me or whatever. I would not and could not be such a sheep. If everyone's smoking when I was a young girl, so I must smoke? No. I never did and never will. When and how can we get people to believe they have an intelligent mind and the power to say yes or no.

22. The ultimate and best competition is within yourself. I like golf because you are not only playing others usually, but you are mainly trying to improve yourself. You know your strengths and weaknesses better than anyone does and I do endorse the novel idea of grading oneself. I am more interested in how God grades me. Yet the exercise of me looking at me and trying to move to new levels is a positive and fascinating thing.

23. One should not be judged on the amount of riches one has, but on the responsibility one takes for himself and others.

24. Most fundamentalists think Catholics are misguided and the Catholics think the ardent fundamentalists are like a cult. I'm beginning to wonder and I feel a little ashamed to admit, if religious intolerance may not be the greatest sin that has plagued the human race?

25. One extreme to the other seems to be the nature of mankind. In 1915, a magazine listed the rules for women who were schoolteachers: "You will not marry during the term of your contract. You are not to keep company with men. You must be home by 8 p.m. unless you are attending a school function. You may not loiter in ice cream stores. You must get permission from the school board if you travel beyond the city limits. Riding in a carriage or automobile with a male is forbidden, unless he is your father or your brother. You may not dress in bright colors. You may never dye your hair. You must wear at least two petticoats. Your dresses must not be shorter than two inches above the ankle."

These are all ridiculous requirements. We cannot force our stupid moral ideas on others. But the point I am making is that women have gone to extremes. For example, dresses are a foot above the knees not ankles and bathing suits cover as little as possible to avoid complete nudity. Is not there a reasonable common sense balance in all of this hokum? I hope so and I believe most women know so.

26. Are many people so morally bankrupt that they must watch "Big Brother," "Survivor" and similar voyeuristic television trash? Is this much different than going to a strip show which many of them would never consider?

In many ways, it may be worse than strip shows or nudist gatherings because children watch it. What next? Group marriages on TV? Yep. People would watch it play out in compounds. TV has gone downhill at a fast rate. There are still some good programs, but the ugly is overcoming the decent.

27. Mosaic or assimilation. Why not both? America and the rest of the world have lots of both. If people would keep their nose out of other people's business, it would work fine. We are ethnically divided and we are a melting pot. The many benefits of separate cultures are obvious in architecture, music, the arts, customs, dress, festivities, and other practices. And, the blending in of cultures has many advantages. The key is to let it flow. Don't force it either way.

28. On December 25, 1916, the British and the Germans stopped World War I long enough to sing songs together, but it would end at midnight and they would have to kill each other again. The moratorium worked like it has in other wars. Why not call for a moratorium on all wars just for one century, then maybe one would not go back to it seeing we could live together in peace?

29. The great Helen Keller said it is not possible for civilization to flow backwards while there is youth in the world. There will always be a large core of each generation that will meet the challenges. I believe that statement and I desire to support every young person I possibly can to move their life and humanity forward.

30. The term "teenager" took hold after World War II. Before the war, the people in that age range were roughly referred to as "young persons." Now it is a tough era to go through because a teenager is stereotyped by adults and subjected to commercial power and exploitation. Then there are the negative idols and heroes teenagers are suppose to "just love" regardless of whether they are dope takers with no morals or whatever. They encourage each other to ignore their parents and all adults. Forget the rules. Get what you want.

31. Some horrible disasters are beyond our control. We have horrendous earthquakes, killing hurricanes, typhoons, tornadoes, volcanoes, floods, droughts, and raging fires started by lightning. We may never be able to control these calamities, but we can control war and we can reduce violence and suffering and we must.

Long live the organizations who help out during these disasters like the Red Cross, the Salvation Army and others all over the world that we have not even heard about. A sympathetic heart is like a spring of pure water bursting forth from the mountainside.

32. We have gone too far technically in our extreme effort to take God out of our society. To satisfy one or two, who are

complaining in a community, we yank out Christmas plays, prayer over the sound system and prayer on the athletic field. "In God We Trust" is in the capitol of the US and on coins. Benjamin Franklin led the group in prayer after the Declaration of Independence and legislature chaplains pray for lawmakers at the beginning of sessions. A fact not generally known is that the Capitol building was used as a church and religious services were held there. This is verified in the Congressional Record of 1800 and the diary of John Quincy Adams.

On the one hand, the top level of government supported by tax money, has prayer and worship in their building and our youth are forced to forego this privilege. The Christian religion was the prevailing religion along with the Ten Commandments which are no longer legal in schools. What an erroneous tragedy! Oh consistency, thou art a jewel. Cannot our CODE recommend an end to this nonsense?

33. The challenge of a mobile society. The experience of losing a loved one is the number one stress producing event. Divorce is number two and moving out of the city to another city or state is third.

The characteristics of the new location give a sense of strangeness and incongruity that cause increased anxiety and depression to many people, pre-occupation with one's self, often somatic changes, a general withdrawal laced with suspicion and even hostility. Some people adjust well and rapidly. Others can grow ill or experience marked discomfort and develop intense disorders in mood; they never adequately adjust. Some use the move as a means of gaining attention and increasing control.

Rational reasons should be shared with all involved in the move, especially children and friends left behind. Immediate effort must be made to identify the positives of the new place and gradually get involved with the community, church, sports, whatever. Be friendly and interesting to establish new friends. Do not be a complainer and hark on how great things were where you moved from. Otherwise, you may be told the same road that brought you to the new community can carry you back to your lost paradise.

CODE 3-M should recognize the large and increasing number of people who are moving. Those who are established should be neighborly in perhaps a cautious way until a more solid relationship is desired by both parties. The practice of knowing and appreciating neighbors is a lost art. We are social beings and as an individual, you need to extend the hand of friendship remembering the Golden Rule.

34. The Prodigal Son syndrome has gone too far. We are glorifying people who have hit bottom on dope, sex and crime who make a comeback. I appreciate their recovery, but the wrong message is being sent out to young people.

All sorts of glamorous people — even Betty Ford — became alcoholics or drug users. It shows you can hit bottom, be rehabilitated and become a hero. The truth is only a tiny fraction ever licks those problems. The Betty Ford Clinic is a great institution for a few wealthy people.

The problem is overwhelming and the impression that almost everyone experiments with drugs or alcohol like Clinton, Gore and Bush is the wrong message. Why can't we make heroes of people who never got into this stuff to influence our youth in the right way?

CODE 3-M should establish a guideline for individuals to praise those who have the intelligence and courage to say no in the first place.

35. There are billions of people who receive assurances that if they serve their God and die in the faith they will be with family and friends gone on before. There is great comfort from this belief. Even if it were not true, why would atheists attempt to discredit this sacred belief?

36. Let's have sensible gun control. There is a proper balance in the gun issue. Strict registration and background checks are essential, but just as important is the prosecution and punishment of law violators.

Over 2,300 years ago, the Greek philosopher, Aristotle, considered arms ownership the single most reliable indicator of whether a society was free. Plato, who believed in a benevolent dictatorship, took the opposite view considering ordinary people too reckless, too ruled by emotion, or not intelligent or judicious enough to be trusted to conduct their own affairs.

I side with Aristotle, though it is a political issue which it should not be. The individual has a right to own a gun if he or she is worthy.

37. War is war. All sides commit despicable acts, some worse than others. I am humiliated and embarrassed by massacres and atrocities inflicted on humans by other humans. This is an old sordid practice in military conflicts.

In 1565, a fleet of French ships led by Jean Ribault attacked St. Augustine. Pedro Menendez, the founder of St. Augustine, led the defense. A storm wrecked the French ships, but most of the soldiers and crew made it to shore. Ribault signed unconditional surrender after being promised mercy. The French were tied up and marched ten at a time behind the sand dunes. There all of the forces including Ribault were massacred. Thousands of such hatred and mercilessness acts have occurred. War is war and humans may have to be transformed into an animal like revenge killing creature. God help us to stop war!

38. If the African Methodist Episcopal Church can elect female bishops and Pentecostals have been ordaining women for over a half-century, why do the Catholics and Baptists forbid them to be pastors?

39. Inconsistency in religion fuels the non-believers. When I get through this project, I would like to see a CODE for religious people also. There must be more cohesion and common ground.

40. Crowd fervor and crowd fever. I have participated in huge religious crowds and shared the collective fervor and enthusiasm of the crowd. I have also gone to sports affairs, political affairs and noted some of the same dynamics.

It is compelling to do what the crowd is doing and many are just aping the crowd. However, this does not mean that some people are not really worshipping or enjoying the spectacular blocking moves of the athletes.

Large TV crowds orchestrated by skillful preachers like Billy Graham, Oral Roberts, or Benny Hinn do some good as people need numbers to bolster their faith. However, the exaggerated claims of soul saving and healings turn many Christians off. The prearranged prayer-warriors that run to the altar to get others to come and the falling out when touched only by the lead preachers raises doubts to others.

Anyway, I've learned to accept the true and real and to discern the false and improper. This type of worship and all types of worship are within the authority of the individual, so what style works for one may displease another. It is an area where we should live and let live.

41. Respect for all veterans because they deserve it. Anyone who has even donned the uniform and served his or her country is worthy of respect. Any war veteran, regardless of which war, deserves equal praise and respect. One can love and respect the participant even if they disagree with the war!

42. We should show compassion for the sick, especially the terminally ill. Why is it when one is sick, few will come to visit and encourage them? When one dies, why does everyone show

up at the funeral? It is right to care for and show compassion for people when they are alive and need it.

43. Faith is a strong thing. Some people believe that they can walk on hot coals and not be burned, lie on spikes and not be pierced, swallow swords and not be killed. Others believe they can handle snakes, be bitten and not die. I would not venture any of these things, but I do know my faith in God is strong enough to lead me through my whole life and get me to heaven!

44. Hollywood idols. Most people in Hollywood are plastic and hypocritical with their egos out of control. They develop a strange personality due to their fear of the roller coaster heading down swiftly anytime.

It is so hard for them to enjoy success. They have psychiatrists on call, go to psychics and practice yoga and ancient Asian crafts that the average person knows nothing about and cares nothing about.

Money and fame have claimed their souls to the extent that they will play any part regardless of its negative impact on youth. Most of them go the alcohol and drug route and don't realize their life style is being followed and admired by millions.

There are a few wonderful exceptions to the norm in show business. They have my utmost admiration because they bloom pure and white as the lily does surrounded by mud. Whatever happened to Shirley Temple and Roy Rogers movies? They were discarded as old fashioned, but Bambi and a number of other good movies have been made like E.T.

The problem is money. If the public refused viewing movies with so much sex, violence and blood, Hollywood would soon switch to what they would patronize. It is that simple. So the CODE must encourage each individual to see the best and avoid the rest.

45. Maximum individual choice is the democratic ideal. We must not just be regarded as consumer-creatures, surrounded by standardized goods, educated in standardized schools, fed a diet of standardized mass culture and forced to adopt standardized styles of life.

Let CODE 3-M strike a powerful blow for individual power and potential to blaze a separate trail and not be a rubber stamp to every dress style, housing style, automobile conformity, or whatever. The important thing in life is to use your own intelligence, conform if you wish or be independent if that appears to be your best choice.

46. What age will we be in heaven? I know it is not religiously or politically correct for a born again Christian to raise a tough issue, but above all I want to be as honest with myself and everyone else as I can. I am a strong believer, but I do have doubts. In the choir we sing, "I was walking along through that city when I spied an old couple I knew." The old couple was my mom and dad as the song goes.

Would I look old when my family and friends see me on the streets of gold? How old would my great great grandparents look? Will we all look at our peak — say 28 years old?

Then how will we "meet our friends and loved ones over on the other shore" as we lustily sing? Oh well, I just put my questions and doubts in the hands of the Lord when they arise. He will work out all of these logical questions according to his will. After all, he is God and I am just his child with a finite mind.

I then sing, "after we've been there 10,000 years a million or two, look for me for I will be there too." I believe that.

47. Cataclysmic changes when "born again." I personally have seen people I knew that smoked, drank and lots of other sins hit the altar in a tent revival or church, "pray through" and never do those things again. The power of God to change people who repent can be documented millions of times. They did not taper down or wear a nicotine patch. They were delivered. It can and it does happen! Did I hear someone say amen?

48. It is impossible to understand our present existence or look through a small window in the future if we do not master a general basic knowledge of man's past. In our obsession with gadgets and technology, we need not neglect to reflect on where we have been. The trail we see is both heart breaking and inspiring.

Let us cling to the principles that inspire and attempt to avoid the pitfalls that lead to heartbreak. We will often fail, but we can keep pressing toward the goal.

49. Dignity. The United Nations Declaration of Human Rights, Article 1, declares, "All human beings are born free and equal in dignity and rights." Webster says dignity is "worthiness or nobility."

I'm glad I looked that up because I had never before thought of a little baby born on the mountains of Peru as being noble. I knew the baby was worthy, but now I know it is noble and I want to treat everyone as I would nobility. What an inspiration!

50. Maturity can sooth rage. We now have road rage, air

rage, raging parents who kill each other at little league sports, players spitting on umpires, and dugouts looking for fights.

Rage is the sign of our times. Rage about war, murder, and starving children is what we need and act upon that rage. However, a mature adult will not rage if a discourteous or drunken driver cuts in front of his vehicle. Set an example, cool it. People are gauging your maturity level.

51.   One does not have to ever drink wine. Some say it is good for your health. The ingredient that may help the heart in wine is also in non-fermented grape juice. It is called cate- chin and is one of many flavoraids found in plants and non- alcoholic wine as well. This helpful nutrient doesn't work as well in alcoholic wine as in non-alcoholic grape juice because it is eliminated faster from the body. You cannot justify drink- ing wine for health reasons when alternatives are better.

52.   Moral relativism. I believe in moral absolutes that are eternal. There was a time in our history that if a president admitted to any kind of sex in the Oval Office or near there that he would have been not only impeached but also removed from office in disgrace.

Nowadays people are so-called more tolerant about private matters. After all, it didn't put the country in jeopardy. It did put the country in moral jeopardy when almost every teenag- er in the land saw what happened and knows he was allowed to remain as president. He did make a negative unerasable lega- cy for history.

Can our morals be so easily adjusted? Wrongs don't fluctu- ate and right moral things stand steady through every gener- ation. We did agree on thou shalt not kill, didn't we?

53.   The Apostle Paul said he learned to be content in what- soever state he was in. If you are not content most of the time in your circumstances, you probably will never be content without a radical change in your outlook on life.

54.   I have to wonder if people in places like Afghanistan don't despair of the culture in America that has so much crime, sex and mayhem. Do they wonder if the American way is the right example?

The example of Islam in American has not gained much ground. Louis Farrakhan adheres to his own brand of Islam, which is not exactly like most Muslims follow in the Near East. I hope that when people observe my life and actions, they will want to be a Christian. What one does speaks louder than what one says.

55.   Should there be an atomic war that spread around the

world, the major cities would be leveled like Hiroshima and Nagasaki. A few humans here and there would probably survive. I would hope they would devise a CODE and their first article would read, "Never again will humans fight a war. We will settle our differences in a peaceful manner through love and understanding because there is dignity and nobility in each baby that is born."

56. Like any other sweepingly successful invention, the computer has brought unusual positive contributions as well as disgraceful negative uses. Child pornography and hate groups rank among the very highest drawbacks.

We must teach avoidance to our child, youth and adults. Again, we do teach that it is dangerous to drink poison and people have to learn to refrain from doing it or they will die. If you discharge a pistol pointed to your brain, you will die. You have the choice not to join or be swayed by a herd mentality. Society cannot keep dangerous things completely away from people. We can't outlaw all ice picks and butcher knifes. We must teach people not to hate!

57. Predestination. I often worry about the fact God knows whether I am going to heaven or hell. Is it preordained? If He knows it, how can that be changed? At this moment I am slated for heaven or hell. God knows the answer. Most people are going to hell according to the Bible. Am I in that number or among the chosen few to got to heaven? Only God knows. But I just sing that hymn, "I can, I will, I do believe that Jesus saves me now." You can have doubts and still be a Christian if you do not surrender to the doubts.

BRIDGETTE
THOMPSON'S
LIST

Bridgette's mind kept wandering while she labored to make her list as concise as she could. Would David ever really become serious about her? Were his words about loving everyone of any race really genuine?

She caught herself and remembered that men use the saying, "Another streetcar comes along every 15 minutes," if ladies did not show their "hoped for" level of interest.

I know streetcars are the same for women as they are for men, she thought. However, this is an unusual streetcar and I don't want it or him to pass me by. What more can I do to help and yet not screw it up?

"Oh well," she mumbled out loud, "I've got work to do"

1.   Interracial marriages should be encouraged if both persons are in love and desire to spend their lives together. Today, only 2.2% of the world's marriages are interracial because of the tremendous pressure against it, both racial and religious.

Race baiters like Al Sharpton, Jesse Jackson, neo-Nazis, the KKK should be ignored in favor of Jimmy Carter, Jeb Bush, Colin Powell, J.C. Watts, and Ward Connelly. We do not have to eliminate any distinct race and all become tea-colored, but a much better percentage of interracial marriages would be a positive thing for the separate races. This increased understanding has occurred in families in most instances where interracial marriage has occurred.

2.   We endorse truth whatever it may be regardless of what system it may offend. People who burn books and stifle ideas, sane or wild, retard the progress of mankind. If only we had the written accounts of men that were made, we would be

much more informed about our history.

Thankfully, today it is impossible to eliminate books like the old religious leaders did in large bonfires. Computers have helped tremendously, but the facile method of printing has flooded mankind with all types of information and ideas. No one person or entity owns truth and so much of truth is still in the gold mine waiting to be extracted. And, so much of what we have blindly accepted as truth needs to be put in the volume of fables and myths.

3.   Reject mean, vengeful deities that are always threatening people. Why this "payback" personality if you disobey whatever they command on the one hand and teach forgiveness on the other hand?

Serve me or destruction will come upon you forever and forever. Fear God who hath the power to cast you into hell. He could not even cast Lucifer into hell. Why should I fear him? All kinds of punishment and an ending in hell fire are the fear tools of God.

Did God give "payback" to the Kennedy family because of old Joe's sins and liquor operations? This is nonsense yet the Bible God promised to punish the third and fourth generations for their ancestor's sins.

Others say God cursed Ham and turned him black, thus the Negroid race. The so-called Kennedy curses and Ham curse do not measure up to truth. If God did do it, why would any rational person choose to serve him? Hundreds of examples exist of deities being mean and vengeful and we are admonished to be God-like. This is incredulous!

4.   Celebrate what humans are and what we have accomplished. We know this for certain. Realize the power of man's creativity, not the imagined and unproved greatness of God.

Libraries are full of the accomplishments of men and women. God has not revealed anything he has accomplished except through the guessing and fantastic imagination of man and that through a series of conflicting writings and so-called prophets.

If you want to talk to me about God, which God? If you tell me to live right or else, whose view of what God says is right is accurate?

5.   Religions have called upon people to offer all kinds of sacrificing gifts to their deity. This must be condemned by the CODE.

Just one example tells us that five hundred years ago, on top of one of South America's highest peaks, the Incas sacrificed three children as a valuable gift to their gods. Recently, a team of archaeologists from the US, Argentina, and Peru found the near perfect remains of the two little girls and a boy between the ages of eight and fifteen. They were buried with dried meat, pottery used for ceremonies, along with miniature statues made of silver and gold. Freezing conditions on Mount Liullaillaco in the Andes 22,057 feet high preserved the bodies so well that most of the children's internal organs and body fluids remained intact.

These mummy-like precious children had no choice and no chance due to the stupid religious beliefs of their adults. Most everyone on earth now is shocked by this religious act, but how different is this from the previous and succeeding religions. The Hindus have thrown babies in the Ganges River and a thousand cults have killed people and animals on altars and crosses.

When will the human race rise up and say enough to all of this inhumane practice? No CODE for human behavior should fail to berate and condemn this damnable practice.

I realize what I am going to now raise as an issue in this sacrificial, killing concept to appease a God is very delicate. I do not wish to hurt anyone's feelings, but if I am wrong, it really matters little what my perspective may be. If I am right, and help uncover a truth, there should be a positive effect.

Believing with all your heart in something does not make it truth. Jesus being a so-called sacrificial lamb to God dying on the cross is the center-point of the Christian religion. One person is supposed to have allowed Himself (He could have called on ten thousand angels to come to His rescue) to be hung upon a Roman cross, bleed and die for all the sins of the world, each person's sins were to be covered by His blood.

The Jews who influenced His death and the Romans who carried out this terrible deed hardly realized the effect of their actions. The Christians evidently did not know this was a heathenistic custom dating back to ancient times. In fact, there is so much contamination in religions from the occults and tribal cults that an honest person really does not know what to believe. At any rate, sacrificing a human being to God whether it is Jesus or someone else is repugnant.

6.   One must, I know, start from what he or she truly knows and cannot doubt. Such things are numbered in the millions and are being enlarged as I write these words.

For example, I know I am alive. I know I can see. I know I can walk and talk. I know that two added to another two makes four. It does on earth and it does on the moon. I know water seeks its own level. I know hydrogen and oxygen combined produce water and so on.

Yes, there are many irrefutable facts. Therefore, we need to be very careful ascribing personal knowledge to something that is not a fact. We must distinguish between what we may think we believe and what we know. We may know what we believe at a given moment or for a lifetime. But if the belief is not true and not a fact, we cannot know it as truth.

Most, if not all, religious people are constantly proclaiming that they know their God is real. They know they have been saved. They know that they are going to heaven. What is more incredible is that they get a little hysterical and claim that they know God has spoken to them or told them in the spirit certain things. And topping that off, they expect rational people to accept their testimony or revelation. Well, I don't know God has ever spoken to anyone in any fashion and I know no one's God has ever spoken to me. Some people who make the claim that God has spoken to them and directed them to do this and so may be sincere.

However, many are simple charlatans who push their own personal agenda and wallet with these claims. The TV evangelists who say they know God works through their right hand or through their ministry because they know God gave them a special anointing are to be regarded as dangerous. They don't know any such thing and yet build financial empires, always begging for more money.

It is a pitiful situation all around the world. People send in money by the tons and say they know this is a man of God. Now the women have gotten into the act and appear on TV as celebrities on religious channels. Aimee McPherson led the way for these fakes years ago.

People do not know that God has spoken to them, much less anyone else. In fact, they don't even know there is a God. They can say, "I know I believe there is a God." Of course, some are sincere and some are not. They are flat lying concerning what God has told them to do. One person's defense for murder in court was that he knew God wanted him to kill his wife. The defense attorney could cite the Bible over and over where God ordered killings. This type of astounding ignorance tears up and destroys society. It does not fit in any decent human behavior map.

7. You do not need anyone's God to do the right and decent thing. You can love your neighbor and treat them like

you would like to be treated. You can list a thousand do's and don'ts and follow them if you, yourself muster up the strength.

George Washington said the nation needed religion as a source of moral power. Why then, did he own people? People from any religion or no religion know slavery is wrong and condemn it in their heart whether the religion does or not. Many other religious men owned slaves. There exists a superior morality that most religions espouse.

If you want to believe in something, believe in yourself. You have a brain. Do not loan it to people who did not even know the world was round. Do not mortgage it to screaming TV evangelists. You never have to take dope, drink whiskey or any other stupid, harmful behavior. You, in the final analysis, have to stop these behaviors or continue to choose wrongly. It is within the authority of the individual.

One must realize that good decisions will bring good consequences and vice versa. But in the end, one will have protected the integrity of his or her own mind. A mind is a terrible thing to give away; keep it always as your most precious asset.

8.   Cults. One cult, the pagan group Wiccans, performed a spring rite at an Army Base in Ft. Hood, Texas. Some politicians ranted and raved about it.

The fair and sensible question arises, where does religious freedom end? How many followers must a religion have in order to do its thing? The folly of the whole practice of giving deference to any religious practice brings on the consistency argument. If you give deference to one, should you not give deference to all?

Well, it seems to me that the thoughtful and fair solution is to refrain from giving deference to any religion, anytime, anywhere, if others are shut out. We must love and appreciate the people — not give special favors to their religion. This has proven to be a fatal move many times in human history.

Americans should take "In God We Trust" off the coins and currency because they are financed and used by everyone. We should stop praying in Congress — any type of prayer — because atheists have to help sponsor the salary of some cleric, politically appointed, to drone out meaningless words that certainly have little or no effect on the actions of Congress.

It is wrong and probably unconstitutional to give tax deference to mosques, churches, synagogues, religious schools, and colleges. In essence, the government is requiring people to support religious efforts and most of them are in conflict. One church possessed empty tax-free property on 37th Avenue in

Miami, Florida. Later it was sold for tremendous profit. These cases are legion. Whether legal or illegal, it is wrong!

9. Cruelty, torture, sadistic actions, though completely incomprehensible must be addressed. Laws do help prevent much cruelty. However, we must be more diligent and consistent in punishing each individual who perpetrates their terrible crimes when the person is guilty. Slick lawyers using unreasonable technicalities with rotten judges accept and encourage such behavior.

When leaders of nations who are cruel have a military force they can command, it is an awful situation that results in untold suffering. Human history is lined with indescribable torture and massacres. Much of it evolves from our fear and insecurity that another religion will triumph.

If the Jews were responsible for the crucifixion of Christ because of religious reasons, how can anyone, anywhere justify this torture? The Jews, until recent days, have tortured the Palestinians to get information even in these so-called modern times. Recently, they tried to outlaw torture, but many see this as an accepted modus operandi if the suspect is involved in terrorist action, which is also a cruel sadistic act.

All sides historically have used some form of torture. Terror breeds terror. Torture breeds torture. There should be consequences — perhaps death, but torture, no. We cannot claim to be civilized if we endorse torture of animals, let alone human beings.

I know all Jews are not uncivilized. Most are wonderful, decent, highly intelligent and productive individuals, but the ones who torture human beings are committing uncivilized acts. Have they not heard of the Holocaust where the Prince of Torture, Hitler spread this venom? It makes no difference if cruelty and torture is committed by atheistic tyrants or religious fanatics; it is anti-human and anti-civil and must be eliminated!

10. "God chasers," in my opinion, are just one of the recent efforts to gain notoriety and make money off religion. There are a thousand examples of this type of exploitation that decent people should condemn. Bumper stickers, t-shirts, jewelry, clothing, etc., certainly do not jive with Jesus throwing the money changers out of the temple, driving them with a scourge of whips.

There seems to be no end to the books published that are sold outright or sent as a gift, if you send money. These books and pamphlets make all sorts of wild promises of healing if you believe. If you do not receive healing, it is not the fault of the wealthy evangelist; you just did not have enough faith yourself or it was not God's will at this time.

If you have faith the size of a little grain of mustard seed, you can move mountains they scream, but I don't see any mountains jumping around, never have and never will. According to this nonsense, you could put all the faith of all the religions in a thimble, which would hold lots of mustard seeds.

The pitiful part is laws favor this medicine-man type of conning people out of their money. "You can't outgive God," they say with great fervor. So, send me a little "seed money" and God will prosper you. If there was a fiery hell, there should be a center spot for people who exploit weak-minded people for their personal financial gain.

Just the names of these charlatans, both men and women, would fill a good-sized book. Their sense of fairness has been seared with a hot iron and the litany of rationalizations they spew out is sickening. People who need to feed and clothe their own children better often send money in the mail to support these "worldwide ministries." If we could get an accurate total of what is sent in and what pitiful amount is given out, we would be disgusted beyond imagination!

11.   The war on drugs is a joke as long as alcohol and tobacco are legal.

12.   Illegal immigrants from Haiti are sent home immediately. Mexican illegals have gotten away with crossing the border and later even received amnesty. Yet, every politician in Washington claims they are not racist. Clinton intervenes in Bosnia, Kosovo, wherever whites, Jews or Arabs are in conflict to stop the carnage, but omits the wars in Africa. No wonder he will go down in history as the expedient president without consistent principles.

Most people in the world just don't treat the black or Negroid race like they do the whites or even the Asians. This is a fact that CODE 3-M should address. It is at least a worthy goal for human behavior to treat every human on an equal basis.

13.   We must abandon the human obsession to live forever. We make movies like "Cocoon" because our doubts of the traditional heaven are so strong. We overly crave something to shore up the ridiculous streets of gold, pearly gates, walls of jasper baloney that has been laid on us.

We need to focus on present living and contributing to others and forget this eternal life obsession. It is a concept that has done immeasurable harm to humanity, perpetuated largely by religious leaders for their own interests. This life is where it is. Live right here and if there happened to be a future, one would fare well.

14. The witch movement, in my opinion, is a farce. Though similar and just as ridiculous, the witch surge here and around the world may contain more danger because of its history and far-reaching nature.

The local covens, perhaps with 30-50 adults sitting around in a circle in black capes is a dangerous joke to mankind. Witchcraft is ancient and has seen many forms and claims. One woman near Providence, Rhode Island, that thrusts a sword above her head and exhorts the circle to raise a circle of energy around then and makes ridiculous claims.

Federal court rulings have recognized witchcraft as a legal religion. A positive veil has been spread on witchcraft to fool the courts and the people. It is a neo-pagan movement that regards nature as being charged with divinity. Since it has no Bible or essential text or authority, there are a large number of historical beliefs of the Egyptians and Greeks. Some refer to themselves as Druids.

The Internet is one of their tools listing 900 covens. They have an October festival in Washington. Tens of thousands of followers are known, but many more follow this religious group who are afraid to "come out" because of job and social reasons.

Some people still believe that witches are associated with black magic. The old 1486 book, *Hammer of Witches,* was written by a couple of Germans and served as a persecutor's manual. Many thousands of suspected witches were burned.

Other religions fight this religion like a rattlesnake. Some quote the Bible as saying there is a way that seemeth right to man but the end thereof is death. Of course, they apply this statement to anyone and any belief that disagrees with their little concepts of the correct religion.

The whole religious situation is astounding! There are so many people chasing a black cat in a dark room, it is worrisome to any caring person. Some of the witches grab positive ideas and incorporate these concepts into their darkness like extreme feminism and extreme environmentalism and other isms.

We are challenged as thinking human beings to accept any proven truth and reject any falsity. However, it is essential to make progress in our list of truths. The main reason I am an atheist is the strong similarity of characteristics I find in all religions whether Baptists, Catholics, Pentecostals, Jewish, Muslims, Buddhists, Hindu, Confucius, cults, or witchcraft.

All of them want to brainwash your mind to accept only their view and possess you and threaten you openly or obliquely if you don't adhere. A pox on each of their houses! In the final analysis, they have more in common than the sum of their differences! You can find some good in all of them if you seek it. Likewise, you can find a whole lot of fantasy and incredulous ideas in each of them if you are honest.

15. The deep hate held by religious people against each other is wrong and CODE 3-M must condemn it! There are millions of examples of this deep hatred. A recent one involves the visit of Pope John Paul II to New Delhi, India. A huge demonstration against the ailing, old Pope ensued. The Pope tried to declare the right to freedom of belief and worship.

One wonders how this highly educated person could not remember the denial of this freedom by the very organization he represents. The coalition of Hindu groups would have none of his pompous declarations. They called him a pimp for Christianity and compared the Christian conversion of Hindus to rape, calling for a halt in forced conversions. They demanded that the pope apologize for the historical abuses by the Roman Catholic Church.

The Pope said, "Let no one fear the church." This must have made Martin Luther turn over in his grave not to mention the multiplied thousands killed in the long, tragic years of the crusades. You could feel the hate in the crowd in this backward, populous country. The Hindu religion spawned Buddha and his beliefs. These religions and others have stifled science and any creditable search for truth.

The Pope went on to say God had commanded the gospel (his view, of course) was to be preached to all the nations in the world. The radical Hindu groups should not have acted like a bunch of wild people against the Pope, who is honest in his strange beliefs. The Pope had no business going to India to try to convert Hindus from their strange beliefs where many people are equally honest and sincere.

This obsession to convert the world is inherent in almost all religions with the possible exception of the Jewish people, who simply proclaim they are God's chosen people. Then they wonder why they have been persecuted down through the history of man. When you arrogantly claim there is but one God, Jehovah and he favors you and will enable you to endure against all enemies, it doesn't exactly set up a climate for peace, love and acceptance!

The more I study religions, the more I realize what a detriment they have been to mankind. We must find a way to erase fear from man of death and the obsession for eternal life or man will continue to invent religions as he has in all history.

We, who do not believe, cry out to the religionists for humanity's sake, stop hating one another! Can't you see you are causing conflicts and wars that take away the precious, innocent lives of men, women and children everywhere? Believe what you must, but don't hate others because they do not believe like you believe. Is not this the greatest sin of all?

16. The ACLU has supported some weird things, but there is a need for this maverick group. They provide a legal bulwark against a religious takeover and ruining America. We are supposed to have religious freedom and freedom not to be religious.

17. Non-religious people have a duty to see that no particular religion gains control of the society and to set an example of decency and love. We must ensure that the bloodshed caused by religious groups is eradicated. This may be too tall an order to fulfill, but a millennium is a long time and it is certainly the right direction.

18. Each individual should ask, "What do I want out of my life and what do I want my life to do for others?" What is the legacy I wish to leave? Will a little bit of the world be better off or worse because I lived? Or, would people have been better off if I were never born?

"Have I been concerned for my health and happiness or carelessly committed slow suicide? Will people remember me as one who would go the extra mile for the right thing? Will these people who knew me miss me as a positive, happy person or will most people be glad to see me go?"

19. Racial hatred within the same race is a double curse that is morally wrong and devastating. Probably the worst example in human history was the caste system in India. Unfortunately, strong vestiges of that terrible and inhumane system still exists. But the caste system spirit is in all races.

Comedian Chris Rock is humorous if you don't care who is being offended. He is black, but rails out to his audience, "I love black people, but I hate n——."

He claims he does not add to the problems by declaring the heightened hate he seems to generate is only enjoyed by mal-

adjusted people. He chides the black middle class for reject-
ing the black underclass. He warns not to hate gays because
you might have a gay son. He mixes in other fair and sensible
admonitions like take personal responsibility, take care of
your kids, do the right thing, but counteracts the little bit of
good by taking potshots at the NYPD and joking about hating
whites. Educated blacks often hold illiterate blacks in total
disdain. Many blacks manage to keep the caste system alive
by the lightness/darkness skin color, which white plantation
owners fostered with no shame.

When the federal government in DC finally began to push
for more black employees, the extremely light skin were the
first to be hired. Yes, there was a military Chief of Staff, Colin
Powell. Look at his skin color. Consciously or unconsciously, a
pretty light-skinned Negroid girl gets the job over a coal-black
unattractive black girl, especially if a white man is doing the
hiring.

People need to lift their head out of the sand and face some
realities in this extremely sensitive area. An individual has
absolutely no choice how dark his skin may be or the color or
texture of his or her eyes, and a thousand other gene-related
traits.

This is what I call "aesthetic prejudice" and it occurs in all
races and between races. To hate a person who is not handsome or beautiful according to your ideas of beauty is a terrible thing to do. We cannot all look like Liz Taylor, Tyrone
Power, Lena Horne, Denzel Washington, Connie Chung, Bruce
Lee or whoever is aesthetically pleasing. We must learn to see
the inside as well as the outside.

Barbara Jordan did not appear to most people to be as
attractive as Diane Sawyer. Which one would have made the
best president of the United States? I could write a book on
this point, but this is supposed to be a list with a brief clarification comment.

Okay, don't hate people that are not pretty to you. You may
not be so pretty to them. Remember that it works both ways.
Stop hating yourself and you can stop hating others.

20. Help only those people willing to put forth the effort to
help themselves as much as possible. We have created a new
type of slave in America, which bridges all races. We give people checks that are able-bodied and capable of work who won't
work; they play the system like a violin. Yet, they are miserable because they have no real self-esteem. They are "dependency slaves."

There has been some progress in this area, but the people on the dole in America are a national disgrace. Those of us who try to make something of ourselves and make the effort to get it together are sick and tired of the no-goods who brag about not working and making babies. In many instances, the government encourages this new slavery. The decent people in society are very willing to support cases where people try and cases where it is impossible to succeed because of sickness, old age, or handicaps. We are all disgusted with the laziness and lack of interest in helping themselves of millions who are capable of becoming taxpayers instead of leeches on those who work hard.

21. Recognize that modern psychology is not all positive. We have invented words for all sorts of conditions that are rarely real. The first time a little crisis occurs, we allow people to be depressed. Stress has been magnified and accepted beyond belief. Every job in America causes stress to someone in it.

Most of us have experiences that are difficult and present tough challenges. It does not help oneself to wallow in self-pity and yield to the temptations of facing so much stress that one cannot function.

Of course, there is real clinical depression and true stress situations. However, we have developed into an emotional "sissy" society, unwilling to shake off tough situations and move on like our grandparents had to do. Not everyone has the makeup and will to overcome and some do need professional help, but it has become a silly fad to run to a therapist of some kind almost every time we break a shoestring.

There are too many lawyers ready to sue on almost anything and too many therapists ready to take your money on little nothing things that an eight-year-old could solve.

It is not chic to have your own psychiatrist on call. It is a sign of failure to develop your own self-esteem in most cases. The field of psychology has in a fair overall appraisal, been worthwhile but it is being prostituted by so many on both sides of the desk that, if not checked, it will be more of a joke than a sensible way of treatment.

Teachers have, in many instances, swallowed up this trend. One teacher told me 82% of the children in the third grade had attention deficit. I thought to myself that this must be a very dull and unimaginative third grade teacher. Children are being over-medicated in their early years for being "polar" or "hyper."

If one truly has a problem, the professional better have true expert credentials if a correct diagnosis is made. "Everybody and his dog" now give out psychological counseling and much of it is very detrimental. If we don't identify this trend and fad of being stressed out and depressed, we will have more patients than so-called normal people. We may have turned that corner so the norm may be what I have described. I sincerely hope this is not the case.

22. What if just half of the money spent on religion was given to medical research. We could probably conquer heart disease, lung disease, breast cancer, prostate cancer, diabetes, colon cancer, and ovarian cancer — the seven highest deadly diseases. There are no affliction or disease entity research efforts that do not desperately need more support.

The next time you are tempted to send a TV evangelist one hundred dollars, please think of this and send fifty to research. It will, in my opinion, certainly benefit all humanity more!

23. The plight of women around the world must be improved. Raped Muslin women in Kosovo and some other cultures are expected to commit suicide so that blood could cleanse the family. This is just one example of the terrible things that women have to endure.

I know it will take time and education, but can't the UN or some powerful ruler put an end to such madness? Of course, CODE 3-M will endorse human rights. Women and children are human also.

I must say that the emphasis on blood in so many religions gives them a ghoulish element that could be very unhealthy for young children. Ceremonies use blood. Sins are supposed to be forgiven by blood and the horrible Roman crucifixion cross has become an ornament to remind us of the blood of Jesus; we are supposed to be healed by the shedding of his blood. This, to me, is a throwback to primitive and heathen practices.

24. We spend too much of our lives trying to get to heaven yet we doggedly slave to get a better car, a bigger house thinking that big day will make us happy. We face a million struggles and say heaven will be worth it all.

We must learn the value of the view across the mountains; the sand between our toes; the smile of the three-year old; the gleaming eyes of the child licking an ice-cream cone; the sun rising, shooting its silver arrows across the sky banishing the darkness of night and sending a brilliant array of colors as it sinks in the west; teaching a kid how to tie his shoe and ride a bike; holding the hand of an elderly lady crossing the street; reading the face of a boy carrying his little sleeping brother on his back — these are the things that make heaven.

It is not the gnashing of teeth in fear worrying about what comes after death, but tasting the tiny moments of life that bring us so much joy and peace on earth. The principle for CODE 3-M is short and sweet, learn to enjoy and cherish the wonderful moments of your life.

25. Death. The death of loved ones and friends, even celebrities, forces one to reflect on one's own frailties and mortality. CODE 3-M should encourage a renewal of its principles to score a higher grade since this gives meaning to one's life. It is tangible and reassuring.

If you know you have a passing grade or a very high grade by living these principles, everything is going to be okay. Some strange religious beliefs require faith of a perceived god and obeying his commands. Often its followers seem to die in doubt and great fear, wondering if they really will get to heaven and be saved from an eternal hell.

26. The human species is noted for lying about others, fantasy scenes, and wild imagination. We even lie to ourselves. Is this characteristic really the basis for religious beliefs?

27. Ponder the wonderful exciting things of the future if we can stop murders, serious crime, and wars. Over 90% of life on our planet is in the sea. Walsh and Piccard went seven miles deep in the *Tryst* and stirred up the sediment on the floor. The phenomenal pictures made by a Japanese robot indicate new vistas of understanding.

Meanwhile the space telescopes are sending back so much data so quickly we cannot analyze it fast enough. We cannot fully envision what metaphysical puzzles might be solved in our lifetime by future explorations nor do we dare prophesy the wonderful benefits that can come to mankind.

We can break the shackles of the past and declare war is not inevitable. Let's be a world family and live together and enjoy all of the wonderful things that exist and the things to come. Sure, there are problems, but let them be transformed into challenges. Let's get on with it!

28. Billions of people live or have lived on earth pay great homage to Abraham. He was a wealthy cattleman, so-called friend of God and an ancestor of the Hebrew nation and other religions. However, outside of the Bible, little if anything is known about Abraham. This holds true for so many patriarchs

of the various faiths. Yet, enshrouded in mystery, this seems to stir up more followers who accept myth after myth.

We should really apply common sense to all of the weird claims of all religions. And, if we do, they will fade away perhaps back to the people who made them up in the first place. One does not have to believe any of these suppositions to be righteous, decent and honest.

29.   The philosopher Krishna said, "Let the motive be in the deed and not in the event. Be not one whose motive for action is the hope of reward."

30.   Don't jump off a tall building. Don't take drugs. Don't touch a red-hot stove. There are thousands of do's and don'ts that we teach children.

I just wonder if the big deal we make of drugs does not make it the proverbial forbidden fruit. People are enticed to do drugs because of the emphasis we make to just say no. I don't know. I do know we have tried just about every technique and we are losing the war on drugs.

Why don't we have a war on people jumping in front of trains? Because not many do it. It seems the only effective technique we have not tried is to tattoo on the forehead of all druggies, "I am a fool and do drugs."

Of course, that won't happen but it might be pretty effective. CODE 3-M must address all addictions with prevention and perhaps we should ask why people don't run around purposely touching hot stoves.

31.   Making this list for CODE 3-M is challenging, interesting and exhausting. I never thought about devising a workable living code for all humans outside or aside from a religion, although I subconsciously follow certain principles. Getting them out on paper for others to see takes more courage that I thought I had.

Edmund Boeke wrote, "All that is necessary for the triumph of evil is that good men do nothing!" I believe I am a good person, so I am trying. I believe in this project even though I sometimes seem like a maverick in this group. I like everyone here. That tells me something.

32.   Smart people see life differently than other smart people. Jesse Ventura may have a dozen I.Q. points below George Will or William Buckley, yet he is smart and he says religion is for the weak-minded.

Brilliant attorney Clarence Darrow said, "I am an agnostic; I do not pretend to know what many ignorant men are sure of. I may say what they believe is preposterous and incredible, but I would not call religious people ignorant."

I would shudder to think where the world would be if it was not for the many positive and wonderful contributions of religious people in science, medicine, music, art, physics, space vehicles, and any field that you might name. Men who accept religious ideas or atheists who don't are found at every level of the intelligence scale — intellectually impaired to sparkling genius. Arrogance on either side of the issue and cutting down the individual on either side is unseemly.

33. We should increase the interchange of peoples, especially those whose governments are estranged from one another. This is already being done and producing very positive results. The Olympics is a shining example. The Berlin Wall would have toppled sooner had President Carter not refused America's participation in Moscow. This was the case of a good man being too rigid and a great opportunity lost. It happens in all levels of human interaction.

Out of thousands of examples, I will briefly mention one. Zhang, better known as Ah-Mei, in her twenties, is an entertainer from Taiwan. She put on a show in Mainland China; 45,000 screaming fans came to the Beijing show. It was a Madonna-type presentation with a "no holds barred" attitude, a real rock concert! The young people loved it and asked, "Why should we invade Taiwan? Ah-mei lives there and she is the greatest of all!"

It seems paradoxical that this relatively wild show, a far cry from the usual staid music in China, could unite so many young people and serve as an instrument for peace. If peace on earth ever comes, it will be through the young people of the world who become thoroughly disgusted with the hates and prejudices of their forebearers.

34. In extreme cases, the guilt laid on an individual can help cause personality distortion making the person anti-social — sometimes criminal. Various types of mental illness have been traced to extreme beliefs.

I have searched in vain for a religion that was not laced with extreme and goofy ideas. Thankfully, most adherents ignore or tacitly accept these incredible concepts, but some cannot handle the extremes and simply do not adjust.

The concept of an eternal, fiery, hell where people burn for trillions of years and the burning has just begun blows the mind. Some adherents say this is not really so. It is only an illustration. Even Pope John Paul II cannot swallow this terror.

Yet, multiplied millions do. If you want a miracle, here is

one: the fact that more people do not lose it when they think and worry about hell every day.

35. The more radical the religion, the more hate and negative action follows. This fact is so clear it needs no clarification.

36. The overwhelming obsession for quotas in race relations is wrong. I am considered black by most people just because I am not all white or all Asian or all Hispanic. It really doesn't bother me, but I am concerned that anyone would demand a near exact number for any endeavor that reflects this race.

What if all-white people demanded a quota on professional basketball teams or other sports? Why demand a quota on university faculties? Why not let each individual who has the best qualifications gets the job?

There have been great black quarterbacks and great non-black quarterbacks. Most great football quarterbacks have been white. Do you think in a money driven operation like football that this is racial prejudice? The Hall of Fame is open to all. McGuire, Aaron, Sosa are shining examples of fairness here since McGuire and Sosa will also make it easily.

Diversity is a wonderful thing, but artificial window dressing for the races has been more detrimental than helpful. Joe Lieberman shouts, "Diversity is great," but is it only for people in America? How many non-Jews are in official jobs in Israel?

Of course, non-whites can do anything as well as whites and it does not have to be proven by quotas. The Olympic teams all have only those whom earned their spot. Race has never been a factor!

Black people say to whites that the whites will never understand their feelings. True. And by the same token blacks will never understand the feelings of good modern-day whites who are set aside to let blacks get the promotion just because they are black, even thought the white person is far more qualified for the job and has far more seniority. Not understanding hurts and disappointments is a two-way street.

We must be done with the nonsense of quotas and support the individual with the best qualifications and the most deserving. Sports have led the way for other human activities. If whites, blacks, yellows, browns, reds, whatever, can stop voting as a block, we will see all kinds of presidents and that includes women.

Any of the above, if better qualified, should be president. A handicapped person, FDR, was one of our greatest presidents. He should not have been elected because no polio person had ever been president but because of his qualifications. JFK should not have been shunned or elected because he was Catholic, but because he was the most qualified and so on. When will everyone see the value of the individual aside and apart from his or her religion, no religion, or skin color? These artificial classifications have plagued humanity.

The dream team for the basketball Olympics had diversity. What sports numskull would say Michael Jordan (black) or John Stockton (white) did not belong on the basketball dream team for the Olympics? We need to foster a dream-team attitude for all of our activities.

37. The gullibility of the human species certainly is one of the world's greatest wonders. From witchcraft, medicine man, cure-all tonics, pills claiming to cure anything, or special prophets of God, we line up as blind followers.

Our older people are being fleeced each day by some fast-talking, lying con-artist. Young people leave a bar with a stranger to meet abuse or death. Oral Roberts buys the old Barnum and Bailey circus tent, claims he feels the healing power of God through his right hand and builds an empire. And he is preceded and followed by thousands of such so-called special people who have a real "in" with God.

It is pitiful. Most anyone can make a wild claim, put it partially under the umbrella of any established religion and make hay. In fact, they can start an altogether new religion as Buddha did and amass huge numbers of followers.

And, looking at the Jimmy Swaggerts and Jim Bakkers in this dubious mess causes one with an ounce of common sense to say this is a farce. But others are arising to outdo them like Benny Hinn who touches people and they fall out flat on the floor or sometimes he just waves and they fall out. You talk about hysteria and mass hypnosis. These few examples are the tip of the iceberg without even mentioning Jim Jones, Heaven's Gate people, and the Davidians.

We tend to draw a line on the latter way-out cults, but the psychological dynamics of all of them are somewhat similar. CODE 3-M needs to encourage people to stop being so gullible.

38. Do not underestimate the power of youth to bring humanity together if the adults and older people would step aside and encourage them to solve some of the age-old problems. Children of all races and religions do well together until some prejudiced adult warns them against their closeness.

Children have no mean agenda.

39. I wonder if the higher species— like apes, elephants, dolphins — worship. I doubt it, but they do follow their leader. Perhaps they do if they fear death like most humans. They may think of humans as superior entities or gods. No one really knows and it may be that no one cares. However, as the chimpanzees learn to push buttons and communicate better with humans, one day we may find out. Exciting idea.

40. Only truly defensive wars are to be fought. Will Rogers quipped, "You can't say civilization is not advancing. In every war, they kill you in a new way." And Will knew nothing about the atom bomb.

41. Harry Emerson Fosdick wrote, "God is not a bell-boy, for whom we can press a button to get things." This strange idea of God for many people is unproductive because it flies in the face of personal responsibility and self-development.

Why did not some believer push a button and say, "God, please bring peace in Viet Nam and never let another war happen"? Would not this be more appropriate than a prayer asking God to give you a wonderful spouse, a house and a good job? It would certainly be less selfish. Why are most prayers selfish?

42. Our youth are the first to go to war on the front lines. It takes about 18-21 years to make a man and a split-second to destroy him. Should not the boys and girls in service, as well as Congress, have a say in declaring war? The problem in the last half of the century is that not even Congress has a say. The ego of a President to leave a great war victory legacy, I think, is a big cause of an aggressive war.

We scoff at Hitler, Mussolini, Stalin, Napoleon, Caesar, and the like for we feel certain their inflated egos were a factor in the carnage they left behind. We must be careful we don't create the same tyranny here or anywhere again. World pressure by good people can help prevent these phenomena.

43. Loyalty to an organization is fine until the "us versus them" spirit causes you as an individual to fail to treat any individual who is not in your group unfairly. We must show great care in identifying with any group that can set us against another group.

Gang participation is a perfect example of loyalty gone bad. When you dissect the psychological foundations of the extreme groups, you see them operating in a huge amount of other human activity.

44. An individual has the responsibility to develop self-

worth and self-esteem. If he and she needs help, they have the responsibility to seek help. People who constantly cut down others, who are almost always negative and seek pity for themselves in an unreasonable manner, can cause lots of heartache among others. When they claim a religion despite all of these problems, one wonders why can't their God help them out?

45. Innate decency and fairness in humans. I believe and trust that a vast majority of humans have a reservoir of decency and fairness. In some cases, an environment needs to be created to bring it out. Yet, isn't this the hope of the world?

46. Moral relatives. People adapt to morals that give them comfort especially if they can apply their standards to others. No one is certain whether many issues are moral or amoral. The application of morality that varies from situation to situation has intrinsic dangers. This is why we need to try to find some common ground.

Isn't it always immoral to throw an infant in a river to please a god? Sure it is and you can't accept the excuse that the person did not know any better or the mother who did this was too poor. There are standards that should never be breached by anyone and no excuse should be valid.

47. We pour countless millions into church edifices far beyond the need of houses of worship. I've always felt the purpose of large cathedrals was to leave the individual awestruck and reduce true thoughts and questions.

As a little girl I noticed the mass hysteria of hundreds and sometimes thousands of people caught up in a style of worship. How could little me dare do anything but go with the flow?

Isn't this kin to everyone yelling their heads off, when the home team scores a touchdown? Are not the same mass crowd techniques viable in almost any huge crowd? The larger the crowd, the more the individual is intimidated. Multiplied billions are spent to propagate conflicting religious viewpoints while half the world is in severe poverty and disease.

Poor Africa, they have 50% of the AIDS cases in the whole world. On top of that scourge is the fact that over five million have died in Africa from senseless wars. I do believe that some people care, but they are told to support the local church and the ministry. If we had the money that has been poured into buildings, ministries, bingo games, church schools, and the like, millions upon millions might not have starved to death.

I know you have to draw the line somewhere, but I do recall some religious leader saying it is more difficult for a rich person to go to heaven than it is for a camel to go through the eye of a needle. We have a worldwide pathology on our hands. The three wealthiest people on earth have assets that are more than the total of at least 45 least-developed countries.

People in Europe and North America spend $37 billion a year on pet food, perfumes and cosmetics. This $37 billion would certainly help provide basic education, water, sanitation, basic health, and nutrition for all of these needs for practically every person deprived of them. This is more conducive to war than peace. The UN studies such things.

There is no easy solution, but the astounding inequities of the distribution of wealth are alarming. Religion and Communism have failed. Population control and basic opportunity for each person may be part of the answer.

48. Most religions could not exist without overwhelming the individual followers with fear. If you removed fear from the people, how many followers would still go to church, synagogues, whatever?

Is a state of fear best for humans? No. Unconscious fear may be the cause of many diseases, both physical and mental. Fear of the wrath of God, fear of a burning hell, fear of being stricken with sickness rendered from heaven, fear of not living up to the religion, and a hundred other fears can ruin one's health. Fear is a very negative emotion.

49. We deplore the devastation of the atom bomb's effect on innocent people, especially children and babies, yet the God of the Jews wiped out the whole world save Noah and his family. If one can believe he marched male and female of all the species of the world on that little boat, it would be easy to believe reindeer could fly Santa Claus all over the world in one night.

God utterly destroyed whole cities like Sodom and Gomorrah. Were the two-year-olds all defying God as well? When we consider that Christianity claims the most followers in the world and accepts this vengeful God as part of their trinity, it boggles the mind. If just the religious people got together against war, it could cease. Why not all religions adopt an edict, "Thou shall not go to war." These vicious gods, in the so-called holy ranks claiming to want peace, are a sad puzzle.

50. Keep holy the Sabbath. There were some questions whether Christians should follow this ancient Jewish law. St. Jerome and his group went to church on Sunday and then they

pursued their occupations. The American Sabbath was born in Scotland after the death of John Knox who played bowls on Sunday.

Handfuls of fanatics without reason or any global perspective have from time to time forced their religious dogmatic views upon the people. The "blue laws" on prohibitions of Sunday activities became rampant and some of these stupid laws are still on the books in some states. One of the first breakthroughs was allowing baseball after 2:00 p.m. This was thought to be a concession by the religionists, but they were hoping that people would never miss Sunday morning church.

The funny thing today is most churches have no Sunday evening service and some radical Pentecostal churches even show the Super Bowl football game on the Sabbath in part of their tax-free church property.

My, how things change especially when people finally get tired and sick of unfathomable religions fanaticism that tries to put a tight control on its adherents. People just won't put up with much of the ignorance they once proclaimed. Yet so much remains. Church leaders are frantic about how to keep control of their old creeds and rules and still keep the people.

51. Cease giving any child low expectations.

52. In 1995, the First World Conference on Women was a good idea, basically eliminating all forms of discrimination against women. The US signed on in 1980, but a 2/3 vote required in the Senate was never brought to a vote. However, 165 other countries ratified CEDAW (Convention Eliminate Discrimination Against Women). The US was in the company of Afghanistan, North Korea, Iran, Sudan. What a disgrace!

53. Religion fails our youth by not emphasizing ethics and morality but mostly worshipping a deity. Fifty years ago 10% of high school students admitted to cheating on tests in school. Now 80% say they cheat and it is no big deal.

54. The Songs of Solomon has Bible scholars in an uproar. Sensual ones may have been written to honor a female in one of his many polygamous weddings. Some say it was satire because of Solomon's many acquisitions and exploitation of women. Why is this material in a Holy Bible which people are to reverence?

55. Book of Revelation — vivid imagination of a deteriorating John means basically nothing. "Anointed" men of God interpret the prophecies in opposite manners. It should not be taken seriously.

56. How many millions perished while calling on God? Yet,

if someone lived it is a miracle. Baloney!

57. Religion is like building a house with playing cards. Pull out one and whole thing falls.

58. Worship nothing. Imagined God, totem pole, statues, or movie stars. Give allegiance to ideals of ethics and morality.

59. True believers in all they are supposed to believe in their religions are very, very rare!

60. "One person can make a positive difference" should be taught to every child.

61. Saved only by calling on the name of Jesus? What happened to the 20-30 billions who lived before he was born, all burning in hell? How about the millions now on earth who never heard?

"The blood covers all," "God treats them as children," "in God's hands," and they will be okay. Why then send missionaries to tell of Jesus? If they don't serve him, they will burn in hell whereas if left alone, go to heaven. Doesn't anyone have compassion for people's souls outside of their own narrow faith?

62. Acting and religion. Did not Jimmy Swaggert sing and preach beautifully while using a prostitute? Is not Barbara Streisand at her usual inspiring manner singing "Ave Maria"? Cannot Hollywood actors portray effectively any side of any religion? Of course, most religious leaders are simply good actors and we don't know what they really believe.

63. There are 181 or more different denominations that say they use the Bible as the word of God as their spiritual constitution. Which interpretation should an honest citizen of the world follow?

64. Humans try to create a type of immortality — Egyptian boats in tombs; Indian wampum and tomahawks in graves; imaginary mansions in the sky with streets of gold and walls of jasper.

Why would the New Jerusalem need walls? On and on religions plays on the fears of mankind promising gifts greater than Santa Claus and punishment greater than Hitler.

65. Historical lessons are many, but let me list some important facts that cast doubt on ethnocentrism which seems to be increasing around the world instead of decreasing. In New York, in the Teens and Twenties, the Irish fought the Italians until they started marrying one another. Then both fought the Jews until a significant number of Jews married Italians and the Irish.

Later the same thing happened with Hispanics, Orientals

and other ethnic or religious groups. Marriage between these groups and blacks has never gained much momentum, though at least it is not illegal and there has been some advance. The groups feared that their group identity was threatened and propounded a philosophy that a mosaic was much better than a melting pot.

I do not know if they truly meant for those of us who are melted to be ostracized like the mixed children in Viet Nam where so much blending and melting occurred between the French soldiers and Asians, followed by the American military, both black and white. The mix made quite a gene recipe. The treatment of these innocent children is a blight on human history.

Do any of us think we had control on who our parents happened to be? The mosaic philosophy may last on the globe for several centuries, but it is as doomed as the dinosaurs eventually and the sooner the better it will be for all human-kind. I am not for any forced cross-race or cross-religion romances, but if a boy and girl find true romance and true love there, who has the authority to say it should not lead to marriage? No one has that authority, but plenty people as individuals and groups assume that it is patently wrong.

Again, this is a desperate plea for each person to be tolerant and understanding and support the right for any human to marry another of the opposite sex regardless of race, nationality or creed.

66. "Servants should be obedient to their masters" is another Jesus teaching that makes me see red. There should exist no such thing as a master-servant relationship.

67. If there is a judgment day by God, then I would hate to stand in the shoes of Father Divine, Daddy Grace, Oral Roberts, Benny Hinn, Jim Bakker, Jimmy Swaggert, and thousands of others whose ministries have left the impression that if you supported their ministry, God would reward you.

So many poor gullible people continue to send in hard-earned money to these types of self-proclaimed special servants of God who drive expensive cars, wear expensive garments and live royally. The old fear-and-greed scheme remains a devastating ruse and abomination. How would any fair judge treat this activity if we did not have special preferences for religions?

68. War's awful devastation and destruction has been portrayed many times rather eloquently in films and books, but nothing takes the place of the actual experience of the real

indescribable fear and anxiety.

The PTSD patients from war and the permanently physi-cally wounded deserve our highest praise and admiration. So do those who returned in relative good condition and not only went on but excelled in their lives and continued service to others. How could anyone support war unless they were hon-estly convinced not going to war would destroy America? This should be the criteria for sending our youth to give the best years of their life.

69. I know of a family that hold hands and offers secular grace before meals. They thank the people who have made the meal possible and the people who have provided them the ways of earning funds to pay for it.

If God is to be thanked and praised for the food, who do starving people thank? Do they pray, "Oh God, we thank you for allowing us to go hungry and starve to death and suffer so much from malnutrition." No, of course not. Do they say, though they are not Jewish, "Would you rain down food from heaven?" It does not make sense to me that a fair, compas-sionate loving God steps in and distributes food to one family and lends a deaf ear to another. That just does not compute in my mind.

70. We should be concerned, even frightened, by the pos-sibilities of bio-genetics. Very large modifications of animals are being made. Some efforts go toward enlarging the IQs of domestic animals with implanted electronic controls in their brains to increase intelligence. This has been done with bulls.

Humans are in the animal species. Will the day come when humans are controlled electronically by devices implanted in their brains? Will we create zombie-like soldiers to wage war? We have got to get a grip or the human race can be changed fundamentally by genes and electronics.

71. The Bible glosses over slavery by telling servants to obey their masters. It says to pay taxes to a despot and many, many other bad teachings. It reduces women to a level far below men in admonitions like "wives obey your husbands" and "let the woman keep silent in churches." It could not be the word of any merciful, compassionate, just God.

72. Many people are filled with serious doubts about their religion. They are not gung-ho; instead, they stay just inside the fringe to keep it as an insurance policy. This will keep them out of hell and help them escape the awful wrath of God, not as a means to treat their fellow-man with love and under-standing. "Fear God who has the power to cast you into hell"

is the theme. They also recall one of the thieves being cruci-fied with Jesus who said, "Lord remember me" and everything was okay.

73. I propose a wordwide convention of teenagers. The delegates could be in proportion to the total population of their nation with a minimum of five per nation. Let them simply free associate for two or three days with electronic language computers. Let them meet in Athens, Rome or Cairo to feel a sense of history.

On the third day, divide them into groups of 10-15 and give them about a dozen topics that are pertinent to world peace and prosperity. Have adult advisors on call nearby for expert advice if needed, but limit any one advisor's time to 15 min-utes with the group.

Consolidate the main ideas and thoughts and marvel at their love and appreciation for each other and the wisdom of their thinking. They could inspire the adult world to cool it and learn to live together.

The details, of course, are flexible, but the concept is fool-proof. Humans don't want to fear and kill each other. Tribal days are gone. The prejudices of the preceding adults and glory seeking leaders has to go. We must share equality and respect for everyone on the planet.

Adults in the UN are there to ensure the selfish interests of their country. The youths are to be told they can be the start of something big — a true emotional uniting and honest accep-tance of everyone in the world. A million naysayers and crit-ics would scream "It won't work," but even those negative voices know that it might work and would be a great service! Well David, you called for ideas.

Now what person would sponsor such a convention? Per-haps a Rupert Murdock, Martha Stewart, Ross Perot, or Don-ald Trump? Sponsor such a convention. We might be surprised. It is a dream I have had for many years.

Our hope for the Third Millennium is our youth who have been freed from the shackles of former hatreds and selfish goals. We need a worldwide youth convention on World Peace!

Chapter VII
Compiling Individual Lists

It had been quite an interesting and fun time creating the individual lists. A lot of energy and research went into some of the items. It was a monumental task to attempt to critique the human race. The group considered its origin, its purpose, the route for individual happiness and achievement while exploding peculiar myths and untruths replacing them with common sense, scientific and rational precepts. No one expected the majority of their items to be in the CODE, but all hoped that their main ideas would make it.

All the lists were piled on the captain's conference table. "Since we have listed several hundred nuggets of wisdom for CODE 3-M and a brief clarification for some of the items, let me suggest the following," David said.

"First, that we do not extend the time frame. If we did, we could have another 600 or so and never be able to boil the ideas, comments and suggestions down to a workable report or document.

"Second, we will make copies for all members to study. If there are any items that you require further clarification, ask the person who authorized it to explain more about it to you.

"Third, there will be some duplication of ideas, but that will not matter since each member will checkmark the ones that he or she feels is worthy to be placed in CODE 3-M. There is no need to mark the others. You should mark your own list and check the items you would give priority because most ideas are not going to make the next level.

"We can have another week to consider these lists, discuss it with anyone and turn in your marked lists when we reconvene the group in seven days. Are there any suggestions to improve the plan? Hearing none, I suppose you all agree," David concluded, glancing around the conference table.

Rachel spoke, "I like the procedure very well. I wonder if we could receive two copies of all lists, one to turn in and one to keep for ourselves. This way the balloted list can be shredded and the secrecy of votes will be kept intact as we have followed."

"That's a splendid idea," Al agreed. "I would like a personal copy of the items so I will have the ones that made it and the ones that did not."

"Without objection, we will supply two copies to each member," David motioned. There were no objections and he added, "Just because an idea does not make the CODE does not mean it isn't a good one. When the cut comes in pro football from 60 to 40, the 20 who were cut may be better individually than an individual in the 40 that made it. It is a judgment and honest consideration call. All of us will struggle as we realize we have to reduce the lists. Some items will be easy for some of us to discard and some will be so very difficult. Pardon the pun but we are all in the same boat."

"When will we receive our two copies of all the lists?" Rev. Hayes asked David.

"They will be delivered to you tomorrow morning at breakfast. Any more business? Meeting adjourned."

Lu moved quickly to chat with David. She asked if her many items were too much. David noticed how delightful she looked and the scent of her perfume was very beguiling. "No," he replied. "Some, as you will see, had less and some had more like me."

"That's nice. As long as I'm close to you, I'll be okay and I mean that in a romantic sense as well," whispered Lu.

"I'm flattered. We both know there is great chemistry between us. Certainly I can sense your beauty on the inside and well as your striking attractiveness on the outside."

Just then Captain Davis came in and asked, "Say David, did you send for me?"

"Yes. I need you to do us a big favor."

Lu drifted on out the room rather disenchanted by the interruption. She reminded herself that she had already taken a giant step forward. Maybe it was good enough to leave well enough alone.

"What?" inquired Davis.

"I want you to have two copies made of these long lists for each of our seven members. And when the items are checked off by them, I want you and two or three of your crew to tally the items that are checked and then destroy all of the lists. We will each have unmarked lists and this way, we may guess but we will not know who checked off which item to be included in our report. I do not want to know either or I would do the leg work."

"No problem. When will the lists come back checked?"

"In seven days," said David.

"Good! We'll have plenty of time to get set up and do a quick job," said Davis as he walked over toward a porthole gazing at the sea. This was a man who would not be content doing anything else.

"You know," said Davis, "I have never had such a nice group aboard *The Quest*. I must say that I am amazed how you seven people blend in work and pleasure."

"Thanks," David agreed as he thought he needed to balance in a little more pleasure.

David wandered to his favorite spot atop the wheelroom. He relaxed in one of the canvas chairs and tried to come to grips with his heart and which way it was leaning. He had deep feelings for all three ladies, but he knew one stood out in his heart more than the others. As he pondered his next romantic step, he saw Rachel climbing the little vertical ladder.

"Hi," she said nervously. "I don't mean to bother you if you are in deep thought."

"No problem," he said. "I was in deep thought but not about the CODE. I know we are headed in the right direction. Everyone has been creative and honest with their lists, and together we will forge something meaningful and positive."

"Well, why were you in such a serious state of reflection? Are you homesick?" asked Rachel.

David chuckled, "I had rather be here than any spot on earth." He wondered just how much Rachel knew about his feelings for Bridgette and Lu. Perhaps he would find out in a subtle way. He knew women have an uncanny ability to evaluate other women. Maybe this little meeting tonight could really clarify the mixed emotions in his heart.

"You know," David began, "I have to say that Mr. Morgan really picked a near-perfect group for this project. John, Al and Tony are true gentlemen and scholars. I have already learned so much from them. The three ladies are just as bright and a lot better looking! Seriously, I've been impressed with all six of you and somewhat surprised at the in-depth insights of both Lu and Bridgette. I knew you were a heavy-hitter."

"Oh, flattery will get you everywhere, David. I too have been favorably impressed. Although there are seven distinct personalities and styles, each person is striving to craft a report that will make Rudy proud of this undertaking. I sense, however, you want my opinion of my two competitors."

David was startled and his body language showed it. He was surprised for two reasons. First, she had easily figured out he was trying to come from left field, but most of all because she referred to Lu and Bridgette as competitors in the present tense. She did not use the word "former" before "competitors." David could discern his usual steady composure was falling apart. In fact, he was in uncertain territory.

"I'm sorry," he said sheepishly. "Now I'm not sure what to say."

"Don't say anything for a few minutes and I will really set the scene for you. First, I am not going to trash Lu or Bridgette. They are both fine ladies and I can see why you have deep feelings for each one. But I do wish to restore my name on the ballot.

"I have agonized more about what I said to you about being 'unequally yoked together' more than any rash statement I have made in my whole life. I know you can feel how much I care for you; I was presumptuous to block you out of my long range plans for my life. I apologize and sincerely ask you to put my name back in the pot so I can start sleeping at night. Can we kiss and make up?"

"You know I would enjoy the kiss and the hug and the closeness of sweethearts, but I am afraid I would be the cause of you breaking a sincere religious principle. I could not live with that. I fear all though our lives together you would be thinking about putting me ahead of your beliefs and be tormented by that decision. I will always care for you as a friend and wish you the best. You can easily find someone better looking than me, smarter than me and a man with a lot more money than I will ever have."

Rachel was crying. She climbed down the stairs very slowly. No other words were spoken. David cried. While he felt he had been overly abrupt, he knew he could not lead her on if there could be no future for them. He had done the right thing, but it really did hurt both of them.

Rachel walked meaninglessly by the rail of the ship. In a short while she found herself at the tip of the ship's bow. She paused and felt the warm, soothing winds flowing in her face. She turned her head towards the heavens and silently prayed for almost a half-hour. Then she bowed her head very low and headed toward her room.

David had watched the whole scene from his vantage point on top of the wheelroom. He had wanted to rush down, put his arms around her and comfort her, but he knew that was not the right thing to do. He thought of the song, "Breaking Up Is Hard to Do," and just sat there gazing up as Rachel did hoping she had received some solace from up above.

Several days passed and a stop was planned at Palm Coast just north of Daytona Beach. An exact replica of one of Columbus' three ships, the *Nina*, was sailing into the inlet to be placed on display for a week.

Captain Davis asked David if he thought the group would be interested in following it and going aboard the *Nina*.

"Everyone would be thrilled; let's do it!"

It was a most pleasant little side visit. The entire crew except Columbus slept on deck at night or wherever they could. The tiny ship was only 66 feet by 17 feet and had one bunk bed (for Columbus). The rest was used for supplies. They had two horses and a few other animals aboard headed for the New World. David stood behind the wheel and turned the crude rudder just behind him about 10 feet.

Although he could not really know how Columbus felt as the storms came and the crew got sick and afraid, he thought of the determination Columbus must have had.

David mumbled to himself, "Sail on, sail on!" He realized again that despite the setbacks in life, one must muster up courage and "sail on." He had received renewed purpose from this little ship.

Chapter VIII
An Adventure to Remember

The time allotted for the moratorium for the group sessions had ended. Everyone had reviewed the suggested lists of the other six members. Each participant wondered which of the hundreds of ideas or guidelines would survive the very rough critique of the group and rise to the level of CODE 3-M.

Each thought of the honor it would be to make a substantive contribution for a human road map or guidelines to follow, if possible, throughout one's lifespan.

The level of excitement had reached a new high crescendo as Al, Bridgette, David, John, Lu, Rachel, and Tony entered the Captain's conference room. It was early in the morning. The group loved to eat breakfast and watch the sun rise. Just about the time the last one, Tony, was pulling up his seat to the table, there was a large commotion going on up on the deck.

One member of the crew had been peering through his telescope to try to locate a school of dolphins when he saw a flat boat-like image way off on the horizon. He yelled, "There's something floating out there several miles away. It could be a boat!"

Captain Davis quickly grabbed his powerful binoculars and gazed carefully in the direction that the crewman had pointed. He soon spotted the thing, whatever it was, and turned the wheel to guide *The Quest* in that direction. After all, they were just going here and there with no destination at a time certain and more importantly, if it was a vessel of some type, they might be able to use some assistance.

He checked his bearings and noted *The Quest* was about 25 miles offshore from a spot between West Palm Beach and Ft. Lauderdale. He headed south at a fast rate using a favorable wind and his powerful inboard motor. In a few minutes, the people on *The Quest* with binoculars and telescopes could see that the floating object was indeed a vessel and furthermore it was crowded with dozens of human beings. The craft did not seem to be moving much at all. There was no sail. Captain Davis put his engine on its highest speed and said beneath his breath, "Hold on, I'll be there soon."

The excitement of everyone was so full and genuine that it almost compared to Columbus spotting land on the New World. One huge difference was that all had eaten well and lived in luxury on this ship and they knew where they were and had no fear of their safe return.

"Oh my God in Heaven," shouted John. "Let us get to those people in time." He could see now through his binoculars that the people, no doubt Cubans, were jammed together like sardines and seemingly were going nowhere.

The crew was magnificent as they carried out the Captain's orders. David asked Captain Davis if the group could help in any way.

"Yes. Assign a person to six crewmen to assist them as much as they can. You stay here with me. Can you speak Spanish?"

"Yes, not perfectly, but I understand it very well and can communicate pretty well in the language."

"I've got a feeling you will need it. I speak German and French and know very little Spanish," said the Captain.

David could see the Captain was very calm under the circumstances. This gave him a sense of assurance that whatever the situation might be, things would work out. However, as they came within a mile two or the flat barge-like vessel, it was apparent that it was sinking with about two or three times the number of people it could carry.

"How many extra people can we take aboard *The Quest*?" David asked.

"About 20 if we have to take that many."

"But there looks like almost a hundred on that barge, sir, and I believe it is sinking! How did they ever get this far? Why didn't they go to Key West?"

Captain Davis explained, "Many Cubans trying to get to America know Castro's ships will intercept them and often kill them on the obvious closest route to the United States. They try to sail to Nassau and sometimes go way up to the Ponce Inlet Lighthouse area near Daytona Beach before they head for shore. There you can see old inner-tubes lashed together with rope with a piece of plywood or tin for a deck and a piece of tent for a sail. These are some of the bravest people in the world. Many drown in the ocean before they get home."

"It seems that no one cares except their family and friends and the Cuban community in Miami," David reflected, softly and reverently.

The Captain handed a battery-driven bullhorn and told David to go down on deck and talk to these poor desperate people whose lives were at stake. David hurried down the steps and as the engine was cut off and the sails lowered, *The Quest* drew within 50 yards of a very pitiful scene.

There were about 90 people on board the barge and it was slowly sinking. The Captain had radioed for help, but no ship of any kind was in sight.

Speaking through the bullhorn, David asked, "How many people do you have on the barge?" One man who seemed to be the leader yelled back at the top of his voice, "We have 76 adults and 16 children — 92 in total."

The Cubans on the ill-fated barge were wild with joy that the big luxury yacht had come to their rescue. Did they realize the depth of the peril they were still in at this moment? The barge would probably not float over an hour. None of the ships that had responded to the distress call could get to the spot in less than three or more hours. Finally, *The Quest* could take on board only a fraction of the number on the barge.

Captain Davis explained the situation to David who relayed the information to the Cuban leader. "We will start with the mothers and children. Captain Davis will tell us when *The Quest* cannot possibly receive another person or it will sink also. Calm everyone down and explain the situation to them. Tell them to be as silent as possible and move quickly according to this plan. We have two lifeboats that will hold six people each. Then we will figure out something. I don't know what."

The anchor had been dropped in deep water, but it was dug in and holding. The two-foot wide gangplank type bridge extended to the barge. Fortunately the sea was calm this particular morning. Everyone seemed to realize the gravity of this dangerous and perhaps fateful moment.

Even the small children were attentive and orderly. The 16 children and 10 mothers marched briskly across the makeshift lifesaving bridge. *The Quest* began to go down farther in the water.

"How about 10 more women?" David cried out.

"I'm not sure, but try it."

Ten women came aboard with the other 26 people. Now both vessels were in danger, but the barge was still going down. The stern was sinking faster than the front of the old half-rotten barge. How in the world did they ever think 92 people could make it on this death trap? How did they ever come this far?

The leader of the Cuban group explained they planned to take only 40 adults and 10 children. As they started to leave Cuba in the middle of the night, another 20 men found out about the journey.

"We just couldn't refuse to let them on board, so we had 70 people and two sails. Both sails were eventually blown down and into the sea. We tried but we could not retrieve them. The next day we saw people floating around in the water holding on to boards. A few had life jackets. What could we do? We took 22 on board.

"They told us they had started out in three little canoes and wooden boats with 10 in each boat. They had oars and made it for about 40 miles together until hit by a lightning storm. They managed to huddle together, but eight drowned and were never seen again. We took them on board and our barge, already overloaded dangerously, began to sink.

"We knew we should have stuck with the original 50, but we just couldn't leave people in Cuba or in this dangerous ocean. I know we are in deep trouble now, but you can get to shore with 36 of us, so go ahead. We will just hope and pray we can get picked up before this barge goes to the bottom of the ocean."

"Forget it," David said. "We are not going anywhere. We are not going to leave 44 people here to die. All the women and children are on *The Quest.* Twelve men are in two lifeboats. The barge is not sinking quite as fast, but it is still going down by inches. I have a plan if Captain Davis will agree."

David cut off the bullhorn, ran upstairs and laid out his plan to him. He asked if he could take all of the Dacron sails from *The Quest* to the barge where everyone could pitch in, sew the sails into floating pontoons and lash them all around the barge.

"Great idea!" said the Captain. "Then I can tug the barge in slowly if we can put some adults now on *The Quest* on the barge."

"Now, you're talking sir," David agreed. As the crew of *The Quest* hurriedly unleashed every sail and brought up a couple more from the hold, David told everyone in English and in Spanish what was going on.

Every one of the seven participants in the think tank volunteered to go on the barge and help sew the sails into pontoons. They would remain on the barge for the 25-mile trip to shore. All of the crew on *The Quest* also volunteered, but Captain Davis ordered three to remain on *The Quest* to help him.

It was a group of courageous people working against time and how they worked. David asked Josh of the crew from *The Quest* to take over the sewing project and he would do what he could. Some of the Cubans could speak a little English. This really helped matters as Josh arose to the task screaming out friendly orders but with a tone of urgency all could understand.

Since the barge had taken on water in the storm, a gas pump and emergency generator were taken from *The Quest* and began pumping water out of the barge. This helped but she was still going down an inch at a time. Finally, the first sail pontoon was completed and lashed to the rear of the barge and almost immediately the rear of the barge leveled up.

There was a great hurrah from both vessels. This first success really inspired the men and three women, Rachel, Lu and Bridgette, on the barge; they worked feverishly to raise the barge slightly or at least cause it to cease sinking!

The two lifeboats were tethered to the stern of the barge. The anchor was hoisted to the deck. The engine was started and *The Quest* began to pull this strange cargo very slowly towards land. Shouts of hope and victory filled the air. Songs were sung in Spanish and English at the same time. It was a glorious wonderful feeling and though they were not on land, the promise was so inspirational that everyone cried for joy.

It wasn't easy, but they all made it. Some in the Cuban community in Miami had known of the planned escape from Cuba. However, they had almost given up hope when an airplane spotted this unbelievable sight and radioed the media on the mainland.

Small boats and big expensive yachts headed out immediately to meet them and take them on board their ships at about eight miles off shore. What a beautiful sight! Charter buses were waiting with tables of all kinds of food and clothing lined up beside them for the refugees.

After a short while, the 92 boarded the buses to Miami and freedom with their American cousins. Mr. Morgan saw the rescue on television in New York and phoned Captain Davis to congratulate him, the crew and the group.

"I'd buy a hundred sails in a New York minute to save these precious people," he exclaimed.

"Thank you. Thank you, sir, but I want you to know it would

have been a terrible disaster if David Preakness had not come up on the spot with the idea of sail pontoons. He is the group leader and you could not have picked a finer group. They worked as hard as a crew on a pirate ship to get those pontoons made!" Davis said proudly.

New sails were fitted and *The Quest* checked out to sea on its important mission. It had become more important than they ever dreamed it would be!

This group continued talking about the rescue. When *The Quest* was about three miles off shore, David borrowed the bullhorn from Captain Davis and announced, "Okay gang, enough sightseeing. Let's get to work pronto!"

The participants gathered again around the large round-table. The tally sheets were handed out to each member to review. There were 104 items with at least four votes to survive. David said he thought some of them could be combined so the abbreviated CODE would be about half that number or a little more. All agreed so the group for the next three sessions hammered out the wording for 60 items.

Chapter IX
Guidelines for CODE 3-M

PREAMBLE:

We human beings, having set upon a quest for truth and understanding concerning the purpose of human life, its responsibilities, strengths and frailties, have in this document, fashioned a type of road map for each individual on earth to consider and hopefully follow to the best of their ability.

We need some guidelines to enable us to thread our way through life with reasonable assurance that we are doing the right things. We trust the dedication to these principles, if chosen, will bring intrinsic happiness to each individual and further the yearning for genuine peace among all people on our planet.

It is an amazing and beautiful planet that has experienced many important eras of change. It is still changing. The awesome formations of seas, land, lakes, mountains, volcanoes, and huge rivers winding their way to the seas create a geological kaleidoscopic wonder! Features underwater and above water are still to be explored and mapped by humans.

Enhancing this marvel is the almost infinite number of plants, trees and flowers. The inspiring blanket of the botanical world has been ingeniously cataloged by man over the centuries. New elegant examples are presented in each passing decade.

As we behold the universe of living, moving species like fish, fowl, animals, and man, we stand amazed in the presence of this phenomenal place. The incredible photographs and videos from space vehicles of our planet reveal its fantastic blue, pristine beauty. We are so fortunate to live in this fabulous, extraordinary environment.

Here we are, born a separate unique individual placed on earth not by our personal decision. The precious gift of choice is our birthright as humans with intelligent minds. Our ongoing challenge is to select the right alternative when choices appear. The goal and purpose of our lives is contentment, fulfillment and contributions to others.

1.   Guidelines may be followed coupled with any religion or no religion as long as that allegiance does not cause the individual to hate or kill people of other religions because their beliefs are different.

2.   CODE 3-M does not promote any particular religion nor is it hostile toward any. No deity is required for individuals to do the ethical and moral thing.

3.   All humans are born equal regarding their rights, responsibilities and obligations to others in the human society without regard to race, sex, language, religion, nationality, or any other remarkable difference. Brotherhood and human family are the concepts we must practice in all instances.

4.   Each individual has responsibility to promote peace and refrain from violence and war except in rare cases of defense. The heartaches of war go on and on after one side surrenders and each individual must be responsible for their actions.

5.   Most religions have many positive teachings and CODE 3-M seeks to incorporate these principles for its road map for human living.

6.   Each individual should value truth, when supported by reason, logic, science, and common sense, above mythical speculation.

7.   The urgency of CODE 3-M springs from the fact that religions cannot agree on a proper road map for human living but seek to destroy others' faith by evangelical efforts, governmental control or war. CODE 3-M is an effort to promote reasonable common ground in order to eliminate violence and war.

8.   Respect yourself and realize you are a unique individual with a mind only you should control. No other person has precisely the same DNA as you.

9.   Respect others. Show compassion for people who suffer. You are no better than anyone else is and no one is better than you. You cannot love others until you have learned to love and accept yourself and appreciate your own uniqueness.

Compassion for all other humans is the key to happiness and peace. Never discriminate on any basis. Honor and respect women and men and all humans.

10. Respect your body. Do not abuse it with tobacco, alco-

hol or any other drugs except for medical purposes. Do not mutilate your body.

11. Respect your mind. Do not use mind-altering drugs, gaseous fumes or any form of surrender to the occult. Do not let anyone or anything enslave your precious mind.

12. Practice as much as possible common virtues that have almost universal acceptance like love for family and friends, trustworthiness, friendliness, courtesy, reasonable thriftiness, charity, duty, gratitude, honesty and truthfulness, ethical behavior, humility, patience, loyalty, cleanliness, helpfulness, honor, courage and bravery, modesty, confidence, and other proven positive attributes that humans display. These qualities make for good moral character.

13. Treat people in the manner that you would like to be treated — the Golden Rule. This is the basis of human civility and freedom. We need to clean up our overuse of foul language especially vulgarity and respect religious people enough not to use God's name when they curse.

14. Be understanding of other people. They have a mind and emotions like you and all humans. "Walk a mile in the other person's moccasins." (Native American proverb)

The amount of trivial lawsuits is ridiculous. More understanding and arbitration is sorely needed.

15. Honor thy father and thy mother if they deserve honor.

16. Do not kill except in defense of self or others.

17. Be a peacemaker in all situations.

18. Do not steal for any personal or selfish reason.

19. Do no bear false witness against thy neighbor.

20. Do not covet the possessions of others nor be unreasonably jealous.

21. Be faithful to your commitments including such things as marriage, business and important promises.

22. Refrain from adultery and fornication is the ideal. However, it is within the authority of consenting adults.

23. Recognize everyone has civic duties like helping one's community and paying lawful taxes within reason.

24. Evaluate your actions. Strive to score not only a passing grade in virtuous living but also a very high grade. Remember two things: others grade you also and no one makes a 100. You can make the honor roll and to respect yourself you must score above 70. Your own self-appraisal, if balanced, will generally be accurate.

25. Be forgiving and merciful in practically all things done against you as you will need forgiveness at times in your life.

However, some things are unforgivable like murder, child molestation and slavery. The Holocaust should never be forgiven by anyone.

26. Recognize that people are not born good or evil but with the wonderful gift of choice. Strive to make good choices and correct the bad ones you make if possible. Do not blame others for your unwise choices. Personal responsibility must be emphasized.

27. Abortion is not ideal, but it is within the authority of the pregnant individual to make that choice. Government and religion should not interfere.

A woman has the decision for her own body whether or not someone else concurs. Adoption is ideal. Birth control is within the authority of the individual without the interference of church or state.

28. Be a productive individual. No one likes a lazy person and you can make the choice to do something productive instead of being a parasite.

29. It is unseemly for a religious person to mock the strange and unusual things in another's religion because all faiths have incredible beliefs.

30. Slavery, whenever and wherever it occurs, is a terrible, disgusting practice. No person should ever try to own another person. It is wrong when nations enslave other nations and wrong when individuals own slaves whether Washington, Jefferson or any person lowly or great. It is next to murder and should never be tolerated anywhere.

31. Homosexuality. There are two categories. One is the biological imbalance of hormones and the other is the learned homosexual. At the present state of medical science, the individuals in the first category are not responsible for their inheritance any more than the color of their eyes.

The second category chose that lifestyle and can choose to become heterosexual on their own or if they seek assistance. The authority rests with the individual. Their legal rights and employment rights should not be infringed. Gays should not flaunt their abnormality and should not recruit children to engage in their lifestyle. Biological gays should not be penalized in their life score. "Choose to be" gays are a different category and they would score higher if they chose the normal way of human sexuality.

Coining the word "homophobic" does not change the facts. CODE 3-M recommends civil and cordial treatment of gays but does not endorse their lifestyle and condemns silly parades and the like and any recruitment of children.

32. Marriage and family values are essential to a stable, healthy society. Monogamy is the ideal and a positive goal for mankind. Until that goal is voluntarily reached, religion and lawmakers should be tolerant of individuals who believe and see it differently. Consenting adults must be given authority in this area.

33. Divorce is a sad action. It is usually not the ideal, but in some cases necessary. Individuals should not be judgmental. It could happen to them

34. Change is inevitable. Try to hold on to the true and essential while adapting to new territory. The ability to adapt is the highest form of intelligence. There are some scientific and moral absolutes.

35. You can choose to be happy and optimistic.

36. Support things that unify humanity. Avoid all divisive actions as much as possible. The Internet is already crossing national boundaries. It is a great unifying force despite some negative aspects. There are hundreds of positive efforts like student exchange, chess championships, the Olympics, Miss Universe, various sports cups, and the like that merit broad support.

CODE 3-M enthusiastically endorses any effort to unify human beings. Whither thou goest, human race? Each person has an equal claim on its promise and if we are united there are no limits to our potential.

37. Assisting death can be moral in selected cases. CODE 3-M does not suggest a death on demand whimsical, impulsive, capricious, fickle approach to this important issue. Only applying rigid criteria should a life be snuffed out mercifully. The individual has that authority and government nor religion has no dominion. Use of heroic measures is within the authority of the individual or family.

38. Support sensible laws regulating biogenetics. The line must be drawn if attempts are made to basically change what a human being is like in the year 2000. Religionists would be concerned if the part animal, part human had a soul. Government would be concerned about a large array of legal aspects.

CODE 3-M recommends drawing a line to preserve the human race.

39. World citizenship is a worthy goal. A web of interdependency is fast developing and far-flung nations are becoming neighbors due to air travel. We can guide economic cooperation and devise a better government from existing ones

that will truly insure equality and justice, fairness and compassion. Total globalization is inevitable. The only question is when.

40. Death. Fear it not. Score well in your life and death will be nothing to fear as you die courageously.

41. Truth stands on its own merit. Support any honest search for truth, scientific or irrefutable facts.

42. CODE 3-M suggests a loving commitment to one person as the ideal in sexual relations. This is achieved by many humans around the world. The authority of consenting adults should not be abridged by religion or government. Sex should be a private and personal matter. The CODE suggests an ideal.

43. Religion has no business in government and government has no business in religion. If separation of church and state had been followed throughout history, millions of young lives would not have been taken. These wars proved nothing.

The religious right vote, the Catholic vote, the Jewish vote, the Buddhist vote, the Mooney vote, and others are antithetical to any democracy. It is an undemocratic disgrace. Individuals should vote their own conscience, not the herd instinct of any religion or special interests.

44. Abuse of spouses, children, the elderly, animals, and any other kind of abuse should be held in the highest condemnation and receive appropriate punishment.

45. Respect for planet earth and environs. Each individual has the responsibility to protect the environment and ensure that the important things are preserved. Extremists who say the ozone layer is not being affected or the other extreme who get a little "snaildarter fish complex" should be avoided.

Strike a sensible balance. Our water tables are falling. The temperature worldwide is rising and the rain forests are shrinking. It took human history to reach a world population of 1 billion in 1804. It reached 2 billion in 1927, 3 billion in 1960, 4 billion in 1974, 5 billion in 1987, 6 billion population occurred in October 2000. That many people must treat our environment properly or we are down the drain and we must slow population growth.

46. "An eye for an eye and a tooth for a tooth" is a good foundation for criminal justice, which must have major reform to show there are consequences for dastardly crimes. Enforcement must be fair to all.

47. Food for everyone is a requisite for peace. Population increases should be discouraged at least until we can catch up and prevent starvation. The dignity and nobility of just one

human being must be realized.

48. People are born neither righteous nor evil. There are good choices and wrong choices that continually confront the individual. Do the right thing because it is the right thing to do. Be fair, ethical and moral as much as possible as you live you life.

49. What the world needs now is love somehow. Love suffered long and is kind; love envieth not, vaunteth not itself; is not puffed up; does not behave itself unseemly; seeketh not her own; is not easily provoked, thinketh no evil. (New Testament)

50. The whole world is an ever-increasing melting pot of races and cultures. Overall, this is a wonderful happening because it will help prevent war.

However, we should preserve the positive things from each race and culture. Melting or blending should be voluntary. It will take many centuries; hopefully, it will never be fully completed because the loss of so many traditions will be sad.

However, the huge majority melting will bring more positives than negatives. The cessation of war will be a trump card that will make any loss fade from view.

51. List all the rights to which you feel you as a person are entitled. Then give each of those inherent rights and privileges to every individual in the world. This spirit, if adopted by most of the world's people, will prevent war.

52. Ambition is worthy as long as it does not carry the sinister agenda to control others. "Who we are" is more important than "what we have." Strive for excellence in all things. The fact that you know you are doing a good job bolsters self-esteem; a passionate person knows no boredom. Believe in good causes and work hard for them.

53. Humanity has entered a number of new eras and we are on the verge of realizing a positive world that is beyond our wildest dreams if we can stop fighting and killing each other. The "us versus them" attitude has to cease and we must adopt "them is us" and "us is them" philosophy in our hearts.

54. Laughter is positive. Laugh often. Laugh out loud. Laugh at yourself, never at others when inappropriate. Laughter is contagious. Build a good sense of humor. Life will be more enjoyable.

55. Into each life some rain must fall. Everyone will face overwhelming negative situations. How one is able to respond to bad things happening to a good person is the key. First, real-

ize that you know some people have had more tragedy than you. Do all you can to improve the situation then have a heart-to-heart with yourself and move on with your life. Wallowing in a lake of despond is the wrong response. Moving on despite setbacks is the right response.

56. Sensible balances in all things may be the best advice you will ever give or receive.

57. Prohibition of mind-altering substances is almost impossible because people can make "booze." Too many people in high places drink alcoholic beverages. Therefore, prohibition of marijuana and other "drugs for kicks" merely taxes decent people more to construct more jails for the users and sellers. The same for heroin, cocaine, and a dozen other drugs used to get high.

The consistent and logical action is to legalize all of it coupled with a powerful education program. We teach our children not to drink poison or cut their throat with a butcher knife. We can and must teach and monitor them about tobacco and drugs, which include alcohol. Driving a car off a cliff will kill you and don't jump off a tall building.

If the individual can take personal responsibility not to kill himself or herself in that manner, they must take personal responsibility not to do alcohol, drugs or tobacco. Consistency is essential.

58. Age is an artificial issue. Performance of required tasks is a legitimate issue. Aging is a process shared by each individual. It is sheer folly to foster animosity between groups based on age. This type of discrimination whether against the young or the old is just as wrong as race discrimination or any other discrimination.

59. Immortality. Many believe in a soul that never dies. Many believe in reincarnation. Many believe you are immortal as long as your children live and make a family lineage; part of you keeps going through chromosomes and genes.

Many believe immortality is found in anything that endures like a music composition or an inspiring poem. "I think that I shall never see a poem lovely as a tree" brings a kind of immortality to Joyce Kilmer as the "I have a dream" speech does to Martin Luther King, Jr. Many believe that man's ego will not allow him to face an end to himself.

CODE 3-M does not endorse or condemn any notion of immortality but challenges each individual to leave a beautiful and meaningful legacy.

60. A good eulogy goal for any individual: "This person

passed the test of a positive caring life and many people in the world are better off in many ways because this person tread upon it. This person lived an enjoyable life of contentment, contribution and fulfillment."

All seven made a little speech about CODE 3-M and the theme was the same. They could wholeheartedly support the purpose and the vast majority of the guidelines but still, to be honest, they had reservations concerning a few of them.

Nevertheless, they had been delighted to work with each member of the group. It proved that people with 180-degree divergent views could work together.

Chapter X
Romance Blooms

The report had been compiled. The brief CODE 3-M items had been meticulously created. Words are so important and each member felt some vital words were omitted. Yet the process of secret voting was faithfully followed so no one complained outwardly to the group.

CODE 3-M was faxed in total to Rudolph P. Morgan in New York City. The members of the group were all hoping that Rudy would find the CODE worthy and substantial. None would want to admit thinking about how they would spend or invest their very nice bonus if Rudy gave them one. All were hoping and could not help but think a little about where this generous bonus would go.

Rudy had made up his own mind about the CODE 3-M report, but being the careful, meticulous businessman he was, he gave copies to everyone in the building including his top educated staff, the janitors and maintenance people. He asked them for a paragraph on their reaction to the CODE.

Without exception all agreed that overall, it was a blockbuster, interesting and substantive and expressed the exact feeling that Rudy held. Although they did not agree with a few of the items, overall they would not only give it a passing grade but a very high grade. The average grade was B+.

When Rudy assembled the CODE 3-M group and told them the results of the people and his own appraisal, the group let out a whoop that startled even the seasoned crew members on the beautiful yacht. They waited breathlessly for Rudy to say something about a bonus.

"I'm sorry about the $25,000 bonus," Rudy teased. "The $25,000 bonus is out." An embarrassed silence swept over the room where the members were listening so intently.

"Oh, I forgot," chuckled Rudy, "the $25,000 bonus is out but the $40,000 bonus for such splendid work is in. Your individual checks totally $150,000 are on the way. Pick them up in Miami. I really appreciate the intellectual ferment you have created. Goodbye and thanks again for your outstanding work. I hope to see all of you again. I love you all!"

Each member expressed their appreciation to Rudy for this unforgettable opportunity. There should be a stronger word than celebration for what happened on that yacht. The festive mood called everyone, crew and group, to turn up the music all the way. They danced and frolicked for hours as Captain Davis headed *The Quest* towards Miami.

David had been doing some serious soul-searching in the six-hour trip back to Miami as he had ever since the three beautiful ladies walked on the ship. He wondered how any man could be so lucky as to have such an opportunity. He had reached the juncture in his life where he was ready to settle down, marry someone with whom he could love forever and raise a family.

He knew some people would accuse him of a shipboard romance. So what. He had used his best judgment in being honest with Rachel. He had visited with her one Sunday morning at a charismatic Pentecostal church while new sails were being fitted to *The Quest*. It was quite a negative experience.

Now, there were two great girls left and he needed reassurance that his pick between Lu and Bridgette would be the right one. He had been alone with each of them for many hours. He finally decided and felt in his heart of hearts "that special one" would be the answer.

With her, the nights were full of passion and the days seemed like interesting adventures. There was always a satisfying closeness when he touched her and a love, even when transmitted in silence, was mutually received in a manner that tingled his whole being.

David remembered she had told him that she had rather live with him in a shack than in a mansion with anyone else. She also said, "It's not only how I admire you and love you, but the person you make me to become when I'm with you."

He would call a friend in Miami, have him purchase an engagement ring just like the sketch he would fax to him and have it waiting when *The Quest* docked in Miami.

David made the call. The friend said he knew a first-rate jeweler in downtown Miami and could get it done easily in a couple of hours.

David leaned back in his comfortable deck lounge and welcomed the next exciting chapter in his life. Still he owed it to one of the ladies to tell her of his plans to become engaged to the other. Breaking up with Rachel was difficult. This second experience of romantic honesty was so emotional it drained both of them.

A few hours later, everyone was leaving reluctantly what had been the best time in their entire lives. David saw his friend, got the gorgeous ring, and turned in time to see his beloved leaving her cabin. He rushed to her door.

"Can we step back inside for just a moment?" he asked.

"Oh sure," she said, expecting to get a wonderful goodbye kiss. When inside alone, David pulled her close to him and kissed her long and passionately. With both hands clasped firmly around her waist, he spoke softly with great feeling.

"When I look into your eyes, I feel some strange but warm magnetism. I feel drawn to the most wonderful girl I have ever known. I love you so much. I just wish I could find the words of love to express my deep true feelings for you. I know that I want you passionately and that I need you more than I can say. You are the girl of my dreams in every way. You are so beautiful, so kind and caring. Your innerself even exceeds your outside beauty and I know now that my life would be empty without you. I want to grow with you, protect and cherish you as long as I have breath. Will you marry me and be my loving sweetheart forever?"

"Oh yes, oh yes, oh yes, I will," she exclaimed while raising her voice.

David opened the little box. Her gorgeous brown eyes glowed as much as the expensive diamond.

"It's so beautiful," she sobbed through tears of joy. "And so are you. I love you with all my heart."

David's heart was thumping like a bass drum. As they left the yacht arm in arm, a large cheer of congratulations arose from the group and the crew members. Everyone approved wholeheartedly.

– THE END –